Jem Tugwell is a crime fiction  from City University. **NO SIG** iMe series and follows his thri Jem is inspired by the fascinating possibilities of technology, AI and the law of unintended consequences. In a past life, Jem had a successful career in investment management, and he now lives in Surrey with his wife and dog. He has two great children. Outside of his family and writing, Jem's loves are snowboarding, old cars and bikes.

🌐	www.jemtugwell.com
✉	jem@jemtugwell.com
🐦	@JemTugwell
f	@JemTugwellAuthor

Praise for Jem Tugwell and the iMe Series

'No Signal, an immersive, entertaining high-octane thriller set in a plausible interconnected world. Well-written, thought-provoking escapism. Perfect for fans of Black Mirror & Philip K. Dick.' Adam Hamdy

'A vision of the future that both **chills and entertains**.' Jake Kerridge (*Sunday Express Magazine*)

'...**exhilarating and provocative** debut crime thriller with a twist.' *The Malestrom*, 4 of the Best Beach Reads: Summer 2019

'Very topical, terrifying, superb concept for a crime novel.' Stav Sherez

'A darkly **twisted crime novel** set in a future world that seems to grow closer every day. Fantastically imaginative and gripping.' Angela Clarke

'An **ingenious and highly plausible** look at crime in a future with 100% surveillance.' Claire McGowan

'**Compelling, relevant** and chilling. Is this where we're heading?' Abi Silver

5* Review 'The writing hurtles along like a runaway train and **you can barely pause for breath**. What renders it **original** and ingenious is the background of embedded technology called "iMe" (how perfect is that?!) It's a crime thriller and it is very thrilling.' Gill Chedgey (*NB Magazine*)

5* Review 'I must admit that I finished the book with a prayer that I will never see something like iMe in my lifetime - **the idea is just too terrifying**' Breakaway Reviewers

'5*s from me as the **storyline is brilliant**... Plenty of discussion topics here for bookclubs!' EmmabBooks

'Jem Tugwell's outstanding description of years too close to ours to my taste **left me speechless.**' Meggy, Chocolate'n'Waffles

'A brilliant book, an excellent thriller and 100% entertaining. Highly recommended. **Really can't wait for a follow up! Genius.**' Books from Dusk Till Dawn

No Signal

Jem Tugwell

SERPENTINE

BOOKS

First published in Great Britain by Serpentine Books
This edition published in 2020 by
Serpentine Books Limited

www.serpentinebooks.com
info@serpentinebooks.com

A CIP catalogue record for this book is available from the
British Library.

ISBN 978 19 1602 233 1

Printed and bound in Great Britain by Clays Ltd,
Elcograf S.p.A.

This book is a work of fiction. Names, characters, businesses,
organisations, places and events are either the product of the
author's imagination or used fictitiously. Any resemblance to
actual persons, living or dead, events or locales is entirely
coincidental.

Part 1

Selection

Chapter 1

'For the sceptre of wickedness shall not rest on the land allotted to the righteous, lest the righteous stretch out their hands to do wrong.'
(*English Standard Bible*, Psalm 125:3)

Serge pushed the barrel of the gun hard into Antoine's cheek, forcing his head to turn towards the corner of the room. Towards Antoine's girls. Towards their fear.

Marie had little Sadie enveloped in her arms as if her will alone could deflect a bullet. Her stare blazed back at him: How could you put us in this danger? Little Sadie's wide eyes tore a hole straight through him: Yes, Daddy, how?

Antoine's shoulders slumped in shame. This was all his fault. His fingers were slick on the joystick, his grip not as light and controlled as normal. Today he needed to be better than normal. He needed to be perfect. The pressure from the gun released and he turned back to the screen. He wished he was in another long session on a game where losing a life simply meant starting again and doing better. But this was real.

Saliva flooded his mouth and Antoine swallowed. He tried to shake his head clear of everything except his joystick and the screen in front of him that showed the image from the drone he was piloting.

He couldn't let his girls pay for his stupid mistakes.

The timer at the bottom of the screen showed one minute to the coastline, and the black waves of the English Channel flashed under the drone as it skimmed only a metre above the water. He nudged the joystick in his right hand to correct for a gust of wind, but his movement was clumsy and the drone almost touched the sea.

Serge stifled a cry and leaned in. His breathing sounded like it had a distant rattle, as if something small was trapped in his lungs and vibrated with each breath. With a sour tobacco cough, Serge controlled his laboured breathing and said, 'Careful. Don't cause me more delays.'

Antoine risked shooting another glance towards his girls. Marie was sobbing and kissing Sadie's head, whispering to comfort her. Each sob scratched a deeper wound. Saving them was everything.

Antoine brought his fingers to his shoulder and wiped his fear onto his shirt. Hand back on the joystick, he repeated the movement to dry his other hand.

His grip was better now – his control more precise. He tried to shrug some of the tension out of his shoulders. At least tonight the sky was clear, and the water was calm. No waves to snatch his drone like last time. No defence drone to shoot him down too soon. No pilot error.

Last chance.

He took a deep breath and blew it out, collapsing all his senses down, leaving only his eyes and fingertips. He was the drone.

As the white cliffs appeared, he pulled back on a joystick to slow the drone and edged it in as close to the cliff as he dared. Deft fingers feathered the joystick and the drone began a vertical climb, hugging the irregularities of the cliff.

The drone peeked over the high security fence at the top of the cliff and showed a green field edged by a coastal path. Serge coughed in Antoine's ear and said, 'There. By that pile of stones.'

Antoine edged his joystick and the drone jumped over the fence and into the United Kingdom. He pushed forward and the drone accelerated, skimming the grass. As it flashed over the pile of stones, he pressed the button to drop the box the drone carried.

'Destroy the evidence,' Serge said.

Antoine eased the altitude of the drone up and away from the stones. Ahead and to the right, he saw a Border Security drone rise into the air and swing towards his drone. Two lines of tracer fire erupted from the defence drone and scorched a path across the clear sky. Antoine flinched as the image on his screen jumped, flashed and then blanked out.

'Perfect,' Serge said.

Chapter 2

DI Clive Lussac had only been at work for an hour, but he looked at the Proximity Crime Unit's '*Requiring Action*' message queue for the hundredth time. Still empty.

The message queue took up half of his Head Up Display, or HUD as everyone called it. It was part of his embedded iMe device. The same iMe every adult had. Its virtual screen projected information about a metre from his face. It had everything he could ever need. Work, personal, news, maps.

His location.

iMe knew where everyone was. It saved their signal so that it also knew where everyone had been. There was nowhere to hide.

On the other half of Clive's screen, Uniform's message queue ticked over slowly with the occasional trivial case where, despite knowing they were certain to get caught, someone's emotions had raced ahead of their logic.

Clive glanced at the clock in the bottom corner of his HUD. He knew it was a mistake. It only seemed to slow time, stretching and blurring the minutes. Watching it definitely didn't make the day go any quicker. He groaned at the thought of seven more workless hours to go. A detective's work had all but disappeared.

I'll do another lap of the office, Clive decided, standing and stretching out the knotted and aching muscles in his back that were caused by the cheap chair's poor design. He strolled past the empty desks, trailing two fingers in the dust, leaving parallel tracks on the surface. He reached the window. The grime crusted onto the panes obscured most of the outside, so he didn't pause to gaze out.

Walking made his beltless trousers settle. Since Mary, he couldn't look at a belt, let alone wear one, without seeing her face, so he hooked his fingers into the vacant loops on the waist of his brand-new trousers and hitched them up. He turned and completed this lap of the office. Walking around the office was a complete waste of time – but that was the point.

Sitting on the edge of his desk, Clive looked at the office door, remembering when DC Zoe Jordan had burst into the room with news of Karina's body. The excitement of those few weeks had dimmed over the last year like a setting summer sun. Clive's new Off-Grid Crime Unit had waited for a wave of new style off-grid crimes, but they never arrived. Zoe's frustration at doing nothing had ramped up and up, and when they both had been merged back into the Proximity Crime Unit, it was the final straw. Zoe had wanted some action and had transferred to Cyber Crime.

Now, only the dent in the wall from the door handle remained. It was almost like it never happened.

**

The PCU office door opened and DC Ava Miller appeared, one hand on the handle, the other holding a glass of water. A zero-calorie, sugar-free protein bar dangled from her mouth, like a huge antique, Cuban cigar. At twenty-three, she was too young to have seen anyone actually smoke a cigar, but she would have been bombarded with all of the health risks when she was at school. At five foot two inches tall, her lack of physical size made the protein bar seem even bigger.

Mouth still full, Ava sat opposite Clive, and raised her eyebrows in a silent question. Clive pinched his fingers in front of his face to 'pick up' the *Requiring Action* queue. He pulled his hand back and pretended to throw the queue at the office's display wall. The wall's scrolling health and safety directives paused, leaving an *'Avoid HUD eye: Don't forget to blink and focus on something else'* instruction for a second before being replaced by the *Requiring Action* queue. Now Ava could see the empty work queue and fully participate in the inactivity.

Ava had worked on Karina's case when she was a trainee, and now qualified, she was the latest officer forced into a three-month rotation into PCU. When she had arrived, Ava had kept herself busy with her TrueMe, the secure and identity-assured replacement for all the old abusive, stalker-friendly, and insecure social media. Her hands danced on her virtual keyboard as she typed message after message. Clive would see her smile at a lot of the messages, but the occasional frown and dismissive shake of her head sent her blonde ponytails swishing. Somehow Ava managed to make doing nothing a high energy activity.

Clive was used to keeping his real self – the conflicted, struggling, depressive – hidden behind the body the world saw. When he had watched Ava, fully immersed in her world, something about her seemed similar, as if the image she projected, with bouncy, happy ponytails, was an act. Like she thought that's what the world expected because of her age and stature. Her self-confidence seemed to depend on her TrueMe, and dipped and rose with the flow of external validation.

As tentatively as if he was tiptoeing past a sleeping lion, Clive had tried to get Ava to talk about herself and to work on building her inner-confidence. Clive could talk a good game on the subject, despite the obvious hypocrisy. To his surprise, Ava had opened up and they had talked and talked. It wasn't like they had much else to do during the empty PCU workday. Ava's breakthrough, unlike the Nazirite Samson, had come when her ponytails were cut away and replaced by a stylish bob cut. She embraced a strength-oriented exercise regime and a more 'take me as I am' attitude.

'How's the wrestling going?' Clive asked, nodding at Ava's protein bar.

'Brilliant,' Ava beamed. 'Nothing better for the soul than sending a six-foot bloke flying.' Rolling her sleeve up, she clenched her arm. Muscles jumped to her command and bunched into impressive mounds and ridges all along her arm.

'Wow, you're getting scary,' Clive said, making no move to roll his own sleeve up. The comparison wouldn't have been flattering for him.

As they waited for work, Ava alert, Clive, eyes half shut, mouth half open, he wondered what all his old colleagues were doing. Ava was into her final few weeks and Clive was going to miss her. He felt like he was drifting away from shore, away from people. *No man is an island*, he thought, but his life was a very good impression of one. Mostly his own fault. He didn't really bother to try to contact people unless he felt lonely, and then it was too late to reconnect.

He typed out a message to Sophia, but changed it again and again, failing to find the right tone. It had been difficult dating Zoe's mum when he and Zoe worked together, but now their relationship was getting rocky and Clive's depression was returning. It was leeching into his relationship with Sophia. He settled on a lame, *'Hi, can I come over tonight? Miss you,'* and pressed *'Send'*.

No response.

He typed out another message. *'Zoe, how's things?'*

'Can't talk, Boss. Snowed under with a cyber attack,' flashed Zoe's reply. Clive's disappointment lifted slightly at Zoe still calling him boss, but plummeted at the message he received from Sophia: *'Sorry, busy.'*

'When then? I need to see you,' Clive typed. At least the pleading tone in his mind didn't translate directly into the text. He had the Sentiments on his HUD turned off on purpose. Having a little graphical figure representing his exact emotional state for all to see was too much information. Too embarrassing.

'Not sure, I'll call you.'

Where was she going? Clive wondered. Who with? When would she call? Would she even call? She'd started going to Church of the New Modelists recently. She said they helped simplify her life, but Clive didn't get it. He churned and whirled the possibilities. Failing to grasp any positives, he gleefully snatched at the negatives and let them run free.

Clive jolted fully awake at a bing. The tone was distinctive and he and Ava both knew what it meant.

Ava used to be so timid that she would wait to be told to take the message, now it was their personal game. Their hands shot forward, trying to grab the message from the action queue, like two politicians trying to snatch the last exemption for a dodgy expense claim.

Ava beat him to it and slid him a smile. 'Too slow, Boss,' she said, her fingers dangling the virtual message in front of her. Clive could see the icon of the message rocking on the display wall. Ava opened her fingers and the message disappeared from the wall. Clive knew that she had dropped it onto her empty work queue on her HUD.

'Share–' He broke off as he was interrupted by a small figure, his Buddy, running across the bottom of his HUD and rolling out another warning banner.

'Oh, fuck off, Buddy.' He waved an angry hand, as if he was swatting at a fly settling on his food. His Buddy looked sad.

'Boss? You OK?'

'Fine.'

'If you're sure,' she said with a shrug and threw her HUD display at the wall. It redrew to show an 'Incident' message from Uniform. It described the beating of a man by four others. She picked up the whole Incident and dropped it into the Monitor window of her HUD, selected the time of the assault and pressed 'Search'. A small animated representation of Ava, her Buddy, ran across the bottom of Ava's HUD trailing out a banner that said 'Searching'. After a couple of seconds, her Buddy packed the banner away, threw the search results onto Ava's HUD screen and scampered off.

The results opened with a map of Old Racecourse Road in Epsom. The racecourse was long gone – too dangerous for horses to race, and the tax on risk-taking was way too expensive for the jockeys to afford. The area was all housing now, and a dot representing the assaulted man appeared on a path in front of a block of flats. Four other dots crowded the man – one right next to him, the other three in a rough semi-circle. Ava dragged the dots representing the four men back into the Incident, which loaded with all their details and IDs. Ava marked them all for arrest. The three bystanders were equally guilty for failing to prevent a crime as the attacker was for the punches.

Ava pressed *'Send'*, and their work queue was empty again.

***

Clive gave up on his high-powered inertia of waiting for something to do, and rather than complete another aimless lap of the office, he sauntered along the empty corridor to the office's snack area. The vending machine stretched across one wall and connected with Clive's iMe as he got close to it.

'How can I serve you, Clive?' it said in a happy, but stilted synthesised human voice.

Clive scanned the rows of food and drinks, trying to decide what would satisfy his craving.

'Your iMe reports: you are inside all of your Freedom Unit allowances. You may choose anything,' the machine encouraged him.

The Model Citizen, as defined by the government, set the optimal levels for calorie, sleep, risk, fat, and the other categories that everyone was measured against and had to live up to. It was for your own good.

Freedom Units gave the pretence of choice where you could 'spend' your allowance of excess: chocolate, fruit or chips, the choice was yours. The quantity wasn't.

Your consumption was taxed and enforced through iMe. When you checked your status, there was meant to be a solid, conformant green column showing in every category. You were allowed a small amber tip on some columns where you were outside the Model, but still inside your Freedom Units allowance.

Clive's eyes settled on a small bar of real chocolate, and lingered. His mouth started to water. He tore his eyes away from the chocolate, it would blow his calorie allowance for the next few days.

The machine had a new Choco-Lite bar. The gold wrapper shimmered behind the display glass. It promised all the flavour at a fraction of the calories. Should he give it a try?

'Choco-Lite,' Clive said.

'Certainly, Clive.' The machine whirred and a gold wrapper appeared in the dispensing slot.

Clive took it with a dubious look. Could it really be as good as the adverts? As good as the real thing?

He tore the top of the wrapper away and bit into the chocolate. Instead of the crisp hard ecstasy of real chocolate, the bar crumbled like sawdust swept off the floor. Whatever the brown flavouring was, it wasn't chocolate.

Clive spat and scraped at his tongue.

'Give me some water. Quick.'

Chapter 3

In the damp morning air at the top of the cliff, Jay could hear the drone somewhere ahead of him. Maybe this time it would actually arrive and make the delivery. He waited as the noise got louder and then he saw the drone peek nervously over the fence.

The drone swooped low, skimming the grass and accelerated to a pile of stones. Jay saw his delivery drop, then the drone rose, gaining height. Surely a deliberate act of suicide.

Jay watched as red tracers flashed across the sky from the Border Security drone that lived in the darkness of the small wood. The tracers thumped into the delivery drone with small flashes, followed by the rumble of an explosion. Then silence. It was like a very brief and disappointing Firework's Night display.

He scurried towards the stones with Kevin barking and bounding behind him. The dog was a fawn pedigree Great Dane and his mix of genetics had produced a one-year-old puppy who was already massive. Each of Kevin's huge strides covered a couple of metres, and his over-sized paws thudding on the coast path warned Jay that he was still growing.

Kevin flashed past Jay and beat him to the box the drone had dropped. Kevin pushed the box with his eager nose as he sniffed at it, pulling in the scent. Jay reached the dog and nudged his shoulder to move him. Kevin didn't budge, so Jay pushed harder and the dog reluctantly yielded half a yard, his nose still busy.

Jay shot nervous glances all around him, then grabbed the box. He reminded himself that he had a valid reason to be here if the police questioned him. For the last ten months he had walked Kevin here in the early morning. Jay's signal would prove it. 'Of course I was there,' he would say, 'I always go there' – just a normal day, like any other. He hoped it was enough.

'Come on, Kevin,' Jay called as he turned from the stones. He puffed his chest out to convince himself that he couldn't feel the fear worming through his guts.

Jay was a talker, not a doer. His stories began 'I'm going to…' and his wife would sigh, 'Of course you will.'

But he didn't.

He talked – of change, of inequality, of unfairness, of a new ideal. He met with like-minded idealists and talked of action, safe in snug, private rooms. Safe with other talkers. They all agreed that the time for change was *now*. It always was. Every time they met.

He thought that all his talk was well away from anyone who would actually expect him to *do* something, but that changed a year ago.

He still had no idea who had listened to him talking and then slipped the note into his pocket – his call to arms he had never expected or wanted: *'Live up to your words. The cause needs you.'*

Now his life was run by secret notes and furtive drop points in deserted parks, like he was in an old Cold War spy story, but with iMe monitoring every message and your location, what choice was there but to go backwards in time?

Kevin must have sensed Jay's anxiety and shoved his head under Jay's spare hand.

Jay fondled Kevin's head and ears, and allowed the velvety touch to soothe him.

He had done the pickup – told himself he was a helping hand in the great change. An activist.

Clasping the box tighter to his chest, he headed for his car.

He hoped they wouldn't need him again.

Chapter 4

Clive had suffered another restless night, and now the sun streamed through the loose weave of the bedroom curtains' fabric and lit the room with a spring morning's hope of new beginnings. He groaned, turned his back on the window and pulled the duvet over his head. Trying to resettle, Clive willed himself back to sleep, but the pressure in his bladder became more insistent.

'Fuck's sake,' he shouted, throwing off the duvet and rushed for the toilet for the fourth time that night. Stumbling through the discarded clothes of the previous few days like a kid kicking autumn leaves, he made it to the toilet in time, savouring the bliss of the release of pressure.

He could feel the effect of the broken sleep in his gritty eyes. His body seemed too heavy for him to hold up. He glanced in the bedroom mirror and quickly looked away. All those creases and lines on his face seemed to have got much worse overnight. He looked grey and exhausted. He felt drained.

'You're not meant to wake up knackered,' he muttered, and headed back towards the bed, but his Buddy skipped along the bottom of Clive's HUD trailing a banner: *'Good morning, Clive. Time for your voluntary exercise session.'*

Clive hesitated, longing for bed. He wanted to ignore the exercise and get more sleep.

His Buddy packed away his banner and rolled out another: *'Exercise is an essential part of a healthy lifestyle.'*

Clive gave up, turned and headed to the lounge and its treadmill. Despite his exercise being 'voluntary', Buddy would keep reminding Clive, again and again. And again. His Buddy had infinite patience and so many inane banners. *Less effort to exercise than fight a battle I'm bound to lose*, Clive thought.

He trudged over to the pile of clean exercise clothes sitting on the clothes processor. A year ago, he would have pulled on dirty, smelly kit, but he had tried to up his game since he started dating Sophia. He threw on some shorts, trainers and edged into his *Spirit of the Honey Badger* T-shirt, careful not to pull any of the holes bigger.

The treadmill started moving and his clothes released a mild lavender smell. He flicked through the video streams on his HUD. He swiped past a couple of ancient comedies, past Miles Raven standing in front of yet another demonstration and calling, *again*, for the country to embrace eco-socialism. Clive clicked past more comedies and settled on the news.

An earnest-looking woman, dressed all in green, was talking.

'The Model Citizen is clear; we are meant to live green in every category... we cannot allow our children to consume excessively and be tainted with amber.'

The image widened to show the woman and a slick, but greying presenter. He put on a frown and raised his eyebrows, 'OK. Thank you, Reverend,' he said.

The director zoomed in on the presenter, who shook his head as he said, 'We'd love to hear what you think of the growing popularity of the Church of the New Modelists. Please get in touch in the usual way.' He paused and his face changed as he switched on his sincere, concerned look. 'The month-long environmental catastrophe demonstrations continued today, with the police complaining that the protests were taking all available Uniform officers from other duties...'

The treadmill sped up and Clive had to stop watching to avoid falling over. His Buddy jogged along the bottom of the HUD, and unrolled banner after banner: *'Go, Clive.' 'Aim for a personal best.' 'Super Clive!' 'Awesome, dude!'*

Clive trudged through the sweaty and exhausting session, *encouraged* all the time by his Buddy's grating superlatives and colourful banners. As the treadmill stopped, his legs seemed to have turned to jelly and he had to grasp the handle to hold himself up.

Buddy trotted across the screen of his HUD, the latest banner was one he couldn't ignore. *'Your hospital appointment is confirmed for 10am tomorrow.'*

His Buddy crossed his arms in a protective, concerned gesture and then gave a hopeful thumbs up.

Chapter 5

Serge liked to work in this room. The high ceilings and large windows gave it a bright, airy feel with plenty of natural light.

He loved to stare at the River Seine as it curved through Rouen. Especially at night as the city's lights reflected and danced on the water. He tapped away at his computer and finished his tweet.

'To all you Reece Witherspoon fans, just finished watching "Overnight Delivery".'

He allowed himself a smile, relaxed a little and pressed the *'Send'* button.

Getting the box into the UK successfully had taken months, much frustration and failure. Now they could move on.

He could feel the tightness and rattle in his lungs, but he didn't reach for his asthma inhaler, instead he picked up another cigarette. It was his choice and besides, he liked smoking too much. He took a long pull, savouring the sensation, then the inevitable cough covered the noise of the mouse click that opened a new window.

He didn't really understand augmented reality gamers, but that hadn't stopped him building his online profile and credibility with them. Slowly at first, he'd organised simple games, but always with a dangerous edge. He discarded the weak and unfit. They were useless to him. He encouraged the athletes, and the more adventurous. He followed the brave and the reckless. The games got harder, more dangerous, and demanded more physical sacrifice to succeed. He dared the gamers to be more extreme and rewarded them well. Now, he had his favourites. The ones who would accept this call for the supreme test of their strength and nerve. He had done it all remotely, using others. Now finally he would meet them.

He pasted the pre-prepared message into the window, pressed *'Send'*, stood and went to the kitchen.

His computer screen still showed the message.

The AR game you have waited for is here.
'Forbidden Island'
The select few will get the call.
This ultimate game requires a supreme sacrifice.

Chapter 6

Lilou ran straight at the three-metre-high wall and jumped. She used her momentum and four short strides to scrabble up half of the wall's height, then stretched out her right hand. She grabbed the top of the wall, hung for a fraction of a second and effortlessly pulled herself up with one hand. She didn't care about the lashing Parisian rain that had everyone else heading towards the office block huddling under umbrellas. She vaulted up onto a handrail and jumped across to the other side, landing with perfect balance on the balls of her feet. She hopped down, strolled into reception and towards the lift.

Other workers crowded around her in the lift, shaking coats and complaining about the rain. Lilou smiled as she replayed the moves of her parkour commute. She gave her hair a flick, sending droplets flying. She ignored the complaints and tuts.

The lift doors closed, and the smell of her damp clothes filled her nostrils. She was desperate to see if there was news, but her phone was buried at the bottom of her small rucksack.

She wanted to be part of it.

She craved the impossibility of it.

***

Lilou's skin tingled from the shock of the heat of the shower after the cold rain, and from the after-glow that pushing her body gave her. Now, sitting at her desk, she devoured her work, feeding on how her whole body felt alive. The other lawyers seemed to take an age to get up to speed in the morning.

Lilou started ahead of them, and they never caught up with her – just like in her Olympic triathlon. But tapping keys and pushing paper was an empty victory, she ached with her need to replace the purity and intensity of Olympic competition.

She allowed herself a quick break, reliving the surging buzz of achievement from standing on the top step and kissing the gold medal. She lifted her phone from the desk and checked her messages.

Nothing.

She wasn't top of the gamers' chart because she had too many work commitments to compete in them all, but she thought she was the best. Surely, she would be selected. If not automatically, then at least on the short-list.

She shut her phone and refocused, channelling the buzz into her work until lunchtime.

Still no message.

Not that she was worried. Yet.

Lunchtime passed with Lilou at her desk, eating carefully selected proteins and vitamins, and reading about new technologies aimed at improving personal fitness and performance. They promised that she could be better than human. She could upgrade herself.

She allowed herself to dream of a modular body.

Still no message.

Lilou switched back into work mode and immersed herself. Somehow, when she took a second to look up, the day was almost done. The light had faded, and the office was almost empty.

She decided to call it a day and headed for the changing room. Her Lycra running suit was still a bit soggy from the morning, but she pulled it on, having to wriggle a little more than usual to overcome how the dampness made the fabric grabby.

She opened her rucksack to put her day clothes in and picked up her phone. One last check before leaving.

It was there.

She jumped onto the bench, launched herself at the lockers and took two strides along them, finishing with a backflip onto the floor. She was chosen. She was one of The Ten.

The thought of it made every jump longer and every turn higher on the way home. Every landing was perfect.

She would play in the Forbidden Island.

She would win.

Chapter 7

DC Zoe Jordan banged through the front door and pushed it shut with her foot. 'You home, Mum?' she asked.

'I'm in the lounge with Clive,' Sophia called in reply.

Zoe let out a small groan and kicked her shoes off. It had been another crazily busy day at Cyber, and all she wanted was to collapse and chill for what was left of the evening. She didn't want to have to be polite and talk. She didn't want company.

She hesitated at the bottom of the stairs. It helped her transition out of work mode to get out of her suit and into home clothes. To change into her favourite baggy top and jogging bottoms, and lie on the sofa and relax, but she wasn't comfortable, even a year after Clive had rescued her from that cage, with letting him see her like that. Zoe didn't want him thinking that she wasn't coping with her new job. Sure, he'd supported her transfer, but she knew that he wanted her back and always laid a guilt trip on her.

She shuffled towards the lounge, dragging it out, savouring the alone-time. A snail would have overtaken her.

'Hi, Boss,' she said at the doorway.

Clive stood, crossed to her and hugged her. 'How's work?'

'You look tired, darling,' Sophia said.

'Busy – like always.' Zoe dropped into her usual chair.

'You can always come back to PCU,' Clive said. He shrugged, like he was trying to soften the words and make it sound less desperate.

Zoe rolled her eyes. 'I can't. I'm joining a joint Terrorism-Cyber special unit.'

'Congrats.'

She knew Clive meant it, but could see in his eyes that he was contrasting her success with his stagnation.

'Still easy going at PCU. Plenty of downtime,' Clive said, trying to recover and sound positive. He failed.

'How's Ava doing?' Zoe asked.

'She's really starting to come out of herself.'

***

19

It was nearly ten, and Zoe couldn't take it any longer. Something was going on. Her mum and Clive used to sit and chat with a gentle contentment, but recently it was more stilted, and tonight there was a definite edge. The gaps were longer, and the suppressed fizz of an unresolved argument hung in the air.

'OK, what's going on?' she said.

'Well…' Sophia started, but a fierce glance from Clive stopped her.

'Nothing,' Clive said.

'Doesn't look like nothing. What are you fighting about?'

Clive repeated his 'nothing' and glared at Sophia.

Sophia crossed her arms. 'Clive's not well, and he doesn't want to deal with it.'

'It's nothing,' Clive said.

'It's *not* nothing,' Sophia protested.

'I said I don't want to talk about it,' Clive shouted.

'You need to believe in something other than yourself.' Sophia glared at Clive, but he was studying the floor. 'The Church of the New Modelists has helped me, you should–'

'Don't start with that again. I'm fine.'

The room dropped into silence. Sophia and Clive both sat with arms crossed and no eye contact.

Zoe looked at them and shook her head. She slipped out of the room, not wanting to be caught in the frosty lounge or cajoled into acting as their mediator. She was shattered and needed some rest. The threat level in the Cyber department never seemed to drop below 'Imminent', and the pressure wave of probing attacks seemed to grow and grow. They came from everywhere: Russia, China, Pan-Europe, the US. From governments, companies and hackers living with their parents. They all had different ultimate goals, but the same mission – hack iMe. With everything online and interconnected, if you got past iMe's defences, you could hack a whole country.

You could hack every single person.

Chapter 8

Serge ducked his head as another blast of wind buffeted him. He was halfway across the Pont Boieldieu, holding on tight to his coat. No point having an umbrella today. Not when the wind and rain hit him almost horizontally. He could feel the cold wetness soaking into his trousers. Pushing forward, he aimed for the shelter of the buildings on the other side of the bridge, pleased that his preparations for the next stage of the game were nearly complete. A couple of jobs remained, but most importantly, he had his ten.

The warmth of his apartment hit him after the stinging rain, and he pulled off his coat and left it on its hook by the door to drip. Serge dipped into the coat's pocket for his cigarettes but even in his coat, the box had taken on water.

He headed for his desk and his spare cigarettes. Halfway across the room, he paused and dropped the damp cigarette box onto a chair. He hopped and pulled at his wet trousers, struggling to get them off his shins before putting them over the back of a chair and pushing it next to the radiator. His soaking socks joined the trousers, and he left them to steam quietly.

Finally at his desk, Serge lit a dry cigarette and switched his computer on.

One by one, he crafted a separate email to each of The Ten, before attaching a document containing their different joining instructions for the selection process. The Ten would know where to go and when to be there, but not the identity of the other nine. Not yet anyway.

As he took a long pull on a second cigarette, he chuckled to himself. He must look like a pathetic old man, sitting in his underpants, leaving damp footprints on the wooden floor, but *he* was about to unleash the game.

He scanned the list of the challenges he planned for The Ten. Not very subtle, but then neither was Serge. He was sure they would be quick and effective. Feeding off the competitive nature of The Ten.

His only doubt was the final step. Despite their past performances and all the assurances they had given him, did they really have what it took? Would they live up to their bold words?

The test would find out for sure.

The last job was the status report he sent to the man he called Jack Jackson. Obviously, not his real name, but a carefully chosen pseudonym. His *nom de guerre*. Jack was the real architect of the game. The one with the vision. The man with the belief and the cause.

Serge typed out the tweet.

'Hi to all you film fans, horrible day outside so I'm going to settle down and watch "10 Items or Less". Should be exciting.'

Chapter 9

Femi had slept fitfully on the flight from Durban to Paris, having to squeeze and contort his legs into the tiny gap to the seat in front. Now on the train from Paris, he couldn't face more sitting down. The other passengers stared and shrugged at him, looking confused as to why he walked and stretched instead of sitting and watching the countryside roll by.

Finally, the train bumped to a halt in Gare de Rouen. Femi jumped off and bounded along the platform, free of the constraining train. As he strode out on Rue Jeanne d'Arc, he felt pleased to be outside and moving. Some early spring sunshine tried to warm him, but it was only yesterday he'd been at least 10 degrees warmer, running on a Durban beach with his Dinah, his wife, then enjoying a braai with his parents. He smiled at the memory.

Despite longing to be home, he had to be here. Not because he was top of the AR gaming championship table. Not because his selection would be assumed by the community. No, he did this for his family. He earnt much more doing AR games than was possible with a real job. His success so far had pulled first himself and Dinah, and then his parents out of the townships. His sister and brother were still there with their families. He helped them when he could, but winning now would mean he could buy them a new future as well.

Femi checked his watch, he had time in hand, so he lingered in the greenery of Square Verdrel, looking up through the trees at the sky and watching the ducks contented paddling on the still pond. Then he turned and glimpsed the spire of the cathedral between the rooftops of the nearby buildings. Time to go.

When he reached Place de la Cathédrale, he stared at the facade of Rouen's Notre-Dame Cathédrale, marvelling at the Gothic excess and intricacy of all of the carvings and figures in the stone, the slight yellowing of the Butter Tower. Only the

Church had enough money for such a symbol of power and wealth.

Walking towards the right-hand arch of the cathedral, he stepped through the doorway and left the sunshine of the square behind. The small entrance area was empty of tourists and Femi pulled the inner door open. He frowned at the second door that stood immediately in front of him. It would have almost touched the first door when they were both closed. Holding the first door open with his foot, he pushed the second open and was greeted by the cool and distinctive smell of a church. Musty air that didn't circulate enough, mixed with burning candles and stone.

Inside, the cathedral was massive, with huge, high ceilings, every pillar and surface intricately carved. The scale and detailing spoke of the enormous effort needed to build such a structure, before cranes and power tools. It would have been a lifetime's work for so many.

Femi headed down the walkway, admiring the skill needed, but thinking about the contrast between the wealth of the Catholic Church and those who carved the stones.

He walked to the end of the cathedral and followed the walkway as it curved behind the main altar. He passed a small set of tables, covered in books for sale, guarded by a nun in a pinkish habit who was looking at a mobile phone. He hadn't expected a nun to have a phone.

The complaints of a tourist's bored child echoed in the air, followed by a swift 'Sssh!' from a woman.

Femi continued and found the meeting point – the small Chapelle du Saint Sacrement. It was Stop Eight on the cathedral's tourist trail. The tiny chapelle within the cathedral had two rows of pews and a large stone altar. He tiptoed past the rows of flickering candles and sat. The chapelle's pews were empty. No one there to greet him.

After a few minutes, Femi started fidgeting. There was no mistaking the chapelle, so he must be in the right place, but where was the person to take him to the game?

Then an old man paused at the entrance. Femi caught the smell of cigarettes oozing from the man. He didn't look important enough. He didn't have the presence suitable for the Forbidden Island. He looked like a thug who preyed on the tourists.

'Please,' the man said, one hand waving towards the exit of the cathedral.

Femi paused; this man couldn't be the beginning of the most prestigious AR game ever. He looked around, searching for someone more impressive.

The man looked annoyed, a flash of anger lighting up his eyes. 'You're Olufemi and you're here for the Forbidden Island.' He looked directly at Femi. 'I won't ask again,' he said, repeating his wave towards the exit. 'Do you want to fail your family before you have started?'

The taunt was enough to unstick Femi's feet and he followed the man to the exit of the cathedral, across the square and into Rue du Change. A couple of cars were parked on one side of the road, behind them rested an old white van.

The man must have been waiting a while, or smoked a lot, thought Femi, looking at the pile of cigarette ends under the driver's window.

The man opened the back door of the van and waited.

Femi hesitated again. He had expected more respect. More comfort.

'OK,' the man said with a shrug, starting to close the door again, but Femi grabbed the door and hopped in the back.

The door slammed shut, leaving Femi in darkness other than the faint smudge of light from around the edges of the doors and the rotating ventilator on the roof.

Femi sat on the floor of the van, his back to the wall, and bounced and rolled with every movement. The aeroplane had been much more comfortable.

His doubts rolled with him.

Chapter 10

Sully sat in the tiny room with two doors, tapping his hand with frustration at being made to wait so long. His gold ring made a tinny note on the plastic arm of the chair with each angry tap.

Sully glanced behind him again. The purpose of the two doors had been made very clear. The open door behind him invited him to walk back out and to quit.

The closed one in front of him was the entrance to the game.

The game was too big. He couldn't walk away.

Sully stood and reached towards the door in front of him. It was still shut, but he tried the handle again. As before, it was locked. No way to progress in the game except by waiting.

He paced around to burn some of his outrage and irritation. *I shouldn't be made to wait*, he thought. *Not one of the best AR gamers.*

Sully sat again, crossed his legs, and looked at his new white trainers. He muttered more annoyance, licked his finger and wiped a small scuff mark from the side of his left shoe.

His ring started to batter the chair's arm again, its pace increasing with each passing minute.

***

Sully straightened in his chair when he finally heard activity on the other side of the door, and jumped up as the handle started to move. He pushed through the door before it had finished opening and stepped into a large room. The floor was swept concrete, but showed multiple dusty footprints. Sully looked at the metal walls and up at the high metal roof, recognising it as a large farmyard barn. Then he heard footsteps to either side of him.

He glanced around and behind. The door he had pushed open was part of a long wall that stretched the full width of the building. Nine additional doors punctuated the wall, each held open by what looked like a farmworker. Nine other people stepped through the doors and into the room. *This must be The Ten*, he thought.

His competition.

But he was the one. The winner.

The others repeated the same visual tour of the space that Sully had done. Their body language changing, becoming more upright, more assertive as they concluded that the people were the other players. The people they would have to beat.

Each of The Ten had taken three paces into the room and stopped at the yellow painted line on the floor. They formed a line, unsure of what to do next. The ten farmworkers stood with bovine stillness.

One door stood closed in the wall opposite them. Sully stared at it, waiting for whatever dramatic entrance the organiser had planned.

Nothing happened.

The Ten all looked at the door, all making the same assumption, then turned and stared at a scraping noise from the side of the building. A pedestrian door, cut into the metal side wall slid open and a man stepped in and crossed to the centre of the room, looking at them.

Sully's irritation flared again. It was the scruffy smoker who had driven the van. Even now he had a cigarette in his left hand, the smoke twirling lazily up his yellow fingers. *He can't be in charge.*

'I want to talk to the organiser,' Sully said.

'Yeah, this is bogus,' someone else said.

The smoker ignored the protests. 'I am Serge,' he said. He gave a shrug as if he didn't care what they thought. 'If you were expecting some big Disney production then you're in the wrong place.' His eyes swept The Ten. 'Feel free to quit anytime.'

The room dropped into silence; they had all reacted to the threat in the tone of Serge's voice.

'OK then. You've all played my other games. You've done well,' Serge said. 'You've been specially chosen. You're the best AR gamers,' Serge said.

Sully nodded. Of course he was.

'But those games were nothing.' Serge spread his arms wide. 'This is Forbidden Island.'

The Ten smiled at the name and the promise of the place.

'This is the ultimate game, for the ultimate prize,' Serge continued. 'Much preparation has taken place, much money spent, and many people have put themselves at risk. We do not do this lightly. We need to be sure that this is the greatest game of all time. We need to be sure that you'll give everything to the game.'

'Yes,' Sully shouted, 'bring it on.'

Serge shook his head. 'Words are easy. We need you to *prove* your commitment.' He paused. 'And only four can play.'

The others shouted complaints and questions, but Sully smiled. *No problem*, he thought. Ten or four, he would beat them all anyway.

Serge ignored the protests and waited until the room fell silent again. He let it drag on, then glanced up at the pattering on the roof. The noise got louder as the rain fell harder.

'There will be three tests to find our players. They will turn ten into four. They will find the righteous. The rest will go home and reflect on their lack of commitment. Their unworthiness.' Serge took a long drag on his cigarette. 'You will have no help, no devices, no money. Nothing but you.'

I play by my own rules, Sully thought and puffed his chest out.

'The first test will prove that you have the desire and skills to get around with no help,' Serge said, raising a finger. 'The second will show that you can evade capture.' Now Serge had two fingers raised and a third joined it. 'The final test will prove how serious you are. It will strip away all the pretence and bravado. It will expose the real you.'

'Bring it,' Sully said. The others joined him, each demanding the start of the game. Each sure of themselves.

'More words, more boasts,' Serge said, shrugging his indifference. 'We will see who lives up to them. Leave anything you have in your room. The van leaves in five minutes. Wear something warm.'

Chapter 11

Clive had woken up tired and irritable again, and his mood wasn't helped by the insistence of his bladder. His mouth was so dry that his tongue seemed glued stuck. *The human body has a design fault*, he thought. He needed a drink and his body clearly had enough liquid in it, yet here he was heading to the toilet to get rid of it. Why couldn't his urine be recycled and then he wouldn't need to piss or drink. Obviously not external recycling. He cringed at the thought of the people who drank their own urine. *That can't be a good idea.* Years ago, he would have complained that bad beer tasted like piss, but he was pleased that the comparison wasn't based on actual experience.

Clive's Buddy rolled out a banner with the reminder of the hospital appointment, then another banner. *'Your car is booked for 9:30am.'*

Maybe I don't need to go, he thought. He pinched his fingers on a menu item on his HUD, then clicked and swiped until he got to his health summary page.

'Crap, not again,' he said.

***

In the car, sitting with his usual rear-facing view, Clive scrolled through the medical articles on the screen. As the car approached Windsor, he turned slightly and took in the Long Walk. He loved the tree-lined pathway stretching down to the castle in the distance.

Today's blue sky contrasted with the feelings of dread he was fighting. The articles he was reading added to his fears. The car completed the journey five minutes before his appointment time, and Clive got out.

The King Edward VII hospital's cream facade, royal crest and statue made it seem like a country club, but as Clive stepped into the reception, that hospital smell of disinfectant and old cabbage hit him.

The hospital's automated registration system recognised Clive's iMe signal, and his Buddy rolled out a banner detailing the consultant's name, room number and re-confirmation of his appointment time.

The waiting area had an aura of calm, with only a couple of people in it. As Clive sat, it struck him how different it was now. Eleven years ago, before iMe, he would have brought a book, and expected a long, long vigil in a crowded and unpleasant waiting room. Even worse at an A&E department. The minimum four hour wait meant that you could get through a lot of chapters. Now iMe did the triage automatically, and sent people to the pharmacy drop-in, GP or hospital. Everything diagnosed early and booked in advance.

At 10am, the green light over the door labelled Exam Room 5 blinked and Clive stood and hesitated. Did he really want confirmation of what he already knew? His Buddy flashed him a new banner *'Don't waste precious resources. Being late for your appointment by more than 5 minutes will result in a £500 fine for each ten-minute period.'*

It was enough for Clive, he stepped forward and opened the door to the room.

The consultant sat behind a metal topped desk by the window, and the angle of the sun lit up her long dark hair and one side of her face. The swirls caused by the cleaners in the metal desktop glinted. Clive's gaze settled on her white doctor's coat and the angular NM badge on her lapel.

She stood and waved Clive in and pointed at a chair opposite the display wall of the room.

'Mr Lussac, hello. I'm Dilani Adhya,' she said as she crossed to Clive and shook his hand before walking to the display wall and touching a button on the side. 'We have a problem.'

Clive said nothing. He knew he had a problem.

The display wall redrew with his health summary. Now he could see his problem. The flashing warning said it all. *'High blood sugar level.'*

'What I can't see, is an obvious cause,' Dilani said. 'Despite the records of your consumption being pure green, your blood sugar seems to have risen over the last year, along with your weight. Has anything changed?'

Clive shuffled uncomfortably in his chair. 'Not really,' he muttered, thinking of how often he used the Health Bank bracelet he had 'borrowed' from the PCU evidence store and how it masked his consumption. It couldn't mask the side effects.

'That's strange. You used to be given Excess Consumption Orders, but there's been none in the last year. That's very good, so something else must be going on.' She looked at Clive, her eyes alive with questions.

Clive shook his head and dropped his gaze.

'Your fasting blood sugar level has been over the diabetes threshold several times recently.' Dilani paused and her fingers danced in front of her face as she typed on her HUD.

The display wall redrew, showing a pre-iMe era hospital letter confirming Clive's Type 2 diabetes diagnosis. He groaned. Dilani then swiped the wall and he saw a second letter. This one was dated a year after the introduction of iMe. Dilani used her finger to highlight a sentence on the second letter *'Your type 2 diabetes appears to be in remission.'*

'That's no longer true,' she said. 'As your insulin levels seem normal, we need to work out what is causing your high sugar levels.'

Clive nodded. He was back where he started through his own weakness.

'I'll schedule some other appointments, but we have rules...' she said and paused, dropping her gaze to the desk. 'I don't want to do this, but as there's no obvious medical cause for the change, and with your history of excess consumption, the Ministry of Well-being and Health will need to be informed.'

Shit, thought Clive. That meant meeting Winter, the FU Enforcement Officer again. It wasn't going to go well.

***

Back in the sunshine of the hospital car park, Clive groaned again and slapped his palm against his head. 'Idiot!' he screamed at himself. The bracelets were a gift, well, a stolen gift, Clive admitted to himself, and he had taken them for granted. It wasn't only the diabetes. Well-being and Health would be all over his Freedom Units allowance. They'd find out about the chocolate. He'd owe so much in FU tax.

His car pulled silently into the car park and stopped beside Clive. The door opened and he got in. The PCU office was already programmed as the destination, and the car started off.

Clive couldn't put it off, he'd stolen a bracelet for Sophia as well, not that she used it now she had the Church of the New Modelists. He touched his jaw to make a call. 'Hi, Sophia, how are you?'

'How did it go?' Sophia asked. Clive could hear the concern in her voice.

'OK.'

'What does that mean?'

'Sorry.'

Clive couldn't find the words to tell Sophia that her bracelet would put her in the shit as well.

Chapter 12

Tatsuko guessed she had been in the van twenty minutes. All her possessions had been taken and locked in her room in the barn – the one with the big number five on it.

She braced her body and held on as the van took another corner. The Ten were all in there, perched on two box seats that ran the length of the van's sides. They had no padding or cushions, just a flat metal top that was both uncomfortable and slippery. No seat belts. They slid and returned with each movement of the van, like waves lapping at a beach.

The Ten hadn't talked amongst themselves. Instead, there were glances: assessing, competitive, uncertain, some hostile.

We're all here to win, but it doesn't need to be like this, Tatsuko thought. She was going to break the ice.

But she could hear her mother. *They're not your friends, stupid girl, they're the enemy.* Whatever she did was never good enough. She wasn't good enough. She had tried everything to win approval from her mother. Even after her mother had died, she couldn't shake her mother's voice from her head. It still drove her.

'Hi,' she said to the middle of the van. They all looked at her but said nothing. She saw a couple of the gazes were interested. 'I'm Tatsuko,' she said. 'I'm *ReflectiveAndRightous* on the forum.'

'Don't care, Yankee,' a man by the door said. From his accent, olive skin and dark hair, Tatsuko guessed he was Italian. 'I'm Sully, but you'll never catch up with me to use it.' He glared at her, like he was trying to bully and intimidate her. He had the look of a spoilt brat.

'Lilou,' someone said.

Tatsuko blanked Sully and spun to a friendly French voice.

The woman opposite Tatsuko flashed a smile. '*Parkour179* on the forum.'

Any opportunity for conversation ended as the van braked hard. Everyone grabbed what they could to stop themselves flying forwards, then the van crunched into reverse, and they all lurched back. The van stopped and the doors opened.

***

The van was parked a little way off the road, up a rough, small track cut into some trees. Its back doors were open, and Serge sat on the floor, using the open doors to shelter his cigarette from the wind. The Ten stood waiting, apprehension on their faces. Not a group. Definitely not a team. Ten silos.

Tatsuko waited, focused, watching Serge, but Sully shoved her, sending her off-balance and her left foot splashed into a deep puddle. He smiled.

Before she could retaliate, Serge coughed and said, 'This is the first task. In Forbidden Island, you will need to travel a long way without being caught. No phone, money, no devices. Just you. Now we have a practice. Come and get your bag.' Serge beckoned them forward.

Tatsuko could see the bags behind Serge, each with a number on the front. She stepped forward and was given one with the number five on it.

'You have a map and a compass. A torch and a little food. Please get the map out,' Serge said.

Tatsuko pulled her map out and swung the bag over her shoulder. The wind caught the map and it flapped, like a bird trying to escape. She grasped the map and sheltered it with her body.

'We are on the D61, near Forges-les-Eaux,' Serge said. 'It's marked.'

Tatsuko and the others all checked the maps to find the start point.

'You have to get to Parkeerplaatst aan de haven in Plage de Saint-Valery-en-Caux. It's about eighty kilometres.' He looked at his watch. 'About 16:30 now, you get there by 08:30 if you walk.'

Tatsuko was already using her finger to trace a rough route.

'This test is not only about speed.' Serge paused so that they all looked up. 'We will have cars out looking for you, we don't want to see you.'

Serge stood and dropped his cigarette. 'You start when the van goes.' He walked around the van and climbed in. 'Only seven make it through the test,' he called as the van drove away.

Tatsuko walked off the track and onto the road. There was a small junction a few metres away. She jogged to it. Three signs. The left pointed along a narrow, tree-lined road and said *'D61 – La Ferte'*. Right said, *'D61 – La Balliere'*, and pointed along an identical tree-lined road. The sign ahead said *'D9 – Le Fosse'*. She looked at the map again. *Time for planning, not running*, she thought. After a few seconds, she had decided, and followed the backs of the other competitors running along the D9, but she didn't follow them for long. Instead, she cut left, jumped over the green and white pole that acted as a gate to another track, crunched along it for a few metres and headed into the trees.

***

Tatsuko stopped for a sip of water, leaning against the sign marking the exit of Bacqueville en Caux. The town's church clock had called three in the morning as she skirted the buildings, with their sleeping people and their barking dogs, and trudged across the fields.

Why are you wasting time, lazy girl, her mother's voice said.

Tatsuko flicked her torch on, sheltering the light with her hand, and played the light across the map. Time for speed, she thought. The roads would be quicker, and she would see the lights of an approaching car miles off. She started jogging along the D152 road.

***

Tatsuko stopped again. It felt like her left big toe was beginning to blister, maybe because that pig Sully had pushed her into the puddle and the water had softened her skin. She hadn't seen any of the other Ten since the beginning. She walked on, wincing at each step as her foot started to ache.

She clenched her jaw. 'No surrender,' she said to the fields.

***

Tatsuko turned and saw car lights in the distance. The landscape around her was all open green fields. Nowhere to hide. She jogged on and as she came around the corner, she saw a clump of trees ahead.

The car was louder. Closer.

She ran, arms and legs pumping. Reaching the trees, she glanced behind her, the car's lights were turning the corner. She jumped into the trees, and lay, panting.

The lights and the noise of the car flashed by. As she looked up through the trees, glimpsing the night sky, she thought of her mother, searching for a gentle, warming memory but her mother's mantra echoed in Tatsuko's ears. *You won't get anywhere in life laying around, lazy girl.*

She took another breath, jumped up and started running along the road again.

***

Tatsuko's stomach tightened and her legs felt heavy with dread as she jogged along the promenade at Plage de Saint-Valery-en-Caux. She could see the waiting van. And the people around it. She counted them.

Too many people.

Seven of The Ten were already there. She was eighth and only seven go through.

The brisk sea air ruffled their hair, and she could taste the salt in the air. The bitter taste of failure.

Sully leered at her. 'Thanks for playing, Yankee. You're a bit late.' He raised one finger in the air. 'Guess who was first?'

***

Now, back in the barn, The Ten were in a line again, their backs to their numbered doors, waiting for Serge to speak.

Tatsuko shuffled and waited for the verdict. She expected to leave and heard another *useless girl* taunt from the voice of her mother replaying in her head.

'As I said. Only seven go to the next test.' Serge shrugged out a fake apology. 'The first two people leaving us are…' He paused for dramatic effect, playing it like the elimination on a TV cookery show. 'Four… and One.'

The woman to Tatsuko's left groaned and turned, joined by the man at the end. Both headed to their now open numbered doors in the back wall of the barn.

'The final person leaving us is either Five.' Serge looked straight at Tatsuko. She felt her legs give, but Serge continued, 'Or… Nine.'

Tatsuko held her breath. Please don't let this be over before it's begun.

'Five you were slower than Nine, but we never saw you… Nine you were quicker, but you blunder around like a drunk bear. So, the third person leaving is…' Another long pause. 'Nine.'

Tatsuko let out a long gasp.

'You were lucky, Yankee,' Sully said.

'Shit, man,' Nine groaned as two of Serge's assistants stepped forward. As they escorted him to the door, Tatsuko twisted and watched him go. His shoulders sagged in defeat and shame at being sent home so early. Her mother's whispered sneer bounced around her head, *You bring dishonour on me, lazy girl. You're too slow.*

I'll win, mother.

'Next test tomorrow. Eat and rest.' Serge turned and left.

***

Serge sat at his desk, the smoke from the cigarette balanced on the edge of the ashtray curling lazily upwards.

He tapped on the keyboard as he typed out the tweet.

'Hi to all you film fans, quick poll. Which film do you prefer? "Se7en" or "The Magnificent Seven"? Both classics – you decide.'

He pressed send.

Chapter 13

As Clive arrived in the PCU office, Ava flashed him a bright, white smile. She looked annoyingly healthy and youthful. Her vibrant yellow shirt seemed to have brought the sunshine inside with her. He felt as grey as the hospital corridors he had left behind.

'Morning,' Clive said, dropping into a chair.

'Wow, Boss. You look awful,' Ava replied.

'Can't seem to sleep.' Clive rubbed his hand back and forward, pulling at his face, but couldn't wipe away the feeling of exhaustion. 'Anything happening?'

'We've got an Unchip. How can the parents be so selfish?' Ava threw her HUD at the display wall so Clive could read the details.

The Sacred Chant School had reported the parents of one of their pupils for failing to present their daughter for iMe insertion. The fourteen-year-old was still using her iMe Lite Child Tracker bracelet.

'What's their defence?' Clive asked.

'Parental concern over the kid being vulnerable to cyber-bullying and them wanting to control video stream access.'

Clive's eyes drifted to the far wall. He had stopped listening and replayed the hospital appointment. *Why do I always make things worse for myself?*

'Boss? You OK?'

'Fine.' Clive tried for a smile, but it only got to about a tenth of the intensity of one of Ava's. 'The parents must know they can't win.' He pushed back his chair and stood. 'Let's go and sort it out.'

As he took a step, his head emptied of blood and he stumbled. He dropped his hands onto his knees to ride out the wave of dizziness.

'Sure you're OK, Boss?'

Clive waited for a second and then stood up. 'Got up too quickly.'

He headed for the door, muttering and grumbling, as Ava swiped and clicked to book a car.

Chasing the parents of some Unchip kid should be a job for Uniform, not a DI, he thought, but at least doing this would keep him occupied instead of staring at an empty work queue all day worrying about his health.

***

'Summer was fourteen yesterday and *you* called the cops today. Shame on you.' The woman emphasised her point with a jabbing finger pointed straight at the teacher.

Clive could see her details on his HUD. She was thirty-four, named Dani, mother of Summer and the head of a large department in a media firm. Her lawyer husband nodded along behind her, happy to let Dani do all the confrontation.

Summer stepped backwards towards the classroom wall, clutching her Mobi. It was the child's mobile version of an adult HUD, and when paired to her iMe Lite Child Tracker, it provided Summer with the gateway to her electronic world.

'It's the law and my duty,' the teacher replied, her chin high and proud. She wore a grey suit and white shirt, but it was the bright-green lapel badge with the angular NM letters she touched as she spoke. Certainty radiated from her.

'Legally, we have five days after her birthday, so we've done nothing–' the father said.

'No, you don't.' The tips of Ava's bob waved in time with her head shake. 'You're required to have booked the insertion *before* her fourteenth birthday. Which you didn't. The five-day allowance is for the actual insertion appointment.' She sat back and crossed her arms.

Clive thought that Summer's parents stopping her becoming an adult had got to Ava and she had opened up and cut the father in two. Clive couldn't help but smile at her growing assertiveness.

Dani's withering glare turned on him.

'Well…' the father flustered.

'Without her full iMe, Summer isn't an adult,' the teacher said. 'She'll have no vote, no tax record, no young-adult benefit payments, no access to the legal stimulants and drugs.'

'And that's a good thing,' Dani said.

'You know she can't abuse them. We encourage all our students to stay green.' The teacher touched her badge again.

Clive thought back to his own childhood, long before iMe, getting served beer underage, drinking too much and pebble-dashing the floor or pavement with his vomit. In those days, the beer stayed inside him for such a short period – piss or puke, he only seemed to rent alcohol by the hour.

'I thought you all wore green,' Clive said to the teacher.

She nodded. 'Usually, but religious clothing is banned inside the school in case it offends anyone. One item of symbolic jewellery is permitted.' She touched her lapel badge, as if drawing strength from it. It seemed to empower her.

'Pure green?' Clive asked and the teacher nodded. It explained her calling the police. The Church of the New Modelists was clear on the subject: *Conformity is Contentment, Conformity is Peace.* You can only conform to the Model Citizen directive if you have iMe – not the Child Tracker.

Children didn't have FUs to keep up the pretence that they had free will. They couldn't be measured. You needed the full iMe to prove that you lived your life according to the Model. Or to prove that you 'lived green' or the even more extreme 'pure greens' who had never been outside the Model.

'But all the cyber-bullying and adult video streams,' Dani said.

'Summer's an adult,' Ava said. 'She can view what she likes, and block bullies.'

'Or ignore them,' Clive said.

Everyone turned to look at him – disbelief on their faces. Clive shrugged. He had grown up in a 'sticks and stones may break my bones, but words will never hurt me' era. 'Don't give the bully the power,' his parents had told him. He didn't understand how people these days allowed words to cut deep wounds into them, how everything was labelled abuse, and everyone was a powerless victim. 'Words only have power if you let them,' Clive tried, but he could see that they didn't believe him. He had only recently reconnected with these words and his own beliefs, but along with the therapy for his depression, it was helping.

'But…' Dani said. 'She's still my baby.'

Summer cringed at the word baby. 'Mum,' she complained.

'Irrespective of your feelings,' Ava said to Dani, 'Summer is an adult and is required by law to have an iMe. As she doesn't have a pre-booked appointment, we'll have to take her today for an emergency insertion. It will be at your cost, not the government's.'

Clive and Ava stood up and crossed towards Summer. Dani stepped in front of them to protect Summer, but stepped back again as her husband pulled her arm.

Dani's crying still echoed along the empty corridor as Clive and Ava escorted Summer out of the school.

***

Clive was back in a hospital waiting room again, grateful that this time it wasn't for him.

Summer perched on the chair opposite, biting her bottom lip as Ava held her hand.

'We can let your parents know where you are,' Clive said, but Summer shook her head.

'I'm an adult now,' she said. 'And they don't understand me.'

Clive leaned forward and asked gently, 'Can we talk about your diagnosis?' He'd noticed how thin her legs were in the walk along the school corridor, and was pleased that it had been empty of the prying eyes of other students.

Summer nodded.

'I know the insertion seems scary, but it might help a bit.' He waited until Summer looked up and he continued. 'Your doctors can adjust the Model Citizen to allow for your anorexia. You'll be able to see that you're eating exactly the right amounts of the right things. No more guesswork.'

'Maybe,' Summer said.

Clive knew that iMe wouldn't address the underlying mental health issues, but at least Summer's doctors could monitor her health and target her weight gain now. It was a big improvement from the days of sectioning anorexia patients and locking them in hospital.

Two double doors banged open and made whooshing noises as they swung back and forth before they settled closed.

'Summer Tailor?' a nurse said.

The girl stood, looking more like a small child than the adult she was.

The nurse took a step forward. 'We're ready for your iMe insertion.'

Chapter 14

'We lose two more of you today,' Serge said, once more sitting on the floor of the open van.

Lilou watched his eyes pan across the remaining Seven, and stiffened as Serge met her eyes. She straightened and lifted her head. She needed to win this one.

The van was parked on the side of the road of a sleepy French town.

'For today's test, you start at the church behind you,' Serge said. Lilou turned and saw the drab, brown church, black metal gates and the blue sign: *'Eglise Evangélique'*.

Serge tapped some sheets of paper beside him. 'Come and get a map and compass.'

When they all had their single sheet, he continued. 'We are in Saint-Saëns, and you need to get to the V1 rocket launch site at Val Ygot.'

Lilou found both places on her map. A big green area was drawn on the map between them with the name 'Forêt d'Eawy'. There was no clue of how dense a forest it was.

Serge watched a second van arrive and park in front of the church. Lilou could hear dogs barking inside.

'It's only about eight kilometres. Nice and simple race.' Serge paused for another drag on a cigarette. 'But we'll pretend you're on the Forbidden Island and are being chased.'

Lilou felt elated. This was about strength and evasion. Speed and running. This was designed for her. She bounced on her toes, warming her muscles. She touched her chest where her gold medal had hung.

Serge nodded to the van with the dogs. 'We give you ten minutes head start. Go!'

Lilou bounded forward, beating the others off the line. She flashed past Sully, who stuck a leg out to try and trip her, but it was easy to avoid such a clumsy obstacle. She reached the gate to the church first, grasped the top rail with her left hand and vaulted over.

Landing easily, Lilou ran up the hill and left the others still climbing the gate.

***

Lilou bounced easily on her toes, enjoying the running. The trees pressed in around her, but she greeted each of them as a parkour barrier and skipped over and around them. The earth smelt damp and she splashed through the mud. The sound of the dogs' excited barking seemed closer. She ran faster, trying to keep her rhythm.

When Lilou broke cover, she saw the sign for the rocket launch site across the empty road. Crossing the road, she jogged through the car park and up the shaded track to the launch site. She stopped at the rocket, touching the cold, grey metal of its wing, and bounced on her feet, elated to be the first competitor here.

She turned as she heard clapping. Serge sat on a bench and smiled. 'Fast time,' he said.

Lilou shrugged. It had been like a training run and not any serious competition. She walked to the end of the launch pad and looked along the length of the rocket, like she was aiming it.

Straight at the Forbidden Island.

***

Lilou kept stretching to make sure her muscles cooled down properly as she waited. Three others had straggled in, minutes after her. Femi, then Tatsuko, then Jose, whose muscled physique was built more for strength than speed.

Still they waited. And waited.

Finally, Sully panted his way up the path and stopped, breathing hard and covered in mud. He had somehow won the longer test easily, but now he looked unfit. Lilou couldn't work out how he had done it. She was still wondering when Serge stood and said, 'The dogs have the others, so they are out.'

'But they're OK?' Lilou asked.

'Of course. The dogs are trained to grab people by the arm, not the neck.' Serge beckoned them all towards the road, 'Come my final five, we can go.'

They followed, eager steps, jostling to be the first behind him.

Some of their swagger disappeared as Serge said, 'But if you fail the next test, today's losers will be back to take your place.'

***

The man who used the name Jack heard the chime of a new message arriving on his TrueMe account. His heart quickened – the tone was unique to Serge's tweets.

He pinched his fingers to pick up the tweet and threw it at his HUD. The little TrueMe icon turned, like an old-school spinning newspaper, and opened to the text of the message.

'Hi to all you film fans, enjoying a sci-fi classic today. "The Fifth Element".'

Jack smiled, down to five already. The selection was going well.

After all his plotting, soon it would be time.

His destiny.

Chapter 15

Zoe pushed on the frosted glass door and took a tentative look inside. The usual pre-meeting hum of conversations stopped as people turned, but started again when they saw it was only the newbie arriving.

It was her second day in the Terrorism-Cyber special unit. The first had been a round of introductions and briefing notes to wade through. Today was when the work started. This meeting was the kick-off.

Zoe headed for an empty space against the back wall and weaved around the other team members who slouched on beanbags or perched on balance balls. She reached her spot and nodded to the man next to her. What was his name? Sam? Josh? She hadn't had a chance to memorise them all. As she rested her back against the wall, the door opened again, and Detective Chief Superintendent Bhatt strode in. The noise in the room vanished – part respect for Bhatt, part anticipation.

Bhatt slowly and deliberately tracked her eyes around the room, making sure she caught everyone's eye.

'DI Alexis Sawyer is heading up this special group,' she said, nodding to the person standing to her right.

Sawyer straightened at the mention of her name.

'She has my complete backing.' Bhatt paused and waited – demanding all their attention. 'I came today to emphasise the importance of your work.'

With a small nod to the room, Bhatt marched to the door and was gone. *Typical*, Zoe thought, *straight to the point and no unnecessary chat.*

'OK, team,' Sawyer said as she moved to the centre of the room. 'With the cyber threat level at "Imminent", we want to catch any hint of terror attacks from the electronic traffic – real or virtual. It's going to take intense data grinding, but we can make a real difference. You've all seen the briefings. There are plenty of possible leads.'

Sawyer repeated Bhatt's slow track of the room with her eyes. It didn't have the same intensity, but Sawyer still got her message across – this was serious work with no option of failing. Sawyer took the rest of the meeting emphasising the point and describing everyone's work assignments. She finished with Zoe.

'Zoe,' Sawyer said. 'Welcome to the team. I've heard good things from DCS Bhatt.'

'Thank you, Boss,' Zoe replied, conscious of everyone turning to look at her again. She flashed a smile, but kept her eyes serious. She would make herself central to the team.

'I want you to start by looking for correlations between the number of messages sent into the UK and any of the recent cyber attacks. See if you can find anyone who's more active just before an attack.'

***

While Zoe was settling to her task, Clive's call was disintegrating, and he banged his hand on the screen of the car as it turned into the King Edward VII hospital car park.

'I'm fine,' he said for what felt like the fiftieth time, losing the battle to keep the sulk out of his voice.

'You're clearly not,' Sophia countered.

'Look, Sophia, I can handle it.'

'If you could, you wouldn't be going to the hospital…' She went silent and then said, 'Oh, do what you want. You will anyway,' and hung up the call. If she had screamed at him, he could have taken it, but the resigned coldness in her voice ate at Clive and forced an involuntary shiver.

His appointment was due in five minutes, and he tried to shake the call out of his head as he repeated the check-in process and pushed open the door to Exam Room 5 when the green light showed.

Dilani Adhya sat at her desk, her hands moving in front of her face as she typed on her HUD. She used her eyes to motion

Clive to the empty seat opposite her and mouthed a silent, 'Sorry, just a minute.'

Dilani's dancing hands were still visible in the corner of his eye as Clive scanned the room. It didn't take long. A sterile hospital examination room – display wall, cupboard, narrow bed to lie on, flimsy curtain, desk and two chairs. His eyes caught a flash of reflected light as Dilani twisted to reach for something on her desk, and Clive noticed that Dilani's NM badge was silver in colour and not green like Summer's teacher's badge.

Finally, Dilani's hands dropped and she turned to face Clive.

'I'm sorry, Mr Lussac,' she said. 'I think you may have had a wasted journey.'

Clive looked bemused.

'I had planned to run a series of tests to try and see why your blood sugar level has been spiking with no food intake.'

Clive said nothing. He knew why his blood sugar spiked. His stolen Health Bank bracelet hid his eating from the sensors in his iMe. His FU allowance didn't allow for chocolate, but his craving couldn't be denied.

'Unfortunately, the Ministry of Well-being and Health have only just replied to me. They're saying that because this is a pre-existing, self-inflicted condition, you should be put on the low priority list. I'm not allowed to run the tests today.'

'What can I do?' Clive asked. Even though he knew the cause, he didn't want his diabetes back and unmanaged.

'As you're a police officer, you're in a protected occupation. You need to talk to police Employee Wellness and your boss. Get them to raise it with the Ministry.'

'No way you can do the tests today?'

Dilani shook her head. 'But I'll set you a new diet.' She hesitated and looked around the room.

Clive's eyebrows raised, she seemed to want to say something else. 'What?'

She let out a little cough and said, 'In cases like yours, the New Modelists can provide guidance and a supportive framework in this difficult world.'

She stopped when she saw Clive's head shaking back and forth like an overactive set of windscreen wipers.

'Not you as well… sorry, thanks anyway, but I can't,' Clive said, stood and left.

As he walked out of the hospital, the rain stopped, and he caught the smell of damp tarmac. Clive's Buddy jogged onto his HUD, trailing an *Urgent New Message* banner. Clive clicked on the banner and his Buddy threw the message text onto his HUD.

The name of the message sender crashed into Clive, stopping him dead. 'Special Investigator Winter, Freedom Unit Enforcement, Ministry of Well-being and Health.'

Clive knew that Winter would be coming for him, but the message text made Clive's legs almost give way.

'Inspector, it is with great anticipation that I am re-opening my investigation into your Freedom Unit abuse.'

Chapter 16

Serge smoothed the green, satin fabric cover draped over the boxes on the middle of the table and nodded to his assistants. They each went to a door in the back wall and unlocked it. The five remaining contestants stepped out. Serge motioned them forward to the yellow line on the floor.

He lifted his hands and placed them on top of the cover, knowing the motion would draw their attention. All eyes looked at the cover.

'Congratulations,' Serge said, smiling. 'You have proved that you have the skills to perform well in the ultimate augmented reality game.'

Sully looked up and pushed his chin forward. 'Too right.'

Serge gave a small shake of his head and said, 'You can all count. The game is for four players and there are five of you... so we have more challenges. We keep going until there are four.'

The Five flicked glances at each other, and Serge could feel their excitement and nerves at being so close. He made them wait.

'But before that, let's talk about the prize. The first is obviously access to the Forbidden Island and the chance to play the ultimate game. Along with that is the glory and fan worship you will get. The forums will shout your names.'

Although Lilou, Sully and Jose beamed, Femi and Tatsuko stayed focused on the table.

'There are different motivations – maybe honouring the memory of a parent.' Serge looked at Tatsuko. 'Or helping your family.' Femi lifted his eyes, as though he was picturing a favourite scene.

'We all need money and there is a prize fund, paid in Pan-European dollars. Five million to the winner.' Each of The Five smiled, seeming to be spending the cash already. 'Three million to second place, one million to third, and half a million for last.' The Five winced at the word *last*.

'But the main prize for playing the game is special.' Serge tapped his hand on the box under the cover on the table, and all eyes snapped back to it. 'This is unobtainable to mere civilians, but I have contacts. You think that you are already able to do things others can't. You are already part of the AR elite, but...' Serge grasped the fabric cover and started to slowly drag it off the boxes, 'I offer you the chance to be superhuman.'

With a flick of his hand, Serge completed the reveal. The Five whooped and cheered and crowded up to the table.

'No way,' said Tatsuko.

'Magnifique,' sighed Lilou.

There were two simple blue boxes on the table, nothing to get excited about in themselves.

Except for the logo. Everyone ached and yearned for products wearing that logo.

The initials BST shone in red with a gold leaf background. A red border made in a diamond shape surrounded the letters. It looked like a stylised version of the Superman and Superwoman logos from the films. The B and T letters smaller, next to the bigger central S.

'Obviously you know of BioSuperTech products.' Serge picked up the smaller box and opened it. He pulled out a small sleeve-like object with a solid end. 'This is the universal mount. We will take your measurements and customise it to your arm and skin tone.'

They nodded, waiting for the bigger box. Serge could taste their anticipation. BST was everything.

'My contacts have access to the latest generation products.' Serge opened the bigger box, placed the lid on the table and turned it so that The Five could see the contents. All five moaned, a low 'ooo' noise of longing and desire.

'I have four,' Serge said.

The box held a hand. But not a real hand. Much better – a BST synth-hand. The shape was hand-like, but on this BST model, the little finger and third finger were replaced by a second thumb and index finger giving a huge range of grips and possible uses. The hand's simple satin finish hid all the technology and bionics that BST was famous for. Ten times the strength and sensitivity to the touch of an inferior human hand.

'You can choose any finger configuration or finish you want. Something bright and obvious or a subtle colour match to make it look natural if you prefer a stealth look.'

Serge offered the box, and eager hands grabbed for it.

'One each for the final four.' Serge beamed like a generous Father Christmas. Then his smile dropped.

'Time to see if you have the will and determination to earn your prize. Return to your rooms and wait to be called.'

***

The tiny side room to the barn held two chairs and a small table. A simple light dangled on the cord over the table and cast yellow light on Serge and the sawdust covering the floor. A cigarette balanced on the edge of an ashtray sending a lazy spiral of smoke up towards the light.

Serge was fighting for breath as his chest tightened. Something in the air at the farm always made him worse. He pulled his inhaler from his pocket and took another long pull. The drugs eased his chest a little. He needed two more for the tightness to pass.

He was glad Jose hadn't arrived yet. Serge didn't want to show any weakness. He stuffed the inhaler back in his pocket.

The door opened and Jose entered. Serge nodded to the chair opposite him and Jose lifted it effortlessly and sat.

'I think you will need an extra-large from BST,' Serge said, but Jose was looking at the table and didn't seem to hear him.

'Jose,' Serge said louder, and Jose looked up. 'You have been impressive so far, but it is time to show commitment and not just strength.'

Jose nodded and kept staring at the guillotine on the desk.

Serge placed his hand on the guillotine's release lever and paused. The blade shone and he watched Jose's eyes follow the wires from the blade up to the large, heavy counterweights and down to the lever.

'Please place your hand through the guillotine until your wrist is under the blade. Left or right – your choice.'

Beads of sweat appeared on Jose's brow, his hands remained glued to his side.

'Where did you think the BST hand was going to fit?' Serge asked.

Jose said nothing. Instead, he licked his lips and moved his hand. Not towards the guillotine, but up to wipe his brow. Finally, he said, 'I know, but I didn't expect to do it now.'

'Time to choose,' Serge said and waited. Allowing the pressure to build.

'Umm… OK,' Jose said, as one of the drops of sweat broke the surface tension on his temple and started to roll down his face.

Jose moved his right hand towards the guillotine. The motion stopped halfway as Jose seemed to change his mind. His right hand withdrew to the edge of the desk and safety. Jose's left hand inched forward and under the blade. Still he fidgeted.

'It's for the game, the money and the BST hand,' Serge said. 'And the fame.'

It seemed to take a lot of effort for Jose to crack a smile. His head dropped in a tiny nod and he said, 'OK…' Then with more conviction. 'OK. Do it.'

Serge's hand moved, drawing the lever down.

Jose's whole body tensed as he stared at the blade. Waiting for it to drop.

As Serge's hand moved again, the pin holding the blade came free with a small metallic click. The blade moved and Jose's eyes bulged. The blade started to accelerate down towards his wrist and Jose's arm trembled. The blade reached halfway, and Jose yanked his arm back and away from the guillotine, clutching it to his chest and rubbing the wrist where the blade would have bitten.

With a clunk, the blade finished its drop and bounced off a hidden stop. It vibrated at the sudden deceleration, a good 50mm above where Jose's wrist would have been.

'You're not committed enough. You're out. Go home and reflect on your weakness,' Serge said.

Jose's chair scraped back, leaving trails in the sawdust and he trudged out, still clutching his wrist to his chest.

After Jose left, Serge reset the mechanism and waited for Tatsuko.

He let out a low 'hmmm' noise from the back of his throat. The first one was weak and had failed. Now the others must all pass, otherwise he'd have to bring back some of the eliminated ones to fill the remaining slots. Compromise wasn't a word he liked. Jack wouldn't be pleased. Worst still if they all failed and he had to run another selection process. The delay would be a disaster.

His thoughts were interrupted by Tatsuko arriving and sitting down. He explained the challenge to her, and waited for her reply. It didn't take long, the lure of the money and BST prize were more than enough for her. She nodded and adjusted her position. There was a slight shake in her hands that she couldn't control, but she took two deep breaths and closed her eyes. She opened them and looked straight into Serge's eyes before nodding again.

Serge pulled the lever, and the blade dropped, but Tatsuko didn't flinch. She looked at Serge the whole time, a challenge in her gaze. The blade bounced to a stop with a soft thump. Tatsuko glanced down at the blade wondering why there was no pain. The hand she thought she must sacrifice for the game was still attached with the blade resting safely above it. Frown lines knotted her brow as she looked back at Serge.

He smiled. 'Congratulations, Tatsuko, you've passed the test,' he said. 'Please return to your room.'

Chapter 17

The guillotine had been stowed away, replaced by his laptop, the sawdust swept up. The yellow light in the small room remained. Serge pressed send on his latest tweet. *'Hi, film fans. Going old-school and watching "The Fantastic Four" tonight.'*

He let the relief wash over him. Jack wouldn't have liked the delay. Only one contestant had failed the third challenge, and Serge had his Four. They were waiting for him.

Serge rubbed his face, feeling the ends of the bristles from the days of growth of stubble. He wanted to get back to his apartment, have a shower and shave, pour a glass of wine and pull on a cigarette and watch the river flow by. But that would have to wait.

He scraped back his chair and pushed his hands into his lower back, arching and stretching to ease the grumbling pain. Opening the door, he stepped into the main hall and saw The Four sitting around the long table that held the BST universal mount and hand. He tapped the smaller box in his trouser pocket to double-check that he had it.

'Congratulations,' he said as he stood in front of The Four again. 'You are the chosen elite. You will become legends.'

From the smiles that greeted him, they clearly believed his words. Especially Sully. He looked like he thought himself a Roman Emperor surrounded by peasants.

Serge pulled the small box out of his pocket. 'I need you to decide which inferior human hand you want to upgrade with the BST device.'

He looked at The Four, seeing some frowns on faces, some glances at hands trying to decide. 'BST recommend the weaker hand as a first replacement to give you the most immediate functional benefit.' The frowns became nods. 'Place your chosen hand on the table, please.'

As The Four each placed a hand on the table, Serge opened the small box, and pulled out one of the strips of transparent film. He placed it on the back of Lilou's wrist, then repeated the process with Sully, Femi and Tatsuko. Each transparent strip started morphing in colour, going lighter and darker, trying to adjust to the specific skin tone of the wrist it was on. The fluctuations in colours started slowing as the strips got closer to the solution. Eventually each strip matched the skin tone of the wrist it was on, even adjusting for the density and spread of Lilou's freckles. Only the slight sheen of the strip's material made it visible.

'Please write your name on the back of the strip.' Serge picked up the special marker from the box that held the strips and passed it to Femi.

While he wrote his name and passed the marker to the next in line, Serge pulled out four small transparent bags and four more strips. 'Now peel off the strip and put it in a bag,' he said and waited for them. 'Now put the second strip on a different part of your wrist.'

Serge watched as the four new strips repeated the colour changing convergence to the wearer's skin tone. When they had all finished, he said, 'Add your name to the second strip and put it in your bag.'

'What are these strips for?' asked Tatsuko.

'They are used to make sure that your BST universal mount matches the skin tone,' Serge replied.

'But why do it now and not when the game is over?'

Serge ignored the question as he scooped up the four bags and put them in the box. He slid the lid shut, then picked up the box and returned it to his pocket.

'Let me explain the basis of the game,' he said.

The Four all straightened in their seats, their eyes alive with excitement.

'Obviously, you will travel to the Forbidden Island.'

'Yes,' Femi shouted. 'But how can there be a game there with all the tracking.'

Serge smiled. 'We have been planning this. All will become clear, but imagine a game where you run free of tracking in the Forbidden Island. Free to go as you please.'

He looked at four hesitantly nodding heads. They didn't believe it was really possible. 'Would we give you the BST device and money for nothing?'

He left them considering it and shuffled in his pocket again. This time he brought out a cigarette and lighter. The flame flashed and he drew a long breath, holding the smoke in his lungs before exhaling and finishing with a choked cough.

'The game is a race. You will all start at different places. You finish at different places, but the distance is about the same.'

'But that's not fair if I get a longer distance,' moaned Sully.

Serge shrugged as he dismissed the objection. 'The routes we will choose later. You might get a slightly shorter one.'

Sully didn't appear to like the answer. He seemed to be churning the idea over, sensing some conspiracy against him. He stayed sullen and silent.

'If we are all going to different places, how will we know who wins?' Lilou asked.

'Ah, a sensible question,' Serge said, glancing at Sully.

'We will give you a device for the game. It will contain the details of your finish point on it. Once you are free of the Island's control, it will provide GPS positioning and will tell you if you win. It will provide your fans the ability to subscribe to live updates on the game. They'll be able to watch your progress. Watch you triumph.'

'Yes,' they all said. Even Sully's sulk seemed to have evaporated.

'How will we travel when we are on the Forbidden Island?' Femi asked.

'You know that the island controls its citizens. The control also allows them to pay for travel. Once you are in the game, you will not be controlled – so you will have no money.'

Serge could see them all thinking it through.

'Think about the selection tests we made you do… How do you think you will travel?'

Chapter 18

Jay's self-drive car trundled up the M40 towards Birmingham. Ten miles ago, the car had flashed a low battery warning onto its screen, and now it was in the inside lane, a link in a long chain of cars heading to the service area. They were all so close together that they could have been a stack of supermarket trolleys. Their speed and the distance to the car in front controlled by algorithms that churned through data and possible personal injury claims.

Eventually, his car peeled off the motorway with some others and headed to the recharging area.

A mass of white, generic cars waited on the tarmac, each in a neat, marked bay. The red box painted on the road showed the dangerous area where a car would go, and was flanked by a safe green, pedestrian striped area.

Jay couldn't tell which box his car would choose, but as he had selected the 'fewest stops' option on the route guidance, he hoped that it would influence the car's decision.

His vehicle seemed to have made up its mind, and it turned towards a bay. The car that was already in the bay looked like the one he was in. They were all identical. His car inched into the red box, and Jay saw the new car's lights come on and one of its doors opened.

His car stopped and Jay opened his door. He grabbed his bag and checked that the box was still inside. *Where else could it be?* he thought, but he couldn't afford to leave it behind. It was too valuable.

He stepped out, careful not to incur a fine by walking outside of the green, pedestrian area, and got into his new car. He checked the car's information screen. The old car had passed over the details of the journey, and the new car showed more than enough charge to get him to his destination. He settled into his new seat, the door closed, and he started moving again. The old car edged forward and took his car's place. Jay knew that a charging dock would attach itself to his old car so that it was ready for the next person. Charging the car batteries still took a long time, but one car handing the passengers to the next, like the baton in a relay race, meant there was no waiting around.

His car joined the motorway, and Jay moved the bag from his lap to the car's centre table.

Genetics, he thought, and slipped his hands into the bag and onto the box.

It was cold to the touch and heavy. The box was sealed, not that he would dare open it, and he imagined what was inside.

He was on the front-line now – an activist.

Making a difference to the world – but feeling exposed and vulnerable. He shivered. iMe knew where he was, even if it didn't know he had the box. Could it know?

'No,' he said to himself. Even so, he glanced around him.

Despite the carefully controlled ambient temperature in the car, he started to sweat again. He knew he wouldn't survive the penalty if he was caught. If only he had kept his mouth shut at the meetings, but how could he when his dad had died like that? Drifting away, each day the hope diminishing.

Jay shut the thought down and stared out of the window. Trying, but failing to stop the tears forming.

He rubbed at his eyes, catching the sullen stare of a boy in the car travelling in the lane next to him.

He could have given the boy the finger, but with all the cars travelling at the same speed, the boy could be there the rest of the journey. Besides, from the look of his miserable parents sitting opposite him, perhaps the child had reason to stare out of the window.

Jay pulled the box out of the bag and put it on his lap. It had taken so much risk and planning to get it to him – so much danger. Its contents made the risks worthwhile.

***

Walking into the Coronation Gardens in Dudley, Jay clutched the bag containing the box to his chest.

He was a couple of minutes early, so he did a lap of the garden, gazing briefly at the cenotaph, before returning to Apollo's Fountain. He wanted his signal to look like he was killing time before his real, official meeting.

Jay sat on a bench. It looked almost new and he flicked his hand to shift a couple of leaves that had settled there. He put the bag on the bench and waited. His view of the fountain was Apollo's back and green buttocks.

Occasionally, a passing pedestrian crossed his gaze. He could feel the sweat on his brow again. The open space made him feel so exposed and vulnerable.

Jay caught sight of a woman coming towards him and he looked down at his shoes – black and generic. Suitable for an office meeting, not running from a trap set by the police.

He tried to calm his breathing.

'Greetings, Brother,' the woman whispered as she sat on the other end of the bench. 'I thank you for the gift you bring.'

Jay kept his gaze down as he had been briefed. It was best to make it look like he didn't know her.

He heard the woman stand and leave.

The bag and its box were gone.

***

Jay waited. Each minute crawling by – feeling more and more exposed. What if she didn't come back? What would he do?

He glanced around, but he didn't really know who he was looking for. It could be any of the women. They were all slim. iMe saw to that.

And that was part of the problem. Since iMe, everyone lived longer. No lifestyle illnesses forcing premature deaths, no careless accidents or car crashes.

No organ donors.

Jay thought back to his poor old dad, waiting for a liver transplant. Of course, iMe reduced all the self-inflicted illnesses, but it couldn't help a genetic abnormality. A fault in the genes that led to illness and despair. It couldn't manage the demand for no-fault transplants.

All it did was manage the supply. Down. Not enough deaths now to fill the demand. Priority given to the young. He understood that, but it didn't help when he had to watch his dad die a little every day. Waiting for the inevitable. Seeing the pain and the suffering. Seeing the fear.

They would have put a dog down, but they left the people to suffer.

He thought again about the box and wondered what it held. Hearts? Eyes? Lungs? Something else?

This was why he joined the cause. iMe-free Europe had plenty of supply. Plenty of smokers and car crashes.

He would have preferred only to give his moral support, but here he was. Sitting on a bench in Dudley, waiting for the box to come back.

He had already made one drop, another after this. Then he hoped they would say he had done his bit. He could go back to talking and walking with his dog, Kevin.

'Greetings, Brother,' a man said.

Jay almost jumped. He was too wrapped up in his thoughts and hadn't sensed the man's approach.

The distance to the man's shoes meant that he was on the other end of Jay's bench.

He heard a soft scrape and assumed that it was the box and its bag being returned and pushed along the bench.

'Thank you for your help in our struggle,' the man said, and his shoes turned and left.

Jay stretched out his hand and found the handles of the bag. He pulled it protectively towards him.

As he had been briefed, Jay waited a minute more and then stood, lifting the bag, feeling for changes.

It was still heavy, most likely from the technology needed to keep the organs fresh and usable. Jay was sure the bag felt lighter and that meant that someone else had been helped.

He walked out of the gardens, trying to get his nerves under control. He wiped his brow and slowed his walk before heading down Priory Road and turning into Priory Street. By the time he reached Dudley Town Hall and the official reason for his trip here, he felt much calmer.

He imagined a family beside a loved-one's hospital bed. Hearing the unexpected but fantastic news of a suitable organ.

The glow of it warmed him through the tedious meeting and the discussion on the details of new accountancy standards that all councils needed to use.

Chapter 19

The two days sitting around since they had been measured for the BioSuperTech universal mount had felt like weeks to Femi.

He couldn't stand waiting. The two runs out along the local roads with Lilou had helped pass the time and kept his body moving. Worryingly, they had also proved she was a serious opponent. When Femi had first seen Lilou in a French Olympic team tracksuit top, he had thought it was a replica and the talk of triathlons and parkour was just that – talk.

Their first run had changed his mind.

Her back disappeared into the distance, then the gap closed as she jogged on the spot waiting for him, before disappearing again. At the end of the run, Lilou seemed fresh, still bouncing as she stretched to cool down. Femi, his hands on his knees as he gulped in air, wished his legs would stop shaking.

'Same time tomorrow?' Lilou said.

Femi couldn't find enough breath to speak, so he nodded.

On today's run, Femi hadn't done much better.

Now he lay on the narrow bed, his feet dangling over the end. Like most things, it wasn't designed for someone six foot six inches tall. Despite the metal bed frame pressing into his calves, his eyes were closed, and a small smile played on his lips as he daydreamed that he was back home cooking for his family, savouring the smell of the ocean mixing with the smoky sizzle of beef.

A bang on his door crashed him out of the warmth of his dreaming and into the cold, stark room.

'Meeting in five minutes,' a voice called through the door.

Femi stood and stretched, hoping that this would be the real start of the game.

***

The Four were back in the main hall area, standing in a line in front of Serge and the long table. Femi deflated a little when he couldn't see the BST hands on the table. Instead, four folders were stacked in a neat pile. The top one had the letter 'A' on it.

He rubbed the back of his leg to ease an aching hamstring and waited for Serge to finish yet another long pull on a cigarette.

Serge's eyes locked briefly onto Femi's before scanning onto the others.

'So, this is goodbye,' Serge said in a breathy voice.

Femi wondered how much practice it had taken Serge to be able to talk and blow the smoke out of the side of his mouth at the same time.

'But first we have the details of the game to discuss,' Serge said as he slid the folder with the 'A' on it off the pile and along the table. The folder now on top of the pile showed the letter 'B'. Serge repeated the sliding of the folders until all four were laid out.

'I said before that there are four starting points, four routes and four finishing lines.'

The Four nodded.

'Now we choose.'

Sully jumped forward, his hand extended as if to grab a folder, but Serge shouted, 'Wait,' and he motioned to someone at the back of the hall.

Sully's hand stopped for an instant, then he smirked at the others before staring at Serge, defiance in his eyes. Sully moved his hand forward again, but as his fingers touched folder 'C', two large men appeared at his shoulder. Four hands found a good grip on Sully's shirt and he was jerked back into his position on the line.

Sully struggled against the restraining grip, but the two men held him fast.

'It's not for you to choose the order,' Serge said.

Sully glared and pushed his bottom lip out into a pout.

'We choose in the order you finished the second test. Lilou first.' Serge waved her forward, and as she stepped towards the desk, Sully tested the grip of his restrainers again.

Lilou's fingers brushed over the folders, trying to sense the best one. 'Can I open them?' she asked.

Serge shook his head.

Lilou ran her hands over the folders again, her head tilted to one side.

Femi saw her head tilt back to vertical and the muscles in her right shoulder tense as she grasped folder 'A'.

'Femi next,' Serge said.

Femi stepped forward and he picked up folder 'D'. No other choice for him. 'D' for Dinah, his wife. His soul.

'Tatsuko,' Serge said when Femi had stepped back into the line.

She took a pace forward, hesitated over folder 'C' before picking up folder 'B'.

'I don't want to give Sully his choice, but I'm from Boston so it seems destined.'

Sully beamed. 'Got what I wanted,' he shouted. The four hands gripping him released him and he shot forward to grab folder 'C' and clutch it to his chest.

'C for cash,' he sneered. 'First prize for me, losers.'

Serge looked at Sully and crinkled his face in disgust, like he had caught the smell from an open sewer.

'In your folders you will find details of your start point and everything else you need. You will be given your finish point when you're in place. Please.' Serge nodded towards the folders.

Femi pulled the flap open on the folder and looked inside. The top sheet of paper showed a map with an address. The starting point.

The second sheet of paper showed details of two flights. The first one from Paris tomorrow.

Serge fished in his pockets and pulled out four passports.

Femi could see his green South African passport on the bottom. Serge gave them out quickly and Femi flicked through his passport. He stopped at the page showing the stamp of a large entry permit.

The stamp showed the words 'United Kingdom – Border Security.'

He was going to the Forbidden Island.

'Let the game begin,' Serge said.

Part 2

Game – The Forbidden Island

Chapter 20

Ava was in an advanced self-defence training session for the whole morning. *She certainly fills every moment of the day now*, Clive thought.

He sat alone in the PCU office, with only the scrolling health and safety messages on the office's display wall for company. The message about HUD shoulder made about its tenth appearance in the last hour. Clive rolled his shoulder as instructed and felt the click and crunch of muscle near his shoulder blade. Typing and browsing on a HUD with your hands in the air meant that your shoulders carried the whole weight of your arms. It got tiring. The muscles knotted in complaint at the abuse, and HUD shoulder crunch was the inevitable, audible melody. In a busy office, the shoulder rolling would give an orchestral sized soundtrack of clicks, cracks, and groans.

It was nearly 11:30 am and he had 'solved' two cases already: one robbery and one assault – stupid crimes committed by stupid people who knew they would get caught. Solved with a simple drag and drop and search. Mindless, skill-less work. Not like the old days.

He knew he was on borrowed time in the police. Ava could do the job easily. Any of the trainees who rotated through PCU could do it after only a few hours. Clive bent to the desk drawer and pulled it open. His hand scrabbled around the bottom of the drawer, disturbing the old, unused police pencils, pads, and even an old phone charger that had somehow survived in the far corner. His fingers found the thicker booklet he had discovered one boring afternoon when he went foraging in the office cupboards and desks.

He laid it out. The spine of the booklet had a form of muscle memory and fell open at the page Clive kept rereading. The heading on the page was *'Detective Constable Job Description'*.

Clive knew the opening sentence by heart, and repeating it out loud brought it to life.

'Being a detective is all about uncovering the truth. You'll do this by analysing evidence, talking to witnesses and building trust within the community,' he said, staring into the distance. It had been so long since he had analysed actual evidence.

Clive tried to ignore the craving his brain fired when he was bored – chocolate and coffee. He gave in and pushed his chair back in preparation for the walk to the vending machine, then stopped.

Two problems. One was that the machine probably wouldn't give him what he wanted as he was now on a restricted diet. The second was his recent trip to the hospital. He couldn't risk the flare in blood sugar.

Clive tucked his chair back in, still pushing down on the craving.

After a few short minutes, Clive was ready to try the vending machine anyway. The walk would kill some time. *No, think of your health*, he thought. He dithered in his chair while engrossed in mental arm-wrestling.

He was saved by a bing in his ear and his Buddy jogging out onto his HUD screen trailing a message: *'One new item in your work queue.'*

Clive clicked the banner and the PCU queue opened. Sure enough, there was one unread item.

'Oh, no,' Clive said. 'Give me some real work.'

What had his job been recently? Taking a little girl to have an iMe implant against her parent's wishes. Moving a mouse to solve trivial cases. Now today's highlight.

He clicked into the case and read the details of an American tourist who was out of time and needed escorting to the airport. iMe classified him as off-grid even though his iTourist was still working, and so he was Clive's problem.

This wasn't police work. He banged some of his frustration into the table, making the booklet bounce.

'Problem, Boss?' Ava asked.

Clive looked up. 'Just this life,' he said.

Ava's forehead wrinkled in confusion. 'Err…'

'Don't worry. Get your coat, we've got a serious criminal to catch.'

***

Clive and Ava's car rolled to a stop outside one of the many Costa Health Drinks in Kensington. They got out and headed to the glass doors, which hissed a welcome as they slid open.

'That him?' Clive asked, nodding towards a figure crouched at a table in the far corner.

Ava's fingers moved on her HUD as she checked the display of iMe signals. 'Yep.'

'You want to handle it?'

Ava half paused, then nodded. 'Sure.'

They walked over to the figure, Clive dropping half a pace behind Ava. All he could see was blond hair and shoulders covered in a white shirt.

'Hello, Brett,' Ava said. 'You should have gone home yesterday.'

Brett looked up, revealing blue eyes and a thin face. His right hand was clasped tight on his left wrist. 'No, not me,' he said.

Clive shook his head and Ava said, 'Really… "Not me". That's it?'

Clive looked in pride at Ava, when she had started at PCU she would have been meek and used her happy-bouncy tone. Now she was hard-edged steel.

When Brett didn't move, Ava snapped, 'Stop pissing us about and show me your wrist.'

Brett jumped to Ava's command. Clive took a half-pace to the side to watch. Ava had this in the bag.

The iTourist was like a thin electronic bracelet clamped tight to Brett's left wrist. It flashed red.

'Not me,' Ava mocked. 'Let's go.'

She reached across and pulled at Brett's shoulder, encouraging him up.

As he shuffled towards the doors and the waiting car, Brett said, 'How did you find me?'

Ava groaned and said, 'Not too bright this one, Boss.'

Clive's smile broadened.

***

The car weaved its way through the afternoon London traffic and headed towards Gatwick airport.

Brett had spent the first miles in silence, but now seemed to have decided that Ava cared about him and wouldn't shut up.

'So, I was at this party. I knew my flight was due, but I thought "fuck it" and carried on partying. There was this girl, and–'

'I don't want to know,' Ava said.

Brett looked offended that his story wasn't the most interesting thing in Ava's world, but carried on anyway. 'Then at midnight this iTourist thing starts flashing red,' Brett said, waving at his wrist.

Ava rolled her eyes. 'You were told it would at immigration.'

'Yeah, but the girl said don't worry I can stay at hers. Then the payment thing wouldn't open the taxi and she had to pay. Guess I misread her. She was just being friendly, and I spent the night on the sofa with her dog.'

'Poor dog,' Ava said.

Brett took the put down badly and spent the next few minutes looking out of the window.

Ava smiled at the silence and started tapping at her HUD.

'SaladWay,' Brett laughed. 'That's Subway at home. This place is crazy... and what's with all the closed burger joints. I couldn't get a McDonald's anywhere.'

Ava's eyes pleaded with Clive to take the next stream of Brett's consciousness. She'd taken the brunt of it so far.

'Too much sugar, fat and carbohydrate,' Clive said. 'The tax on all that means it's too expensive. Also, no red meat during the week.'

'Crazy,' Brett said, shaking his head.

'Yes and no,' Clive said. Sure, the food was healthier, but why was it always the things that were bad for you that tasted so good?

***

The car rolled past a group of eco-protesters holding *'Air travel kills the planet'*, *'You're stealing my future'* and *'Flying? You're a carbon criminal'* placards. A group of Uniforms corralled the protesters and kept them off the road. A gang of young kids in blue school uniforms sang the popular 'Save the World' song, conducted by a man with long dark hair. *Could be an Environmental Studies class from a local school*, Clive thought. The kids sang well, so maybe it was choir practice instead.

The sounds of song faded as the car climbed the ramp to Gatwick's East terminal, and Brett's eyes flashed.

'I was meant to go to Rome,' he said. 'You can send me there.'

Ava groaned and said, 'You needed to have paid more attention, Brett. If you outstay your visa, your iTourist stops your money and you get deported. Not to wherever you fancy, but your point of immediate departure prior to entering the UK. You confirmed all this when you came into the country.'

The car stopped next to two UK Border Security officers and the doors opened.

'Yeah, but I'm meant to go to Rome,' Brett moaned.

'Tough,' said Ava as she got out of the car.

'You should have left yesterday,' Clive agreed.

They beckoned Brett out and as he stood by the car, Clive grasped Brett's left arm and held it out to one of the Border Security officers.

'You'll enjoy this one,' Clive said. 'He wants to go to Rome.'

'Righty-oh,' the larger officer said. 'I'll talk to American Airlines. Get you a nice first-class window seat and access to the executive lounge.'

'Cool. Thanks,' Brett said, perking up. Not getting the sarcasm.

The officer winked over his shoulder at Clive and Ava, then steered Brett towards a battered grey door in a low, windowless building.

Chapter 21

Lilou looked out of her aeroplane's window at the twinkling lights of night-time Birmingham. She always loved a city at night, the sparkling house lights, the tiny stream of lights from the cars – red in one direction, white in the other, tracing the routes of the roads.

As the plane approached the airport, she tried to stay still and appear calm, but for every drop in altitude, Lilou's excitement grew. She was nearly there. After hours on the train to Paris, a wait, a flight to Berlin, more waiting and then a flight to Birmingham.

She was tired, but the game was about to start. Finally, she was nearly on the Forbidden Island. Her pulse quickened and her nerves ticked in her legs as she stretched and then clenched her calves and thighs to ease the tension. She needed to be up and out of this seat to feel better. Much too much sitting around for one day. She needed to go running.

***

Inside the terminal building, running wasn't an option. Lilou pushed up onto her tiptoes to see past the man in front of her and along the corridor towards the front of the queue. All she could see was a line of people that snaked ahead and then turned left. She had no idea how close to the front she was.

Lilou looked up to check she was in the correct lane. Her line was marked '*All Other Passports*' and wasn't moving. The other lane was marked '*UK Citizens Only*' and people in it walked quickly and easily past her.

It took fifteen minutes for her to shuffle, pause, repeat her way to the corner. As she turned the corner, she groaned. The corridor opened into a large hall with a high ceiling and more signs. The line she was in continued into a lane marked with retractable barrier tapes suspended by movable posts on either side. The barrier tapes traced out a snake that crossed the hall, did a sharp 180 degree turn and crossed back across the hall. It seemed to twist and turn forever. Lilou looked up above her head at the sign: *'Average wait time from here 90 minutes.'* The sign crushed what little of her excitement remained. She settled in for a long wait.

***

When Lilou eventually got to the final turn in the line, she was numb with boredom. She had seen all she could ever want to of the back of the man in front of her. The half-smile to the same people she passed on each traverse across the hall had lost its novelty early on.

She stared enviously at the UK Citizen's Only section. People strolled up to a row of glass-doored booths, each the size of a toilet cubicle. As each person approached, the front glass door slid open, the person stepped inside the booth and out through the second door that seemed permanently open. It took each person only seconds to get through the cubicle. Then they turned and walked past a group of about ten idle, uniformed UK Border staff.

'I've had enough of this,' someone said behind her and a second later a rude shoulder pushed past her and a man in his fifties ducked under the tape. 'Those guys are doing nothing. They can serve me,' he muttered and marched towards the UK only booths. Lilou was tempted to follow, but she was within touching distance of the front of the queue.

The man seemed to grow in confidence as the glass door to the booth he had chosen slid open, but as he stepped into the booth, the door in front of him snapped shut as did the one behind him. A red light in the top of the booth started strobing lazily.

Nothing happened for a few seconds. The UK Border staff still seemed to be chatting as the man banged on the glass door. Finally, two staff members pushed themselves off the wall they were leaning against and ambled towards the booth with the same lack of urgency as the strobe light.

They got to the booth and the door opened. The man stepped forward and he said, 'Do you know how long I've been waiting and you're standing here doing nothing.'

The two UK Border staff shared a quick glance and spun the man around, grabbed his arm and frogmarched him off towards a solid black door.

Lilou was glad she hadn't copied him and looked towards the front of the queue. Her eye on the prize, she waited.

The man hadn't reappeared when a UK Border officer finally ushered Lilou forward.

'I'm Sam, and I'll take you through the immigration process today,' the officer said, pushing his lips into a flat, compressed line that Lilou thought might have been a superficial smile. She imagined that he had a checklist to run through, and Sam's mouth movement satisfied the 'Greet each visitor with a welcoming smile' requirement.

He took Lilou through all the basic dos and don'ts, then a lot of medical questions about her health and the details about what would happen if she overstayed her time limit or ran out of money. All delivered with a passive-aggressive threat born of Border Control and multiple repetitions each day.

'You've got a visa for two weeks to cover your stay,' Sam said. 'You need five-thousand pounds per week as a minimum security deposit to cover your expenses while you're here.'

Lilou gulped. She had no money. Serge had said it was all arranged. 'I think my firm has already paid,' Lilou said, trying to keep the nervousness out of her voice. She didn't want to fail the game before it had started.

Sam looked annoyed and moved his hands around in front of his face as Lilou had seen other staff and the people in the UK Citizen's line do.

After some finger pointing and swiping, huffing and with some loud foot tapping, Sam said, 'Oh, yeah. Here it is.'

She let out a sigh of relief.

Sam opened a box from a long pile of identical boxes, and pulled out a thin bracelet-like strap. The black fabric of the strap shone with what looked like embedded metal strands. On the top surface were five buttons. One with a £ sign, one with a simple clock face, one with a little car on it, one with a little 'i' in a circle, and the last with a red cross.

'Which arm?' Sam demanded.

'What?' Lilou stammered, caught off-guard by Sam's tone.

'For the iTourist. Which arm do you want it on?'

Lilou could hear Sam's frustration at dealing with another slow tourist. 'Left,' she said, holding out the same arm she had told Serge.

Sam placed the iTourist onto Lilou's thin wrist and centred the five buttons. Next, he wrapped the free ends of the bracelet under her wrist and slid one end along the other. With each movement, Lilou could hear a tiny tearing noise a bit like pulling Velcro apart. Sam pushed and smoothed the ends until the iTourist was tight on her wrist.

'Put your wrist on the pad,' Sam said, pointing at a shiny section of his desk.

Sam did something Lilou couldn't see and the bracelet tightened even more and pulsed twice, sending two static shocks along her arm and making the fine hairs stand up. The iTourist glowed blue and then the light went off.

'OK, it's working,' Sam said, and launched into another well-practised speech. 'You can see your balance at any time by pressing the pound sign button.' He waited. When Lilou did nothing, Sam sighed and said, 'Go on then. Press the pound sign button.'

Lilou pressed and '£10,000.00' flashed up on a little screen in the iTourist that she hadn't seen before.

'Put your iTourist on the payment pad to pay for anything you want to buy, and the balance will go down. When it gets to six-hundred pounds, it will flash amber. Go to a bank to add money to it. If the balance gets to zero, the iTourist will flash red and you get deported. No arguments, no second chances. OK?' Sam stared at Lilou, waiting for a response.

'OK,' she said.

'You press the clock to see how long your visa has left.' Sam paused, and this time Lilou knew that Sam expected her to press the button.

The screen showed '*13 days, 23 hrs, 58 minutes*' before blanking.

'Report to the police if you want to apply for an extension. It flashes amber when you've got six hours left. If it gets to zero, it flashes red and you get deported. OK?'

Lilou nodded.

'Press the car button for a taxi. The screen will show you the wait time. Your taxi will stop in front of you and the door will open. If a car stops and the door doesn't open, it's not your cab. OK?'

Lilou nodded again.

'The little i in a circle is for information. All sorts of stuff: location, health, routes. Press it and follow the prompts.' Sam didn't pause long enough for her to play with the button as he said, 'Final button with the red cross is for emergency medical help. Don't press it if you've got a cold, don't press it for a pre-existing condition. Even if you didn't disclose it earlier, if it's pre-existing you won't get treatment. If you're not well, go to a pharmacy, they'll help, but they'll charge you. OK?'

Lilou nodded yet again. Sam passed over a small tablet and got her to click in a long list of places to agree to all the entry conditions. She even had to confirm her shoe size. *Why is that necessary?* she wondered.

'You'll get a copy by email,' Sam said and looked over Lilou's shoulder. 'Next,' he said.

Lilou stepped forward and crossed a yellow line on the floor. She was on the Forbidden Island.

Chapter 22

Tatsuko had stood in a similar length queue at Portsmouth docks. She had travelled south through France, and into Spain before catching a ferry from Bilbao to Portsmouth. The Bay of Biscay had been unforgiving and Tatsuko didn't mind the wait for Border Control. At least the floor didn't move under her, and it gave her stomach time to stop swishing from side to side.

Tatsuko said, 'Left,' when she got to the question about which arm she wanted the iTourist on. She listened to the same warnings and threats about getting deported.

She smiled. They had no idea that she was part of the greatest game ever and her progress would be cheered on by thousands of online fans. *Deport me?* Tatsuko thought. *First, you've got to catch me.*

'Will this thing break?' Tatsuko asked.

Her UK Border Control officer wore a name tag that said 'Rohit'.

Rohit smiled at the familiar question. 'You can't damage it,' he said with a small shake of his head. 'It's designed to withstand cutting, drilling, burning – but all of those things would hurt your arm more than damage the iTourist. You can wear it in the shower, swim in it. It's safe in medical operations, MRI scanners, everywhere. Worst damage I've ever seen is the cap of one of those little buttons coming off.'

Tatsuko nodded. Good to know.

When Rohit gave her the tablet with all the boxes to tick her agreement, Tatsuko stopped at one and asked, 'What does "take part in exercise directives" mean?'

Rohit smiled. 'Exercise is good for you, so you're asked to take part in daily exercise.'

'Like what?'

'Your hotel will give you the details and provide the necessary facilities and clothes.'

'What if I don't? You can't force me.'

'No, we can't force you, but it's important that tourists have equality with UK citizens. We have to do the exercise, and so do visitors. It would be discrimination otherwise.'

Rohit smiled and pointed further down the text on the tablet. 'Also, there's a heavy daily fine if you don't, and the hotel will be very, very persistent at reminding you.'

Chapter 23

Clive stared out of his flat's lounge window. The early promise of a blue sky was being reneged on by dark, threatening clouds. A roll of thunder in the distance sounded like heavy booted thugs kicking at his door. He turned from the window as the first fat drops of rain hit it.

'Happy birthday to me,' he said.

Harry the Hoover tracked across the floor and bumped into Clive's foot. 'Hello, Harry,' Clive said.

Harry wasn't technically a hoover. He was a robotic cleaning assistant, but the name 'Harry the RCA' didn't have the same ring to it. Harry spun away from Clive, tracked left and turned again, trying to work out how to get past the obstruction of Clive's foot.

Harry bumped into Clive's foot again.

'What's that, Harry? Happy birthday,' Clive said, sounding like a character from an old *Lassie the Dog* film. 'Thanks for remembering, mate.'

Harry tracked left again and trundled off obliviously.

Balloons started rising from the bottom of Clive's HUD screen, fake fireworks exploded, and Clive's Buddy ran along the bottom of his HUD trailing a *'Happy Birthday, Clive – 50 today'* banner. Buddy stopped running and starting clapping and jumping up and down.

Buddy's cheering stopped and he rolled the banner away. The balloons disappeared and the fireworks faded. The celebrations were over before they really started.

But Buddy made an unexpected return a few seconds later. This time the banner said, *'New message: Happy birthday'*.

Clive clicked on the banner, wondering who had sent it. His shoulders slumped as he saw the sender – *iMe*.

The message was the standard, cringeworthy birthday greeting. All positive words and upbeat tone. All completely fake and impersonal, merely a function of a computerised calendar and some programming code.

Clive shuddered at the final sentence: 'You've left the Fabulous Forties, and you've lived five great decades, so we welcome you to the amazing and super awesome "High 5'ers".'

It felt like the end of something, rather than the beginning of a new phase. A year ago, Clive would have been angry and swearing at the inane labels this society attached to everyone. He was amazed at how many pigeonholes he could be put in. Each category fed into the diversity measurement and tracking, but it seemed like all the labels gave people more and more reasons to focus on their differences, rather than bringing them together.

At least the sender underneath Buddy's next new message banner made Clive smile.

'Happy birthday, Clive. See you tonight, Sophia x.'

The smile stayed frozen on his face. She used to call him darling, not Clive. There used to be three kisses at the end of each message, not one.

I'm screwing things up with Sophia, he thought, seeing the same downward spiral that had led to his divorce from Mary.

***

The sun hadn't dared to make a reappearance during the day and the clouds had been biblical in delivering on their threat of heavy rain and thunder. *The weather seems really messed up today*, Clive thought, but he had the same thought every day.

He closed the apartment's front door, pleased to be shutting the workday behind him.

Not that it had been an especially bad day. The problem was that it was typical. Lots of button pressing and nothing to think about. Nothing to challenge his brain. He knew he couldn't go on like this. He needed a change, but what could he do? His skill set wasn't exactly in tune with modern needs. He'd have to talk to Bhatt about retraining before she told him about 'voluntary' redundancy and the exciting opportunities outside the police force.

Harry had been busy all day and the apartment was clean. Clive stooped to give Harry a little pat of thanks as he went into the kitchen.

He opened the left-hand wall mounted cupboard and pulled down two battered cardboard boxes. Both had *PCU Evidence* stamped on the side. Clive opened the boxes and looked at each of the Health Bank bracelets he had taken from the evidence store. They may have hidden Sophia and his own consumption from FU enforcement, but the evidence was still visible in Clive's blood and waistline. He'd need to find a better hiding place in case Special Investigator Winter made an appearance.

***

'Happy birthday,' Sophia said, clinking glasses with Clive. She had brightened a little since yet another argument at lunchtime.

He took a sip of his sparkling, zero-calorie rose water. *Some birthday*, he thought, grimacing at the taste.

'Did I show you the birthday present I got from my doctor?'
Sophia shook her head.

Clive pinched his fingers together to pick up his HUD screen and threw it at the display wall in the lounge. It paused the music it was playing and redrew to show his HUD.

Clive pointed and swiped his way around the menus until he found the page he wanted.

'Ouch,' Sophia said, but Clive could see her unsaid 'and it's your own fault' in her eyes.

In the top right of the screen, his '*Active FU allowance*' page showed a last modified date of today and the name Dr Dilani Adhya as the author. Worst for Clive was the '*Valid until date*' which showed '*Indefinite (Medical advice override)*'.

'No alcohol,' Clive moaned putting down his rose water. 'And that calorie intake limit means no chocolate. I'd be able to eat more if I had an Excess Consumption Order than on this diet.'

'It's for your own good,' Sophia said. 'How are your levels today?'

'Better,' Clive said, reluctant to find the positive.

'Show me,' Sophia said, with a hardness that told him he didn't have a choice.

Clive shrugged and clicked to his *'Health Overview'* page. The screen redrew to show his heart trace, oxygen saturation, blood sugar and twenty other levels.

'Looks better,' Sophia said.

'S'pose.' Clive shrugged and clicked a button on the bottom of the page. The display wall redrew to show his deviations to Model Citizen. Green bars showed everywhere on the report. No amber or red. He was within model everywhere and wasn't using any of his FU allowances.

'You should join me at the New Modelists,' Sophia said, her voice softening. Her eyes pleaded with him to make the first step.

'Maybe.'

Sophia looked shocked. 'Really?' She smiled and then frowned. 'What's changed?'

Clive looked out of the window again, not wanting to confess.

'My doctor recommended it…'

'What? I ask you again and again and you say no, but your doctor mentions it and you want to go?' Folding her arms across her chest, she continued, 'Is she pretty, this Dilani? Is that why you want—'

Sophia was interrupted by the front door opening. Zoe hurried in, flustered from rushing. 'Sorry I'm late, Boss,' she said.

'Hi, Mum.' Zoe crossed to Sophia and gave her a quick peck before heading to Clive.

She enveloped him in a hug. 'Happy birthday, Boss.'

'Thanks, Zoe. But I keep telling you, I'm not your boss anymore.'

'You'll always be Boss to me.'

Zoe paused as she caught the underlying tension in the room. 'What?'

'Nothing,' he lied. 'Please. Sophia?' Clive tried a lopsided half-smile. 'Sit down both of you.'

He headed to the kitchen to fetch the first course, the urgent whispers between Zoe and Sophia chasing him from the room. He tried to push the argument away and thought of chocolate. He picked up the plates, feeling embarrassed to serve this for a birthday meal, but what choice did he have?

Zoe laughed when he put the lettuce and plain grilled chicken down. 'Reminds me of that pub where the barman offered you whale music instead of beer.'

Clive chuckled at the memory and sat down. At least then he had a real case to solve, but then the memory morphed into Mary and that belt. He shook the image away and looked at Sophia, but her mood hadn't thawed.

'How's PCU, Boss?'

'The same. As always.'

Zoe nodded in sympathy.

'But Ava showed more of her real self the other day. She's a tough little cookie.' Clive recounted the tale of Ava and Brett and Zoe nodded along. 'How's your Terrorism-Cyber special unit?'

'Hectic,' Zoe said. 'So much to do. It's like there's a constant wave of cyber probes and attacks. They've got me checking forums and potentially suspicious chatter that all the web-scanning software finds.'

'Anything interesting, darling?' Sophia asked, brightening for Zoe.

Zoe shook her head. 'No, today was a whole load of gaming nerds getting all excited about an augmented reality game.'

Chapter 24

Femi's flight from Rome touched down at Dublin airport ten minutes early, and he strolled through the arrivals checkpoints with barely a pause. He was channelled through the 'Intra Pan-Europe Arrivals' lanes and the Border Control staff didn't show any interest in him.

Now he stood at the Avis car-hire desk, listening to the clerk's impossibly fast typing on her console. Each clack of the keyboard was harmonised with a click of her long, bright-green fingernails. She looked up and flashed Femi a smile.

'OK. You've booked an automated drive car. Yes?'

Femi nodded a confirmation.

'It's cheaper if you drive yourself. No, wait...' The clerk rechecked her screen. 'Sorry, the booking says you need an iMe compatible car. That's right?'

Femi nodded again.

'OK, that's much more expensive. As you're not a UK or Irish citizen, you'll have to get UK Border Control to link the iTourist they'll give you to the car. It's a bit like this one.' The clerk touched a green bracelet she wore on her left wrist. The colour matched her nails. 'This is the Irish version, so we don't have a hard border with the UK. You'll get a different version.'

The clerk took Femi through the rest of the booking process and passed him a key. 'You'll need to use the key when you're in the car here. The iTourist will take over when you have it.' She smiled. 'Have a good trip.'

Femi hesitated. He'd never used a car that drove itself, but he picked up the instruction booklet and headed in the direction the clerk had pointed.

When he was ten metres from a car, it sensed the signal from the key and flashed its lights. He walked over to it and the door opened. Femi dropped his bag on one set of seats and climbed in. Habit had him looking for the steering wheel and controls, but there weren't any.

His mouth felt dry.

'Ya,' Femi said, flicking to the instructions on defining a destination. 'Car... Destination.'

'Howzit, Femi,' the car replied. 'Where do you want to go, Bru?'

Femi smiled at the greeting, a little bit of home here in a windy car park in Dublin. He wasn't sure if the car had recognised his South African accent or had used his nationality from the rental booking details, but it was a nice touch.

Femi gave the address of the hotel Serge had arranged and the car confirmed it. 'Do you want me to check you into the hotel?' the car said.

'Sure.'

'Please put on your seat belt. Movement is not possible until you do.'

Femi did as he was told, and the car closed its door and started moving. He clutched the seat belt with one hand and the side of the chair with the other. He held on tight. *I prefer to drive myself*, he thought.

He gripped even tighter as the car approached a busy T-junction with cars crossing in both directions ahead of him. He realised that he was holding his breath, but didn't breathe out until the car stopped safely. He released his grip a little as the car waited, sensed a gap and pulled into the traffic.

'Freaky,' Femi muttered.

'Command not recognised. Please repeat,' the car said.

***

Femi relaxed in the car now he had been in it a while, and the traffic thinned as it travelled north out of Dublin. He lost the feeling that the car was going to crash into everything that moved. It helped that the car drove on the same side of the road as at home, unlike Serge's driving in France. It helped even more that it went so slowly.

After about three hours, the car slotted itself into the left lane. It seemed to be following the 'N2 – Derry. Non-local or UK traffic' signs towards the border near Aughnacloy.

'Border delay – estimated twenty minutes,' the car said as it crawled to a halt behind another car. The cars in the local-traffic lane sped past him, free of such worries.

The car inched forward periodically and counted down the delay. At the border, the car stopped and said, 'Please leave the car for Border Security.'

Femi did as he was told, but before he had a chance to get his bag, the car closed its door and drove away.

'Hey,' shouted Femi at the diminishing back of the car.

'Don't worry, sir,' a mellow voice called to him. 'It's going to the bag check area. It will meet you on the other side.'

Femi turned to face the voice. A tall woman with a large UK Border Control badge above her left breast waved him forward. 'This way.'

Femi followed the guard into a small arrivals hall, with desks arranged along both sides. It could have been the Avis rental area other than all the warning signs and the soldiers.

Although he didn't know it, Femi completed all the same steps as Lilou and Tatsuko when they entered the UK.

'All done,' the UK Border guard said after Femi ticked his acceptance in the last checkbox on the tablet. The guard waved Femi forward and towards the doors at the rear of the hall.

The doors slid open as Femi approached them and his car seemed to have a second sense as it was already moving and nearly at the kerb. He arrived at exactly the same moment the car stopped and the door popped open.

Femi was relieved to see his bag was still in the car, even if it was on a different seat now. He settled back into the car and it headed off. It seemed to be going quite a bit slower than on the Irish side of the border. 'Journey time to Derry 87 minutes,' the car said.

Femi wasn't in any position to argue and he spent the next part of the journey pulling and tugging at his newly installed iTourist bracelet. It didn't move.

***

While Femi was crossing into Northern Ireland, Sully was pressing the Taxi button on his iTourist.

He'd been told that Glasgow was usually cold and wet, but the sun warmed his back as he waited.

'Taxi arrival time, 30 seconds,' the display on the iTourist showed and counted down.

As the display clicked to zero, a car stopped in front of Sully and opened its door. He climbed in and followed the instructions for setting the destination.

He was curious about what the car's instructions described as 'Status display', so he said, 'Status display... on.'

The screen in the middle of the car turned on, showing a map, estimated distance and journey time.

Sully pouted at the screen when he saw the words 'Tariff: Tourist' in the top left corner and the fact that the car had already taken £20 despite still being in sight of his departure point.

Chapter 25

Clive and Harry the Hoover were finishing clearing up from Clive's birthday meal last night when the doorbell chimed.

He wasn't expecting anyone, and when he checked the apartment's display wall, Clive saw the last person he wanted to talk to.

'Special Investigator Winter, Freedom Unit Enforcement, Ministry of Well-being and Health', showed on the display. Reluctantly, Clive clicked the door release.

Winter burst into the room. He was about forty and his hair was shaved into short stubble. Clive was sure it was part of a plan to look more intimidating. Winter's eyes glared a cold menace and his suit bulged with muscle.

'I didn't get a birthday party invitation,' Winter said.

'Wonder why,' Clive said.

'Don't be like that. Now you're mine again, I wanted to pop in and remind you how much a Health Reorientation Camp would transform your outlook on life, Inspector.'

Winter prodded at Clive's waist. Despite Clive clenching every muscle he had, Winter's finger made inroads into Clive's soft flesh.

'Oh yes, Inspector. You've magically put on weight. You need some nice long route marches to burn that off.' Winter smiled like a shark before continuing. 'And if you don't, then there's the aversion therapy to help recalibrate your mind.'

Winter was full of smug arrogance. He loved his job.

He moved over to the fridge and peered in. 'Shame you can't eat that.'

'It was only restocked yesterday for my new diet,' Clive complained.

Winter shook his head and said, 'Maybe, but I talked to your doctor. She was too lenient given your history. I persuaded her to change it.'

Clive said nothing and Winter seemed disappointed that he didn't get a reaction.

'I'm watching you, Inspector,' Winter said. As he turned to leave, Harry bumped into his foot. Winter lashed out a kick that sent Harry flying into the wall.

***

Clive turned his back on the door and approached his fridge. Not a casual, easy saunter, more like a man edging down a dark alley towards three loitering men.

'Hello, Clive. The restock will take place in five minutes,' the fridge cooed.

Clive wasn't friends with his fridge, but in an attempt to change his life, he was trying for a less antagonistic relationship with it. He had changed the fridge's voice from the *Dr Who* Dalek to what the instruction manual labelled *'Female voice six'*. The voice was meant to be soothing and positive. It was the best of a bad lot.

The fridge did her best, but Clive had spent the years since iMe introduction fighting and trying to buck the system every time it constrained him. It was his body after all. If he wanted to eat too many chips and chocolate, and drink too much caffeine, then that was his choice.

And what was too much anyway? He should decide and not a group of doctors and lawyers studying statistics and research papers.

He looked at the fridge, the glass door and rows of compartmentalised food containers. All his favourites, even sausages.

All the things that Winter had made Dr Dilani Adhya's new food prescription deny him.

The doorbell rang again, and this time Clive could see two food technicians at his door. Not the ones from yesterday, maybe a different shift.

'I'll let them in,' the fridge said.

Clive heard the door click unlocked, then footsteps and the rumble of trolley wheels on the hard floor. One of the wheels must have been damaged as there was a juddering wobble sound every fourth footstep.

The technicians came into the room. They gave Clive a curt nod and smiled when the fridge said, 'Leyla, Anil, how're things?'

'Like your new voice,' Leyla said. 'Better than that robot thing from before.'

'Dalek,' Clive said.

'What's that?' Anil said.

'The voice – it was a Dalek. From *Dr Who.*'

Anil rolled his eyes and glanced at Leyla. Both arched their eyebrows and turned their backs on Clive.

Anil unclipped two bollards from the side of one trolley. He put them down about three metres from the fridge. From the top of the first bollard, he grabbed one end of a long handle and drew out a wide green and yellow tape with the words *'Food Tech – Do not cross'*. He slipped the end of the tape onto a special clip on the side of the fridge. Leyla was repeating this on the other side of the fridge with a second bollard. Finally, Anil pulled one tape from the first bollard and stretched it and clipped it onto the second.

Leyla, Anil, the fridge and the two trolleys were on the inside of the taped-off area.

Clive was definitely on the outside.

Pretentious gits, he thought, snarling at the similarity of the 'Food Tech – do not cross' tape with the 'Police – do not cross' tape he had used.

He glared at them as they both touched the fridge door and the whole front hinged open.

'Now your diet excludes a lot of the stuff in here, we can't allow all this good food to go off. You'll get a bank transaction for any difference in value,' Anil said as he removed Clive's favourite sausages from the fridge and packed them in the trolley. A faint condensation cloud seeped over the edge of the refrigerated drawer the sausages had gone into.

Clive watched in despair as all the last remaining food he wanted to eat was removed and replaced with even more healthy rabbit and bird food.

He agreed with avoiding food wastage, but he still felt an irrational pang of personal loss.

Leyla and Anil shut the fridge, packed away the tape and the bollards, and left.

'That's better. How about a nice mixed salad for dinner, Clive?' the fridge cooed.

That did it. Clive was sure he could hear a mocking tone in the fridge's voice. He stormed over, touched the status display and scrolled to the voice selection menu.

He knew he had to eat better for his health, but this felt like he was caving in. He felt complicit. He felt a fraud.

Dr Adhya's prescription gave him no choice on food, but the fridge's voice was a tiny thing in his life that he could control.

Clive selected *Restore last used voice'* on the fridge and pressed *'OK'.*

'How about a mixed nice salad for dinner, Clive?' the fridge said in a Dalek voice, once more sounding like *'the emotionless master race bent on domination, utterly without pity, compassion or remorse'.* At least in a Dalek voice, the mixed salad sounded like a threat.

'Do I have a choice?' Clive said.

'No other options are available under the prescription.'

'So give it to me,' he said, smiling despite the anger in his tone.

Clive heard the usual motors whirring and the compartments opening. The serving drawer at the front of the fridge slid open holding a container with the carefully weighed ingredients of his meal; lettuce, carrot, tomato, cucumber and a lot of other green rabbit food that a nutritionist's algorithm had decided must be good for him. No dressings.

Clive picked up the container and pushed his hand in to stir the ingredients around. He tipped the contents of the container onto a plate and returned the container to the fridge.

At least the meal took no effort, he thought.

As Clive crunched the first piece of lettuce, he heard the fridge cleaning the container and stowing it. The food provided more noise than flavour, he decided, as he bit into a raw carrot.

Still chewing, Clive clicked on a message banner that his Buddy rolled out and he unfurled the message text:

From: Dr Dilani Adhya

Subject: Tomorrow night

'Clive, just a reminder that the new member's meeting is tomorrow night at the Windsor Church of the New Modelists. Don't worry, you don't have to be a member, all are welcome. It's a chance for people to share their stories and see how the Church can help you break free of the negative. Free from the battle against the Model. I really think it will help you in your ongoing health issues. Staying in-Model is a fulfilling lifestyle and we are a supportive community. Please come and give it a chance. Dilani.'

Clive stared at the message, his thoughts accompanied by the crunch of what he thought was raw radish. Maybe it was worth a go. What would it cost him? Sophia would be going so he could go with her and try to patch things up. It might even help him.

His eyes touched the bottom of the screen. It looked like there was more to the message. Scrolling down, he read:

'P.S. Sorry the new prescription is so tight, but Special Investigator Winter from Freedom Unit Enforcement was really insistent that I made your menu stricter than I originally intended.'

Chapter 26

Serge felt happy to be back in his own apartment after the selection process. The air was better for his chest. He took a deep breath, but it started him coughing again.

His active part was done for the moment. The Four were travelling and he allowed himself a cigarette watching the Seine slide by.

He was interrupted by his phone vibrating softly on the desk. He picked it up and looked at the screen. A message from Sully on a one-use phone. No text. Instead it showed a long hexadecimal number – his iTourist serial number from his immigration paperwork. He was the last to arrive.

Serge balanced his cigarette on the ashtray and shook his computer's mouse to wake it up. The fan started and the computer beeped a couple of times before the screen flashed up a password prompt.

He pushed his face closer to the computer's camera, the facial recognition software did its thing and logged him in. Even with six days of beard growth, the software recognised his face. Impressive.

Serge brought up a window and clicked through multiple connections, trapdoors and throwaway accounts. It would look like his computer was in Chile when he opened the iMe window.

He logged into his account. He was 'Chile Gaming Services, Inc.' as far as iMe knew while the Forbidden Island was running. Typing in Sully's iTourist ID with one hand, he took a drag from the cigarette, head cocked slightly to one side. He was distracted by the piece of paper under the ashtray. 'Merde.'

With all the excitement of the game, he had forgotten to take his prescription to the pharmacy and collect his new inhaler. He was sure there was an old one in the bathroom. It could wait.

He focused again on the screen and pressed '*Submit*', knowing that the account had been funded sufficiently to pay for the location search. The money came from an untraceable Cayman Island account. He would look like any number of overseas employers running a check on their UK based staff.

Seconds later, the computer screen redrew with a map of the UK. It showed four signal dots: Sully in a taxi near Glasgow, Femi driving into Derry, Lilou near Birmingham and Tatsuko in the south of England.

Happy to see all his players in motion, Serge minimised his iMe window and tapped on the keyboard to send his latest tweet to Jack.

'Hi to all you film fans, I'm watching "The Departed" and enjoying every minute.'

***

As the fifth cigarette stub joined its siblings in the ashtray, Serge finished his work. He was whipping up a storm on the gaming communities. Each message he sent was forwarded on again and again. The first game ever on the Forbidden Island was what the whole community had been waiting for. The huge vacuum of game supply was now fed by this one game. It sent the community's fervour spiralling.

Serge logged into the local bank account for Chile Gaming Services. The numbers at the bottom of the screen ticked up and up as each gamer paid their fee to gain access to the news and status updates from the game. It was already well past five million Pan-European dollars.

He would let it get to eight million before he locked the rest out. Denial of access would drive desire, and when he opened the subscriptions again for each of the 'limited time' offers, the cost for entry would double.

And then there was the gambling revenue. The game would be a very profitable venture. Serge would have to give the lion's share to Jack of course as it was his plan, but Serge's cut would still be substantial.

Serge knew that Jack would be desperate for news of The Four, but wouldn't be able to risk running a search inside the Forbidden Island. He couldn't move without them knowing. He couldn't search without leaving a trail that would lead straight back to him.

It had been more than a year since they had started on the plan. Serge shook his head. He wouldn't have had the patience. But he wasn't Jack. He didn't have the vision.

Serge's plan would have been direct and blunt. No hiding behind a game. Simply send The Four to the end points, but Jack had explained his bigger vision at their last meeting.

Serge had arrived first and entered. As always, he stopped to watch the light flooding through the large stained-glass wall and diffusing colour into the church. Serge walked down the white stone steps and approached the altar, he genuflected and headed to the curved wooden bench pew against the white back wall.

A tall man in an expensive looking blue suit followed Serge's route down the steps and approached the altar, stood for a few minutes in contemplation and then took his place on the pew next to Serge, head bowed in prayer.

'It's been a long time, old friend,' Jack whispered.

'You look well. How did you get away?'

'I told my hosts that I needed some time for a personal tribute and what better place than here. My security wasn't happy that I came in alone, but I told them nothing could happen in a place of God.'

'And they believed you?' Serge laughed.

'They're too suspicious to believe I'm safe anywhere, but they stayed by the door.'

They had talked for a while, Jack describing what he wanted and Serge listening.

'Why this game?' he asked when Jack stopped.

'The game will generate enough money to cover the costs and then a nice present for us both.'

'Sure, but the game adds so much risk.'

'If we simply make four deliveries, then of course it will generate news, but the iMe traces will find all of our supporters who helped and they'd be sacrificed. I need them, and the game adds so much more shock and drama. All those desperate gamers following the updates, and then tweeting their shock and outrage. The news will generate a huge storm in the media. A global focus.'

Serge nodded his appreciation of Jack's vision. 'As you wish.'

'Life's so easy for the young. No war, no hunger, no shortages. The number of friends on their TrueMe account is all that matters to them.'

'It's the same here in France,' Serge agreed.

'They don't need to make any sacrifices. All they offer back to society is selfies.'

'But you want to give them a game to watch?'

'Exactly. Life's a game to them – so we'll give them a game. They'll flock to it.'

Jack stood and bowed towards the altar. He started to walk towards the exit and paused next to Serge.

'There are no martyrs anymore, Serge. If this place teaches us anything, then it's the power of a martyr.'

Serge looked up and nodded.

'We'll give them martyrs,' Jack hissed.

Chapter 27

Tatsuko couldn't believe the convenience. It was nothing like at home in Boston. Or France. Or Spain.

The last hotel she had stayed in was in Bilbao. She had flagged taxis, walked, queued at the check-in desk, presented her passport, filled in a lot of her details and given her credit card all before she was checked in. They gave her a key for the room's door.

Here she had pressed the Taxi button and a car appeared and knew all about her.

'Hello, Tatsuko,' it said. 'Shall I take you to your hotel?'

'Errh... yes,' Tatsuko said, slightly unnerved by the familiarity of the taxi compared to the silence and distance of the people.

'Sorry, I need to go on a slight detour as some of the roads are closed for the ongoing eco-protests,' the taxi said.

'Tell me about them,' she replied.

The car did before offering her a 'tour guide' option. She accepted the option, and chatted with the taxi as it pointed out the notable sites as the journey progressed.

Tatsuko felt the taxi was almost a friend by the time she was dropped at the hotel door.

She climbed out of the car and the hotel doors opened. As she stepped into the cool of the reception area, she started to head to the desk, but was stopped by a tingle on her arm where the iTourist was attached. The display screen showed a scrolling message: *'Check-in complete... Room 537... Fifth floor.'*

Tatsuko shook her head in wonder at the contrast to Bilbao. She diverted from her path towards the desk and headed to the lift. When she got in, the lift said, 'I'll take you to your floor, Tatsuko.'

Room 537 was halfway along a carpeted white corridor. Small sections of the corridor lit up as she walked through them and snapped off as she passed. The carpet was deep enough to silence her footfalls, but not so deep as to snag the wheels of her case.

She reached the door of 537 and stood, unsure of what to do. She had no key and there wasn't an obvious handle – only a small red light glowing above a metal push plate. She reached out and was rewarded by a small click from the door and the light turned green. Tatsuko pushed the door open a small amount against the heavy spring mechanism. She pulled her hand back, the door swung closed, the door clicked, and the light turned red again.

Cool.

Tatsuko's head swung both ways along the corridor, a furtive check for other people. Seeing none, she took a pace right and stood outside room 535. She reached out and pushed the door. There wasn't a rewarding click this time. The light remained a defiant red and the door stayed resolutely shut.

She stepped left to her room and went inside.

A large screen on the wall clicked into life as she entered the room. After saying 'Welcome, Tatsuko' for a few seconds, it redrew with a window showing her 'Status'. Like on the iTourist, she could see the credit she had left, and time left on her visa. It also showed her pulse, blood pressure and other vital signs as well as details of her check-out time and the hotel's menus.

Tatsuko touched the iTourist in admiration. *Very cool.*

She dropped onto the bed, feeling the days of travel catching up with her.

'Please schedule your voluntary exercise session,' the display wall said.

Thinking that some exercise would wake her up and shake the travel out of her, she pressed *'Start in five minutes'*.

'Only approved footwear is allowed on the treadmill.'

'Er…' Tatsuko said, looking around for a treadmill. There wasn't anything obvious, but then a small trap door in the floor slid open to show the base of a treadmill. In a box at the end, she could see a pair of shoes. They looked similar to ordinary trainers, but each sole was split into multiple sections.

Tatsuko pulled her case onto the bed and rummaged around for some clothes loose enough to exercise in comfortably. Finally, she offered up one of the shoes to her foot. It seemed the right size, so she put them on. They fitted perfectly. Now the question on the immigration form made sense.

The display wall started counting down to zero and told her to get on the treadmill.

When she did, the treadmill started and Tatsuko ran. The display wall took her through a thirty-minute cycle, adjusting the speed of the treadmill to keep her pulse in an aerobic range.

At the end of the session, the treadmill slowed and stopped.

The display wall flashed a yellow warning triangle and it said 'Issues found. Say "OK" to view.'

Tatsuko was really fit and strong, so she couldn't think what the issue could be. Intrigued, she did what she was told and said, 'OK.'

The display wall redrew to show a screen with the representation of the soles of two feet and the heading 'Gait Analysis.' The display wall said, 'Say "OK" for details.'

Tatsuko said 'OK' again and the display wall went through details of how she landed on each foot, contrasted it with how she should land and the muscular impact analysis if not corrected.

Tatsuko dropped into a chair, stunned at the details. Everything here was brilliant. *Why do the people who live here complain so much?*

***

Energised by her impromptu exercise session, Tatsuko headed out into the evening. The temperature had dropped, and the sunshine had been replaced by low grey clouds and a persistent drizzle.

She had programmed the names of the shops she wanted to visit by following the prompts under the iTourist's 'i' button.

She selected *'Program Route'*, chose the *'Return to start point'* option, and watched an hourglass symbol as the iTourist worked it all out.

The iTourist's screen redrew to show *'Route calculated'* and scrolled through the route, showing the shop names in the order it had calculated. It finished back at the hotel.

She pressed *'Start'* and the iTourist showed the first shop as only four hundred metres away. Having seen the rain, she tried to use the Taxi button.

Don't waste money when you can walk, lazy girl, her mother said, and the iTourist agreed, telling her that the journey was too short, and it was healthier for her to walk. She strode out, starting to feel damp from the drizzle.

The first shop she wanted was in an arcade and the walk didn't take too long. As she entered the arcade, she saw a small shop selling umbrellas and raincoats. She detoured in and found a lightweight one-piece raincoat with a hood. It came with a neat little bag the raincoat could be stuffed into and a handy hook to attach it to a belt.

Useful for the walk back to the hotel. Useful for the game, she thought.

She headed to the shop she was aiming for and found it tucked in the back of the arcade.

The assistant glanced up from her book and smiled, seeming pleased that someone had actually come into the shop rather than ordering whatever they wanted online and getting it shipped. She looked to be in her early sixties, with greying hair and laughter lines.

"Elp you, luv?' she said.

Tatsuko described what she needed.

'Few in the back. They're all out of date obviously with everything on iMe.'

Tatsuko found the section and chose the newest map. It was nine years old and must have been the last of its breed. It covered southern England, with both road maps and more detailed town plans. She looked at the page detailing London, but the scale of the map was too small to be useful. She scanned the adjacent shelves and picked out an old *A to Z Maps of London*. She knew she shouldn't buy it, but the other map wasn't detailed enough.

She weighed up the risk of her purchase being tracked, versus the risk of not finding her way. She needed to get to the finish and London was a big place. She took both maps to the front desk.

She paid and headed out of the arcade. It was still raining so she slipped on her new raincoat and put the maps into a pocket.

She would need them. She couldn't use her iTourist in the game.

She headed for the next shop on her route, keen to get the rest of the things she needed.

Chapter 28

Clive's Health Bank bracelets allowed his hedonism to be cost-free, and for chocolate to be his substance of abuse. And his diabetes to return.

He hadn't admitted it to anyone. Wouldn't admit it to anyone, but he was scared. Diabetes was serious. He'd escaped it all those years ago, and now it was back. Bucking and fighting the system hadn't got him anywhere. He knew, deep down, that he couldn't win.

Maybe he needed a different outlook. If only he could find a way to live inside the system and its rules *and* be happy. If not happy, then at least accepting of it, his life would be easier and more contented.

A year ago, Clive would have thought the idea crazy. Even two weeks ago before the hospital, he wouldn't be going to a meeting at the Church of the New Modelists.

'I can't believe you're finally here,' Sophia said, 'even if it took *Dilani* to persuade you.'

'Sophia, please. Can we put it behind us? I'm here with you and I'm going to try.' And he actually was thinking positively about the situation.

Clive hadn't been to the Vansittart Estate in Windsor for years, and even then, it had been run down, and on a downward trajectory. A victim of newer, bigger, better developments. When Sophia had told him the address of the meeting, Clive had done a double-take, it seemed so unlikely.

As he scanned the area, he couldn't quite believe the transformation. The old buildings had been demolished and replaced with a large irregular structure.

'Who are they?' Clive asked, pointing at a group of six people climbing out of a van. They all wore multicoloured hoodies and carried placards. They didn't look like eco-protesters and as the group formed in a ragged line and raised their placards, Clive could see the messages for the first time – *'Don't be a slave to the Model', 'Leave out the control', 'Leave in the convenience'*, and three *'Liberation, Empowerment, Responsibility'*. He felt a stir of genuine interest and empathy. These were his sort of people.

'Ignore them, they're Control Rebellion. They always come.' Sophia grabbed Clive's elbow and pulled him away and they joined a stream of people heading through the arch and towards the church.

Clive marvelled at how much time and effort it would have needed to build. The structure almost looked handmade, or at least made from recycled materials, but it had to be a professional build. Not even a church could use volunteers on a building site and conform to all the regulations and health and safety.

The roof appeared to be a living sea of wild grasses and flowers that swayed and sang in the breeze. Along one wall that led to the large, arch-shaped entrance, the Church's mantra was emblazoned: *'Conformity is Contentment, Conformity is Peace'*.

They filed through the door. The use of recycled products continued on the inside. Lighting dangled from an uneven ceiling, but whatever building materials had been used were strong enough to provide a large circular room with no obstructing pillars.

In the centre of the room, two people fussed at a circular table covered in a green cloth. They both wore jackets and trousers with one half-green and the other half-black. Circles of chairs rippled out from the table, in ever increasing diameters. Some in the strange half-green, half-black colours, others pure green, and the rest a uniform grey.

Clive stood at the outside edge of the chairs as Sophia chatted with people she knew. He scanned the people arriving and saw Dilani coming through the archway with a group of others. She waved and headed over to him.

'Clive, so glad you came,' she said.

'Hi.' He touched Sophia's arm to bring her into the conversation. He knew that talking to Dilani without introducing Sophia would be a disaster.

'Sophia,' he said, 'this is my doctor, Dilani.'

Sophia stared at Dilani, who seemed confused about why she was getting such a frosty response. Clive began to wonder if this was such a good idea.

'Citizens,' a loud voice said, amplified around the room by little speakers. 'It is time.'

All the conversations in the church snapped off like they were controlled by an invisible switch, and people started shuffling to find a seat. Clive headed towards the nearest chair.

'Not there,' whispered Sophia, grabbing Clive's elbow and steering him away from the half-green, half-black chairs and also from Dilani. 'Ultras only.' Sophia's grip tightened on Clive's arm. 'You didn't tell me Dilani was so pretty. Is that why you changed your mind?' Sophia hissed.

'I hadn't noticed,' Clive said. 'Anyway, what's an Ultra?'

Sophia hissed, 'Sure you didn't notice,' and edged Clive past the green chairs and towards the mass of grey ones.

Clive settled into his chair and the room waited in silent anticipation. Clive scanned the expectant faces and saw Dilani on the other side of the hall.

Sophia's elbow nearly tore a hole in his side.

A young woman approached the circular table with the green cloth in the centre of the room, and picked the large wooden pole off its ceremonial supports. It must have been heavy as she needed both hands to hold it and place one end on the floor. Wrapping both hands around the top of the pole, she lifted it and, still holding on with both hands, let it drop.

The pole made a booming, echoing thud on the hard floor.

Clive spun left as he heard a door open. A column of people, two abreast and all dressed in green emerged from a large door painted in a matching green.

The pole boomed on the floor again and the column took a stride. Boom, stride, boom, stride. About forty people, all Pure Greens, made their way across the room to the green chairs and sat. Clive recognised the teacher who had reported Summer to the police.

The silence resettled, before the woman lifted the pole and allowed it to drop again. A second door, painted half-black and half-green opened and this time, the booming pole heralded the entrance of a single file of eight, dressed in green and black robes.

Clive, guessing these were Ultras, made a note to ask Sophia later.

The Ultras settled and the young woman replaced the pole on its supports and scuttled off to take a lowly grey seat.

An older woman, maybe sixty, sitting in the middle of the front row of Ultras stood and approached the table.

'Citizens,' she cried as she reached it. 'Let us pray.'

All heads bowed, and Clive followed suit.

'Hallowed be the Model Citizen for it shows us the path of enlightenment,' the Ultra said.

The congregation muttered, 'Amen,' in response.

'Let the purity of a life conforming to the Model bless each of us.'

'Amen.'

'Modern life has no purpose, but the Model takes away our fear and uncertainty.'

'Amen.'

'When everything is dangerous…' the Ultra said, raising her voice.

'The Model keeps me safe,' the congregation replied, matching her volume.

'When temptation faces us…' Louder.

'The Model keeps me pure.'

'When the planet is overpopulated…' Louder.

'The Model keeps my footprint small.'

'When exercise is needed…' Louder.

'The Model keeps me healthy.'

Clive heard everyone around him stand and Sophia's hand pulled at him to rise. He stood and watched the Ultra raise her hands to the ceiling.

'Praise be to the Model Citizen, for our choices are simple.'

'Amen.'

'To follow the Model is to follow the light.'

'Amen.'

The congregation sat and Clive followed them down. He hadn't expected such an atmosphere of devotion and belief. No, it was beyond simple belief, it was real faith. Sophia's face beamed with joy.

The Ultra waited for the room to settle, and silence to return before starting to pace slowly around the table, facing each section of the room in turn.

'We are under attack again from the unbelievers,' she said. 'The lazy and the risk-takers. They call us heretics. They call our Model Citizen a false prophet.'

'No,' the congregation hissed.

'What have the Christian, Muslim and other religions ever given their followers? Look back at history and try and count the number who have died in the name of their faith.'

'Shame,' the congregation hissed. 'Tragedy.'

'They seek to deny us the utopia of freedom. The freedom not to worry. The freedom not to battle conflicting health and lifestyle choices.'

'Praise the Model,' the congregation chanted.

'The unbelievers breed and breed and endanger our planet with their gluttonous hoards.'

'One child per union,' the congregation implored.

Clive zoned out the Ultra and watched the rapt faces of the congregation. They were more devout than any church service he had seen. Despite sitting next to Sophia, he felt more distant from her than ever.

The Ultra's sermon went on for a long time before she paused and then said, 'Let us hear from those who had fallen, and now follow the light.'

Clive felt a sudden rush of panic. Surely they wouldn't want him to speak? He relaxed when he saw a group of No-Tucks –

people who were much fatter before iMe managed away their weight, but couldn't afford the cosmetic surgery to remove their excess skin.

Each No-Tuck spoke of their personal story of salvation. Stories of excess. Stories of weight gain from lack of exercise. Stories of how the Model saved their life.

At the end of the confessions, Sophia dabbed a tear from the corner of her eyes and said, 'Beautiful and inspiring, isn't it?'

Clive wasn't sure what to say. The No-Tuck's stories had been uplifting and emotional, but he was worried about the tone from the Ultra. There was an edge to it that went past a hint of anger to full on threat. 'What's an Ultra? I thought Pure Greens were the most devout followers of the Model?' Clive said.

'No, the Ultras set the Church up. They think the Model is too lenient. They think the government could do much more to save the environment by lowering the population and consumption. They only take half of the Model's allowance. The rest they see as excess that brings death to the planet. That's why half of their robes are black.'

Clive frowned, feeling more unsettled by Sophia's explanation.

***

The meeting closed, the congregation started to drift away.

As Sophia said goodbye to her friends, Clive hung back, inching towards the rear of the room. He crabbed sideways, his back to the wall as he made his way to the green and black door.

He reached for the door handle and tried to turn it, but it was locked.

As he removed his hand, the handle snapped down and the door flew open. A man in green and black filled the doorway and towered over Clive.

He snatched Clive's arm and gripped it hard. Squeezing and twisting as he walked him towards the exit.

'This room is reserved for Ultras, Citizen.'

He shoved Clive in the back, sending him off-balance out and into the night.

'Not for you,' the Ultra snarled.

Chapter 29

Sully's mood was worsened by the wind and the imminent threat of the heavy rain from the morning returning. He didn't know where the other three were, but it must be better than this. Each folder was a secret, but his folder 'C' had taken him to Glasgow and then this small place called Dumfries.

The others must have known this was the worst place, he thought. *That's why they let me have the folder.* 'Conspiracy,' he muttered. But he'd show them. He'd already left a message on the forum using his hotel's internet connection and a one-use only account. However this all played out, he was heading to Gretna Green.

For now, he had to pretend to conform. The folder had given him his instructions and so he was heading to the athletic centre, following a small group of locals who all seemed immune to the weather. He missed the clear, blue skies of Tuscany.

Arriving at the low brown brick building of the athletic centre, Sully followed the group and the signs around the side of the building and along a long, drab brick wall. The clouds seemed to get darker, and pushed the afternoon into impersonating the night.

At the entrance to a field stood a man wearing a thick waterproof coat. He held a small tablet device and each of the people in the group ahead paused to read it before carrying on up a small incline to a field.

Sully approached and the man smiled. 'We don't get many tourists, but you're more than welcome all the same.' He pushed the tablet towards Sully.

He took it, he felt a small buzz from his iTourist and the tablet flashed *'Entrance fee paid – please accept waiver to enter.'*

Sully read the waiver document and acknowledged that any injury or fall wasn't the organiser's liability, and that getting struck by a ball was an inherent risk of attending a football match, and neither the centre nor the players could accept any blame or liability.

He tapped his agreement into the tablet and trudged up onto the field.

The players were already on the pitch and the referee stood over the ball and blew her whistle three times. 'I have inspected the pitch and I am declaring this a "Wet Pitch". As such the slip hazard risk is confirmed as "Severe", and the risk mitigation plan demands no running. This will be a "Walk Game".'

The referee ushered a player forward, she blew her whistle again and the game began. The players walked around, kicking the ball and Sully turned away.

'Pathetic,' he said, and headed towards a group of trees and bushes on the other side of the pitch.

'I'm too good for this,' he muttered to himself. 'I'm one of The Four – the winner of the ultimate game. They should pamper me and bring things to me. Not make me walk around in the rain.'

Sure, Serge had explained it all. The helpers would be tracked. When the game started the police would rerun his routes, see everywhere he had been and see who else had been there. Anyone coming to him to give him what he needed would be tracked and caught.

But he was Sully. He was worth their sacrifice.

The parcel he had to collect was meant to be in the bushes. Thrown from a safe distance so that the police couldn't know who delivered it.

I make a sacrifice for the game – so should they, he thought, but there he was. He had no choice if he wanted to be in the game. He would win the money, the BST hand and everyone would hail him as a champion.

Sully stepped over a low bush and straight into a muddy puddle. 'Shit.'

He scanned the bushes, looking for his parcel. He started to panic when he couldn't see it. Was this more conspiracy? They didn't want him to be in the game.

He strode around in the low bushes, sweeping his hand over the tops of the bushes to see if the parcel was hidden underneath. His only reward was a wet hand to join his wet foot.

Then his toe hit something solid.

'Yes,' he said as he bent and picked up a parcel. It was wrapped tightly in plastic against the weather and had the letter 'C' written on it in black ink. The parcel must have been there some time, some days even, as the 'C' was streaked and dissolving.

Sully pushed the parcel under his arm and hurried towards the exit, ignoring the questioning glances of some of the crowd.

***

His mood hadn't improved when he followed the iTourist's route from the athletic centre to his start point.

He pushed against the door, feeling the resistance from the disused, rusty hinges. No glamorous location, no adoring crowds. Instead, he stood alone in an abandoned room. A thick wooden table was the only remaining furniture. Its top was scarred with hundreds of cut marks and stained with a red tint.

Part of the roof had come away, and water dripped through the gap and down the wall. The room was darker than the afternoon outside so Sully tried the light switch. Nothing happened.

The information status on his iTourist said 15:47. Thirteen minutes to go.

Sully let the thought grow in him, feeding his anticipation.

The game was his.

He put his parcel on the wooden table and started to tear at the wrapping. Despite being thin, it was strong and stretched rather than tore. He pulled and stretched and stuck his fingernails in to try and break through the seal.

Finally, he got through it, and unpeeled the parcel's layers, like pulling the bandages off a mummy.

The waterproof, outer covering looked to have done its job, as the box inside was dry and undamaged. Sully snapped the catches on the box's lid open and lifted the lid, feeling his excitement grow.

On top was a towel. Sully took it out and unfolded it, spreading the folds flat on the table.

His hand returned to the box and pulled out a large lamp. He clicked it on, splashing the table with a harsh blue-white light.

Sully put the lamp on the table and pulled out the next item.

He gasped, gulping down his fear. He knew it would be in the box, but seeing it and holding it was something else. Something real.

The machete's curved blade flashed with the reflected light of the lamp as he twisted it in his hand. He touched the edge very gently. It was extremely sharp.

Sully placed the machete reverently on the towel, careful to stay away from its edge. Despite its excellent condition, the machete was old. Its handle and blade showed scuffs and scrapes from use. You couldn't buy them now. Too dangerous. Illegal to even own.

The lamp and machete had been sourced locally. He reached into his pocket and pulled out his BST universal mount that had been inside his case on the journey from France. It could go through the security scans without looking like anything other than a piece of clothing.

Sully put it on the table next to the machete which seemed to wink at him like it knew what was coming.

The only other thing in the box definitely couldn't be sourced locally or risked in his luggage. Serge had boasted about the cost and complexity of smuggling it into the Forbidden Island. Something in his voice made Sully think that there had been many failed attempts, but Serge had said nothing and glared at Sully when he asked.

Sully put both hands into the box and lifted the game controller out, like a priest lifting a sacred relic.

It was heavier than he thought, and he placed the game controller onto the towel. He marvelled at it. It had four fingers and a thumb – a hand-like thing, but with a solid base that seemed a perfect match for his BST universal mount. The hand looked almost grey in the bluish light from the lamp.

The screen in the game controller's palm was off. A black, empty rectangle.

His iTourist clicked over to 15:52. Eight minutes to go.

Sully stared at the screen on the controller. Waiting for it to come to life, and signal the start of the game.

It stayed black.

The light outside faded, and Sully could hear the rain start to bounce on the roof. The shadows cast by the lamp deepened, and Sully could hear his own breathing.

Sully glanced at the machete. Should he cheat and start early? No, not this time.

The rain banged down heavier on the roof.

Sully stared at the game controller again.

His iTourist clicked over to 15:54.

Six minutes to go until the world's greatest game.

Chapter 30

For once, Serge didn't have a cigarette on the go as he checked his computer. His breath was shallow, and his chest tightened as the excitement and stress built.

15:54 in the UK. Six minutes to go.

He had spent a lot of money with iMe tracking his Four and he had recently topped up the balance on Chile Gaming Services, Inc's iMe account. The minimum credit took him way over what he needed, but Serge could afford to lose a few pounds to iMe. Sales of registrations for status updates on Forbidden Island had gone better than expected. The last time they had opened the website to allow new registrations, the five thousand slots had all gone in four minutes. The registrations account balance was very, very healthy. The amount they had taken in bets had nearly caught up. It would soon eclipse registrations.

His four contestants were all at their starting points. Serge had watched every move of their iTourist's signals as they followed their instructions. Well, more or less, but these were high-achievers not mindless sheep, so he had expected them to push the rules.

Tatsuko had landed in Southampton and headed to the hotel as she was told. She had collected her parcel from its hiding place easily. She was at her start point in Southampton centre on time, but Serge worried about some of the shops she had been to the previous evening.

Lilou was his favourite. Maybe because she was French. Serge thought that a little patriotic bias was allowed at this stage. There would be none later.

She had made her way to Worcester and picked up her parcel without drama or deviation.

Femi had had the hardest journey, but now waited in Derry.

Sully was in Dumfries. Serge had laughed as he watched his signal thrash around in the bushes. He was a pompous fool, Serge thought.

15:55.

Time to start. He pressed the 'Five minutes' button on the game's master window on his computer.

He waited.

This was the moment of greatest technical risk.

He held his breath.

And relaxed as each game controller hand responded and came online, their positions glowed on the game's master window of his computer. If it was able to show the iMe signals as well, they would be almost perfectly overlain.

He pressed the 'Contestant View' button and the game master window redrew into four segments. Each segment showed the contestant's name and a graphical representation of the contestant's game controller hand.

Each hand-shaped controller counted down. 04:55, 04:54, 04:53.

He could almost feel their tension, imagining the contestants watching their game controllers intently.

Serge checked another page on the game master window. Fifty-six thousand subscribers online and growing. All watching the same clock countdown past three minutes to go.

He knew Jack would be looking at his own clock. Blind to the real-time status. Too high risk. It would be stupid for him to express any interest. He would need deniability.

All he could risk was a quick glance at a tweet.

The timers all hit 00:10. Will they do it? Serge thought. They had all passed the tests, but this was different. They had to do it themselves.

They had to survive.

The clocks all hit zero.

He clicked on his computer to bring another window to the front. It held his latest tweet.

'Hi to all you film fans, a sports comedy theme today. I was tempted by "Run Fat Boy Run", but I settled on "Ready to Rumble".'

He pressed send and clicked back onto the game master window, staring at the screen, willing the game controller hands to move.

Chapter 31

Tatsuko glanced at the clock on her game controller, 04:55. She still had time. She wasn't going to waste it watching the rest of the countdown.

She was in a disused butcher's shop, with a large, scarred chopping bench. The angle of the pale afternoon sun through a window cast a shaft of light across the bench. She had the contents of her parcel laid out on a towel: game controller, machete, lamp. The lamp was off. She had already checked that the game controller fitted her BST mount.

The bench also held some of her shopping. The brand-new, battery-powered multitool balanced on top of its box. She had charged it overnight in the hotel, so she was sure it had enough juice. A flexible metal shaft snaked from the multitool and ended with a small circular base. The base had a light and a spring-loaded clamp that when Tatsuko pulled down on it, she could attach one of the circular cutting discs onto the end of the shaft. When she released the base, its spring forced the base up to grasp the disc. The disc was the hardest and sharpest they made.

To check that the disc was on correctly, she held the shaft in her right hand and used her left hand to blip the power of the multitool.

Instead of the sound of the multitool powering up and the disc spinning, the end of the shaft holding the cutting disc, flashed red. The display on the multitool's casing alternated two error messages: *Error code: 1'* and *Error code: 2'*.

Tatsuko found the error codes in the user manual – no safety glasses detected, and no safety gloves detected.

She checked on her game controller: 03:43. Still time.

Tatsuko pulled the safety glasses and cut-proof gloves out of their boxes, glad now the shop assistant had insisted she bought them.

Relieved that she had charged them as well, she slipped the glasses on and pressed the power button. After a pause, the glasses buzzed and the *Error code: 1* message disappeared.

Tatsuko slipped both gloves on, careful not to cover the iTourist with the cuff of the left glove. She pressed buttons on each glove and was rewarded with a buzz from each and the disappearance of *Error code: 2*.

She must have breathed a bit heavily and had steamed up the glasses. As she pulled them off her face to wipe them, the *Error code: 1* reappeared. The glasses must have a proximity sensor or something she decided.

Glasses back in place, no errors showing, Tatsuko held the end of the shaft and pressed the power button.

This time the cutting disc spun up with an excited whir. She moved the disc down towards the bench, and as it touched the wood, the disc slowed momentarily as it dug into the wood, then cut a neat furrow into the bench, shooting dust away from Tatsuko.

She lifted the disc and turned the power off. The edge of the disc glowed red and the smell of burnt wood drifted towards her.

Perfect, she thought. Now to get rid of the iTourist so she could win the game.

Holding the end of the shaft with the disc in her right hand, Tatsuko turned the power on again. She placed her left wrist onto the bench and breathed in. She willed her muscles to still and calm. The tremor in her hand stopped.

She moved the spinning cutting disc towards her wrist, adjusting the angle so that the disc would cut across the iTourist. The cutting disc touched the iTourist and flared red hot. Tatsuko wrinkled her nose at the acrid smell.

She lifted the cutting disc, but the iTourist was unmarked. She pressed the cutting disc down again harder. The smell got unbearable, but she kept the pressure on, even though she could see that the cutting disc had lost over half of its diameter and her wrist under the iTourist was burning.

She lifted the disc again to check the iTourist. Maybe there was a slight difference in the shine where the disc had been. Maybe not.

She glanced at the game controller.

00:27.

Tatsuko didn't have time to keep trying the cutting disc. Not that it was working anyway.

She tore off the glasses and removed the gloves, throwing them with disgust onto the bench. Then she took a few seconds to calm herself.

00:18.

Unfortunately, it looked like Serge was right. There was only one way to get the iTourist off. Only one way to join the game.

She thought of her mother saying, *work, work, lazy girl*. Work was all she had ever done. The prize money would let her rest a little, and with a BST device she could do so much more. If she won, maybe her mother's voice in her head would finally quieten.

Tatsuko gulped as the timer hit 00:05 and flashed red.

She put her left wrist back onto the bench and picked up the machete.

Chapter 32

Sully's game controller hit 00:05 and he raised his right hand high into the air. Staring at a spot on his wrist above the iTourist.

'Fuck,' he said. 'Fuck.'

He flexed his shoulder and told his brain to send signals to his arm and shoulder to move. They obeyed, the hand moved, gathering momentum. The weight of the machete aiding the acceleration of the hand down towards his wrist.

He willed the blade down, trusting his aim, knowing one clean strike, delivered with all his weight would slice through bone and tendons. Serge had said the BST universal mount worked better with a clean cut.

His brain decided otherwise. Some deep subconscious survival instinct kicked in. Urgent, frantic messages were sent to muscles, and they obeyed.

The machete stopped millimetres above his wrist.

Sully sobbed, part relief, part frustration that his body had let him down. He was brave enough, he told himself. It was his body's fault.

This wasn't like Serge's stupid test. He had heard the others being called before him. Why was he always the last?

Sully had sat in the chair and looked at Serge's guillotine, listened to empty words about commitment. Did he think Sully was an idiot?

Had he heard screams as a hand was chopped off? No, and he would have heard.

Was there blood splattered around the room? No, and they couldn't have cleaned it up so completely.

It was a hoax. A trick. Nothing.

Sully had watched the guillotine blade drop. Even though his brain told him that it would stop, he almost pulled it away. Sweat burst onto his brow, but he kept his hand still. His smile of triumph when the blade hit its stops was cracked and unconvincing.

Now he had to do it for real. Tears formed in his eyes. More weakness from his body. A couple of drops rolled down his cheeks and dropped onto the bench. They soaked into the wood, leaving little dark circles.

He sniffed and shoved a rough sleeve across his face to wipe the tears away.

'This time,' he said and raised the machete again.

His arm wouldn't move. It had failed him.

'No,' he said, firmness filling his voice.

Everyone would laugh at him if he failed here. The whole online AR community would know his cowardice.

He couldn't allow it. He thought of the money and what he could buy with it before he swung his arm hard and fast.

Chapter 33

Lilou's game controller hit 00:00 and beeped. She felt calm. Certain. This was the level of challenge that had been missing from her life for so long.

She didn't hesitate. Not even for a moment.

Her arm swung down and she arched her back to add to the force behind the blow, drawing on the strength of the muscles in her shoulders and back.

She kept her eyes on the prize, the spot on her wrist above her iTourist. The machete's handle was big in her hand, but her parkour had built strong muscles in her fingers and wrist. The machete didn't waver from its course.

Lilou heard a crack as the machete hit her wrist, right on target, and then a deeper thud as the blade sliced through her wrist and hit the bench. The force of her swing buried the machete into the wooden countertop.

The blade's singing vibration was drowned by Lilou's scream.

Her brain exploded with thousands of nerves all lighting up at the same time. All screaming for her attention. Her vision flashed white and she staggered, almost falling.

Her brain was in shutdown. She couldn't see it, but her blood jetted out of her severed wrist, bouncing red splatters off the machete's blade and sending them flying onto the bench and floor.

From somewhere inside her, she forced a message into her chaotic brain.

'Act or bleed out.'

Nothing.

'Act or die.'

Her brain wasted another second in chaos before rationalising the situation, then her vision snapped back on like a display wall coming to life.

She tried to distance herself from the scene. The blade. The blood everywhere – *her* blood.

Her hand and part of her wrist on the floor. The iTourist flashed red all over, still attached to her now departed limb.

'Act,' she screamed at herself.

Time slowed and she spun back to the bench. The BST universal mount waited for her. A few drops of blood had landed on it, but it didn't ruin her grip.

She rotated her left elbow to bring her damaged arm across her, keeping it pointed away from her face to avoid the jetting blood. She twisted the BST universal mount so that the top of it aligned with the top of her wrist.

Twisting it left and right to overcome the resistance, she pushed the mount over her left wrist. Pushing harder and gasping from the effort, she got it all the way on, then stopped to suck in some deep breaths.

Lilou could feel the pressure of her pulse against the end of the mount.

Leaning against the bench, she grasped the end of the mount as Serge had shown her. She pushed and rotated the end, hoping to hear a click as it fastened itself in place.

'You need the click,' Serge had said. 'If you don't, you have to pull it off and try again. Trust me that will really hurt.'

Lilou sobbed. There was no click. Her brain was letting the panic, the shock and the noise of her severed nerves take over again.

She pushed and twisted harder.

Click. The mount slotted into place.

Her brain blanked again at the sensation, and then seemed to reboot into a calmer mode.

The click had released a cocktail of painkillers and clotting agents into her bloodstream.

She stared at the mount and the blood smears along its length. It seemed to be constricting around her arm. The colour of it matching her skin tone almost perfectly.

The nerves in her wrist calmed, some weird movement in the inside end of the mount felt like rubbing the ends of a bristle nail brush against the back of her hand.

One by one, the nerve endings stilled, seeming to connect to a receptor in the mount. The rubbing sensation stopped, and her wrist felt normal.

Lilou stared again at the mount, almost not believing what had happened.

Her brain told her that she still had a hand. She could tell it to move her fingers, but obviously, her hand lay still on the floor.

Now that her brain had been fooled into thinking that nothing had happened to her wrist, she was aware of her pulse hammering in her ears.

She doubled over and retched.

When she stood again, she felt better.

Lilou took in the scene, again feeling distant from it. The blood and hand on the floor couldn't be hers. She was fine.

She turned to the bench and looked at the display on her game controller.

'Attach game controller to universal mount to begin,' it pulsed.

Lilou picked the game controller up, twisting it so that its fake thumb was upright. She pushed the controller onto the connector that protruded from the end of the mount and twisted. The controller rotated into the normal position of a hand and clicked on.

Lilou twisted her arm to see the controller's 'palm' and the display.

'Welcome to Forbidden Island – the ultimate game,' it said.

Chapter 34

The day had scraped by, each dull minute dragged its heels, seeming reluctant to leave. Clive could have run through waist-deep thick treacle faster.

The grimy window of the PCU office hadn't been able to mask the sunshine outside, and Clive's gaze had flicked from the clock on the display wall to the window and back again. Willing time to go faster, like he was a bored school kid waiting for the release of the final bell of the day.

A walk in the late afternoon sun would be a nice end to a crappy day.

The clock on the display wall turned over. 16:00. One hour to go.

Ava sat opposite Clive in Zoe's old seat. He replayed her handling of Brett in his head. Her self-confidence was surging, feeding itself. *She's going to fly*, he thought.

Ava looked up, seeming to sense that Clive was watching her.

'OK, Boss?'

'Yes. Thinking about home time.'

In reality, Clive was now thinking about calling Sophia again. Their relationship had locked into a hard frost since the meeting at the church. Every one of his unanswered messages and calls seemed to drop the temperature a degree.

He didn't want to call with Ava hearing his side of the conversation, so he decided to try messaging again.

'Hi, darling. I don't want to lose what we have. Can we meet? I really want to change.'

His HUD remained blank, then he smiled, and his heart quickened as he saw *'Sophia is typing'* appear at the bottom of his TrueMe window. He waited. Hoping.

Sophia's response cut through him and forced tears into his eyes. He read it again through blurry vision. Rubbing the tears away with a savage swipe of his hands didn't change the message: *'Sorry, Clive, but we need to take a break. After all my care and love, you go to the church because of her.'*

Clive tried to type some words, but it was all inadequate. He'd have to leave the office and try to find a quiet spot that he could call her from. He needed to explain.

He needed her.

Then he realised the truth.

He loved her.

His thoughts were brought to an abrupt halt by his Buddy sprinting onto his HUD. The banner he trailed said *'Urgent: iTourist unauthorised disconnect – Lilou Boudin – location: Worcester.'*

Clive snapped upright. He glanced at Ava, seeing from her face that her Buddy had dragged the same banner onto her HUD.

Her fingers were already up and typing. Always so fast. If this was a gunfight, Clive would have already been bleeding in the dust, holding his chest, with Ava blowing smoke from her gun barrel.

He knew he was beaten, and she flashed a triumphant smile.

'Shall I say it for you?' she said.

Clive shook his head. He tried to steady himself from the shock of the message and the realisation of his love for Sophia. 'Share,' he said.

The PCU office display wall froze, then redrew to show Ava's HUD. She already had the report open and a map of Worcester showing. A small red dot pulsed in the centre of the map. As Ava pinched her fingers together, the map zoomed in until the scale was large enough to show a couple of buildings. The iTourist signal was stationary in the centre of a disused butcher's shop.

Why would an iTourist fail? It couldn't. No more than iMe could.

Then the pain of losing Sophia swamped him.

He blinked hard twice, trying to force some clarity into the jumble of thoughts thrashing around. He needed to focus on work. His mouth was dry, his pulse rising in anticipation. *Could it be?*

This was the first hint of an issue with iMe since Karina Morgan's disappearance over a year ago. This could be the same. It could be the beginning of some real police work.

He tried to think logically, but he couldn't think about anything other than Sophia. *Never any work and now this comes up just as I'm losing Sophia*, he thought. He didn't have time for a call, but typed out a simple message: *'I love you. Wanted to call but work urgent'* and pressed *'Send'*.

Now he had to clear his mind and focus.

'It'll take us three hours to get there,' he said. 'See if Control can tear some Uniforms away from the eco-protests to go there now.'

Ava nodded and started to type out the request message.

'Send a forensic drone as well,' Clive said.

'Really?' Ava queried. 'It won't be anything serious.'

'You remember Karina. That started in the same way.'

Ava had been part of Zoe's 'crew' of trainees working on the case. She had seen the images and her eyes changed as she remembered, showing the same determination that Clive had seen when she dealt with Brett.

Ava finished typing and pressed *'Send'*. Clive watched Ava's Buddy on the display wall, she was halfway through the familiar animation of folding the message into a paper aeroplane and throwing it, when her Buddy froze and sprinted back across the display wall dragging another banner.

'What the fuck?' Clive said as he read the banner: 'Urgent: iTourist unauthorised disconnect – Olufemi Naidoo – location: Derry.'

He didn't even try and compete with Ava this time. She clicked on the message and did the same pinching and zooming. Another unauthorised disconnected iTourist stationary in a disused butchers.

'That's quite a coincidence,' Ava said. 'Same approach, Boss? Uniform and drone?'

Clive nodded. He'd never trusted coincidences. They made him nervous.

Ava hadn't even had time to press send before her Buddy unfurled the next banner: *'Urgent: iTourist unauthorised disconnect – Tatsuko Ito – location: Southampton.'*

Clive's head rotated. 'No, no, no.'

Ava pressed send on the message to Uniform in Derry before sending a nearly identical one to Southampton. 'What's going on, Boss?'

'No idea.'

Could it be the start of a systemic failure? Surely not? A Cyber hack? Clive touched the back of his neck where his iMe was embedded. Was someone there?

'We'd better check with iMe,' Clive said. He touched his jaw to make a call and said, 'Call iMe Tech Support.' He heard the call ring and threw his HUD at the display wall. It blanked out the display of Ava's HUD and redrew with Clive's. Now she could hear the call through the speaker in the wall.

'Tech Support, this is Rob,' the voice said. He sounded flustered.

'Hi, Rob, this is DI Clive Lussac at PCU. I've got three unauthorised iTourist disconnection messages. What's going on?'

'Hi, Clive. We've got them too. Everything seems OK our end, other than the three messages. We're checking. Can't tell you any more at the moment.'

'Not a cyber hack?'

Rob snorted. 'You watch too many films. It's not that easy.'

'Call me back when you can,' Clive said.

'Sure,' Rob said. Clive could hear raised voices in the background at Rob's end of the call. It sounded like panicked questions being thrown around. 'Got to go,' Rob said, and the call dropped.

In the silence, Clive and Ava looked at each other, not sure what to do next.

Clive decided. 'Southampton's closer than Worcester or Derry,' he said. 'Get a car here now. We need to see for ourselves.'

Ava nodded, fiddled on her HUD. 'There's one outside in two minutes.'

Clive was pushing his chair back in a loud scraping noise when ringing in his head stopped him. Ava stopped too. Clive's HUD was still connected to the display wall and they could both hear the call and see the caller ID: *DCS Bhatt.*

Clive raised his eyebrows and said, 'Prepare yourself, Ava.'

Clive touched his jaw to accept the call.

'What's going on, Clive?' Bhatt shouted.

Clive could hear the urgency in her voice. It singed his ears like a fiery blast from a dragon.

'Three unauthorised disconnected iTourists,' Clive said. He knew this bland statement of fact would raise the temperature of the blast from Bhatt, so he added, 'I've sent Uniform and drones to all three sites. iMe Tech Support is checking. They can't see anything sinister. No system wide issues.'

'What else,' Bhatt demanded, sounding like she expected Clive to have solved it already.

'Ava and I are about to go to the Southampton site. It's the closest. Feels like we need to see it for ourselves.'

Bhatt hesitated. Clive could almost hear her thinking. The drones would scan each site and create a perfect 3D model that they could 'walk' around. They'd do a full forensic sweep and compile a detailed report. Did they need to go and incur both the cost of the journey and the overtime? Could the depleted PCU budget sustain it?

'Go,' Bhatt said. 'You'll get a better sense of the place if you're there.'

'On it,' Clive said and dropped the call.

'Car's outside,' Ava said.

'Let's go,' Clive said, standing up straight and heading for the door.

As Clive's hand hit the door handle, his Buddy sprinted across the bottom of his HUD with another message banner: *'Urgent: iTourist unauthorised disconnect – Salvatore Rossi – location: Dumfries.'*

Clive didn't bother to click into it. He knew what it would show. They needed to get moving and they could call and message from the car.

He yanked the door back with enough force to thump the door into the wall. The handle sent a few pink flecks of plaster floating onto the floor.

Clive and Ava ran down the empty corridor, heading for the car.

'I've got a really bad feeling about this,' he said.

Chapter 35

Femi panted out short breaths as his BST universal mount constricted, connected and then rested. One, two, three, four more sharp breaths, and then he stopped and tried to tell himself that everything was normal. That everything was the same.

Why doesn't my hand hurt? he thought.

A human hand for a BST bio-hand was an easy choice. Everyone wanted one, but few got the chance. The scarcity and massive upgrade over an organic 'original equipment' human hand fuelled the desirability to stellar levels.

But starting the process with a machete – that was hard-core.

The game couldn't function with an iTourist telling the police where the contestants were all the time, allowing them to pay for transport, shelter and food. Way too easy. It was day-to-day life, not the game of the Forbidden Island.

Femi picked up the game controller, fitted it onto his universal mount and watched the *'Welcome to Forbidden Island – the ultimate game'* message.

'Bring on the challenge,' he shouted to the empty room.

The palm display of the controller blanked.

Now what? Serge hadn't said anything past this point other than that each of The Four had a different finishing point. The others could be anywhere.

Femi ran his right hand over the controller 'hand'. No obvious sign of buttons or switches. The thing was heavy though. The fingers and thumb seemed to be flexible and hinge in the same directions as a human's. Femi's brain tried to clench his left hand.

'Cool,' he said as the game controller obeyed. It seemed a bit slow, like there was lag in the message or resistance in the joints. He experimented with more finger movements, hand rotations and grips. They all worked, but in a sedate fashion. *Maybe it's like being old*, he thought.

Femi stared at the palm display. It was still blank.

He looked around the room, but other than the bench, he didn't see anything else except neglect and decay.

And an arc of blood.

And his old, redundant hand.

It's the ultimate game, he told himself. It was never going to be easy. The game's designers weren't going to feed him everything. No instructions. No cheat sheets or hacks.

Think like you're in a game. Earn it.

The game controller was the place to start.

He brought it close to his face, twisting and turning it to scan the surface for anything that might help. Nothing but a skin like covering, and synthetic fingernails.

Femi grasped the controller's thumb with the fingers of his right hand and twisted. Nothing. Same with all the other fingers.

He turned his game controller so that the palm was facing the floor and used the thumb and index finger of his right hand to hold the fingernail of the controller's little finger. He pressed. Nothing.

Ring finger. Nothing. Middle finger. Nothing.

He pressed the fingernail of the controller's index finger. In the darkening room, the controller's palm display cast a white glow onto the floor. His brain told him that the finger was tingling, like severe pins and needles.

He let go of the finger and shot his wrist around to see the display.

'Game Controller Active – Let the game begin.'

After a couple of seconds, the display blanked.

Now he was getting somewhere.

He grasped the controller's index finger again and pressed.

He got the same tingling sensation, and the screen flashed white and redrew with the same *'Game Controller Active – Let the game begin'* message before blanking again.

Not that simple, Femi thought, but maybe the screen going off could be to save power. The glare would also be obvious to other people at night.

He spent a few minutes trying all sorts of different grips and movements. Squeezing, pushing and pulling.

He was wasting precious time, but he still had no idea what else to do other than keep trying different actions.

When he pulled the controller's little finger, like he was trying to crack a knuckle, his brain told him that something blunt had been pressed into his little finger. At the same time, the display came to life.

He looked at the display. The message *'Game position – equal third'* showed before the display blanked.

Given that there were only four of them, 'equal third' meant that two were ahead of him and he and someone else were still standing at the start point fiddling with their controller. 'Shit,' he muttered, knowing that equal third meant equal *last*.

He tried to crack the knuckle of the game controller's ring finger. The same sensation of pressure from a blunt object but now in the ring finger. The display's message this time was *'Distance to finish – 70 to 90 miles.'*

That's at least thirty hours of walking, he thought, but the range of distances in the message implied that there were multiple routes.

He still needed to work out where he was meant to go.

Cracking the middle finger gave Femi a display of the game's elapsed time.

Shit, he needed to move, Serge had warned about the police getting disconnect messages and sending drones.

He could work the rest out later. After packing the lamp into his bag, Femi looked at the machete, not knowing why he might need it, but reluctant to leave it in case he did. He wrapped the towel around the blade and stuffed it into his bag.

Dabbing his finger into the pool of his blood and using it as ink, Femi scrawled a message onto the bench, then rushed to the door.

He pulled the creaking door open, smelling the freshness of the late afternoon air after the mustiness of the butcher's shop. He had to make a choice, but didn't know the correct direction. Fifty–fifty.

He turned left, and set off, head down, bag over one shoulder and his game controller stuffed into a pocket.

Two streets away from the butcher's shop, he heard a frantic buzzing, blending with a police siren behind him. He hurried on, looking for somewhere quiet to hide and work out how to get the game controller to tell him where he was meant to be going.

He turned into a small side road with terraced houses stretching away on both sides. He couldn't see anyone, so he risked pulling out the controller from his pocket and cracked the knuckle of its ring finger.

The display showed: 'Distance to finish – 71 to 91 miles.'

He was heading in the wrong direction.

He cracked the little finger: '*Game position – fourth.*'

***

After taking some random turns, Femi stumbled across a small open area. It looked uneven and rutted, with the grass growing in tufts interspersed with muddy tracks.

He found a bench underneath a blinking streetlight and sat. He'd bought an old map of Northern Ireland from an antique shop in Derry and flicked through the pages. The front section contained smaller scale road maps of different parts of the country. The back section had large scale maps of the major towns and cities.

Tracing a finger down the road index, he found the road the open area was on. Square 'C4'. He moved his finger to the square on the map and tapped the small green shape drawn next to the road.

Some small progress but he needed to work out where the finish was.

He tried to think like a game programmer. What they used. What they might think. A double click. That was a common action when using a mouse.

He tried a double press on each fingernail, then double pulls on each finger. They all did nothing.

He looked down at his right hand, his real hand, resting on the map. His thumb was balanced against the tip of his index finger.

Worth a try, he thought and did a double-tap of the thumb against the index finger of the game controller.

The display on the controller's palm flashed and drew a map with a little black and white chequered flag in the middle. It was too small for him to work out where it was. He didn't know how to zoom the map out, but a second double-tap of thumb and index finger changed the display from a map to a street address.

'Finally,' he muttered, conscious of how slow he had been, and how much of a head start he had given the others.

Femi flicked through the map to the page showing the destination, then more slowly through several of the other pages, planning a rough route in his head.

He stuffed the map into his bag and started running.

Chapter 36

As the car trundled along the M3, skirting the edge of Winchester, Clive and Ava ignored everything except the display screen between them.

The screen resembled a low, glass-topped table sitting between two rows of armchairs that faced each other. Its display was split into four distinct images, but four very similar ones. The top of each quadrant had the location name: Southampton, Worcester, Derry, and Dumfries.

Each image was from a forensic drone showing the inside of a disused, shabby butcher's shop. Some in better condition than others, but all with a large wooden chopping bench in the middle, signs of recent blood splatter and, most disturbingly for Clive, all with a human hand severed above the wrist. Each hand had an iTourist bracelet still firmly attached and broadcasting its position in complaint at being so rudely disconnected.

Clive hadn't bothered to chase Rob at iMe Tech Support. This wasn't a technical issue, or a programming error, or even a cyber hack. This was a human hack.

'How did they stop the bleeding?' Ava asked.

Fair point, Clive thought, wishing that Ava hadn't zoomed the whole screen to show a close-up image of one of the hands and its cleanly severed stump. 'Don't know, but there's not a lot of blood, so it must have been done quickly.'

'Would a tourniquet work?'

'Maybe temporarily, but they'd need medical treatment. Walking around with a belt on your wrist instead of a hand is pretty obvious.'

Clive paused to think.

'The hospitals would have reported anyone without an iMe or iTourist who came in for treatment, so we need a list of doctors, both current and retired who are local to each site. We'll need to see if they treated anyone.'

'Surely, they'd report it too,' Ava said.

'Maybe, but four so close together in time must be connected. The similarities are too strong. There's some cause or reason behind it, so there may be sympathisers loyal to the cause.' Clive forced his eyes away from the image of the hand. 'Add vets to the list of people who might have treated the injuries.'

Ava nodded and made some notes on her HUD. 'What sort of cause requires you to chop your hand off?' she said.

Proof of loyalty, proof of compliance...? Clive wondered. Proof of insanity?

'There's a shortage of organ donors,' Ava said. 'But that doesn't work with hands. And even if it was donors, then you'd take the hand with you.'

'There were cases years ago of people using power tools to cut off the hands off a family member, saying it was an accident, asking the insurance company to pay out in compensation while they claimed disability benefits.'

'That couldn't work here. No way you get four accidents this close together. No insurance company would pay out. And why would foreigners do it here?'

Clive had no idea, but clearly there must be a reason. 'So, what could it be?'

'I've run a search on why people might cut off their hand. The top answer was swapping for a bio-hand like this one,' Ava said, sounding like she was testing the beginnings of an idea. She threw a web page at the car's screen that showed an advert for one of the many companies feeding the growing trend of body augmentation. Ways of improving on nature. The bio-hands all looked impressive. Stronger and better than new.

At the bottom, there were comments from users around the world and Clive scanned the first few:

'I'll cut my arm off and my bionic arm will crush the skull of my enemies.'
'That is freaking awesome.'
'I wanna go modular.'
'But can it play Minecraft?'
'BRUH!!! I'M READY TO MOD MY BODY.'
'That thing must give the best handjobs.'

'The usual intelligent input from around the world,' Clive said, shaking his head.

Ava scrolled the display and Clive nearly choked when he saw the price.

'But if you had that sort of money, you'd go to the factory and have it done by a surgeon in a sterile environment with aftercare. You wouldn't chop your hand off in a grubby shop and run. Plus, the drones were at the site inside ten minutes,' Ava said, dismissing her own theory.

'Let's run the signal traces at the sites to see who was there. Start with the one in Southampton as we're heading there,' Clive said.

Ava nodded and found the signal trace for Tatsuko Ito. She threw the trace onto the display, which redrew to show an architect's drawing of the butcher's shop and Tatsuko's signal glowing green in the middle of it. 'She was on her own, so she must have done it herself. This is when the iTourist generated the alert.' The time display on the screen showed 16:02.

'Run it backwards. Let's see how she got there.'

Ava nodded and selected a fast rewind of the signal history. The display screen scrolled, keeping Tatsuko's signal dot in the middle and showing the seemingly random route that Tatsuko had taken from her hotel through roads and parks.

'She doesn't seem to interact with anyone or do anything,' Ava said.

The time on the display stepped backwards through the night, showing Tatsuko's signal in the bed.

Ava skipped the display over the time Tatsuko was asleep. Ava then carried on replaying the trace, following Tatsuko backwards in time on a circular route around several shops.

'What did she get in the shops?' Clive asked.

Ava paused the display and brought up a list of transactions from Tatsuko's iTourist. Ava clicked a button to filter the display to only show purchases.

'A map of southern England and an A–Z of London. A raincoat and baseball hat. Food and water. And a specialist multitool, cutting discs and safety equipment,' Ava read.

'Safety gear didn't seem to help her,' Clive said, but Ava frowned at the inappropriateness of Clive's joke.

***

Clive pushed the door of the butcher's shop open and stepped inside, with Ava close behind.

He was thankful that the Uniform who had got to the scene first hadn't trampled around inside. He had seen the hand and the blood through a window and waited outside for the forensic drones.

Now the drones had completed their sweep, Clive and Ava were free to explore, but they hesitated, trying to take in the scene that they already had seen on the car's display screen. It was different in the flesh. More shocking. The smell of the room mixing with the metallic smell of the blood and the buzzing of the flies feeding greedily in it.

Clive approached the bench. 'Have a look in the cupboards and anywhere the drones can't get, Ava,' Clive said, over his shoulder.

A machete was buried in one end of the bench. Clive snapped on a pair of forensics gloves and reached for the handle. He pulled up, but the machete stayed firm. He pulled harder but it had been driven in with real force and determination.

He looked down, careful to avoid stepping in the blood and looked at the hand. It lay palm up, fingers curling in a half grip. The iTourist status screen's frantic red pulsing reflected along the concrete floor.

Clive put his thumb on one side of the wrist and his index finger on the other side and lifted the hand and placed it palm down on the bench. The red pulsing was brighter now. He pushed the hand against the blade of the machete so that the wrist touched the blade. The angle of the cut in the wrist matched the angle the blade was buried in the bench. Clive peered in to look at a faint mark on the iTourist.

'Boss,' Ava said. 'Here's some of her shopping.'

Clive turned and crossed to where Ava knelt. She had a cupboard door open and Clive could see a tangle of things stuffed randomly into the cupboard.

One was the multitool from Tatsuko's purchase history, with a small, burnt cutting wheel on the end of a shaft.

'No maps or raincoat,' Ava said.

'Can you bring that over to the bench,' Clive said, pointing at the tool.

Ava did and placed the tool on the bench and untangled the flexible shaft.

Clive picked up the end with the cutting disc. 'This has seen some abuse.'

He offered the disc up to a burnt gouge in the bench. The disc slotted in perfectly. Next, he offered it up to the mark going across the iTourist.

'She tried to cut it off,' he said, showing Ava that the faint mark was the same width as the disc. 'Maybe she wasn't as committed as the others. Or maybe she was more intelligent.'

Clive had been to some demonstrations of the destruction testing performed on the iTourist when the Off-Grid Crime Unit was first set-up. They had thrown everything at the iTourist and nothing made more than a tiny mark.

Clive was thinking about why you might not want an iTourist, and what the map of southern England and the A–Z meant, when Ava beat him to it.

'Obviously they wanted to get off-grid, Boss. No tracking and no surveillance. We don't know where all four are, but she's heading to London.'

Chapter 37

Sully had worked out the destination double-tap on the game controller almost immediately. It simply seemed an obvious movement.

The display said '72–78 miles', and he wondered if he had been given a longer route than the others. He pushed the thought aside. It didn't matter. Winning was in the bag.

All those selection exercises involving walking and running. All to get them to play the game the way Serge wanted him too. Trudging alone in the rain. Well, he'd do a bit of that. But only at the beginning.

The only problem with his plan was that he had guessed he would be travelling south and not north. To get to his meeting point in Gretna Green, he was going to head away from the finish and not towards it. Too late now, but his old friend, Davide had lived in England for years. He'd see him right.

Sully had memorised his route to Gretna. An overnight walk along the A75. Eight or so hours walking. He had nearly ten hours until his meeting with Davide. Not fun, but do-able, and he should even have some time for a nap.

He could have told Davide to come to Dumfries, but he had dismissed the idea as too risky. Too obvious to the police if Davide drove into Dumfries. Staying the night in Gretna Green was simpler. Still a risk, but Sully would have won before anyone reacted.

***

Sully shivered with cold. At 1am it had rained heavily, with the wind driving the drops around and down his neck. The rain jacket had done its best, but it was out gunned by the Scottish storm. His trousers clung to his legs and his shoes squelched.

He reached the sign to the entrance to Gretna Green at 3:30am in the morning. It had taken longer than he thought because of all the evening cars on the road. Each time he had seen lights he had jumped into the verge and hidden. He didn't want to risk being seen and people asking questions.

The town seemed quiet, no one about this early. Sully walked along the roads, his dark clothes helping him blend in. At least the clouds hid any glare of the moon.

He only saw the white cross on the junction when he was a few metres away. The Old Parish Church should be up on the right. From his internet searches, the images of the church showed grounds and bushes that he could hide in until he met Davide at 7:15am. He could sleep for a couple of hours.

He reached the church and went past the few mildewed gravestones at the front, through the gate, past the door and into the large graveyard behind the church, where he found shelter under a dark bush.

Sully's clothes were damper than the ground, but he curled up and got himself as comfortable as he could before drifting off to sleep.

***

The plan was that Davide's car would roll down the drive of Gretna Hall Hotel at 7:15. Davide would then turn right onto Gretna Loading, then left onto Glasgow Road by the white cross and pull in to park at the back of the Old Parish Church.

Sully checked the status of the game controller: *'Game runtime 15hrs 15'*.

7:15am.

A few seconds later he heard the crunch of a car door as it closed. *Davide*, he thought, but stayed in his hiding place in case it was a local or someone who worked for the church.

A tall, elegant man came around the corner and wandered amongst the graves, scanning the trees and bushes. *Davide was meant to be looking at the graves not at the hedges*, Sully thought, but he couldn't complain. Davide, smart blue suit and shiny shoes as always, was here and he was on time.

Sully shuffled out from under the bush and walked towards Davide. He stopped in front of his friend.

'I'd give you a hug, but I'd spoil your suit,' Sully said.

Davide looked at him. 'What the fuck, Sully. What crazy shit have you got yourself into?' He whistled through his teeth. 'How did you get the iTourist off? It's meant to be impossible unless Border Control do it for you.'

Sully pulled his left 'hand' out of his pocket and pulled his sleeve up.

Davide clasped his hand to his mouth. 'Holy fuck, man.'

Sully smiled. 'I'll tell you all about it in the car. I'll wait by the church.'

The plan was that Davide was meant to be looking around the old church and churchyard for a research project and then travelling on. He was a naturalised UK citizen and so his signal was permanent. If it got replayed, his signal needed to stay more than a few seconds for the story to work.

Sully spent the ten minutes with his back pressed against the church wall, praying that no one else came.

Finally, Davide came back and walked towards his car. Sully fell in behind him, like a scruffy shadow of the elegant Davide.

The car door opened as Davide approached. 'You get in first. Lie across the seat so no one can see you,' he said.

'Will the car know?' Sully worried.

'Not without a signal.'

Sully climbed in, grateful that the car was hidden from the road, and Davide got in after him. The car door shut, and the heater came on. The warm air was a welcome relief. His right hand had a bluey tinge and was awkward and stiff from the cold. His left hand was fine. An unexpected benefit of an augmentation upgrade.

Davide looked at Sully's left hand. 'You need to explain *that*.'

Sully shrugged and talked about the game and needing to be off-grid. Davide went as pale as his white shirt when Sully said, 'Only way to get the iTourist off is to take your hand off above the wrist.'

'You... you did that?'

'Sure, easy. One clean strike. No problem for me. I'm here to win.'

Davide shook his head in shock. 'No way I could compete with you, man. Able to do that so easily... wow. Respect.'

Sully smiled, basking in the awe.

Davide said nothing for a few seconds, looking like he didn't believe the whole story was happening. 'Can I touch it?'

Sully nodded and Davide put a tentative finger on the game controller 'hand'.

Davide cringed and straightened then said, 'So, where are you heading?'

Sully showed Davide the map on his game controller display.

Davide sat and thought for a moment. 'You want to get there without being tracked?'

'Yes.'

'Then it's better that I take you only part of the journey. I've got a friend who can take you the rest of the way. That way if they find me, my signal won't go anywhere near where you're heading.'

Sully nodded, seeing the logic in the idea.

Davide opened a message window on the car's display screen and typed *You still work in the same place?*, selected a contact and pressed send. Sully watched the screen.

Yes, why? came the reply.

'Favour to ask. Can you meet at the Row at 08:45?' Davide typed.

'See you then.'

Davide programmed a destination into the car then sat back as the car headed off. They spent the next hour catching up on life. It was fun, but Sully had an uneasy itch he couldn't place. From his prone position, all he could see were grey clouds rolling by. 'Are we being followed?' he asked.

Davide spun his head. They were the third car in a 'train' of about twenty, all bunched up close so that the aerodynamic effect of the first car created a slipstream for the others and meant that the others used less battery power. Every so often, the lead car would pull out and drop to the back and let the next car take the strain.

'There are lots of cars, but they all look the same.' Davide shrugged.

Sully's unease nagged at him.

When he saw the first signs for Glasgow centre, Davide said, 'Nearly there.'

***

Sully followed Davide across Rottonrow Gardens.

Davide stopped and hugged a woman in her thirties. She wore dreadlocks and a very formal grey suit and smart black shoes. The conflicting styles in her appearance made Sully wonder about her work. While she and Davide whispered, the woman stared at Sully the whole time, shaking her head and scowling.

She shrugged when Davide stopped talking. 'Only 'cos it's you,' she said.

Davide hugged her. 'Sully, this is Ruth. She'll take you most of the way.'

Ruth ignored Sully's offered handshake and turned to walk away. Davide hugged him and said, 'Good luck.'

'Thanks, man,' Sully said, and hurried off after Ruth.

He caught up with her when she reached her car and stood with the door open. Sully climbed in and Ruth jumped in after him. 'Car... Destination... Office,' she said.

'Destination... Office,' the car confirmed and pulled off.

Ruth looked at Sully. 'Whatever this is, I don't want to know. Stay low and don't talk. I've got work I need to do.'

Sully lay across the two seats, trying to make himself as small as possible.

Ruth started waving her hands in the air the way Sully had seen people do everywhere in this place.

While she was frowning at something and typing, her fingers flying, Sully slipped his game controller hand out from his pocket. He clicked the little finger and glanced at the palm display.

'Yes,' he whispered with a smile.

The message *'Game position – first'* showed on his display.

Chapter 38

While Sully was starting his walk to Gretna, Clive and Ava were back in the car leaving Southampton. Clive checked his messages, but he had nothing from Sophia. He felt a queasy shift in the pit of his stomach. *Shit, I've cocked it up again*, he thought.

The car's display screen was split into four once more, but this time it was mirroring Clive's HUD. He was looking at four UK Border Control profiles. One for Lilou, Femi, Tatsuko and Sully.

'We've got four apparent strangers,' he said, looking at the profile photos. 'One French, one South African, one American and one Italian. But they all chopped their hands off within minutes of each other. They have to be connected.'

'Clearly,' Ava agreed.

'OK. We'll take two each and research as much as we can about them. I'll take Tatsuko and Femi. You take the others.'

'Sure, Boss,' Ava said, and started to swipe and tap her fingers on her HUD.

Clive clicked on Femi's picture and the screen redrew to show his bio, the report from the forensic drone and the UK Border report.

Clive decided to start with the forensic report. He played the video from Derry and saw a similar scene to the one they had left in Southampton.

The same type of disused premises, bench and blood splatter. Femi's bench didn't have the machete stuck in it. Instead, Clive could see a fresh, deep cut in the wood with blood on one side. Femi must have been able to lever the machete out.

Clive swiped his HUD to check the report from the Uniform who had searched after the drone's forensic sweep.

He read the terse report. It didn't add anything much to the forensic report other than to say that there was nothing in any of the closed cupboards. No sign of a machete.

Femi must have taken it. That made him armed and dangerous. So where was he and where was he heading?

The not knowing was frustrating.

Clive swiped back to the forensic report and looked again at the photos of the blood splatter on the bench.

Femi was obviously a very confident and capable man. He'd chopped his hand off in a country he had never been to before and he still had found time to leave the police a message.

Scrawled in block capitals, written in his own blood, Femi's message challenged Clive.

'CATCH ME… IF YOU CAN!!'

***

Clive and Ava spent some quiet miles in the car, searching and collating information, before Clive said, 'Let's look at it another way.'

Ava dropped her head in a small nod and finished typing something on her HUD before she looked up. 'How?' she asked.

'Let's ignore the ultimate reason for them chopping their hands off for a moment and look at why you'd chop it off above the wrist and not below.'

'They all cut immediately above the iTourist.'

'Exactly, but they can't do anything without the iTourist. No travel, no food or water. So, they all bought maps and enough food and water for a few days.'

'They're planning on walking and carrying everything they need,' Ava added.

'And the real benefit of no iTourist is that we can't track them.'

Ava nodded and looked straight at Clive. 'And you moan about how easy police work is with iMe.'

Clive looked away sheepishly. He did hate how easy it was.

He couldn't say it out loud, but it would *really* help now.

'They all got maps. Femi's covers Northern Ireland, so his finish point must be there. Tatsuko had a map of London. The others could be heading to London as well.'

'Maybe.' Clive stared out of the window, lost in thought. 'Femi's "catch me if you can" sounds like it's a chase or a race,' he said.

'Sully's profile claims he's an AR world champion,' Ava said. 'It could be an AR game.'

'What's AR?'

'Augmented reality. The game's players' real-world environment has visual and audio content integrated into it.'

'But a map and food are so low-tech.'

'Yeah,' Ava said. 'That bit doesn't work as AR. Maybe there's something else?'

Maybe, but Ava's idea reminded Clive of something that Zoe had said on his birthday. Something about an augmented reality game.

He said, 'Call, Zoe,' and touched his jaw. The ringtone echoed through the car's speakers.

'Hi, Boss,' Zoe said, the noise of a busy office behind her.

'You still at work?'

'Yep, always hectic.'

'Did you hear about the four tourists going off-grid?' Clive asked.

'Of course. We ran a quick check when the alerts went off, but the four don't have any terrorist or cyber-crime links. We lost interest at that point. Why don't they have a signal? Technical issue?'

'You haven't seen the reports?'

'No, like I said they're of no interest to us, and we're snowed under.'

'They all chopped their hands off above the iTourist.'

Zoe went quiet, but Clive thought he heard her gasp.

'Still not anything for us to worry about,' she said. 'Four one-handed tourists aren't much of a terror or cyber threat.'

'I agree,' Clive said. 'But you mentioned an augmented reality game. Lots of chatter and excitement online.'

'You think it's related?'

'Maybe, can you take a look for us?' Clive asked.

'No chance. Way too busy.'

'Can you send us what you have at least?'

'Don't know, I'll have to check. I'll send it if I can.'

Zoe dropped the call. Clive looked at Ava, who shrugged and said, 'Maybe.'

They went back to their respective silent research into the four tourists. No closer to anything concrete.

Ten minutes later, the PCU work queue filled up with message after message.

All from Zoe.

All about an augmented reality game called Forbidden Island.

Chapter 39

Clive and Ava divided the avalanche of data and messages that Zoe had sent them and set to trawling through it. Darkness crept up on them and by the time the car was driving through Windsor Great Park and past the site of the old Lego Land complex, the only illumination on the case came from the car's interior lighting.

Clive dropped his hands from in front of his face and rolled his shoulders, trying to relieve the ache. He was rewarded with a loud crunch from each side.

'Boss. Do you have to?' Ava said, her nose wrinkling and top lip curling.

'It helps,' he said, and he gave them one last rotation and crunch. He tipped his head to the left to get a stretch into his neck and down his shoulder blade.

'The face you're pulling now is no better.' Maybe it was tiredness, but Ava was using the same tone with Clive she had used with Brett.

He let it slide. He was tired too, and reading all the messages Zoe had sent wasn't helping the case or his own mood.

'There are so many pointless messages. They're like static trying to masquerade as communication,' Clive said. 'Thank you, DataMiner5 for sharing your thoughts *"Forbidden Island – Psyched to the bollocks. It's sick. Can't wait"*. I mean, why bother saying anything so pointless and empty?'

Clive shut his eyes and soothed his temples with his fingers.

Ava grinned.

Clive wasn't sure if she was grinning at the stupidity of DataMiner5, or him moaning. 'You got anything, Ava?'

'A lot of the same, but did you see the subscription fees to follow the game? That's a massive amount of money.'

'I saw. Someone's getting very rich.'

Ava's grin widened, and her hands flew as she typed and swiped on her HUD. 'Thought so,' she said and threw her HUD at the car's screen.

The screen showed a profile picture of Lilou on one side and a message from someone called Serge.

'We have our final four. Our champions. The brave explorers of the Forbidden Island – You can follow Parkour179, TheChampion1, Braai_Bru, and ReflectiveAndRightous. Click the link to subscribe.'

'What?' Clive asked, but seeing the name Braai_Bru he thought he could guess.

Ava's grin was still in place. 'Lilou was an Olympic champion in triathlon, so she could be TheChampion1, but she's now really big into parkour. I think she's Parkour179. Look...'

She clicked on Lilou's photograph on the car's screen and it redrew to show pages of text and details on Lilou and her life. At the bottom was a section titled *'Images'* showing several thumbnails. Ava clicked on a thumbnail and it redrew to show at full size. Lilou was standing on the top step of a podium, beaming and waving to the crowd. She wore a blue vest with a French flag on the left, above her heart. A gold medal hung around her neck, but Clive was staring below the medal. The blue of the vest was interrupted with a white square. On the top of the square were the five interlinked Olympic rings. Most of the rest of the square had blue numbers. Her competitor's number. Number 179.

'That's got to be her,' Clive said. 'And Braai_Bru could be Femi. He's South African and they call each other bru, like we use mate. A lot of the photos that Femi posts show him cooking on a BBQ that he calls a braai.'

'That would mean Sully and Tatsuko could use either of the names: TheChampion1 and ReflectiveAndRightous.'

'Tatsuko's profile doesn't show that she's a champion of anything,' Clive said.

'But Sully's does, and he really loves to big himself up in his messages.'

Clive stared out of the window, seeing the lights from the houses of Windsor pass by. 'It's not definite that these four are here for a game, but Forbidden Island could fit a foreigner's perception of the UK,' he said. 'It's a strong enough link to follow up.'

'If Lilou is Parkour179, then the rest must be in the game as well,' Ava agreed.

'Try that subscription link. Maybe we can find them that way,' Clive said. 'I'd have to get Bhatt to approve the spend, but let's see what the price is now.'

Ava clicked the link and a new window appeared. 'Lists closed. We are oversubscribed and have a massive waiting list, you're too slow.'

'Crap,' Clive said, banging the top of the car's display much harder than he meant. The car said, 'Any non-accidental damage will be chargeable.'

Clive looked sheepish and was relieved to see no damage to the display.

'What now?' Ava asked.

'Not sure,' Clive said, turning his palms up to show he had nothing. 'Tatsuko and Femi have no real history here. A few distant business contacts, but no real friends. What about yours?'

'Lilou nothing, but Sully…' Ava swiped her fingers so that the car's screen redrew with his profile page. The same jumble of text and thumbnails at the bottom. 'There was one picture…' she said as she scrolled over the thumbnails. 'There.' She clicked onto the thumbnail.

Now Clive was looking at a group photo. About thirty people arranged in rows. All in suits and all wearing smiles. 'What's this?'

'Sully's university graduation photo.' She pointed at the third name on the second row. 'Davide Lombardi.'

Sully's name was the fourth on the same row.

'And?' Clive said.

'I found him earlier.' Ava flicked through some menus and opened a 'UK citizen search' window. She typed in 'Davide Lombardi' and pressed *'Search'*. The screen redrew to show a list of UK citizens called Davide Lombardi. Next to the sixth Davide Lombardi on the list were the words *'Naturalised Italian'*.

Ava clicked the name and Davide's Ministry of Well-being and Health's page opened. Ava ignored his health details and found a section labelled *'Education'*. She pointed at some text. 'That's the same university and year as in the photo.'

'Great work, Ava.' Clive leaned forward in excitement. 'Where is he now?'

Ava brought up the iMonitor window. She pinched her fingers to pick up Davide's profile, dragged it over to the iMonitor window and dropped it. She pressed *'Search'*.

The screen redrew displaying a map of a hotel room. One green signal dot glowed at a table in a hotel restaurant.

Ava zoomed out, and the display showed the Gretna Hall Hotel.

'What's he doing there?' Clive said, feeling the first prickle of excitement. 'That's pretty close to Dumfries. Call the hotel and check he's eating on his own. Tell them to be subtle and don't let him know.'

Clive leant back. *This could be it*, he thought. *Catch Sully, and he can lead us to the others*. He listened to Ava talking to the hotel and getting confirmation from the restaurant's maître d' that Davide was eating alone. She hung up.

'Shall I send Uniform to talk to him?'

'No, he'll deny everything. And we need to find Sully.'

Clive thought for a while.

'It's too much of a coincidence that he's so close to Dumfries. Get a Uniform to the hotel in an unmarked car. Tell them to watch for Sully arriving or Davide leaving. And tell them to charge their car. We can't afford any cock-ups with flat batteries.'

***

Clive spent a restless night churning ideas and dreaming of one-handed gamers running around the UK. At 4am, he finally settled.

A buzzing in his head dragged him from a deep and dark sleep. 'Huh. What?' he said, before he woke enough to realise that it was a call. He touched his jaw to accept.

'Boss, Boss,' Ava said. From the return of her bright and energetic tone, Clive guessed that she had slept better than him.

'Ava, what?'

'Davide's on the move.'

This snapped Clive fully awake and he jack-knifed up in bed. 'Where?'

'The Uniform called me. He drove about two hundred and fifty metres and parked at the back of a church. He's still there.'

'Any sign of Sully?'

'Nothing.'

'Get them to stay with him. Tell them to take their uniform jackets off and hide anything that makes them look like police.'

'OK, Boss.'

'I'll meet you at the office.'

***

Clive and Ava pushed a couple of desks nearer the PCU office display wall. Both perched on the edges staring at the screen, like they were in a private cinema.

They were watching Davide's signal trundle up the M74 towards Glasgow.

'Are they sure that Davide is in the car on his own?' Clive said.

Ava rolled her eyes; it was the fourth time Clive had asked the same question.

'As I said before, the Uniforms can't be sure.'

Clive could see the signals on the screen for the people in the cars in front and behind Davide. The Uniforms following Davide were five cars back. It was a shame they couldn't get closer, Clive thought, but the cars decided their order in the line for themselves.

Davide's car was near the front of the pack, so at some time it might pull out and drop back, giving the Uniforms a closer look.

Ava had searched all the recent messages and found Davide's message to an old friend called Ruth who lived somewhere called Milngavie, to the north of Glasgow. She was now driving towards Glasgow and two Uniforms following her in a plain car were joining the train of cars she was in.

'What's your guess, Ava? Where's the Row that Davide mentioned? In Glasgow?'

'Could be,' she said. 'It's the most obvious place.'

As Clive's HUD was connected to the PCU office display wall, when Ava started swiping and tapping on her HUD, Clive couldn't see what she was doing.

'There's a park in the centre of Glasgow called Rottonrow Gardens and a road called Rottonrow. They could be going there,' she said.

'Why there?' Clive's rhetorical question hung in the air and died.

Neither said anything. Davide's car followed the M73 and as it joined the M8, it tacked onto the back of a long train of cars. The Uniforms' car joined the same train, shuffling into the line. They were now eight cars back from Davide.

'Crap,' Clive said and jumped up to start walking back and forward.

Half an hour later and Clive was still walking. Ruth was parked on Montrose Street that bordered Rottonrow Gardens. Davide's car rolled on and turned into Rottonrow.

'You were right, Ava. Get one of the Uniforms to follow Ruth on foot. Tell the other one to stay and watch her car.'

Ava nodded and relayed the instructions, then said, 'Boss, can you sit down? I can't see properly.'

Clive sat, and his leg jigged up and down. He leant forward.

They watched Ruth's signal move towards the centre of Rottonrow Gardens and followed Davide's signal as he got out of the car.

Ava touched her jaw and accepted an incoming call.

Clive stared at her, waiting, hoping for good news.

'The Uniform following Davide says that a second man got out of Davide's car,' Ava said. 'He's got no signal.'

Clive punched the air. 'Yesss. Sully.'

'Shall I get the Uniforms to arrest him now?'

'No,' Clive snapped. 'Let's see what happens. Keep both sets of Uniforms on the line.'

Ava nodded and they watched Ruth's and Davide's signals converge and then separate.

'Sully is following Ruth,' Ava said, repeating what she was being told. 'Davide is heading back to his car.'

They watched Ruth's signal approach her car.

'Ruth and Sully got into her car.'

'Sully's arranged to be taken somewhere. They've handed him over to try and break the trail,' Clive said.

'What do I tell the Uniforms?'

'Get the ones following Davide to arrest and hold him, but shut his HUD down now so he can't warn Ruth.' Clive thought for a minute. 'Let Ruth go, but follow her. We've got nothing on the other three. Sully might be going somewhere that helps us. And get a second car on Ruth. We can't afford to lose him.'

Chapter 40

As Sully settled across the seats in Ruth's warm and dry car, Lilou was scanning left and right, crouching by the side of the road. Rain patted down onto the road and she wiped her hand across her brow before double-checking her map, using her body to shelter it from the rain. In spite of walking hard for hours, she was cold, and the wet was starting to seep through the waterproofing in her shoes.

She'd reached Kerne Bridge and checked the display on her game controller. *'Distance to finish – 42 to 45 miles.'* She'd travelled about thirty-two miles in sixteen hours – a slow two miles an hour. Disappointing if she had stayed on the roads the whole time, but she'd kept mostly to lanes and fields to avoid as many people as possible. When a car did come, she skulked in the bushes and hid. *Doing OK*, she thought and smiled despite the drop of rain on her nose.

She needed to cross the River Wye and worried it would leave her exposed. As she crossed the B429 and followed the sign for Goodrich Castle, she shot a glance at The Inn on the Wye hotel. *It's so close to the bridge, but at least it's quiet. The guests might be at breakfast*, she thought. Her stomach rumbled.

Lilou crouched by the tall gates to someone's house and waited. The bridge had a hump in the middle that she couldn't see over. She didn't know if there were any people or cars coming in the opposite direction. Risking a few steps forward, she saw that on the far side the road approached from her left before it turned towards the bridge and she lost sight of it. Clear.

With near-silent electric cars, she couldn't hear anything coming, but she waited in case there was a car close to the bridge.

She started a fast, half-walk, half-jog across the bridge, praying that she had waited long enough. Despite the pace of her walk, she held her breath and followed the upwards incline of the bridge. Lilou breathed out and laughed when she could see over the top of the hump. Nothing coming.

She ran over the rest of the bridge. Where the walled sides of the bridge ended, steps had been cast in concrete down into a field. She turned off the road and skipped down the steps, past the *'Private Fishing. No day tickets'* sign, and jogged along the edge of the field. Her easy stride was accompanied by squelching noises at each muddy footfall and the sound of her rucksack sliding across the waterproof material of her coat.

The rain meant she wouldn't look like a tourist out enjoying the fresh air by the river, so she sprinted the last few metres of the open field. The hill rose in front of her, covered in trees, but thankfully not so dense that she couldn't keep jogging.

'Get to the top of the hill, then breakfast,' she told herself. She jogged on, breathing harder as the hill climbed. And kept on climbing. It was like one of her old training climbs.

At the top, Lilou stopped and crouched down. She could see houses nestled in the trees on both the left and right. She checked her map and used a compass she had brought from France, trying to fix the next part of the route in her head. The map showed her that the river made a big loop ahead of her and there was a pinch point where the river almost touched the A40, with lots of buildings and businesses. Not good.

She slipped the rucksack off and pulled out an energy bar. She broke off a quarter of it and stashed the rest back in the rucksack.

Not quite the same as breakfast at the hotel, she thought, and popped the piece into her mouth. Chewing slowly, she tried to make it last and feel like a bigger meal. She twisted the game controller and pulled it off her mount to give the muscles in her left arm and shoulder a break from the weight.

She thought through her route options. Maybe it was safer to take a big loop north and then west to stay safely away from the road and buildings.

She was pleased with how she felt. Strong. Fit. Capable. No blisters or aches to slow her down. She thought she had learnt from her mistake of being too cautious in the first selection exercise.

Lilou thought of the others again. Femi and Tatsuko were good, but she was faster than them. She was an Olympian. Sully was slow and lazy. No way he was ahead of her. She still hadn't worked out how he won that first exercise and looked so fresh. He must have cheated somehow, she decided. Especially after how he was in the race to the rocket launch site.

She clicked her controller back onto her mount and pulled at its fingers. 'Merde,' she said, seeing the display: *'Game position – fourth'*.

Fourth? How could she be fourth?

Perhaps she hadn't learnt as well as she thought. *Need to go faster. Take a few more risks.*

Lilou stood and decided. Shortest and fastest route – west across the fields and use the small road she could see on the map to get past the top of the loop in the river. Then stay tight to the river. Try and sneak past the back of the buildings.

Hope not to get caught.

She ran down the hill.

Chapter 41

Serge watched his Game Control window. Three of the gamers were playing the game, making good, if slow, progress.

Sully was way ahead of the others and moving too fast. He must be in a car.

All the betting money had dried up on the other three. Everyone was betting on Sully.

Serge started coughing. He had stayed at his desk all night, watching the game and the rising balance on his Chile Gaming Services, Inc bank account. The bookies paid him a small commission on every bet as their cost of being in the game.

And Sully was cheating, skewing the bets.

Serge's face flushed red with anger. He'd never liked him. All his boasting and confidence were based on Sully's inflated opinion of himself. All based on a lie.

Serge's chest tightened. *The anger and the stress*, he thought. The lack of sleep couldn't help.

The first two puffs on his asthma inhaler didn't make any real difference. His chest got tighter. He was finding it harder to breathe and get enough oxygen into his lungs.

The next two puffs emptied his inhaler.

His anger returned. This time directed at himself for forgetting to get his prescription.

It felt like a giant hand was squeezing his lungs shut. He started to feel lightheaded and staggered to the bathroom, searching for his old inhaler.

He found it and took a puff. Nothing.

He peered at the date. Two years out of date, and when he shook it, it felt empty. He threw it onto the floor in disgust.

The giant hand squeezed down harder on his lungs. Each desperate, wheezy breath pulled in a tiny amount of oxygen.

He could hear his pompous doctor, 'Mixing smoking and stress with your asthma is a recipe for a full asthma attack. Don't forget your steroid inhaler every day.'

But Serge never remembered the steroid inhaler.

The muscles tightened in his neck and chest.

He couldn't breathe.

He glanced at his fingernails. They were going blue.

He needed to get help.

Serge staggered out of his flat, coughing and wheezing and coughing again.

Chapter 42

Sully watched the clouds roll by from his inclined position on Ruth's car's seats. Every minute brought him closer to the finish, closer to glory, but he was conflicted. He churned another thought. The sense of unease he had first felt in Davide's car was growing with each mile.

Had he been right to redefine the rules? To win the game on his terms?

When he looked again at his game controller, he smiled. It pushed the unease to one side.

'Game position – first' it showed.

He was going to win. The money and the BST hand would be his. He would return home a true champion.

The ruler of the Forbidden Island.

His online followers would be able to see how close he was to winning. They'd be putting money on him. Betting big on him to win.

He toggled the game controller display. '*Distance to finish – 5 miles.*'

So close. Who could stop him now?

The unease crashed down onto Sully again.

Serge hated him – he didn't want Sully to win. He would be able to see that Sully was close. He would know that he had broken Serge's rules. Would Serge give his position to the police?

Sully glanced out of the window at the sound of a drone flying overhead. He started to shift his weight and peer out of the car window.

'No,' shouted Ruth, banging her hand down on her seat to emphasise the point. 'There's a police drone above us.'

Sully dropped down in his seat. 'Bastard Serge,' he spat.

'Wait. No, it's a delivery drone.' Ruth smiled. 'The local ones are painted a lovely Scottish blue – like the flag. Very close to the colour of the police ones.'

Sully sighed out his relief, but it didn't release his sense of unease. His gut told him that something was wrong.

What if he won and Serge refused to pay? What if Serge refused to give him his hand?

Dread fought with unease and won easily. What if he had lost his hand for nothing?

'Distance to finish – 4 miles' showed on the game controller.

'I *need* you to stop the car,' Sully said.

Ruth laughed. 'I can't simply stop.'

'I need you to stop the car,' Sully repeated, raising his voice.

Ruth sneered at him. 'I'm doing you a favour and you're shouting at me. Is that fair?'

'Stop the car. Now.'

'Arsehole. Davide is a gent, but you're a pig.'

Sully stared and shouted, 'Stop... the... car.' Long pauses between each loud word. Making it an order she had to comply with.

Ruth stiffened and said, 'Ungrateful pig. Car... Immediate stop.'

'Scanning for safe parking,' the car said and kept moving.

'Why hasn't it stopped?' Sully moaned.

Ruth shrugged, and the car kept going.

Sully lifted his head and stared out of the window. A helpless passenger in the car. He pulled at the door handle that had a small red light next to it, but the car said, 'Error. Doors locked while vehicle is moving.'

Finally, the car began to slow and stopped. Sully pulled at the handle again, but car repeated its error message.

'It's not opening,' Sully said.

'It needs to park,' said Ruth.

The car moved backwards, reversed into a small space on the side of the road, and stopped.

The light next to the handle went out and Sully grasped the door handle again and yanked the door open.

He jumped out of the car and felt like he had escaped a small, moving prison cell.

He could see Ruth's ferocious finger and her mouthing the word 'pig' as her car slid away from him.

He held the game controller. Serge might still screw him, even if he finished the game within the rules.

For the first time, he wished he still had his own hand.

Chapter 43

Femi jogged alongside the B40 Glenedra Road. He had settled into a nice rhythm: run a mile, walk two, and his long stride was eating the tarmac. At first, he had jumped out of the road when he saw cars, but every time he had sprinted and dived for cover and then peered tentatively back at the cars to check if he had been seen, the people in the car were looking at a screen or their fingers waving in front of their faces. Everyone seemed to spend their time in a different world.

Now when he saw a car, he dropped into a stroll and waved at the car as it passed. No one acknowledged him. No one even seemed to notice him. Not even in the occasional sleepy village. Even so, he kept his left hand firmly in his pocket when people were in sight.

The grey clouds had kept their rain to themselves and lifted as the morning progressed. The rolling hills and greenery of the landscape was so different from South Africa that he sucked the view in and looked forward to each bend in the road unveiling a new vista.

He thought he was doing well. A little over forty-four miles in twenty hours. His plans for his brother and sister, and the purity of being outdoors fuelled him. He'd taken a few half-hour naps to recharge. He was going to push on and win the game. He could sleep later. The quicker he won, the quicker he was on a flight back home to his family.

The only bad news was the game controller's display: *'Game position – second'*.

***

Now, Femi was past Lough Neagh and was walking through the elongated village of Moneynick, he scanned the hedgerow looking for a good place to stop for a short break. A mile or so later, he came to a small turning on the right. The narrow lane stretched off ahead of him, green moss down the centre, two black ribbons of tarmac on each side where car's wheels rolled.

He turned off the land and side-stepped down a steep bank, careful not to get tangled in the long grass and brambles. He pushed through a small gap in the hedgerow and dropped down behind it.

The game controller told him he was still second and gave him his precise location.

He pulled a small bottle of water out and allowed himself one mouthful. He rolled the warm liquid around in his mouth, his tongue feeling the furry edges of his teeth. He hadn't wanted to waste water cleaning his teeth or bathing, despite the dampness of his armpits.

He allowed himself five more minutes rest before pulling at his game controller's fingers. 12:17, it told him.

Another finger pull and the display showed: *'Distance to finish – 25 to 27 miles.'*

Maybe eight or nine hours if he walked. It would be dark by the time he got there. He toggled the controller's display and saw he was still second. Trouble was that it didn't tell him how far behind he was. Or how close whoever was in third was behind him.

He'd run his last marathon in three and a half hours. The distance left was about the same.

If he upped his pace he could still win.

He jumped up and scrambled back up the bank and settled into a ground-eating jog.

Chapter 44

Clive and Ava were glued to the display wall in the PCU office as it showed Ruth's car enter the outskirts of Edinburgh. Guessing and double guessing which iconic landmark was Sully's final destination – Holyrood Park, the Scott Monument, the botanic gardens? Further on, the coast or the old Royal Yacht Britannia Museum. There were too many options.

They now had two cars behind Ruth's, each with two local Uniforms in them.

'Approaching Murrayfield Stadium,' Isla, one of the Uniforms in the first car, said.

Clive and Ava obviously knew. They could see Ruth's signal, but a long telephone call where no one said anything was too weird and awkward. Isla clearly thought so, and kept up a stream of unnecessary updates. Ava's HUD was linked to the display wall so that they both could hear and talk.

'Hold on,' Isla said. 'I can see him. He's sitting up... He's looking around.'

'What else?' Clive said.

'Looks like he's arguing with Ruth... Lots of angry hand waving.'

The line went quiet and they could hear Isla's breathing, it was getting louder and faster.

'OK! Something's happening. The car's lights are flashing. It's doing an Immediate Stop.'

'Shit,' Clive shouted. They couldn't afford to lose Sully, and if he got out now, he could run. Lots of gardens and hedges. Lots of places to hide. 'Shit,' Clive said again. He really needed to catch the others.

'OK,' he said. 'If Sully gets out, get your uniforms back on and arrest him. Repeat. Arrest him. Do not let him get away. Confirm.'

'Confirm,' Isla said.

'Tell the other car to do the same.'

'Will do. What about Ruth?'

'We can pick her up anytime. Just get Sully.'

Clive and Ava heard a male voice in the background relaying the instructions to the second car.

Ruth's car slowed, turned left and pulled over.

'What's happening?' Clive shouted.

'Doors are opening... Sully is getting out. Repeat, he's getting out.'

'Get him!'

'Car... Police Override... Stop!' Isla said.

'Car... Stop. Door locks will release when I am stationary,' the car said.

'Look out!' Isla said.

Clive could hear frantic movements of police jackets being pulled on. The car door locks clunked and unlocked.

Clive listened, wishing he was there, but had to rely on little dots on a screen and sound to guess what was happening. The noise provided more details. The Uniforms clambering out. Fast and urgent zips being pulled up on police jackets.

'Stop,' Isla shouted.

Dots started to move on the display screen, and Clive heard panted breaths and footsteps as Isla started running.

Chapter 45

Sully stood under the tree where the car had stopped. It had pulled off the main road at the sign for an Episcopal Church and St George's School.

Murrayfield Avenue the road sign said, and Sully smiled to himself. Murrayfield. He was close to the once-famous rugby ground. Home of bruising games of passion and courage. Now home to a pointless, non-contact charade of a game.

But *his* game mattered. Forbidden Island mattered to the hundreds of thousands following online. They would all see Sully, so close to winning. So close to glory. The first-ever winner of a game in the Forbidden Island would live in history. He imagined the adoration.

As long as Serge let him.

His smile disappeared. He shook the thought aside. He was a long way past the point where he had committed himself.

Trying to get back to visualising his triumph, he pulled his body up straight, head high and proud.

'The path to glory starts with the next step,' he muttered.

He stepped into the road, causing a car to swerve to avoid him. He hadn't heard it coming, but he did hear the clunk of the doors opening. He spun to look at the car. The two people getting out. Two people pulling on blue jackets. The word *'Pol'* on one side of the jacket and *'ice'* on the other. Fast hands on a zip and the jacket halves joining. The word *'Police'* staring at him. Name tags visible: Isla Stewart and Gregor Patel.

Sully froze.

The two Uniforms seemed like opposites. *The smaller woman won't give me much of a race*, Sully thought. The man was much bigger. Slower but stronger. He would have been at home on the pitch at Murrayfield in the old days. He held his arms wide apart. He looked bigger than the car.

If Sully ran towards them, he'd have to dodge and out run them both.

He turned to look up the hill.

'Stop,' the woman shouted.

Sully did the opposite.

He spun away from the Uniforms and ran. Arms pumping, heading up the pavement.

There were too many trees and recycling centres on the pavement for speed, so he skipped across the small grass verge and onto the road.

He ran hard, following the road as it curved.

Shit, he thought as the road started to climb.

He was breathing harder now, but he couldn't lose. He risked a glance over his shoulder.

'Shit.'

The woman was much closer, her eyes focused. The man didn't seem bothered. He was sauntering along the road, like he was on a gentle afternoon stroll. It looked like he was talking to someone.

Sully ducked his head and ran harder, faster. The air sucking noisily into his lungs.

Still the road rose, and Sully could feel his legs starting to complain.

Ahead he could see a side road. *Maybe that way?* he thought.

No.

A second car appeared at the mouth of the road and parked. Two more Uniforms got out.

Sully was trying to work out why they simply leant on the bonnet of their car instead of chasing him, when he heard a noise close behind him.

He glimpsed a blue shape and heard breathing. The woman.

I'll let her get to me, overpower her and make a break for it, Sully thought.

A force like a fast-moving train smashed into Sully's back and sent him flying towards the tarmac.

His hands stretched out to break his fall, but only did half the job. The game controller on his left arm didn't bend and give. Instead, it acted like a pivot, keeping his left side high, pushing the full weight of his body onto his right arm. It bent, unable to take the load. Sully jerked his head left, trying to avoid his nose planting square into the road. He managed, but grunted as air was forced from his lungs. His right cheekbone smashed down and slid along the road.

He gasped, pain from his cheek screaming from the fall, but he couldn't listen to it now.

Shake the woman off and get going, he thought.

He tried to move, but something held him. Incredibly strong. Sully tried twisting, turning. He couldn't move. The big man had been too far behind to be holding him.

Sully jerked his head back and upwards, trying to smash something soft and vulnerable.

Nothing. Then a voice in his ear.

'I've seen all the tricks,' the woman said. 'And from better than you.'

Sully tried to move again, but she held him effortlessly.

Then his arms started to move, but he wasn't in control. He tensed his muscles, locking them solid, but his arms still moved.

He felt a handcuff lock on to his right wrist. No feeling on his left – only the clank of the handcuffs hitting the controller and a metallic click.

A hand on Sully's collar and he started to rise. Again, not his muscles doing the work.

He stood in the middle of Murrayfield Avenue.

Defeated.

Game over.

His face was screaming from the impact with the road and his legs quivered from the running. Sully wished he hadn't bottled out of asking Serge his main question – would he still get the BST hand if he got caught?

The hand on his collar turned him and he saw the male Uniform sauntering up the road.

He stopped in front of Sully. His face split into a huge, beaming smile.

'Och, Isla,' he said. 'That's the funniest thing I've seen in ages.' He tapped the side of his head. 'Got it all recorded for you. I'll send you the video so you can watch it later.'

'Thanks,' Isla said.

Gregor turned and looked back down the hill towards the old stadium. 'Like the old days?'

Isla's breathing was shallow and controlled. 'Much easier.'

Gregor turned back to Sully, leaned in and said. 'That's the most one-sided race ever. She used to play on the wing for Scotland. You never had a chance, but it was fun to watch.'

Sully heard clapping from behind him. He glanced around and saw the other two Uniforms still sitting on their car, applauding.

Isla, a modest smile on her face, took a bow.

'You always were class, Isla,' Gregor said. His big hand shoved Sully in the back. 'Thanks again for the show,' he said to Sully.

They headed down the hill.

Two big smiles, one broken face with streaming tears.

***

Sully sat in a small, depressing room. The floors and walls were all painted a dull grey. A light in the ceiling threw a harsh light into the room and cast a hard shadow. The mirrored wall bounced reflections around. He could smell paint, everything looked new.

He touched his cheek and winced. A doctor had cleaned it, dressed it and given him some pain killers, but it hadn't helped.

Game over, Sully kept repeating in his head. *Failure. A public failure.* Everyone following the game would know.

Tears formed in his eyes, broke free of his lashes and started to roll. The ones on the right of his face, driven by gravity, headed south only to be absorbed by the dressing on his face. The ones on the left of his face carried on unhindered.

The door opened and the two Uniforms from the first car entered the room. The big, slow man and *that* woman.

'Only a bit of gravel rash,' Isla said. 'Nothing to cry about.' She dragged a chair back and sat down.

Gregor pulled a second chair back and dropped onto it. He made it look like a tiny child's chair. 'Normally, anyone in breach of the UK immigration code would be immediately deported,' he said. 'But instead of taking you to Glasgow airport, we've got two officers from Off-grid Crime flying up specially to meet you.'

Sully said nothing and stared at his hands in his lap. He left the tears to dry.

'And they want whatever that is on your left wrist,' Isla added.

Sully thought about brave defiance, thought about giving them the finger, but lifted his left hand and placed it on the table.

'What is it?' Isla asked.

Maybe they'll be gentler on me if I help, he thought. He blinked to stop the tears starting again.

This wasn't just game over. This was total surrender.

'It's a game controller,' he said.

The Uniforms looked blank.

'I'm in a game,' Sully said. 'One of the elite—'

Isla and Gregor's snorted derision stopped him.

Sully straightened, aiming for some last-minute bluster, but his voice betrayed him. 'It's...' *Too meek, too quiet*, he thought and stopped. He cleared his thoughts and tried again. 'It shows me exactly where I am, and how far I've got left.'

Isla and Gregor leaned in to see the display built into the palm. Disbelief etched on their faces. Sully pulled at the fingers, a couple were scratched from the tarmac, but it all still worked.

'*Game position – first*' drew more snorts of derision from Isla and Gregor.

'It still thinks you're in the game?' Gregor asked.

Sully shrugged and pulled a different finger.

'Distance to finish – 1.8 miles.'

So close.

'Take it off,' Isla ordered. She thrust her hand forward and waited. Her tone demanded compliance.

Sully grasped the game controller and pushed and twisted. It rotated as the universal mount released and the controller came away.

He handed it to Isla and watched her hand drop and her eyes widen as she took the controller's weight.

Isla passed the hand to Gregor and he weighed it in a huge palm. His eyebrows raised as he shrugged and gave it back to Isla.

Isla and Gregor scraped their chairs back and stood. Sully dropped his eyes to the table.

He heard the clang of the door shutting and looked at where his left hand should have been.

Chapter 46

Clive and Ava had been lucky to squeeze onto the next flight from Heathrow to Edinburgh.

Their time in the air was less than half of the advertised flight time. 'We're not really early,' Clive grumbled as they got into a taxi at the airport. 'They pad the flight time, so the airline is never late. Never has to pay compensation.'

'It's good to be early,' Ava said. Her tone squashed any comeback Clive might have and his eyes widened in shock. 'What?' Ava asked.

'That told me.'

Ava looked worried she had gone too far, but the corners of Clive's mouth rose. She laughed and told the taxi where they wanted to go.

The police facility in Haymarket was so new that the taxi's map still showed the building as *HM Revenue and Customs*, but it informed them that the taxi journey was only sixteen minutes.

'Boss,' Ava said, breaking the long companionable silence and pointed out of the window.

Clive looked up from the notes he was reading on the car's display screen and saw a road sign: 'Murrayfield Avenue'. It looked quiet and peaceful now. No sign of the earlier excitement. Clive and Ava shared a smile. They had seen some unofficial footage and had both winced at the impact that sent Sully flying.

'Great tackle,' Ava said.

'Time to destination: Three minutes,' the car said. Clive stopped reading and disconnected his HUD from the car.

The car's display blanked and then scrolled through *Disconnected... Purging viewing history... Purging personal data... Done'*, then clicked off.

Now his HUD was private again, he checked his messages. Still nothing from Sophia.

'In Edinburgh with work, talk when I'm back,' he typed, then added *'Love you. Xxx'.* He pressed *'Send'*, hoping the message would find Sophia's heart and she would give him another chance.

***

Isla and Gregor led Clive and Ava across a busy office crowded with Uniforms.

Everything gleamed, new and shiny. No battered desks, no dust. Nothing like PCU.

'How have you got so many Uniforms?' Ava asked.

'Devolution,' Isla said.

Ava frowned.

'Parliament likes to spend on a strong, visible presence here,' Gregor said, his Scottish accent had a harder Glasgow edge than Isla's softer version. 'It's not enough for us to turn up after the event and convict the offender. Parliament wants a deterrent so that the crime doesn't happen at all.'

Ava nodded. 'Makes sense,' she said.

'Not with our budget,' Clive moaned.

They reached a door to a meeting room made from floor to ceiling frosted glass. The door hissed open and showed another new desk, chairs and a man in his late twenties waiting for them. He wore an Inspector's dark blue uniform, which contrasted with his pale freckled skin and ginger hair.

Clive initiated the sharing of contact details and the name 'Alain Robertson' flashed up on Clive's HUD.

They sat and Clive's smile disappeared and he knotted his eyebrows.

'I've read the complaint made by Sully Rossi against PC Stewart for assault and unnecessary use of force.' He glanced at Isla and Gregor. The look on Clive's face made them shuffle on their chairs. 'I've also read the report from all four officers present that Mr Rossi tripped and fell and that is what caused his injuries.'

'True,' Alain said. Isla and Gregor nodded.

'But,' Clive said, 'I also read the doctor's report. The injuries on Mr Rossi's face are consistent with a trip, but the bruising on his back would make it seem like his complaint might have some merit.'

Ava nodded, going along with Clive's interpretation. The locals were all frowning and looking worried.

Clive couldn't keep it up, and his stern face dissolved into a smile. 'Unfortunately for me, I remember PC Stewart only too well. She broke my heart last time I was at Twickenham by running in two tries in the last ten minutes and stealing the last real Calcutta Cup from us.'

Isla beamed at the memory. 'Always a pleasure to score against the English.'

'I'm convinced that the video I have seen is the result of some malicious attempt to discredit PC Stewart with computer-generated images, and that Mr Rossi tripped. The bruises on his back were from PC Stewart's brave and selfless attempt to break Mr Rossi's fall.'

There were nods all around the room.

'Now that's over,' Clive said. 'Where's his hand?'

***

Sully was still sitting in the same chair, looking deflated. This time Clive and Ava sat in the chairs opposite him. Isla and Gregor decorated the wall behind them, flanking the mirror that hid Alain Robertson's presence.

Ava said, 'Tell us about the game.'

Sully's eyes flashed wide. 'You know about it?'

'Forbidden Island?' she nodded. 'Yes, we know.'

'How?'

'Tell us about your finish point.'

'You know where it is. I showed them.' Sully nodded towards Isla and Gregor.

'I know. But why there?' Clive asked.

Sully shrugged. 'We come to your country, break your surveillance and turn up at the heart of your democracy. Your famous places. It's perfect. We show we can get anywhere.'

'Do you think that sitting in a police interview room really shows that?' Ava said.

Sully wilted under Ava's glare. He looked down and placed his right hand over the end of the BST universal mount.

'Big price to pay,' Clive said, nodding at Sully's arm.

'Worth it.'

'Really?'

'Money and a BST hand... *A BST hand.* It's a dream. An easy swap.' Sully made it sound like the most obvious thing in the world.

Clive couldn't agree, even in a hospital full of care and pain management. He definitely couldn't have used a machete.

Clive tapped the box in front of him. 'But this isn't a BST hand.'

'No. A simple controller for the game.'

'We'll find out what it really is. Tell us about the others.'

'Nothing to tell. We were all chosen.'

'How?'

'It started with forum chat about why some games were getting more and more dangerous. Then rumours it was preparation for a game on the Forbidden Island. No one believed it. Then there were more details, it seemed to be getting real.' He looked to be reliving the excitement of the news. 'Then there was talk of ten chosen players. The ten best.'

He puffed his chest out a little at this, then seemed to remember where he was and deflated again.

'What happened next?' Clive said, prompting, wanting more.

'I got an invitation.' Sully's chest puffed out again. 'We were told to meet.'

'Where?' Clive asked.

Sully said nothing and dropped his eyes back to his hand. He shrugged.

'*Where?*' Clive said more forcefully.

'Can't say.'

'I know we're meant to deport you, but any deliberate attempt to damage UK Border Control property is a criminal offence. Minimum five years in prison.'

'I didn't damage anything.'

'A court won't believe you. They'll think you were trying to break your iTourist.'

Sully kept looking at his hand.

'Five years… A little information in return for a trip home,' Clive said and paused. 'An easy swap.'

Sully's head shot up at Clive's reuse of the words he had said earlier.

Clive held his gaze and waited.

Nothing happened.

'A little information and a trip home. You can collect your money, your new hand and live your life. Much better than a prison,' Ava said, as persuasive as the very best con-artist. 'Think of your new life… Italian sunshine or rainy British prison. They won't know you said anything.'

Sully looked at Ava and then nodded. 'Rouen. At the cathedral,' he said.

'OK,' said Ava. She looked at Clive. He nodded for her to carry on. She seemed to be connecting better to Sully.

'What happened?' Ava said.

'The organiser called himself Serge. He met me at the cathedral. He took me somewhere. I was in the back of a van with no windows, so I don't know where. We all ended up in a big farm building.'

'We?'

'There were ten of us. A tiny room each and a bigger space for food and meetings.'

'The ten to play the game?'

'We thought so, but there were tests first.'

'Go on.'

Sully talked them through the first two tests: the long walk to the coast, then the shorter second test.

'You ended up at the site of the V1 rocket launch?' Clive said. The choice of the venue seemed symbolic, like the UK was back in the targets of an attack, not a simple game. But how could the three remaining handless gamers possibly hurt anything other than themselves?

Sully nodded. 'The tests got us from ten to seven and then to five.'

'But there are four of you here?' Ava said.

'Yes, the game was only for four. The last test was to see if we were really dedicated. Serge showed us the BST hands. We couldn't believe it. I mean, I'd never seen one before, let along *held* one.'

Some of the lust seemed to have returned to Sully's eyes as he remembered.

'What was the last test?'

'A fake guillotine. I was called last, but I hadn't heard screams or seen any blood. It seemed like a trick. The blade fell and stopped before it hit. Still, it was scary.'

Clive hadn't realised he was gripping the table tight as Sully talked about the guillotine. He forced his hands to unlock and rested them in his lap.

'We found out later that the first guy bailed. That left four.'

'You, Lilou, Femi and Tatsuko?'

Sully nodded.

'Then what?'

Sully described his round the houses trip to Glasgow, taxi to Dumfries and his hotel. It was all stuff they knew already from his signal trace.

Clive and Ava sat forward in rapt attention when he described thrashing around in the bushes for the parcel.

'And what was in the parcel?' Clive said.

'The game controller, a light… and a machete.'

Clive and Ava were both very quiet, very still as Sully described the ease with which he had sacrificed his hand to the game.

'How did the game controller get into the country?' Clive said.

Chapter 47

Tatsuko thought she was doing OK considering, but her mother disagreed – *Faster, lazy girl.*

The first half of her journey had been good. She'd enjoyed the downs, the fields and the little villages.

She was going slower now as her route became full of towns and people. Mostly they looked through her. Serge called them HUD zombies. The people walking around, typing and reading their HUDs, and not paying attention. Body present, but brain elsewhere.

Very few of them stared at her. Only some of the eco-protesters, with their placards about the evils of air travel, viewed her suspiciously. She didn't think she looked like an American who had flown to the UK. She didn't even think she looked like a tourist, especially as the city was so diverse. Maybe she wasn't subtle enough with her hand and the A to Z map book. Maybe some people were simply unfriendly. Aggressive even. Only the woman in a multicoloured hoodie with a *'Liberation, Empowerment, Responsibility'* placard smiled at her.

Tatsuko huddled in the corner of a shop. Both the windows and the door were boarded up and covered in scruffy and careless graffiti tags. The derelict space gave her the privacy she wanted, but she could have done without the reek of stale piss.

She felt more deflated when she checked her display. *'Game position – Third'.* Her mother's disappointed frown deepened.

She pressed on, finding it easier to blend in with her head down – another grumpy Brit walking along the road.

She decided to stay on the south side of the river, hoping it would be quieter.

Her next target was Wandsworth Bridge, about one and a half miles away.

***

Tatsuko paused on the path and looked left across Wandsworth Bridge. She stopped and wondered about crossing the bridge and approaching her target from the other side of the river.

'Fuckin' 'ell. Don't just stop,' the person behind her said, as he navigated around her.

'Yeah, I must have cost you at least half a second of your fantastic life,' she shouted after him.

He raised his middle finger at her. She turned back and took in the Thames' slow progress and the famous skyline in the distance. She'd see it all much closer soon.

Two cars with strobing blue lights appeared on the opposite side of the river. Tatsuko froze. *Could be nothing*, she told herself, and breathed out when the lights flashed past the bridge and headed north. She ducked her head and hurried on, keeping to her original plan of staying south of the river.

She found a private corner where one wall of a block of flats turned sharply and joined an office block. At least this didn't smell of piss. She pulled out her A-Z and checked her game controller. *'Distance to finish – 4.4 miles.'*

Better, she thought. Maybe an hour and forty minutes. She didn't really want to look, but checked her position anyway. *'Game position – Second'.*

Something had happened. She'd overtaken someone.

She set off again, a bit more bounce in her stride, but the nagging pain in her foot kept returning.

It could be psychosomatic, but she'd had the ache since doing that gait analysis at the hotel. Maybe there was a real issue with her foot.

She caught her reflection in the window of a shop. Not her best look. Crusty jeans, windblown hair, nasty waterproof coat. She could see something different in her stance. Perhaps it was making her foot worse. She looked more carefully in the next shop window.

The weight of the game controller was definitely pulling her left shoulder down, bending her stance a little, pushing more weight on to the aching foot.

Trying to walk straighter and more upright, she pressed on. Her foot felt a little better.

Chapter 48

Femi jogged along Upper Newtownards Road. He was nearly there.

The hard, fast miles he had covered had left him tired, but in this last mile, he felt light on his feet. He would need to try and find a way in. If this was SA, there would be guards and dogs. And unsmiling soldiers with guns.

But there weren't.

There was a roundabout with a large tree in it and Femi followed the road alongside the tall metal fence. The large double gates were open. The sign said that Stormont Estate was a public park – open to pedestrians until 18:00. Just as well that Femi decided to run the final section of his journey, and he had an hour before closing.

He looked along the Prince of Wales Avenue as it rose and saw the huge, white, elegant Parliament Building in the distance. He could see his finish point.

First, he had to get past the Uniform in the small hut next to the road. He turned left after he went through the gates and took the curving path. Two lines of tall, imposing trees stretched away up the hill towards Parliament. He walked onto the grass and up between them, glancing at the back of the police hut as he passed it. No one came to check on him.

Nearly there. He wanted to run. The others could be closer to their finish points. He might lose by mere seconds.

He couldn't risk it. A mud-splattered black man running towards the Parliament Building might be met with force. It would be in SA. Better to finish second than be tackled by soldiers, or worse.

Femi walked on, a longer stride than normal. Faster, more urgent, trying to look like he was late meeting his family.

He covered the ground quickly and reached the roundabout, barely glancing at the white stone with a bronze statue of some bloke on top.

He headed to the final rise, maybe two hundred metres from the finish line.

A couple of Uniforms stood off to the right of the building, watching the approach to the building, alert but not freaked out by anything. Femi dropped his head, not wanting to catch their eye.

He lengthened his stride again.

Risking a glance at the Uniforms, he saw they were looking straight at him. Their casual body language had changed – their hands were on their guns.

'Shit,' said Femi, forcing himself to stop and look back down the avenue. He did a 'tourist absorbing the view' act, rotating the whole way around, taking the chance to double-check the Uniforms. They were still watching, noticeably more relaxed, but with hands still on guns.

Femi started walking again as an open-topped bus trundled up to the roundabout. It stopped and disgorged a couple of loud families. Little kids running ahead of exasperated parents shouting for them to wait.

It proved a good distraction. The Uniforms weren't looking at him anymore.

He got to the bottom of the steps and looked up. Such a fantastic building. Massive white columns supporting the front. Beautiful.

Twenty-five metres to go.

He put his foot on the first step. The Uniforms hadn't moved. Second step. Still good.

Femi climbed, step after step. Hoping. Feeling the eyes of the police.

He reached the top step.

More cries from the parents dragged the Uniforms' eyes away from him again.

He pulled his game controller from his pocket and looked at the display. A large animated chequered flag fluttered in an electronic wind. A gold dot appeared in the centre and grew, morphing into spinning text. The text stopped spinning.

'1st place – Winner!!' it said.

Femi shot both hands to the sky and shouted, 'Yes. Yes. Yes.'

He did a little dance on the spot to celebrate.

'You OK, sir?' one of the Uniforms called, but there was laughter in his voice. All the suspicion gone.

Then he looked up at Femi's hand and his posture changed. He started to walk towards him.

Femi looked at the game controller again. The whole hand was flashing alternate green then red. *Some sort of built in celebration light show,* Femi thought.

It didn't matter now – he'd won. Soon to be back home with his family.

The flashing was red now. Femi looked at the screen, his concern growing as the Uniforms got closer.

He put his right hand on the game controller.

It was getting hot.

Chapter 49

Sully had been left in a cell to mope and pout. His kicking and banging on the door made him look more like a spoilt child than the 'world champion' he claimed to be. Clive, Ava, Isla, Gregor and Alain were all back in the frosted glass office. Sitting around the meeting table and looking at the box in the middle that held the game controller.

'There's no way someone got that controller through a UK Border check,' Clive said.

They all nodded their silent agreement.

Clive pulled the used Amazon delivery box with the familiar logo and half the address label on each flap on the top closer.

The game controller rested on sheets of bubble-wrap. Like most Amazon packages, the box was way too big for the content and it looked like they were discussing how to return an unwanted birthday present.

Clive pushed the box back to Gregor. 'Seal it up.'

The conversation stalled as Gregor did. A rustle as more bubble-wrap went in, a noisy rasp followed by a dull snip, as he pulled the tape and used the nearly blunt safety scissors to chew through the tape. He patted the tape down, sealing the two flaps and entombing the controller.

'If that hand was real, we'd look like old time crooks sending a message to an enemy,' Clive said, smiling at the image.

The others stared back blankly, unimpressed by his attempt at a joke.

'When's the delivery drone here?' Clive said, trying to break the mood of censure.

'Five or so minutes away,' Gregor said.

'You'd better get the box to the pickup point,' Alain said.

Gregor nodded, scooped up the box in a giant hand and whistled under his breath as he stepped out of the office.

'Let's see what the military make of that game controller,' Clive said, looking past Isla's shoulder and out of the window.

He thought he could see a small dark dot in the distant sky approaching the office. 'It's a wild story, having to use the machete,' he said to the room.

He got a reply of nodding heads.

Even if Clive couldn't imagine wielding the machete himself, the four in the game had used the promise of money, a BST upgrade, fame, and the challenge as motivation enough.

'Alain, can you hold Sully in his cell until we hear back about the controller?' Clive asked.

'Sure, I can slide his case into the Anti-Terror holding rules without too much trouble.'

Clive pushed his chair back and stood.

'Ava and I are heading back to PCU while we wait for the military's report on the controller.'

***

Clive and Ava settled into another taxi. Clive being a commuter of habit, travelled facing the rear and saw the wave from Alain Robertson before the car turned onto the main road.

'We've got one of them, Boss,' Ava said. 'Now we need the others.'

'Sully was no help to us.'

'No. It's like they've deliberately kept all four gamers separate.'

Clive scratched at his left wrist. Four firm, quick back and forth movements. The itch didn't justify the severity of his attack. Maybe it was subconscious empathy? *No*, he thought. *Frustration*. A tiny show of decisive action when he had no leads and no ideas.

He stared out of the window, watching Edinburgh suburbs roll by. He hoped that Ava would interpret him looking out of the window as a sign of his deep thinking about the case.

If Ava wasn't busy on her HUD, the slight lift of the corners of his mouth would have betrayed him. Clive replayed Isla's last try all those years ago. The way she shimmied and left the English full-back grasping at air was pure genius. Shame she wore a blue Scottish shirt, but talent was talent whichever side the person played for. Clive had gone to that rugby match buzzing from an early morning arrest. They had cracked one of Doris Barclay's drug cells and cleaned up all the members. Yet Doris had been too clever as always. Nothing led back to her, but the way Clive had followed the lookout to find the drug house, then from there to the money man, and finally to their supplier gave him an idea.

It would need data and big search engines, but iMe had both. They boasted that they kept everything.

'Any news, Ava?' he asked.

'Drone will be at the military site in about fifteen minutes. They're standing by to look at the controller immediately it arrives.'

'OK. Can you throw your HUD at the car's screen?'

'Sure, Boss.' Ava flicked her hands and the screen redrew.

'We obviously need to find the other three, but unless a Uniform sees our briefing photos and spots one of the gamers, we've got nothing.'

'I'll resend the photos to all regions. Give them the hurry up, but they've got all the protests to deal with. A random tourist walking around isn't going to be their top priority.'

'Maybe not, but there are still some good Uniforms out there.'

Clive took a breath to try and shuffle all the ideas that were firing around his head into a pretence of a sensible order.

'Sully said that the talk about this game started months ago. It must have taken a lot of planning. It would have needed people to find the four deserted butcher's shops, plant the parcels, and do all the other stuff. iMe will have the signal history of anybody who went to any of the sites. I think this Serge guy will have expected us to trace the signals, but let's check. The butcher's shops would have the least traffic. We can start with one of those.'

Clive watched the display screen as Ava flicked through some menus and brought up the Monitor window. She selected the location where Sully had separated himself from his hand. Next, she chose a period of six months ending immediately after Sully arrived. Ava pressed 'Search'.

Ava's Buddy trailed out a banner that said 'Searching'. After a couple of seconds, she packed the banner away, threw the search results onto Ava's HUD screen and scampered off.

No surprise that the report showed Sully's signal as the last visitor. Prior to that, someone called Fahad Ahammad had visited twice, each time with a different person. Fahad's first visit was four months ago and the second a month later.

Clive was about to ask who Fahad was, but Ava beat him to it by moving the mouse over his name. A window showing Fahad's details appeared.

'He's the estate agent, poor bloke,' Ava said. 'He did well to get two people to look at that dump.' Ava moved the mouse over the names of the people who had been with Fahad. The details of two local property developers came up.

'Did any of them go near the park where Sully got his parcel?'

Ava selected the three names and ran a search on the area near the football pitch for the same time period.

Ava's Buddy unfurled a 'No results' banner.

'Go back to the shop and widen the search area to a hundred metres.'

Ava did, and the search returned over two hundred names. 'It's not a busy road, but maybe people use it as a cut through,' she said.

'Any of those people also at the football pitch?' Clive asked.

Ava selected all the names and ran the search near the football pitch. Her Buddy rolled out her 'Searching' banner and stood tapping her foot and checking a fake wristwatch. It was a big search and eventually she unfurled a 'No results' banner.

'Looks like they've used different people for different jobs to stop us tracing them. That's going to make finding them difficult.'

They tried similar searches around the other three shops. They had a list of names, but no idea where the parcel pickup point was for the other three, so it didn't get them any further. None of the names had been near Dumfries.

'There are too many possible people,' Ava said.

Clive sat back in his chair. Hunching over the car's display screen had made his back sore. The car slowed, and filtered off the motorway, heading towards the airport.

'Let's start at the other end of the problem. How did the game controllers get into the country?'

'The ports and airports are all pretty tight. It's unlikely that the hands could get past all the scanners and checks.'

Clive shrugged. 'Very unlikely, but we can ask the military to check when they have the controller. If they came in through a port or airport, then we've got no chance of finding who picked them up.'

Ava chewed her bottom lip for a while and then said, 'Could it have got flown over by drone?'

'They get shot down by Coastal Defence.'

'What if a drone dropped a package straight after it got over land and before being destroyed?'

'It would be a big risk. There's every chance that the drone would be destroyed first.'

'Maybe it didn't make a successful drop the first time.'

Clive looked at Ava's eyes. He could see the possibility of a lead burning in them.

'Worth a try.'

Ava shuffled around on menus, looking for the search she needed. She found a *'keyword'* search option and clicked on it.

A new window opened, and she selected the last six months. In the keyword box, she typed *'drone'*. She stopped and thought.

'That's going to find all the delivery drones as well. Millions of results.'

She spent some time searching online for inspiration, and then changed the text in the keyword box from *'drone'* to *'drone destroyed'*.

'Go back a year,' Clive said. 'They needed time.'

She changed her search and pressed *'Send'*.

After a wait, the screen redrew to show a map of the easterly tip of Kent. Small yellow dots marked the site of each drone destruction by Coastal Defence. Not surprisingly, given the distance from France, most were between Dover and Folkestone, but some went as far north as Margate or as far south as Hastings. Most were over open ground, well away from people or towns.

Aiming for secrecy, Clive guessed. 'Can you find if there were people near the sites when the drones were destroyed?'

'Don't know, but I know a man who will.' Ava touched her jaw to make a call.

'Tech Support, this is Rob,' the voice said.

Ava told Rob what she wanted, and he talked her through a complicated series of options and secondary windows.

The car had parked at the airport by the time that Ava was ready to press *'Send'*.

The doors opened, but neither of them moved.

'You have reached your destination. Please leave the car,' the car complained. Clive imagined some frustration in its tone.

They ignored it and watched Ava's Buddy doing her thing with the wristwatch and tapping foot.

'Your flight closes in twenty minutes,' the car nagged.

Clive and Ava shuffled forward to get a closer look at the screen when her Buddy finally threw the results at it.

Seventeen names.

Ava beamed. 'That's a workable number.'

She snatched at the list and dropped them in the search window they had last used to search around the site of Tatsuko's butcher's shop.

'Shit,' Clive said at the *'No results'* banner. 'Try further out in case there were multiple couriers.'

Ava frowned when the searches at five and ten miles resulted in nothing.

'Yes!' she shouted when she tried a fifty-mile radius.

Only four names. Only four people had been at a drone destruction site *and then* near to Southampton.

'Try Worcest–' Clive said, but Ava was already pressing *'Search'* for the four names within fifty miles of Worcester, where Lilou had been.

Ava's smile almost cracked her face. 'Jay Evans was at the drone destruction site *and* in Chichester *and* in Dudley,' she said.

'Get Uniform to arrest him and bring him to PCU.'

'Your flight closes...' the car began, but they were already out of the car and running for the terminal building.

Chapter 50

'What's that on your hand?' one of the Uniforms screamed at Femi.

The Uniform's hand was on the handle of his gun. He was pulling it out.

'It's a controller for a game. No big deal,' Femi said, trying a casual wave to stand the Uniforms down. It didn't work. The other Uniform was now pointing his gun straight at Femi.

'Looks like a fuckin' big deal. Stand still.'

All colour drained from Femi's face.

The game controller was still flashing red all over and showing *'1st place – Winner!!'*, but it was getting hotter.

Why? Serge hadn't mentioned the heat or the flashing. He had told them to get to the finish and wait for the game controller to tell him what to do next.

Femi looked around, his vision tunnelling in, disconnecting from his surroundings. He could see the families with their loud children running around near the bottom of the steps, but he couldn't hear them. The two Uniforms were edging closer, guns aimed at the centre of his chest. He couldn't hear what they were shouting.

He thought of home, Dinah's loving smile, his parents' warm embrace. He couldn't understand why there were tears rolling down his cheeks.

He'd won Forbidden Island. He was rich. He had secured his family's future. He should be celebrating, but he was crying in Belfast with two Uniforms pointing guns at him.

The game controller stopped flashing and the display changed: *'Wait for instructions.'*

His hearing returned.

'For the last time! On your knees or I'll shoot,' the Uniform screamed.

Now all the tourists were staring up at Femi. Mouths open. Some pointing, some filming.

Two mothers were rounding up their children far faster than any sheepdog could reach a stranded lamb. They were pulling their reluctant offspring away from the Uniforms.

Femi stooped and dropped to one knee. Then the other.

'Hands high in the air,' came the next barked instruction.

The shadows of two guns reached Femi, then the shadow of a body. The Uniforms stood over Femi. Guns still pointing at him.

They looked at each other. The second Uniform's left eye greyed as something came up on his HUD. He switched his gun to his left hand and used his right hand to swipe and double click. 'Sarge,' he said. 'Message broadcast from PCU. Look at the second photo. It's him.' He transferred his gun back to his stronger hand.

The first Uniform repeated the process. 'Looks like it. Call it in.' He pointed at Femi's left hand. 'What is that?'

'A game controller.'

'Where's your real hand.'

'I had an accident.'

'What kind of – never mind. What does it do?'

'It has a display in the palm.'

'Show me.'

Femi slowly lowered his left hand, not really trusting a Uniform with a gun in his face. He twisted his wrist to show the Uniform the palm of his controller.

The screen still said, 'Wait for instructions.'

'Take it off,' the second Uniform said.

'I'll need to lower my right hand... OK?'

'Go.'

Femi lowered his right hand and grasped the game controller, flinching at the heat of it. He pushed and twisted, but it didn't move. He tried again, but it was so hot he could barely touch it.

'Take. It. *Off*,' the second Uniform shouted.

'I can't... I'm trying.'

'Try harder,' he snapped.

The game controller beeped when Femi touched it again. He checked the display: *'Game Controller locked.'*

Femi twisted his hand so that the Uniforms could see the display.

They shot each other a scared glance and turned.

They started running. Their haste ripped through the watching tourists. Femi heard screams and watched them panic and start to run.

He turned the game controller so that he could see the display.

It was too late. He couldn't get the controller off. He couldn't run from it.

A strange calm rolled in over him, like pulling a soft duvet over himself on a cold evening.

At the top of the display showed the words: 'Whoever your God is, now is a good time to pray.'

Underneath it: 00:03, clicked to 00:02.

He thought of Dinah.

00:01.

'I'll wait for you, my love,' he called.

00:00.

Femi's world flashed an intense, blinding white.

The light enveloped him.

Obliterated him.

Chapter 51

There was still no reply from Sophia when Clive and Ava's plane touched down back at Heathrow. *How could he make things better?* The dread weighed Clive down, but as soon as the doors opened, they were off and running through the terminal.

They had to slow to a walk to avoid startling the alert mechanisms in the immigration checks. In single file, they walked through the glass booth. A small beep of acceptance was their only acknowledgement, and they were running for the car pickup point.

'Where's Jay?' Clive asked.

'Uniform's last position update was that he's on holiday at Land's End. Local Uniform are going to get him, but it's getting late already.'

'OK. Tell them to go and hold him now, and then get him to PCU for nine tomorrow morning,' said Clive. His breath was more ragged from the running than he would have liked.

Ava scanned around the airport terminal, searching for something. 'I did book you a "fragile traveller meet and greet", Boss. Can't see them though.'

'Very funny,' Clive said. 'Wait till you get to my age.'

'You've got forty more years until retirement, Boss.'

Clive groaned and straightened up. 'Don't think I'll make it,' he said, and headed for the exit. Not a run anymore, but a walk, taking deep breaths, trying to keep them silent. He didn't want to give Ava any more ammunition to fire at him.

'Boss, report of a possible sighting of Femi at Stormont. Two armed Uniforms approaching him.'

'That's brilliant. Just the luck we needed. Two down, two to find.' He beamed at Ava. 'Maybe Jay can help us find the others. Going to be a great day from here.'

He didn't know how wrong he was.

Chapter 52

Serge banged his apartment's front door shut.

His breathing was back to normal. Not good clean breaths, but his normal distant rattle. He had got to the hospital quickly enough and been treated as an emergency on a nebuliser. After ten minutes on the machine, he was breathing again. Then he had wasted hours when the doctors refused to let him go without more checks and lectures about smoking.

He almost ran to his computer and woke it up.

He logged-in and opened the game's master window and stared at the status.

The window was split into the usual four quadrants, one for each player.

Femi's quadrant showed a chequered flag, and the display underneath showed the controller was locked onto its mount and there were only seconds left on the automated self-destruct sequence that started when the controller recognised it had reached its finish point.

He watched the last few seconds of Femi's life tick away, wondering how he had won. Sully had been way ahead.

Serge double clicked on Sully's quadrant to see the map of the game controller's location.

It was miles from Edinburgh. 'Merde.'

They must have caught him.

He zoomed in on the map and swore again. The controller was in a military base.

Serge moved the mouse and clicked on the menu. He selected the *'Retire player'* option, then selected the reason as *'unauthorised location'*.

He pressed 'OK' to confirm the self-destruct.

Chapter 53

Clive relaxed back into the car's seat, rested his head against the headrest and shut his eyes. He needed a few calm minutes to think through the interview approach for Jay Evans.

His HUD thought he was trying to sleep, and shut all functions down. He concentrated on the rhythm of his breathing, and the darkness of vision. No Buddy, no messages, no streaming news updates. Blissful tranquillity.

It lasted four more breaths before Ava shouted, 'Fuck, Boss.'

He snapped his eyes open. For a fraction of a second he had ordinary, human vision, before his Buddy ran across the bottom of his vision and the screen exploded with message alerts. His TrueMe social media account scrolled faster than his brain could cope with, the words blurring as they sped across the page.

He clicked a newsfeed and its video loaded.

A worried newsreader stared at the screen, she gulped and paused, it looked like she could barely believe what she was going to read out.

Her face changed as she tried to control her emotions. Her eyebrows lowered and her forehead cleared her frown. 'We have confused reports of an explosion on the steps of Stormont. There were two armed police officers at the scene, sadly it appears that they were killed by the blast as their signals are now red. Despite no other signals being present at the scene, there are unconfirmed reports of a man standing outside Stormont. Social media is saying that the police officers approached the man and then ran. The explosion seemed to come from this man with *no signal...*'

The newsreader stopped and her eyes lifted slightly. It looked like she was listening to something being said by her producers.

'We have this footage from an eye-witness. Viewers are warned that the following video shows disturbing images.'

The video cut away from the studio and to a video shot from someone's HUD. Two Uniforms, guns raised were talking to a man who seemed to be staring at his left hand. The police turned and started running, but so was the person filming. The view changed to a view away from Stormont, people running, parents scooping up children. The view bucked and jumped with each panicked step and the person's pumping hands could be seen at the bottom of the screen.

The view changed again as the person turned to look over their shoulder.

There was a blinding flash, the police seemed to fly, and the video tumbled and rolled like the person doing the recording had been blown over by a shock wave.

The man looked like Femi. Clive shut his eyes to try and purge the sight of the explosion catching and ripping into the two police officers. Despite the HUD shutting down again, Clive's retinas still reported a blinding white shock to his brain.

'Boss, that looked like Femi,' Ava said. Her voice was unusually quiet and level.

Clive opened his eyes again. 'Yes.'

He'd wanted to find Femi, but not like this. He had dreamt of putting all four gamers onto transport out of the UK.

'Can you get that video on the car's screen and get to right before the explosion?'

Ava nodded and threw her HUD at the car's display and scrolled the video back.

She pressed play and Clive turned away when the two Uniforms got caught by the explosion.

'Scroll back again. There's something at the beginning. Go really slowly.'

This time the video jerked and stepped forward.

'Stop,' shouted Clive. 'Look.' He banged his finger onto the table at the point where the first light of the explosion was visible.

'It's that game controller. It exploded.'

Ava leant in and scrunched the corner of her eyes. She jogged the video display, back and forward in time, trying to find the exact moment of the explosion.

'Definitely the controller,' she agreed.

Clive stiffened and the colour drained from his face.

He jabbed a finger at his jaw so hard that it left a mark. 'Call DSC Bhatt,' he said.

The call was answered but all Clive heard was, 'Wait'.

He shared the call with Ava so that she could hear through the car's speakers.

They could hear someone else talking at the other end of the call, but it was too faint and muffled to catch, even amplified by the car.

The talking stopped, and Clive thought he heard a sniff. *Bhatt doesn't cry*, he thought. *Never cries*.

'Clive,' Bhatt said, a small crack of emotion in her voice.

'Ma'am, it was Femi's game controller that exploded. That means Sully's might explode as well.'

Bhatt didn't say anything, instead, it sounded like the rustling of tissues, then the call muted.

Clive and Ava looked at each other, not sure they should speculate in case Bhatt suddenly unmuted the call.

They waited and listened to the rhythmic thrumming of the car's wheels on road.

Bhatt's voice reappeared through the car's speakers.

'I have a report that the six scientists who were examining Sully's controller have been killed. They were in a sealed room, but they were all using their iMe to record their findings. The video shows their discussion about the controller getting hot, then they were looking at a message on the palm of the controller that said, "Sully has been retired from the game". They were discussing what the heat from the controller meant, when the display changed to "Unauthorised location" and I saw a flash of white.'

Bhatt's voice broke, but she carried on with a croaky timbre.

'All their iMe signals went red and recordings stopped.'

Chapter 54

Bhatt's message, *'Conference room next to my office. Urgent'*, had binged in soon after the call in the car had ended. The car arrived and Clive and Ava rushed to the meeting room. Clive knocked, and they entered.

The buzz of conversation stopped, and heads swivelled to stare. A hostility crackled in the air which left them shuffling nervously on the spot.

This felt like an ambush, not an update briefing. Clive locked his knees to try and combat the jelly that seemed to have replaced his muscles.

The sensation wasn't helped when Bhatt snapped, 'Sit.'

Clive thought about arguing, but Bhatt's right hand was up, palm facing him. He took the hint that was really an order, and sat. At least the chair meant his legs wouldn't fall from under him.

Bhatt turned to a man in his mid-thirties. She had positioned herself so that Clive couldn't see or hear what was being said. It hadn't been a subtle manoeuvre. Clive checked the man's details on his HUD: Chief Inspector Lance Grannum.

Ava sat next to Clive, and leaned across to whisper, 'What's going on?'

Clive shrugged and shook his head. Whatever it was, wasn't going to be good.

As Bhatt stopped talking, she shifted position and opened a gap so that Clive got a view across the conference room. He saw a familiar face hiding in the corner.

The way Zoe dropped her gaze when she caught Clive's eye seemed completely out of character. She should be smiling and saying 'Hi, Boss'.

'OK. Let's start,' Bhatt said in a tone that demanded instant obedience.

Zoe shuffled behind Bhatt, her body half-turned away from the table, like she wished she wasn't there at all. She sat at the furthest corner of the table.

Clive's discomfort ratcheted up a level. The six other people had taken chairs on the opposite side of the table to Clive and Ava. Now it felt like an inquisition.

In the window behind Bhatt, Clive could see thick, dark clouds rolling in.

'We've had two explosions: one at a military base, one on the steps of the Parliament Building at Stormont,' Bhatt said.

They all nodded.

Zoe couldn't look at Clive. She seemed to find the top of the table fascinating.

'Which makes this a terrorism case,' Bhatt said. She paused and looked at Lance, 'Chief Inspector?'

The clouds outside deepened and a roll of thunder rumbled through the room.

'Ma'am,' Lance said. His head bobbed forward in a nod to Bhatt. His hair had a fluffy, cotton-like appearance with tight curls at the ends, and the nod caused the ends of his hair to rock – an added threat.

Lance looked straight at Clive and pursed his lips in a hard line.

'The case is ours,' Lance said. 'You're both off.' He waved a hand at the two people to his left. 'My DI's will run it. You need to give us everything you have.'

A shock of disappointment hit Clive like a breaking wave that he hadn't seen coming. It knocked him over, he went under and resurfaced. He looked at Bhatt for some encouragement or hope, but her eyes told him it was inevitable.

Lance bent forward and looked right. At Zoe.

'Give everything you have to DS Jordan. She knows PCU, so it will speed things up.'

Zoe still wouldn't look at Clive.

'Clive, Ava, you're back on normal duties,' Bhatt said. 'You can leave.'

'But, ma'am, that's not fair. We've done all–' Ava said.

A raised finger and Bhatt's hard eyes told Ava not to push her luck.

Clive and Ava pushed their chairs back to rise. It was obvious really. Why would they leave it to him when there was a huge, well-funded specialist department?

'Run along, old-timer,' Lance said, a sneer distorting his face.

'You could be the biggest arse wipe,' Clive muttered.

'What did you say?' snapped Lance.

'What? Who? Me?' Clive said, holding Lance's gaze. 'I said "Could be in for the biggest lightning strike".' He waved at the deepening storm.

Zoe still hadn't looked at Clive, but a smile flashed across her face.

Lance's face reddened. 'No, you said–'

'Clive, Ava, go,' Bhatt cut across Lance. 'Zoe will come down after we've finished.'

Zoe snuffed her smile out before anyone else noticed.

Chapter 55

Lilou's route kept her on the edge of the Wye valley, and then past Monmouth.

For her, the game had become a personal, internal battle. Like with her triathlons and parkour, success wasn't only about the strength of the muscles in her shoulders or legs. It was down to the strength in her head. She had to block out the fact that her game controller told her that she was still fourth. Last.

Last. The thought cut her like glass in her shoe at every step. She was behind Sully. Sully!

She checked her map, touching her finger where the game controller confirmed she was. She traced her finger south and hit a thick, green line with the word A40 on it. It looked like a big road. Lots of cars and lots of risk, but there was a small bridge over it. She smiled at the name, Jingle Street. It reminded her of a Christmas song her brother liked.

She'd have to go faster, dig deep. She had done it before. She started running.

***

Lilou ran along Jingle Street. The narrow single-track road, with hedges on both sides, was mercifully free of cars. Ahead she could see the road start to rise. *I must be close to the bridge*, she thought.

She dropped her head and pumped her arms faster, accelerating. She lifted her head to maximise the feel of the wind rushing past her cheeks.

When Lilou reached the brow of the bridge she saw that it was still narrow, with a row of little bollards on either side, one side showed red, the other a reflective white. She could see a T-junction ahead, but hedges blocked her view of the road.

Lilou checked her game controller and laughed. *'Game position – third'.*

She hadn't been that far behind after all. Maybe the other two were only metres ahead of her. She had no way to know.

Her world was condensing down to the map and the controller. She had no idea what her family were doing. No idea of what else was happening in the world.

The road ahead was still clear. *Push on*, she told herself. Time to grab second and then first.

Sprinting across the bridge, she flashed past the last of the bollards, then saw a battered farm van turn off the main road and start gliding silently towards her. Bits of straw blew off in a yellow cloud behind it.

Lilou twisted away and prepared for an easy parkour jump, up and over the fence. She was planning to roll down the bank and away from the car, but as her hand touched the top rail, it crumbled and split. Not a hard, crisp crack of new, strong wood, but the dusty, feathering of age and decay.

She pitched forward, throwing her shoulder in an improvised forward-roll. It shot her into a fast and high leap and as her left foot banged back onto the ground, it slipped downhill on the wet grass.

Lilou windmilled her arms, trying to regain balance, but a hole in the bank caught her foot. Her weight and momentum carried her forward, her body overtook her foot and she screamed as her foot twisted and buckled under her.

She finished her descent and landed in a sprawl of arms and legs.

Wincing, she sat up and touched her ankle. 'Merde.'

She heard movement above her and tried walking, but her ankle wouldn't take her weight.

The movement above her got louder.

She hopped across a few metres of grass and into some bushes.

'You OK down there, lovely?' a woman's voice called.

Lilou pulled her arms around her legs, trying to be invisible, and wishing the woman would go.

Chapter 56

Clive looked around his apartment. He could see nearly all of it from his chair in front of the display wall. The sterile open-plan lounge/dining/kitchen, the door to the small bedroom and en suite and the short corridor to the front door. It was a box to exist in, not his home. Sophia was refusing to communicate at all. Even Harry ignored him tonight.

Since he had got home, he'd spent the hours preoccupied with two things: game controllers and chocolate.

Zoe had been gracious and apologetic in the handover of the case to Terrorism. She couldn't fight a direct order, but it didn't help. This was an important case. He should be helping, but he was being told to sit and do nothing.

He flushed red when he thought about it, but the anger faded quickly. Red replaced by black, swirling clouds of depression. They sucked at him, drawing his strength from his body.

He battled up and out of the darkness, looking for a lift. Looking for his favourite thing.

The fridge used to hold chocolate. Milky, velvety heaven. The sort that melted into a dreamy stream on his tongue.

But the Ministry of Well-being and Health set his dietary restrictions and the chocolate had been seized when the fridge was restocked and replaced with rice cakes.

He glanced at the kitchen cupboard where he had hidden his last illicit bar of chocolate behind his Health Bank bracelet. He could put it on and eat all the chocolate he wanted. No comeback from the Ministry.

But it wouldn't help his diabetes.

'Be strong,' he said, but the cupboard called to him, like it had its own gravitational pull.

He walked a lap of the sofa and looked at the kitchen cupboard. He sat on his hands. Dug his nails into his palms. He gave in and walked to the cupboard and half-opened the door.

'No.' He closed the door and went back to the sofa.

He repeated it all. Again and again. His addiction battled his willpower.

He had to be strong. He had to think about something else.

Clive used his HUD to project the TV onto his display wall. He scrolled through bland channel after channel. It seemed like after 23:30, the TV companies put drivel or news on to send people to sleep.

Clive's Buddy seemed to have got the same message as he rolled out another warning banner. *'You need sleep for optimal health and performance.'* Buddy gave an exaggerated yawn and then pretended to fall asleep on his banner.

Clive looked up at the display wall at the mention of explosions. *This might be interesting*, he thought.

The display wall showed a TV studio. A female presenter and her four guests sat at an elliptical desk so that they could all face the cameras, and at the same time, see each other.

'I'm Katrina Bridges, and welcome to this special edition of *Question Hour*,' the presenter said. Her face was sober to match the severity of the image of Femi exploding that rolled across the screen on the wall behind her.

Clive liked Katrina as a presenter. She usually asked difficult questions, but also let the guests talk. So many others seemed to prefer to talk over their guests, like their opinion was the only one that mattered.

'I'm joined tonight by the Minister of Well-being and Health, Karli Neilson. Shadow Northern Ireland Minister, Conor Mulligan. Leader of the Eco-Socialist Democracy Party, Miles Raven, and Issac Townsend, Head of the New Modelists Church.'

Clive settled back in his chair. The four guests were arranged for easy identification of their politics for the viewers. Far left was Miles, the ultimate eco-socialist campaigner, then Conor since the opposition party were only a little left of centre. Katrina separated left from right, and then Karli, whose politics were a tiny amount right of centre. Then Issac, way out to the right.

Conor and Karli could almost be political clones. Their parties were both so close to the centre that they fought hard and dirty over their common ground. If Miles was as far left as possible, the panel was balanced by Issac being just as far to the right. These four were often on TV shows looking for combative discussion. *No one from Control Rebellion though*, Clive thought.

The time on the studio's display wall said 20:00, which meant it was a repeat, but it might still be good viewing, Clive decided, even if it wouldn't be a good, clean fight.

'Minister,' Katrina began. 'How can we have a terrorist attack on the steps of the Northern Ireland Parliament?'

'We don't have the motive for this attack—' Karli started, but Conor jumped in and talked over her.

'What else can it be? Yer man there was a Catholic. A Catholic blowing himself up outside parliament can only be seen as a sectarianism terror attack. This government's record of protecting the interests of the people of Northern Ireland is shameful.'

'Typical, Conor,' Karli fought back. 'Jumping to conclusions and trying to make political capital from the suffering of others.' She nodded to emphasise her point. 'The perpetrator has no links to terror groups, so the motive isn't clear at this time. But what is clear is the need for greater funding and control to be given to the security forces to protect this great country from vile and cowardly attacks – from whatever the source.'

The bulk of the studio audience greeted Karli's comments with boos, offset by a smattering of clapping.

'Always the same from the government. More and more control. Whatever happens – that's their conclusion. Their control is leading to a police-state,' Connor shouted.

'OK, OK, you two,' Katrina said. She waved her hands, both palms down. 'Let the others have a go. Miles?'

Miles smiled, 'The motive is clear to me. The government is a right-wing, racist, capitalist machine raging against the people.

They don't care about worker's rights and equality of earnings. It's about making the rich richer.'

'But the bomber was from South Africa,' Katrina objected. 'Why does that make it about right-wing politics?'

'Many in South Africa battle against the same issues. We need to get rid of the self-serving political puppets and reboot democracy. Capitalism has failed. Eco-socialism is the only morally ethical approach that protects the environment *and* saves jobs and worker's rights.'

Miles stopped and the audience burst into loud applause. He beamed.

Issac waited for the noise to lessen. He was gaunt, like he ate the very minimum that Model Citizen allowed. 'No, no, Miles. You're missing the point. We live in a time of excess. Hundreds of years ago, people had to work for their meals. Food was seasonal. Now it's a simple click and food is delivered.' His voice had a seductive pull to it and Clive found himself nodding, even though he had always fought the Model.

Clive knew he needed to change. Perhaps the Model and the Church were the right way after all?

Issac continued, 'This lazy greed has led us into an environmental and climate catastrophe. We need to consume less. We all need to be Ultra – it's the only way our world can survive.'

'That's shite,' Conor said. 'Typical "purer than you" preaching from the loony church.'

'For once I agree with Conor,' Karli said. 'The New Modelists are a dangerous cult, not a church. They're generating fear about an economic meltdown. We can't sustain the jobs that Miles wants to protect if consumption falls.'

'We need to use this bombing as a shock to the democratic system and demand political change,' Miles said.

'That's giving in to terror,' Issac said. 'The aim of terrorism is to frighten people and make us believe that we are in imminent danger. You don't win a war by killing nine people. If the terrorists had more powerful weapons, then they would use them. Terrorists want to appear powerful and relevant on a government level by being in the news.' Issac paused to lock his eyes onto the camera, his whole body projected hope and salvation. 'Our church can shelter everyone.'

Karli seized on the pause in Issac's flow and said, 'Terrorists want to use the fear from an event like this because they can't win an election with their ideas. And that applies to the others on this panel. They're looking to change the world to fit their vision and using this tragic event to do it.'

'You can't say that–' Miles started, but Clive hit mute.

Despite his hopes for something entertaining, they were all repeating the same old points.

He needed some escapism, not reality.

Clive thought back to his childhood dream of driving a Ferrari and the ride he had finally had in one. Esteban's car had shown him a different life. A life that wasn't ever going to happen for him. He hopped channels again searching for escapism and settled on the ancient film, *Pirates of the Caribbean*. He'd seen it so many times that it didn't matter that it was almost halfway through.

His body relaxed and the stress of the day leeched out of him: his failure to talk to Sophia, the trip to Edinburgh, the explosions and his anger from the meeting and being cast aside.

He dozed, but was jolted out of a dream by his Buddy alerting him that it was 1am and his *'health and productivity would be sub-optimal unless he slept in his bed'*.

His dream had been full of bare-chested pirates, muscles glistening, wearing pirate hats and waving swords, but Clive couldn't work out why one of the pirates was driving Esteban's Ferrari.

He gave up and headed to bed, but the fire and fight in the pirate's eyes warmed Clive.

He'd find a way to get back into the investigation.

He'd find out what was going on and stick two fingers up at bloody Lance Grannum.

Chapter 57

Clive's pirate dream seemed to have infected him, as the next morning he sauntered into the PCU office ready for a fight. He was upbeat, even if his mood fell short of swashbuckling.

'You seem happy, Boss,' Ava said.

'Given our PCU workload is so light, I've decided that we should carry on looking for Lilou and Tatsuko. Especially as Jay Evans is still waiting for us.'

'Cool. Let's do it.'

'Look, Ava, my career is screwed already, but you've got a lot to lose—'

Ava stood and reached out to touch Clive's arm. 'Boss, you've helped me so much… It's PCU against the world. It's us against Lance.'

Clive smiled and turned away from Ava's gaze as tears of pride welled up and threatened to spill down his cheeks. 'Fuck Lance. Fuck 'um all,' he croaked.

'Fuck 'um,' Ava agreed.

**

PCU's shabby and depressing Interview Room One was a million miles away from the luxury of Bhatt's conference room, and a different planet to Alain Robertson's glass and chrome new room in Edinburgh.

It was PCU's only interview room, and no one knew why it was numbered. Maybe it was a subtle hint from the senior ranks that expansion might follow and that interview room two would be needed.

It never was.

The room had originally been an institutional battleship grey, but had been the victim of a corporate re-branding exercise. Social welfare groups said it needed a colour that was more neutral and less judgemental. More suspect friendly and sensitive to their feelings.

The designers had called for Summer Nomadic Desert Gold paint. The painters had Trade Beige in the van and had skipped any pretence of doing a quality job. They ignored all the necessary preparation and slapped beige paint all over the grey before the designers could object.

Now, the years of knocks and scrapes had opened wounds in the beige and the original grey seeped back into the room like a mould.

Clive and Ava were immune to the scarred room, but Jay Evans sat with his hands on his lap, like he didn't want to touch anything in the room in case it stained him.

'Why were you in Dudley?' Clive asked.

'I specialise in accountancy standards and I had a meeting at the Town Hall with the council's accountants.'

'Why get there so early? Journey time plans are reliable these days.'

'I... I wanted some air before the meeting. I can't context switch from car to meeting easily. I need a little time.'

'How did you spend the time?'

'You know where I was.'

'Yes, you were in the park. Plenty of people to talk to.'

'I didn't talk to anyone.'

The room was cool enough for Clive to need a jacket, but Jay dabbed at his temples with a tissue.

'And Southampton?'

'Same. My job takes me around the country.'

'And to the cliffs near Sandwich? Why do you go for a walk there every day on your own?'

'I'm not on my own, I go walking with Kevin.'

'There's no signal for a Kevin,' Clive said.

Jay half-laughed and said, 'No. Kevin's my dog. He's a Great Dane.'

'Funny name for a dog,' Ava said.

Jay shrugged. 'I like it.'

'Yes, you go every day at exactly the same time. You're either very reliable, or you're building an alibi. Which is it?'

'No... I, I'm reliable.'

Jay's hands were back on his lap, his palms turned down, gripping his knees.

'You ever see drones getting shot down?' Clive asked.

Jay shrugged. 'Once or twice.'

'Once or twice? Coastal defence has you at or near the site of six over the last year.'

Jay shrugged again, but his knuckles whitened as they tightened on his knees. Clive could see a small tremble in the fabric of the man's shirt.

'Once might be a coincidence, but six seems planned,' Ava said. 'What was being delivered to you?'

Jay stayed quiet but dropped his eyes to the table.

'What. Was. Being. Delivered?' Ava repeated, emphasising each word. She used the same tone that had worked so well on Brett. Somehow Ava's force of will seemed amplified when it came out of her five foot two inch frame.

Jay blinked rapidly several times as he tried to process the switch from Ava's sunnier demeanour to this inexorable force.

'And don't lie to me again,' Ava growled.

Jay gulped and started wringing his hands together.

'No. Of course. Of course. I got a box the last time. Other times the drones got destroyed in the air or never arrived.'

Ava sat back in triumph. Jay looked like a balloon that Ava had pulled the stopper out of.

'What was in the box?' Clive asked.

'Don't know for sure. I was told not to open it. That I'd damage the contents if I did.'

'What do you think was in it?' Clive asked, but Jay shrugged again.

'You don't look like you'd be comfortable running around on cliffs. You seem like you'd be happier talking,' Ava said, adding a drop of sweetness to her voice.

Jay looked up at Ava, his eyes seemed bigger, puppy-like. 'Yes. I'm a consultant – I tell people what to do. I don't like to get involved.'

'I know,' Ava said and smiled at Jay. He reflected the smile.

She's got him, Clive thought.

'Tell us everything,' Ava said, but this time her voice was as hard as steel. A honey-covered sword that Jay couldn't parry.

'I belong to a group. We talk about what's wrong with the country and how to fix it. Then about eighteen months ago, someone slipped a note in my pocket. It said I needed to live up to my words, and that the cause needed me.'

Jay stopped speaking, but the wringing of his hands continued.

'Go on,' Ava said, flashing Jay a small smile and raising an eyebrow. 'I want to know.'

'It told me to go to a park and where I'd find a second note. That one told me I could do great service to the cause, and it had the address of a different park for the next note. I went several times before there was anything more.'

Jay paused and licked his lips, but ignored the chipped glass of water on the table.

He relaxed his shoulders. 'They told me to collect a package and that I would help people lead better lives.'

'How?'

'This bloody system. It's not fair. It's not right.'

'I know,' Clive said.

'Tell us,' Ava added.

She kept her voice soft because of the tears in Jay's eyes.

'My poor old dad died waiting for a liver transplant that never came. iMe makes everyone live longer and stops all the accidents that provide donors. Then the prioritisation system favours the rich and famous, or the young. Everyone but my dad.'

Clive nodded. This was an argument he'd made a lot of times, but it wasn't what he expected to hear now.

Jay continued, 'We need a fairer system, more transparent. One that helps the poor. So, I helped. I thought that smuggling in donated organs from Europe and getting them to the poor would help the most needy.'

'But the organs wouldn't survive the trip?' Ava said.

'They told me they had all sorts of clever technology in the box. That's why it was so heavy. That's why I couldn't open it.'

'And you collected a box from the cliffs, took it to Chichester, then Dudley?'

'Yes. It was lighter each time I got it back.'

'Then where?'

'Someone left a note saying I had to leave the whole box under a car in a charging point on the M6 services on the way back from Dudley.'

'Where exactly?' Ava demanded and Jay gave her the details.

'Do you want to know what was really in the box?' Clive asked.

'Hearts? Livers?' Jay said.

'Hands.'

Jay frowned. 'Hands?'

'Did you see that guy's hand explode in Belfast?' Ava said.

Jay crumpled in his chair and his head dropped onto the table. His hands came up and cupped his ears, like he was trying to hide from Ava's words, trying to 'un-hear'.

***

'What do you think?' Clive asked Ava when they were back in the PCU office.

'He was used. He was told what he wanted to hear to get him to do someone else's dirty work.'

'Like Femi, like Sully. They weren't in a game, despite what they were told.'

'It will take forever to search for all the people who left the notes, even if we can find any. Too many locations and too long a time period.'

'And we've still got two people we can't track loose in the UK with bombs clipped on their arms.'

Chapter 58

They had released Jay when it was clear he knew nothing. Lance could always find him again if needed.

Clive checked the empty *'Requiring Action'* message queue when he and Ava got back to the PCU office.

What was the point of sitting here doing nothing when there was real work to do? When Tatsuko and Lilou were still out there.

Ava obviously agreed with him. Her HUD was shared with the office display wall. She had a window with the profile pages of the four 'gamers' open, one photo in each quarter.

She touched Sully's photo and dragged it to the bottom. Femi, Lilou and Tatsuko's images shuffled to make room. She repeated the action with Femi's photo. Lilou's and Tatsuko's images now took up the top half of the display wall.

'Girl's on top,' Clive said. 'They're doing better than the blokes.'

'Obviously,' Ava said. She held a pen icon on her HUD and ran her finger diagonally across Femi's face. It left a vivid, red line. She drew a second diagonal line. Femi had been crossed out.

She changed the colour of the pen and put a single yellow line through Sully's face.

'Now we can focus on the others,' she said.

Clive agreed with the conclusion, but the clinical nature of the crossing out shocked him.

He took a deep breath, trying to settle the jumble of thoughts. 'We've hit a dead end chasing the people who delivered the other game controllers. We've got to try and guess Lilou's and Tatsuko's finishing points and try and stop them getting there.'

'Tatsuko started in Southampton. So, a target in the south of England makes the most sense. She could be aiming for Windsor Castle and the King, but she bought an A–Z map of

London. Also, Sully's and Femi's targets were political. And not only political, they're the parliaments. My guess is that Tatsuko is heading to Westminster.'

'I agree,' Clive said. 'Especially when you look at the distances.'

'Boss?'

Clive pinched his fingers and selected a map he'd been working on. He attached it to a message and sent it to Ava. Clive watched the display wall, and saw the message arrive on Ava's HUD. When she opened it, he saw the familiar map of the UK open.

Clive had drawn four stars on the map, one for each of the butcher's shops where the game had started. Four lines started at Sully's shop in Dumfries and took different routes to Edinburgh. A little annotated flag sat above the finish point with the words: '70–80 miles'.

Clive pointed at the flag. 'That's the rough distance for Sully to travel if he had walked and not tried to cheat. Now look at Femi.'

A second set of lines linked Derry and Belfast. Femi's route. The flag sitting over Stormont also had the words '70–80 miles'.

'Same distance,' Ava said.

'Then there's Tatsuko.'

The star at the bottom of the map had four lines starting from it and crossing diagonally from Southampton to London. The third flag had the same text. '70–80 miles'.

'You can't see at this scale, but those lines end at the Houses of Parliament,' Clive said. 'All three gamers had the same rough distance to travel. Enough of a distance to be a challenge with only the food and water that they can carry. Enough to make it look like a serious game.'

Ava nodded towards the west of the map. 'I can see that we agree on Lilou as well.'

'Yeah. She started in England, but the National Assembly for Wales in Cardiff makes sense. They are attacking all four parliaments.'

Clive had drawn a fourth set of lines on the map from Worcester to Cardiff. The flag over Cardiff read '70–80 miles'.

'I did think that she might be going to London as well, but... it's too far. Give me control, I'll show you,' Clive said, nodding at the display wall.

Ava fiddled with menus and said, 'Yours.'

Clive touched the little dot at Worcester and moved his finger, dragging a little cursor east towards London. As he did, the HUD software drew a line that tracked his movements, keeping a straight line between Worcester and wherever the cursor was. The numbers in the flag spun as the length of the line recalculated. When Clive let go of the cursor over Westminster the flag read '110–120 miles'.

'See it's much further.'

Clive's HUD binged with a new message.

'Crap,' he said. 'Bhatt wants us back in the conference room.'

He banged his hand on the desk.

'With that bloody Grannum.'

***

Lance Grannum sneered across the conference room table.

Clive's map with the four sets of lines and distances for each gamer was on the conference room display wall.

'It's a pretty picture,' Lance said.

He leaned to his left and turned his head to say something to the DI sitting next to him. They talked for a few seconds, but Clive couldn't hear what they said.

Lance straightened. 'Well, it's a nice, little theory, but we've discussed it before,' he said, rubbing at the corner of his eye. 'It's plausible, but our conclusion is that a double strike on London is the game plan. Much more chaos and panic to hit

London with a second bomb so soon after a first. More impact than a bomb in *Wales*.'

Lying bastard, thought Clive. They were locked in a London centric view of the world. Especially with the way Lance said Wales. He made it sound like some tinpot village.

Clive looked at Bhatt, hoping she would contradict Lance.

She didn't. 'This is Lance's case,' she said instead. She didn't sound convinced.

Lance smiled. It looked as sincere as a lion inviting an antelope to dinner. 'I do have good news. Terrorism needs all the hands it can get on this.'

Clive shifted in his chair and looked at Lance. Sure, the guy was nasty, but at least Clive would be on the case.

'Ava,' Lance said, 'I've been very impressed with your work and attitude. I need excellent officers in and around Westminster, and you know a lot about the two remaining terrorists. Welcome to the team.'

Ava nodded, then looked at Clive. Her eyebrows arched high in a silent question.

The disappointment burned in Clive, taking him back to being picked last for the playground football matches. He forced a tight smile; she could handle herself now, so he nodded his approval.

Clive put his hands on the arms of his chair, getting ready to push himself up and out. Away from the humiliation.

'Wait, Clive,' Bhatt said and looked at Lance.

'Sure. I said I needed everyone, and that apparently needs to include you, Lussac.'

Clive's elation almost betrayed him, but he jammed his left leg up hard against the bottom of the table to stop a smile. 'Great, I've got all the skills and experience to make a real impact.'

'Yeah, right,' Lance said, almost choking with laughter. 'You hear this guy?' he said to his DI. They shared a laugh. Then Lance continued, 'That's got nothing to do with it. I want dynamic officers that represent the people we are protecting, not some old dinosaur.'

'Lance, that's enough,' Bhatt said. 'You know the rules on bullying in the workplace.'

'Ma'am,' Lance said. As far as an apology went, it was pitiful. But it was all that he got.

Bhatt looked at Clive. 'According to the Diversity in the Workplace laws and the latest anti-ageism rules, Lance doesn't have anyone in the Terrorism department who represents white, heterosexual males over the age of fifty. Because of your recent birthday, you are now the top diversity score appointment in that category.'

'I want to be picked because of my ability, not because of some bogus attempt at diversity,' Clive said, unable to keep the moan out of his voice.

'You can come to the team under diversity, or decline the appointment and stay in PCU,' Lance said.

It should be about who can do the best job, not about scoring points, Clive thought.

He knew he should tell Lance to stuff it, but he needed to be part of this.

'OK. I'll come.'

Ava smiled and shot a playful elbow into Clive's side.

'Fine, *Clive*,' Lance said. 'I've got some really boring paperwork that's got your name on it.'

Chapter 59

Clive looked at Lance. 'Paperwork?'

'Old boy like you should appreciate the importance of paperwork.' Lance sat back and spread his hands. His smile hadn't travelled north to reach his eyes.

Clive gripped the table. He could do without a professional misconduct charge for punching a senior officer.

'Thought so. Ava, you'll get the full briefing back at New Scotland Yard.'

Ava rubbed her hands together before nibbling at her little finger. He couldn't blame her for going. She would be in the centre of it. Part of a team to stop a terrorist attack on Parliament.

The corner of Lance's mouth tipped up. 'Clive, you can stay here. Zoe will send you the paperwork I need doing.' Lance nudged his DI. 'And the head of the busy PCU department can't leave it unattended. Eh?'

Both Lance and his DI laughed.

'Careful, Lance,' Bhatt said.

'Sorry, ma'am.' Lance's eyes danced with laughter. He was like a troublemaker at the back of a classroom causing mayhem and pretending to be sorry.

'Thank you, Clive,' Bhatt said.

Clive stood and walked to the conference room door, back straight, head high, hoping to make a dignified exit.

His head dropped as he shut the door.

Lance muttered something and laughed.

***

As Clive dawdled in the corridor on the way back to the PCU office, his Buddy appeared on his HUD carrying a large sack. Tips of envelopes peeked from the mouth of the sack, and Buddy staggered across Clive's HUD under the weight of his load. He dropped the sack and unfurled a banner *'Multiple large messages received'*.

All the messages were from Zoe. He clicked on the first.

'Sorry, Boss', it started.

'Fuck,' Clive said, as he scrolled through the attachment. It was massive. Anger burned at Clive's ears, it spread and his whole face glowed.

He clenched his hands, digging his nails deep into his palms.

Clive turned the corner of the corridor and stopped in the office's snack area. The vending machine said: 'Clive, my friend. What can I get you?'

'Oh, fuck off,' he screamed. According to the upgrade notice that had been sent while they were in Scotland, the 'happy-go-lucky server personality upgrade will improve the customer experience by reaching out on a truly emotive level'.

Typical Employee Wellness double-talk bullshit, Clive thought.

'"Fuck off" is in my database of abusive and bullying phrases. Your vicious, hurtful and wounding words have been sent to Employee Wellness to add to your file,' the vending machine said.

Clive's eye was drawn to a part of the mural painted on the machine's side. Some trick his brain played on him turned four swirls of paint joining and twisting together into Lance's nose.

'Add this to my file,' Clive said and smashed his hand into the machine on the tip of Lance's nose. A hollow metal bong resonated and echoed in the snack area.

Clive pulled his hand out of the dent he had caused and rubbed his fingers, then shook his hand trying to dissipate the pain.

***

Clive reread the first part of the attachment from Zoe's first message.

It was junior-level admin stuff. Basic, degrading and insulting for an inspector.

Clive closed the message. It wasn't urgent.

The PCU office was quiet and private now Ava wasn't here, so he touched his jaw to make a call. He was about to give up, but on the fifth ring, Sophia answered.

Joy surged through his body.

'Clive, you need to stop with the messages,' she said. 'I can't do this anymore. I need things more stable. I need *someone* more stable.'

His joy evaporated at her words. 'But…'

'Bye, Clive,' Sophia said and hung up.

In the echoing silence of the office, Clive finished his sentence. 'But, Sophia. I love you.'

Tears rolled down his face. He told himself to stop but they kept coming. Wiping them away just spread the wet around his face.

He sniffed and dropped his head into his hands.

After a few minutes, he slowly raised his head. Sniffed loudly and used his sleeve to dry his face. He needed not to think about it. Not now anyway. He couldn't face it, so he wrapped his feeling and thoughts about Sophia into a tight ball of denial. He squeezed it tighter and tighter until numbness replaced his pain.

He sat in the silence.

Maybe this case would occupy him. Stop him thinking, stop him hurting. He nodded to himself and looked at his map again. He could see that there was some logic in attacking London twice, but to attack Scotland and Northern Ireland, but not Wales made no sense. *If you attack all four centres, you attack the whole country*, he thought.

He typed in a series of awkward finger stabs, wincing at each movement. His only regret was not hitting Lance himself. Clive's message explained why Wales was a target, then attached the map to a message and sent it to the only person he could think of who might help direct some protection to Cardiff.

Zoe.

Clive looked again at the long stream of messages that Lance had made Zoe send.

He couldn't face them. Instead, he looked at the grimy window of the PCU office, and late afternoon sun filtering in. He thought about quitting on the day, and heading to the warmth of the afternoon, but he only got as far as his bum coming off his chair before he dropped back down.

He couldn't leave work early when everything was tracked, but it didn't mean that he had to *do* Lance's piss-take work.

Clive clicked onto a news channel, threw it at the office display wall and turned up the volume. The sound echoed in the empty office.

The familiar face of Issac Townsend looked at Clive from the display wall, before the TV programme's director cut to the interviewer.

'What can the Church of the New Modelists possibly do in these dangerous times? When there are terror attacks, how are you even relevant?' the interviewer said, twisting a little hysteria into her voice to suit the producer's editorial message.

'In difficult times people rely on faith. The Church provides an umbrella of faith to our citizens that shelters them. It gives comfort in this fearful and uncertain world. The political elite sell fear to the masses. The media sells fear and fear allows control of the people, but the Church embraces the real issues. Humans are eating and polluting the world to the point of destruction. These so-called terror explosions are the beginning of the people rising against the tyranny of governments who talk about climate change, but do nothing.'

'You're saying that the Church is behind the attacks? Is this the work of the Ultras?' The presenter prodded an accusing finger at Issac.

Issac didn't rise to the bait. 'The Church shows the true, righteous path. The path of minimal consumption leads to total health and constant peace of mind. We can start to save the world by adopting a stricter version of the Model Citizen and adopting a population control programme. The government knows this, but does nothing. The Ultras are committed to making this change.'

Chapter 60

The largest conference room in the New Scotland Yard building was packed with people. Not quite the sardine tin of a rush hour tube train, but close. Zoe was grateful that she still had a few millimetres of personal space towards the back of the room. If she stood on tiptoes, and the sea of heads aligned perfectly, then she could see Ava near the front.

She was struck by two overwhelming sensations: the heat, and the silence. How could so many people be so quiet?

They'd been waiting ten minutes for Chief Inspector Lance Grannum, and the heat had built with each passing minute. The temperature had travelled north, past comfortable, then clammy, staying briefly at uncomfortable before heading on to roasting. Sweat dribbled down Zoe's back, sticking her shirt to her back. She drew her hand up, keeping it close to her chest to avoid touching the person in front of her, and dabbed the tissue onto her forehead. She reversed her hand's movement and pushed the damp tissue into her pocket to join a few others.

Everyone was staring at the conference room's display wall. Photos and profile details of Lilou and Tatsuko took up one half. The other half kept repeating the video of Femi's hand exploding at Stormont, and the image from one of the scientists' HUDs as Sully's game controller wiped out the entire team.

Usually a bit of dark humour would have circulated in the room to break the silence, but the images were too raw and shocking. They had all been bombarded with briefing messages stressing the importance of catching Lilou and Tatsuko before the scenes were repeated outside the Palace of Westminster.

The conference room door opened, and Chief Inspector Lance Grannum strode in. He slowed as the heat hit him. 'Jesus, what's gone wrong with the aircon,' he said and proved that he could multitask by walking, talking and removing his jacket all at the same time.

'It's knackered,' someone said, and the clang that echoed in the room sounded like they emphasised the point by kicking the offending unit.

Lance took in the room, catching as many eyes as possible and nodding to a few of the crowd.

'You've all seen the briefing and seen the videos. You know what we're up against.'

Zoe said, 'Yep,' and added to all the 'Yes', 'bastards', 'right', and other mumbled agreements that filled the room.

The atmosphere changed. They were like dogs who had patiently waited, but now strained at their leads.

'Our job is to stop these cowards attacking Parliament.'

More agreement half covered Lance saying, 'Put the map up.'

The display wall behind him redrew to show a small section of London, with the Houses of Parliament near the top. The River Thames ran vertically down the right-hand side.

'OK. We've set-up a defensive line around Parliament. We're lucky that it's so close to the river on the east side. That gives us a nice natural barrier. Anyone coming from the south has to cross the Thames either here.' Lance reached up with his left hand and touched a bridge at the top of the map. 'Westminster Bridge, or here.'

His hand dropped to the bottom of the map. 'Lambeth Bridge.'

He touched a small pen icon at the bottom of the map.

'They could cross other bridges further away, but we have the defensive line set along Horseferry Road to the south, up Marsham Street, Great Smith Street and Storey's Gate on the west, and then along Great George Street to the north.'

As he mentioned the names of the streets, his finger followed the route of each road and drew a red line on the display wall. When he finished, the map had a rough rectangle drawn on it that enclosed both the Houses of Parliament and Westminster Abbey.

Lance tapped another small icon at the bottom of the screen and the map view changed to a satellite view. All the simple grey blocks were replaced with images of real buildings and the green spaces grew trees and bushes. The optimism of the bright blue colour the map used for the river was now a realistic dark green-grey.

'We don't know exactly when the attack will come and there are businesses in the area. The Prime Minister wants to show that we are open as usual and won't be scared by terror threats. We've been told that we can't enforce an exclusion zone.'

That drew cries of complaint and disappointment.

'I know, I know,' Lance said, his hands up in mock surrender. 'We've got the drones up and I've pulled Uniforms off the eco-protests and put them everywhere along that red line. I need you lot patrolling outside of the red line to try and catch them before they get there. You'll get a message right after this with your assignments, and exactly where you need to go. Questions?'

Zoe pushed her hand back up through the gap. She knew Lance didn't really expect questions and that she should keep her mouth shut, but it needed saying. Her hand reached head height and then broke cover, like a soldier peering out of a trench surrounded by snipers.

Lance saw the movement, frowned and shot an angry, 'Who's hand is that?'

The sea of heads shifted, turned and stared, like they were cult members under Lance's control. Space opened up in front of Zoe and she had a clear line of sight to Lance.

'Jordan,' Lance barked, 'what is it?'

'Err,' was all Zoe could manage and her faced flushed red under the intense, silent gaze of the whole room.

'Get on with it,' Lance said, pulling on his jacket.

'Err,' Zoe said again, but she knew she was committed. Pulling her hand down and saying 'nothing' would be complete capitulation. A sign of too much weakness. 'Are we sure they're both coming to London, sir? What about the threat to Wales? It could be one terrorist for each parliament of the Union.'

Lance smiled as the room exploded into laughter as if Zoe had told the funniest joke ever.

'We have assessed that threat and dismissed it. A double-tap on London presents a perfect scenario for these terrorists.' He said it like it was a proven fact, not his opinion.

Zoe wasn't so sure. Clive's map had some merit.

Lance started to move towards the door, but Zoe knew how to stop him.

'I'm sure you're right, sir, but if nothing is done to protect the Welsh Parliament and there is an attack, then we're open to political criticism. A small force sent to Wales would allow us to say that we tried.'

Zoe knew that Lance would hear the 'we/us' in her statement as 'he'. Lance would be exposed if he did nothing.

Lance stopped and rubbed his hand over his face. 'The politicians would attack us,' he said. After a few seconds, he said, 'London's the target, but a small force would cover the bases.' He thought for a few more seconds. 'Sounds like you're volunteering, Jordan. You can go to Cardiff.'

'It can't only be me, sir. A team would be better.'

Lance started smiling again.

'A team? Good idea, Jordan. That idiot Lussac likes Cardiff.'

'The dream team,' someone shouted. 'The junior and the dinosaur.'

The laughter made Zoe's face glow like a red traffic light on a dark night.

Chapter 61

Tatsuko had forgotten all about the pain in her foot. The simple act of correcting her posture had eased the excess strain she had been putting on the muscles and restored her balance.

Her step seemed to lighten as she walked along the riverside path in Nine Elms. She didn't really need the A–Z now – if she followed the river, she would reach Lambeth Bridge and then the finish point. Her mood was buoyed up by each glimpse of Big Ben as the river twisted and gaps between the buildings opened up.

The walk from Southampton had challenged her, but her mother was always at her side when she slowed – *Lazy girl, how can you win if you don't walk?*

She'd expected the physical and mental strain. She'd prepared for it, but what she hadn't expected was how easy it was to walk around and be nearly invisible. It was like every person knew they were tracked and therefore they assumed she was as well. No need for a citizen to pay any attention to her.

People were complacent, no that was the wrong word. More like secure. Safe.

Even the few uniformed police she had seen and been careful to pass at a distance were fixated on the eco-protesters. Relying on the technology to do their job. Now even they had gone and Tatsuko attached herself to the back of some protesters walking along the river. She tried to blend into the crowd. They had banners and placards demanding action on the climate. Adults held the hands of little children. Songs alternated with frustrated chanting. It almost had the feel of a festival.

As she got to the road at the mouth of Vauxhall Bridge, she looked left to check for traffic, then remembered that cars came from the opposite direction here. There was a gap in the traffic, but she had to stop herself from crossing and instead joined the queue of protesters waiting at the pedestrian crossing. Her UK

Border Control briefing had included the severe fines she would get for 'endangering herself and other road users' by crossing the road outside of a designated crossing point. She could have crossed with no fine now she didn't have the iTourist, but she didn't want to stand out.

Finally, the lights indicated that it was clear for her to cross, and she followed the stream of protesters who kept religiously inside the alternating black and white painted stripes that marked the crossing. Halfway across, she glanced left again. More blue lights flashed at the opposite side, all heading towards the finish line. So were the protesters.

Were the police all rushing and congregating at her target? How could they have discovered where she was heading? Or were they heading there to corral the protesters?

The crowd continued towards Lambeth Bridge.

Tatsuko followed for a while, then stopped and leant on the wall, both elbows touching the wall and her palms facing in towards her body, hands touching. She still wasn't really used to the feel of the controller. No soft, warmth of flesh, only a hard, cold edge. She pretended to do a tourist long, slow take of the view. Her head was up, but her eyes were on the palm of her controller. Her fingers moved and the game controller's display said: '*Game position – first*'.

Her pulse quickened and she had to trap a scream of excitement from escaping her lips. She kept calm and completed the head turning movement with only the smallest pause. She gazed into the distance.

First place meant everything.

First meant she had overtaken someone. Or had they been caught? Did that explain all the blue lights heading north?

Whichever it is, nothing's going to stop me now, she said to herself.

Lambeth Bridge was very close.

Chapter 62

The fields to the west of Swindon flashed by the window of the high-speed train. Zoe faced forwards and, as always, Clive sat heading backwards. It was like a metaphor for their careers. A metaphor for Clive's life.

She couldn't ignore what was happening to him, but she couldn't put Clive ahead of Mum. She'd shut that down as soon as Clive had said, 'Look, Zoe. About your mum.'

Now she had to get Clive to understand that antagonising Lance wasn't going to help him at work. It was all he had left.

The train's table and glasses of water separated them, as well as age and outlook on most subjects, but she liked Clive. She owed him her life, but there was more to it than that. He was a friend. She needed to give him a talking to about how to get on in the modern police force. Or at least, how not to get sacked.

'Bloody diversity,' Clive moaned. 'It's treating me like a charity case.'

'No, it's not,' Zoe sighed, wishing he would drop the topic. He'd been muttering on about it since leaving Slough.

'There are two big problems with diversity: meritocracy and equality.'

'But diversity brings equality.'

'No. The opposite.' Clive sat up and his eyes came alive as he took Zoe's comments as an invitation to launch into lecture mode again. 'In a truly equal police force, you don't need labels. Each person is just that. A person. With strengths and weaknesses. Chosen on merit. Using the best person for each specific job, and that improves the quality of the police force.'

Zoe looked out of the window again, trying not to encourage him.

'But with diversity, you need labels. Male, female, young, old, black, white, short, tall, and so on. Without labels, you can't separate people into different boxes. You can't measure how many of each type you have, and you can't *prove* to the liberals that you have diversity in the police force. These labels force us to recognise our differences and not focus on the things we have in common. It drives us apart, and the more labels you have, the more fragmented the people become.'

Zoe looked back at Clive. 'Diversity has broken down the barriers and prejudices that affected women, different races, the disabled. All the minorities. It broke the chain of conscious *and* subconscious bias in the selection process.'

'And that's good, but diversity hasn't stopped. In fact, it's getting worse. If you use enough labels, then everyone is a minority. Add even more labels and everyone is an island – a minority of one. It's the ultimate way of destroying a community and making the world only about yourself.'

Clive paused to take a sip of water. 'Think about me being chosen by Lance. It wasn't because I was best, it was diversity. Think about all the other police officers. The system has discriminated in favour of me, and therefore discriminated *against* the others. Any system based on discrimination can't deliver equality.'

'But Lance had to choose you despite his prejudice against you – that proves diversity works,' Zoe said, trying to break Clive's flow. He was doomed if he continued to think this way about the police force.

Clive stared at the table but didn't say anything.

She blew out her cheeks in relief at the silence. Now she could force the conversation back to work, she said, 'It doesn't mean that Cardiff isn't right. I think Lilou is heading to Cardiff, not London.'

'Me too.'

A passenger walked along the gap in the chairs, swaying in time with the train's motion over a bumpy section of track. It set the water in Clive's glass slopping from side to side. Some drops escaped over the top and Clive used his shirt sleeve to wipe the table dry.

Zoe rolled her eyes, reached across the table and slid Clive the tissue that was right next to his elbow. He ignored it.

'We've still got to find her, and Lance refusing to support our request for drones and Uniform backup doesn't help. What did he call it? "Minimal risk",' Clive said.

Zoe pursed her lips, 'Yep, but I got one drone and a couple of Uniforms. There's a lot of water around, but there are still too many approaches to protect.'

'We'll have to do tight patrol laps around the building and hope we get lucky.'

Chapter 63

Ava pulled at the collar of her shirt, but she was still hot. Mercifully, not as hot as in the conference room, but the unmarked van she was in now wasn't far off it.

The van was illegally parked on the pavement off the northern corner of Parliament Square. The statue of George Canning looked down on them. Any traffic wardens circling and ready to earn their commission on the next parking offence, were scared away when they approached the van. The signals of Anti-Terror officers inside the van, scattered them like crows hearing a gun.

Ava's problem was airflow. The three tiny discs rotating on the van's roof were meant to allow the hot air to escape, and the air con should be running lovely cool air inside. That was the theory, but Ava didn't think the system had been designed for four people and the banks of display screens all contributing to the heat. Also, the van's battery had a finite life. They couldn't afford for the battery to run flat and all the monitoring screens to click off just as Tatsuko or Lilou attacked. So, the air con was off and the heat rose.

'Can't we open the doors, Sarge?' Ava asked.

'What and have all the eco-loonies staring in and filming us?' Sergeant Evans said.

Ava looked back at the screens in front of her. She wanted to be outside, and not only to avoid the heat. She wanted the chance to arrest the attackers.

But Lance had assigned her to the van.

'You're too small to tackle anything other than a keyboard,' he had said.

'No way,' she shouted. 'I'm great at wrestling and I've done loads of extra unarmed combat.'

Lance stared at her outburst, mouth hanging open.

'A fight is more about will and technique than size,' she continued. Her will stood at least six foot four, compared to her actual five foot two.

But Lance had waved her protests away, she'd complied with his orders and watched the display from the drone on the north-west corner of the rectangle of the defensive boundary. *Doesn't mean I have to stay in here*, she thought.

Ava had three camera drones to monitor: one looked straight up Birdcage Walk to St James's Park, one looked right along Horse Guards Road and the southern edge of the park. The final drone's camera looked left along the top line of the red rectangle and along Storey's Gate.

The other three officers in the van had their own drones to monitor.

They all sat and stared at the screens. And sweltered.

The logic of the briefing said that the attackers wouldn't be able to get into a self-drive car without an iTourist, so pedestrians were the priority. Ava's central screen had the most pedestrian traffic, and every time the drone's camera software detected motion, its positioning algorithm plotted the movement against the signal in the same location. The image of the motion and the ID of the signal flashed up in one corner of the display and was logged.

If the camera detected movement without a signal, it was meant to generate an alert. They should have been able to relax and wait for the alert, but the movement detection algorithm was too sensitive and generated alerts for squirrels, dogs, cats, and even the 'I am 6' balloon of a little girl holding her mum's hand.

Ava's eyes danced around the screen, hoping to be the one to spot an attacker.

Chapter 64

The Albert Embankment's wide pavements provided a simple route for Tatsuko to follow even if the trees set into the path provided natural obstacles that the crowd had to flow around. Everyone seemed to be reading on their HUDs or typing frantically rather than looking where they were going. *Something big must be going on*, she thought as even the eco-protesters' chants and songs had stopped.

If they were distracted by one of the other gamers getting caught, then she'd be more vulnerable. Her photo could be everywhere. They might be looking at it now.

Tatsuko pulled her baseball cap from her bag and tugged the peak low over her eyes. Lambeth Bridge was ahead, and Big Ben was much closer and bigger. Almost touching distance.

By a bus stop, the pavement started to rise on the right-hand side to take pedestrians up to the bridge. The left side stayed lower and continued under the bridge. Tatsuko watched a red London bus roll over the bridge. It passed in front of her view of Big Ben, seeming to cross halfway up the famous landmark. When the bus reached the middle of the bridge, Tatsuko noticed a black drone hovering over the road.

Was it scanning for her? Would it have facial recognition? Would her hat hide her enough? Could she blend in with the protesters?

She didn't know. She walked to the edge of the road and let the crowd flow past her onto the bridge. She couldn't risk being detected.

Another bus pulled up at the bus stop and people jumped off. Tatsuko stepped up to the back of the queue of people waiting to get on. *The bus might hide me from the drone*, she thought, but as she got closer to the front of the queue, she saw that each person who got on touched a big pad and the bus rewarded them with a chirpy beep. Tatsuko spun away, trying to make it look like a last-minute change of mind.

Westminster Bridge was only a few minutes' walk further on. Better to try there and see before deciding to risk walking under the drone.

***

The finish point was so close now, she could almost touch it. A simple walk across Westminster Bridge, and she would be there. Except that it wasn't a simple walk when a big drone hovered over the road. It looked the same type as the one on Lambeth Bridge.

She was closer to this one and could see that although the drone was hovering over the same spot, it wasn't still. It snapped left and right in small jerky movements. Tatsuko watched the drone for a few seconds. Each time the drone twitched, it was always towards a pedestrian or some other motion. It was hunting.

Too risky. *Move, lazy girl*, her mother demanded.

The next bridge to the north was closer than heading back to Vauxhall which was the last bridge she had seen without a drone.

Worth a try, she thought, and started jogging along the path. She kept her head down and the cap low, but even so, she looped wide around the lines of people waiting to get on the London Eye.

She was heading away from the finish point, and the doubt nagged at her, growing with each step in the wrong direction. Would someone overtake her? Did the police know where she was going?

At Hungerford Bridge, she leant her back against a tree and lifted her head far enough to see the sky. No drone.

She ran up the steps to the bridge, taking them two at a time. Each pump of her legs and arms drove the negativity out of her.

Whatever was happening didn't matter. She needed to get to the finish. Anything blocking her path was a challenge, not a problem.

She would overcome.

Chapter 65

Clive and Zoe's meeting with the head of security at the National Assembly building in Cardiff was short, but not sweet.

'I can't shut the Senedd, see, it's a public building, and if I shut it for every threat level of "Minimal", then we'd never be open.'

'But there's a possible terror threat,' Zoe said.

'If the threat level is "Minimal" they'll never agree.' The head of security crossed his arms. End of meeting.

Zoe and Clive weren't impressed with their plan, but they didn't have enough resources to do any better. They were going to protect the immediate vicinity of the National Assembly building. Most of the south side was protected by the water of Cardiff Bay and they'd sent one Uniform to cover the bridge on Harbour Drive. The east side was more water of Roath Basin and their only other Uniform was on the small bridge at Bute Place.

The two bridges were the only access from about three on a clock all the way round to about seven. That was the good news.

At eleven around to about two o'clock was the Millennium Centre that acted like a huge stone in the river. People had to flow one side or the other.

They'd set their drone to hover and twitch at all the movement between two and three on a clock face. It was a wide spread and to minimise the risk of Lilou slipping through, the drone was hovering close to the Assembly. They wouldn't get much warning.

But they could run.

And hope.

That left the west side to protect and Zoe and Clive stood guard, looking out across the open space of Roald Dahl Plass. The trouble was that people could walk around the Plass on the walkways next to the water. The walkways were lower than the pavement and their approach would be hidden.

It was impossible.

Zoe was in constant motion, tracking between the Plass and the walkways. Knowing that she was going to have to be lucky to spot Lilou.

She didn't feel lucky.

The hours ticked by and Zoe's legs and feet were starting to demand a rest.

Her next loop into the Plass coincided with a loop of Clive's. They rested against the red brick mass of the Pierhead building. The horses of the carousel inched around and around, transporting smiling children. People strolled past eating zero-sugar ice creams. It all felt so normal.

'Any sign?' Clive asked.

Zoe shook her head. 'It's impossible. We're too close to the building and there are so many people around.'

'Nothing else we can do. If we're further out, it'd be easier for Lilou to slip through a gap.'

'Do you think any of the groups who have claimed responsibility for the Stormont attack were really behind it?' Zoe asked.

'I don't know. Politics and religion have killed a massive amount of people over history. It could be the Ultras, but the Church preaches peace and a reduction in consumption. Bombs could frighten enough people, but then again, politicians love fear. Makes it easier to drive up their security budgets and pass tighter controls.'

'Let's focus on motive when we've got Lilou,' Zoe said. She checked with the two Uniforms. Nothing. The drone. Nothing.

As Zoe resumed her patrol. The sun came out from behind a small cloud. She heard laughter and carousel music. Pleasure boats chugged away from the quay. A normal day.

Was Lance right all along? Were they in the wrong place?

Chapter 66

'Shit, there are drones everywhere,' Tatsuko muttered.

She had seen one as she came south along the river on Victoria Embankment. She had skipped west along Derby Gate and onto Parliament Street, but another drone twitched about at the end of the road.

She turned west again, along King Charles Street all the way to the end of the road and the edge of St James's Park.

'Thank you,' she said. No drone on Horse Guards Road, but when Tatsuko got to the corner of Great George Street, she could see another one hovering in the distance. Blocking her route.

How long does the battery in a drone last? she asked herself. No idea, but they were busy things with all the darting and twitching. All the cameras and propellers – they would run the power usage up and the battery down. She walked backwards up Birdcage Walk until she was past the small building and the gates, and could lean against a tree on the edge of the park. She could see the drone, but it didn't see her. Its attention was focused on the motion in front of it.

Pulling her rucksack off, she scrambled her hand around for the last fragment of food. She'd save her last two mouthfuls of water for the end.

She put both hands in her rucksack to hide what she was doing and peered in. Her game controller's display said: *'Game position – first'*. She smiled, whoever was still in the game was behind her.

Pulling at a finger, the controller's display changed: *'Distance to finish – 0.2 miles'*.

She could run that in less than a minute if she went 'all in' and left nothing in the tank.

When the battery on the drone went, she would seize the moment and run. Tatsuko knew she could dodge and weave past the people and any police, skip across the green of

Parliament Square and get to the finish point. It wouldn't matter if they arrested her then.

She would have won.

**

After about half an hour, Tatsuko's pulse ratcheted up. She was sure the drone's twitches were a tiny bit slower.

She watched the drone with the intensity of a bird of prey following a mouse, turning the tables on the drone. Waiting for her chance.

'Yes,' she muttered when the movements were visibly slower and smoother. She took the last two mouthfuls of the water and put the bottle in the rucksack, which she dropped next to the tree. She didn't need it, and anything that might slow her down she could lose.

She started walking towards the drone, tentative steps at first. The drone was going, turning away and flying off. She increased her speed. It was her chance, the route to the finish was open.

Time to go.

Her mother's voice told her, *Run, lazy girl* and pushed her on.

An angry buzz of propellers filled the road behind her. She looked up as a dark shape flashed above her. A replacement drone had caught her motion. Why hadn't she thought of that?

A voice barked from the drone, 'Police! Tatsuko, stop.'

There was no point stopping, not this close. If she turned and tried to run away, the drone would track her. No escape. Game over. Literally.

Better to give it everything. One last charge.

Tatsuko ran harder, accelerating, taking to the middle of the road to avoid the people on the path.

The drone chased after her, inches from her head, like an angry wasp.

Chapter 67

Ava looked at her display as it flicked from person to person. No sign of Lilou or Tatsuko. The status bar at the bottom of the screen showed only one bar left on the drone's battery.

No problem, she thought. Lance had commandeered nearly every drone and the backups were all on charge in Green Park to the west.

Ava clicked a message to request a replacement and got an instant confirmation. As her new drone crossed over the top of St James's Park, she added it to her display.

When it reached the end of Great George Street its display locked onto a figure running alongside the road. Ava glanced at the display to check the iMe signal of the runner. *'Scanning'* the display said and then flashed red. Not a false alarm this time.

Ava couldn't see the runner's face, but the hair under the baseball cap looked like Tatsuko's. Then, as the drone caught up with the runner, she twisted her face to look at the drone.

It was her.

Ava pressed a button on the display to enable her voice to be projected from the drone. 'Police! Tatsuko, stop,' she shouted.

The runner paused for a fraction and then accelerated. The image from the drone's camera zoomed in on Tatsuko's head as the drone caught up with her and buzzed her.

Tatsuko kept running and Ava hit the alert button. The inside of the van reverberated with the sound of a klaxon-like alarm.

'Bloody 'ell,' one the other officers shouted, clamping his hands on his ears.

Ava rolled her eyes, it wasn't loud enough to make that much fuss, but she grabbed on a dial and spun it to lower the volume.

The alert would have flash-messaged the team. She knew Lance would be watching the same footage now and she stared at the screen, but the drone was too close to Tatsuko to get a good view of what was happening. Ava jumped up and banged open the door to the van.

'Orders are to stay inside,' the officer who had complained about the volume said.

Ava landed outside the van, poised and in perfect balance. 'Do that then,' she said without turning, and swung her left arm to slam the door shut.

She stepped from behind the van to see two Uniforms standing side by side on Great George Street facing the oncoming runner. The drone was millimetres behind her.

'Shit,' Ava said. She had played enough sport to see it, even if the Uniforms didn't.

Tatsuko's run curved away from the Uniforms and they followed her, but it opened up a gap on the inside.

Running back away from the Uniforms towards Parliament Square Garden to provide a defensive cover, Ava jumped up the two small steps and stood on the grass.

Two more Uniforms ran up the left of Great George Street, looking like they had seen the hole.

Tatsuko was nearly at the first two Uniforms when she cut hard to her right. The Uniforms were moving too fast to react. They couldn't adjust to stop her, and one of them flailed a desperate hand at Tatsuko as she flashed past.

Ava jogged away from Tatsuko and towards the centre of the grass, all the time tracking Tatsuko with her eyes, calculating Tatsuko's most likely approach.

Tatsuko reached the other Uniforms. There was no room to repeat her sidestep move, but she jumped forwards, sending her feet ahead of her, her legs sliding along the road. She timed it to perfection and slid through the gap between the legs of the two Uniforms.

In one seamless move, she was back onto her feet and past the Uniforms who rubber-necked backwards at the disappearing Tatsuko.

Tatsuko shot past the van Ava had been in and over the road. Heading across the grass towards Parliament.

Towards Ava.

Ava rolled her head in a brisk circle to stretch out her neck and rolled her shoulders. 'Come to Ava,' she said as Tatsuko barrelled towards her.

Tatsuko didn't pause, clearly thinking that her height and weight advantage over Ava plus the momentum would burst straight through her.

Ava bent her knees a little, one foot in front of the other and opened her arms, ready to accept her prize.

She saw Tatsuko's eyes flare in surprise, but she didn't falter. Instead, she dipped her shoulder and charged.

Ava waited and then lunged forward. Low and hard.

Tatsuko slammed into her with the hard slap of impact and the sound of two sets of lungs having the air knocked out of them. She didn't fight Tatsuko's weight and momentum. Instead, as they hit, she absorbed the impact, rolling lower and twisting so that Tatsuko's upper body came past her. Ava's arms circled and closed around Tatsuko's hips, dropping lower as her momentum continued. Closing and dropping until they passed Tatsuko's knees.

Ava locked her arms tight.

Tatsuko tried for her next forward pace but her leg was caught by Ava and didn't move far enough. Now the momentum was against Tatsuko as she overbalanced. Arms windmilling but nothing could defeat gravity and physics.

Tatsuko smacked face-first into the ground and slid to a stop on the grass.

Ava heard cheers and feet running towards her, but she held on tight.

Chapter 68

Serge ignored the Seine rolling by outside his window and watched his computer.

The dot on the screen showed Tatsuko's run towards the finish point. She was three hundred metres from the finish, then two hundred and fifty. She must be sprinting to go that fast. The dot drifted left before cutting hard back to the right. It slowed near the corner of Parliament Square and then accelerated.

The dot travelled fast across Parliament Square Garden then stopped abruptly in the centre, as if Tatsuko had run into a brick wall.

He watched, but the dot didn't move.

'Merde,' he said, and flicked to another window that showed trending social media posts. The top tag was *#TinyCopTakedown*.

Serge clicked on the tag and then on a video that came up.

The footage was taken from the edge of the Parliament Square Garden and tracked Tatsuko running hard and straight at a small, blonde woman. It was a complete mismatch. Tatsuko had height, weight and speed on her side. The little woman didn't stand a chance, but as the video rolled forward, Serge let out a whistle as the little woman took the hit and spun, sliding down Tatsuko's body before grabbing her legs. He let out an involuntary wince as he watched her face hit the grass.

He clicked off the video when he saw the crowds of Uniforms and passers-by running to get a better view.

'C'est la vie,' Serge said. 'Close, but not a winner.' She hadn't got to the steps of Parliament, but Parliament Square was close enough.

As he had done when Sully's game controller was in the military building, Serge went back to his Game Control window. He clicked on the dot where Tatsuko still lay. He selected the *'Lock Controller'* option.

Serge moved the mouse and clicked on the menu. He chose the *Retire player* option, then selected the reason as *Player arrested*.

A message box popped up asking him if he was sure.

He was sure.

He pressed *Yes*.

Chapter 69

Ava caught her breath and started to release her grip, but as soon as she did, Tatsuko began wriggling and trying to break free.

'Stop,' Ava called, but Tatsuko kept struggling, trying to get away.

Ava held on tight but pulled her knees up under her. 'Here goes,' she thought, and released her grip at the same time she pushed forward with her feet and spread her arms. Ava shot forward and landed on Tatsuko's back before she had a chance to get more than a couple of inches off the ground.

Ava grabbed at Tatsuko's arms and yanked hard. First the left and then the right pinning them palm up on her back. She placed her knee in the small of Tatsuko's back to keep her down and fished one-handed in a pocket. She pulled out a large cable tie that she looped around Tatsuko's wrists and pulled tight.

The cable tie's zipping shrill stopped when it bit into the flesh of Tatsuko's right wrist and her unyielding left.

Ava wriggled her body so that her knees were on either side of Tatsuko and she sat on her back. She held on to Tatsuko's hand as she blew a stray strand of hair away from her face.

Heavy feet and jagged breathing reached Ava's side. 'Need any help?' came a voice.

Ava looked up at one of the Uniforms who had let Tatsuko get past so easily.

'Not from you.'

She smiled at the ring of faces around her.

'Awesome take-down, dude,' someone said, and her smile widened.

Ava froze when she felt something warm on the top of her leg. Tatsuko's game controller was flashing red and was getting hotter.

'Fuck,' she said.

'Run!' she screamed. 'Run now.'

They frowned but stayed put.

She stared at the Uniform. 'Get these people away from here. NOW.'

The Uniforms turned and started to shoo the people.

Too slow.

'Bomb,' Ava shouted, and the crowd scattered, desperate to get away. Not caring if they knocked someone else flying in the process.

'What bomb?' Tatsuko said.

Dreading what the display would say, Ava looked down at Tatsuko's game controller.

She gasped when she read the display: '00:09'.

No time to get help.

She pulled and tugged at the controller, but it wouldn't move.

She jumped off Tatsuko and looked at the backs of the fleeing crowd.

Tatsuko seized her opportunity and clambered to her feet. Awkward with her hands tied behind her back, she started running towards the Parliament building. Towards the crowds.

Ava looked towards her van and safety, and then back towards the running Tatsuko. Her life versus all those in the crowd.

She sprinted after Tatsuko. She caught her easily and landed on her back.

Tatsuko face-planted into the grass for the second time.

'Run,' Ava screamed at the crowds and this time they did as she told them, but they were still close.

'I'm not a lazy girl,' Tatsuko said as she struggled to get up.

Ava pushed down, covering Tatsuko's hands with her body and closing her eyes. So many things she would never do or see.

'Love you, Mum. Love you, Dad,' she said.

Chapter 70

The woman in the farm van hadn't tried to climb down to see where Lilou was hiding in the bushes. Long, long minutes dragged by before Lilou heard footsteps and a car moving.

She released a long breath and forced the muscles in her shoulders and neck to relax. Reaching along her leg, the first gentle touches found some swelling. Not good, but as she pressed harder the pain didn't explode. It hurt but was bearable.

She explored her foot, fearing one of the many bones was broken. She knew them well, especially from the beginning of her parkour. So many falls, so many twists, and even a broken metatarsal bone. The doctor had shrugged when he saw the X-ray and said, 'Rest.' She had rested, bored and fidgety until the swelling dropped enough to get her foot in her shoe.

Then it was about ignoring the pain. Determination and time got her through.

Now her foot didn't feel that bad, probably only a twisted ankle, but no way was she going to take her shoe off in case it wouldn't go back on.

She pushed herself up, wobbling on the slippery ground as she took all her weight on her right foot. She touched her left foot onto the ground, as gently as a feather landing. She shifted a little weight onto her left side, then a little more.

Pain and discomfort, sure. But she was still in the game.

In the shelter of the bushes, she checked her game controller. *'Game position – second'.*

'How?' she said, as deep lines rippled across her forehead. She had overtaken someone while hiding in a bush.

They must have been caught. She hoped it was Sully.

***

Over the hours of walking, her ankle had eased. The trick was to keep moving. Every stop stiffened it up, and then she had to push through the pain to get it moving again.

She was in Cardiff now, less than a mile to go. The few pedestrians she saw all seemed agitated, fingers waving frantically in front of their faces. Lilou stopped and looked in a shop window as a man walked past her. 'You seen the video? That cop sacrificed herself.'

Lilou's sense of isolation deepened. All she had was this controller and it had no news or connectivity that she could use. She walked on, but her feet seemed heavier. How was she in second place when she was walking so slowly? The elation she expected at being so close to the finish was missing. She was frowning, not smiling.

Her frown deepened when she stopped in a small alleyway and checked her game controller. *'Game position – first'.*

There's no way I should be winning, she thought. Unless she was the last survivor in the game.

She walked on and turned into Pierhead Street. As the road swung around a gentle curve, it straightened and Lilou's view opened up. She could see straight along the road to the red tower of the Pierhead building itself.

She spun and looked into another shop as a young woman came out of the shop dragging a toddler by the hand. 'Come on, we need to get home and safe.'

Safe? Lilou thought.

Then all thought disappeared. Lilou was mesmerised by a small square of a display wall inside the shop.

The screen showed a figure running across some grass. Grand buildings in the background.

Tatsuko running.

At least this video might explain why she was now winning.

Lilou read the caption at the bottom of the screen: *'Terror attack outside Parliament'.* She wasn't sure if the caption was a breaking story or somehow about Tatsuko.

Lilou's eyes flicked up. Her competitor ran on, straight at a small woman. Tatsuko tried to run through her but crashed to the floor. That seemed to be all the excitement in the video, but then all the heat drained out of Lilou, like water flowing down rapids.

As the video continued, the people around Tatsuko scattered and ran. Panicked eyes and screams. The small woman caught Tatsuko again and held her down.

Lilou's knees caved and buckled at the flash of white and the crack of the explosion.

She was still struggling to process what her eyes were telling her when the image changed, and the caption read '*Attack linked to Stormont*'.

Lilou's hand clamped over her mouth. Sobs followed as she watched Femi on his knees as his controller exploded.

She forced herself up and stumbled along the road like an early morning drunk.

Femi's hand exploded – his controller exploded! Two explosions couldn't be a coincidence.

She was meant to be in a game, but they were calling it a terror attack.

She couldn't be part of this. There were people around her, on the road, in offices.

Lilou walked on, trying to see someone to surrender to, but like everywhere, there weren't any police around.

Her hand fell to her controller and she touched the release mechanism and twisted the controller off. She didn't know what to do with it. She couldn't leave it for a child to find.

She saw a small dot hovering above the junction at the end of the road. A drone. That had to be official.

She headed forward and as she got close, the drone twitched and rotated towards her.

Lilou stood still and waited as the drone seemed to recognise her and swooped down.

Chapter 71

Zoe screamed at Clive. 'The drone's got her. She's not running.'

Zoe spun from the carousel and sprinted, losing sight of Clive as she passed the Pierhead building. Clive had been patrolling right by the building, and Zoe could see him ahead of her now. His run was ungainly, but he was making progress.

Zoe was quicker.

She drew level with Clive. He was running and talking on his HUD, struggling to be understood with all his panting. Zoe flashed him a smile. Clive groaned, and flapped a hand to grab her. He missed and tried to go faster.

Zoe could see the drone ahead of her. Lilou stood underneath it, waving her left arm. It was missing a hand. Luckily the few pedestrians who saw Zoe running, turned and ran in the opposite direction.

'I never… I didn't know,' Lilou said as Zoe stopped in front of her.

Zoe took a couple of big breaths and looked at Lilou's truncated left arm. A small connector poked from the end.

Lilou's game controller balanced in her right hand. Her legs were shaking and her eyes wide open.

A car pulled up to a stop and the door opened.

'No. Go, go!' Zoe shouted at the car, trying to get the car's passengers safe, not realising that it was empty.

She heard Clive's ragged breathing right behind her, but instead of stopping he snatched the game controller from Lilou's hand and jumped into the car. Zoe took a step forward. 'Clive, no.'

Clive turned to her and shook his head and waved her away. He started talking and the car's door slid shut.

The car headed away.

She could see Clive staring back at her, clutching the bomb.

Chapter 72

Serge watched the dot on the screen, trying to work out what Lilou was doing.

She wasn't moving and she had detached her hand. She'd done it a few times but doing it while standing so close to the target didn't make sense.

Maybe she was waiting for a gap to make the final charge? Maybe.

The dot started moving again and Serge rocked forward in his chair.

It was too fast for a pedestrian. Sully had been in a car nearly all the time, but why would Lilou do it now?

She wouldn't. And not to move away from the finish.

In his Game Control window, he clicked on the last remaining dot then moved the mouse and clicked on the menu. He chose the *'Retire player'* option, then selected *'Player arrested'*.

The same message box popped up asking him if he was sure.

He pressed *'Yes'*.

Collateral damage was simply a part of the game.

Chapter 73

The tsunami wave of #TinyCopTakedown messages had swamped Clive's HUD as he paced around the Plass, scanning for Lilou. They picked him up and swept him away. Each new message battered him and sent him under the water.

Worse was the truth that grabbed him like a savage current and sucked him down.

He had saved Zoe, but failed Ava.

Down.

He had encouraged Ava to come out of her shell.

If she had stayed timid, she'd have stayed in the van.

Deeper.

She'd still be alive.

Clive's knees gave way and he dropped to the pavement.

Her death was his fault.

It grasped him, weighed on him like a huge ball of concrete. Too heavy to carry, it crushed him.

***

Eventually, Clive's brain began to win the battle with his guilt. More immediate thoughts took hold. There could be no more deaths. He had to stop Lilou.

Was this bravery or a coward trying to avoid more failure and guilt? He couldn't decide, but the motivation didn't matter. He forced himself to rewatch the footage with a logical detective's eye. Tatsuko's explosion was too soon after she was caught for there to be any chance to safely disarm Lilou's controller. Then the drone messaged that it had Lilou standing below it. The news jolted him into action. He ran. It was up to him. There was only one way that gave any hope.

Now, as the car rolled away, Clive could see Zoe's face. She looked distraught, mouthing a long, silent 'No'. He couldn't tell Zoe what he was going to do. She would have tried to protect him. She would have grabbed the bomb herself. He couldn't let that happen. He couldn't carry Zoe's death as well.

An idea flashed into his mind as he ran: a simple journey of only a 0.1 of a mile. He could run it, but a car would be quicker. He hoped that if it wasn't quick enough, then at least the structure of the car might absorb some of the blast.

Only now he was in the flimsy car, did he worry about flying shrapnel after the explosion. Too late – he was committed, so he forced his head clear of everything else and focused on the logistics. It didn't work. All he could see was Ava's face.

Shoving the heel of his palm at his face, he scoured the tears from his cheek. 'Focus,' he muttered.

The car was limited to 20mph in town, so ten miles in thirty minutes, one mile in three. 0.3 of a mile in one minute. That meant his 0.1 of a mile would take a third of a minute. Twenty seconds, then he still had to get out of the car and get rid of the bomb.

Too long, he thought and looked at the controller, wishing for hardware failures, lazy programmers and buggy code.

The other three had all exploded, so he wasn't holding out much hope.

Traditional churches and religion held no power for him, and it seemed hypocritical to start praying to a god he didn't believe in. What did he believe in? Only one thing. So he looked to the sky and chanted the prayer from an old Mayan legend that had always worked for him in the past.

'Ixcacao, Goddess of Chocolate, see my tears and come to my aid.'

He allowed a second for divine intervention, but even Ixcacao failed him now and the game controller started to flash red and get hot.

His breathing had been jagged from running when he got in the car, but now his pulse spiked and he gasped out hard, short panting breaths.

His hands started to tremble, and his knee jigged up and down.

Oh shit, oh shit, spun around in his head. Was this really his end? Would he meet Ava again so soon?

He glanced up and looked out of the car window. He was close but was it enough time?

The display in the palm of the controller started counting down.

Clive's knee jigged up and down faster.

The car stopped and said happily, 'You have reached your destination.'

The door seemed to take a lifetime to open on slow electric motors designed to prevent a door flying open and hitting someone. Clive scrambled out when the door was still only half open.

He still had to cross the twenty odd yards of the walkway before he could get to the Roath Basin.

The Uniform guarding the bridge turned and looked, not sure how he could help.

The display on the controller hit *'00:04'.*

Clive dithered but time seemed to slow as he tried deciding between his original plan or throwing the hand into the car and hoping.

He visualised bits of the car flying through the air. He didn't know enough about cars or explosives to make the right choice.

He could lie on the bomb like Ava. Go out a hero, but the idea grated. Ava was a true hero. She had willingly given her life to save people when she had so much ahead of her. He would be giving up on life. He'd be saying that it was too much for him. He'd be the shrapnel, but it would be suicide, not a sacrifice. It would devalue Ava's memory.

So, he ran, letting his right arm pull back. Like a javelin thrower, except he didn't want a high arcing throw. More a hard and flat chuck, but with no risk of the hand kissing the water and bouncing up like the skimming stones he had thrown as a kid.

He bunched the muscles in his shoulder, still yards from the water, and threw.

'Down,' he shouted and launched himself for the hard slabs on the walkway.

Clive was still airborne when the controller completed its descent, scraping over the edge of the dock before it hit the water.

He hadn't got any real distance in the throw. Not even close to where he hoped for.

Clive heard the controller explode and tensed his body, hoping that whatever came his way would miss.

But the weak throw meant that the controller was close to the concrete of the wall at the edge of the water. The wall took most of the explosion.

A jet of water was forced up and over the wall. All the harder, sharper shrapnel bounced off the wall and ricocheted back into the basin.

A shock of cold water landed on Clive.

He rolled onto his back.

Water, he could deal with.

Ava's face flashed before him, he screwed his eyes shut, but could still see her body as she covered Tatsuko in calm acceptance.

The flash of white.

Someone had to pay.

Part 3

Aftermath

Chapter 74

Clive and Zoe couldn't risk taking Lilou to London on the train. They decided that a car was the quickest, simplest option that also provided a degree of physical confinement.

Zoe sat next to Clive, with Lilou opposite. One end of the handcuffs was shackled around her right hand. With no left hand, the other end of the handcuffs was closed around the fabric of the seat belt. It allowed her a little freedom of movement for the long journey and prevented any attempt at escape.

Zoe didn't like travelling backwards, but Clive had pushed Lilou in first and chosen his habitual direction of travel. Zoe tried to ignore it.

The car moved off and turned the corner. Zoe shifted in her seat to see where they were going, her shoulder and leg brushing against Clive. Water from his shirt and trousers happily jumped across to hers. She looked down at the two damp patches.

'No offence, Boss,' she said, unclipping her seat belt. One of the car's sensors reported the seat belt coming out of its clasp. The car's processor saw that the seat had an iMe signal on it. The programming told the car to report the breach, so it set an alarm off and stopped. 'All passengers must wear a seat belt,' it said.

Zoe half-stood, constrained by the height of the roof of the car, and completed a distorted Quasimodo-like transfer to the seat next to Lilou. The car restarted when her seat belt clicked home.

Lilou remained frozen in her seat. The shock had leached all the colour from her. Zoe studied her, trying to get a sense of this gamer, but it was like looking at a plaster statue in a museum.

Clive's clothes were beginning to steam gently as the heater in the car circulated air. Despite the heat, he shivered. 'My bomb disposal technique was a million miles from the heroic throw I'd imagined,' he said. 'I was lucky.' A shudder rippled through him and his eyes fixed on something in the distance.

The moisture in the air condensed onto the inside of the car windows giving it a damp, laundry room smell, but with a sickly undertone.

Mud from the water, Zoe decided, and shut her mind to any other possible sources of the smell.

'Lilou,' she said with a gentle tone, leaving Clive to his thoughts.

Lilou seemed to wake and her eyes moved, and her head turned a few degrees. She looked like a robot restarting after a recharge – still not fully conscious. She blinked a couple of times and seemed to start breathing again.

'It was a game. Like all the others I've played... not... not,' she said. 'I had a bomb on my arm all along.' Lilou shuddered and tears pooled in the corners of her eyes. 'Are the other players all dead?' She rocked her head back and forth.

'Sully's alive,' Zoe said, thinking this would help her, but he saw Lilou's forehead furrow.

'Why him?'

Zoe explained how Sully had cheated by using a friend.

'Typical,' Lilou said. 'That must be how he won the first trial.'

'His hand killed six scientists,' Zoe said.

Lilou gasped and her hand moved like it would cover her mouth, but the seat belt and handcuff made for a slow, jerky movement. Her hand got there eventually.

'Eleven dead in total, and a few bystanders with injuries from flying fragments,' Zoe said.

'Including Ava,' Clive said with a harder edge in his voice than Zoe used.

Lilou shook her head again before dropping her hand. Her head dropped as well, and Zoe could hear sniffling. Teardrops fell and made small dots on the legs of Lilou's trousers.

'I'd played their games before. Never anything like this,' she said quietly, and then her head snapped up. Her wild, pleading eyes shot between Zoe and Clive. 'You must believe me. I never knew.' Her eyes continued their pleading of her innocence, then with a smaller voice, she said, 'A game. The greatest game ever. And the prizes were enormous. The BST hand and all that money.'

'Was that why you did it?'

'Yes, but also the challenge. Parkour is fun, but not like winning a gold medal at the Olympics. The game was the same level of challenge.' She looked at her left wrist. 'Maybe more.'

'Tell us,' Zoe prompted, and Lilou talked them through the meeting in Rouen, the selection and her time in the UK.

'Were you ever meant to finish in London?' Zoe asked.

'No.'

Zoe glanced at Clive. Clive had been right, so much for Lance's certainty, she thought.

If they were going to get any further with the case, they needed to trace Serge. Sully hadn't been any help. All he had done was shrug and say, 'A man. I don't know – an old, scruffy smoker. I didn't pay attention to him.'

'Could you describe Serge in detail, Lilou?' Zoe asked, and held her breath. This was their only lead.

'Yes,' was all Lilou said, but Zoe could see certainty in her eyes. 'I'll do anything to help find him. He needs to pay for what he's done to those people.'

Zoe moved her hand in an iMe hand dance, and then her HUD appeared on the car's display screen.

At the top of the screen was the title: *FaceFit v4.7*. The rest of the screen was blank.

'Start... Suspect... Serge... Unknown family name.'

The title changed to: *FaceFit v4.7: Suspect: Serge, <no name>'* and the main area of the screen redrew to show four yellow, generic faces. Each face was a different shape. An arrow to the right of the screen showed that there were more choices.

Zoe looked at Lilou. 'You scroll by swiping with a finger. Select one by double-tapping and zoom in and out with a pinching movement.'

Lilou nodded and sat forward in her chair. She moved her hand, but the seat belt's inertia mechanism caught and held her hand away from the screen.

Zoe looked at Clive. His eyes were back inside the car, but it looked he was in deep shadows. He nodded his agreement.

She unlocked the handcuff from Lilou's wrist. The handcuffs slid down the seat belt and settled in Lilou's lap.

Zoe watched as Lilou scrolled back and forth through the face shapes before settling on one. 'This is closest. But it's not perfect.'

'That's OK. Once you've gone through all the options then you can adjust it,' Zoe said. 'Select it for now if that's the closest.'

Lilou did and the screen redrew with a choice of hairstyles.

She chose one, and then did the same for age, eye shape, eye colour, skin tone, nose shape, ear size and all the other possible facial features.

At the end of her selections, a man with a long, thin face and a shock of grey hair stared out of the screen. Lilou said, 'More or less – that's him. It's not perfect.'

Zoe's hand moved as she took control of her HUD. She moved the cursor and clicked a button on the side of the screen that looked like a small, blue cog.

A calm, patient voice came through the car's speakers. 'What adjustments would you like to make?'

'Tell it and it will change the face,' Zoe said.

Lilou stared at the face and said, 'Older. Iller.'

'What illness?' the voice said.

'I don't know, but he smoked a lot and coughed.'

'High probability of asthma or lung cancer. Adjusting,' the software said.

The colour of the face on the screen changed from a healthier pinky glow to a drawn, grey pallor. The eyes sagged and dark smudges appeared under the eyes.

'Iller,' Lilou said.

Zoe sat back in her seat as Lilou talked the FaceFit software through all the subtle changes to the face on the screen.

'Any other changes?' the voice said.

'No. That's him,' Lilou said.

***

Clive typed out a message on his HUD, and then went back and corrected all his typing errors. Some were the result of 'fat fingers' – his careless aim on the airborne keyboard, others were the result of his terrible spelling and reliance on the spelling checker.

He read through the message: 'Urgent assistance required in tracing male, late fifties or early sixties. Known as Serge. FaceFit attached.'

He searched through the international directory of police contacts, narrowing his search to France and then Rouen. He found the entry for an Inspector Bisset, selected the name and pressed send.

Clive's Buddy rolled out a message banner almost immediately.

That was quick, Clive thought and opened the message.

'Thank you for contacting Inspector Bisset. Requests from the UK are routed via our External Foreign Police Forces Department. Issues that relate directly to Pan-European members are given priority. Your request will be given due consideration and if you do not have a reply within five working days, please contact us again.'

'Thanks for nothing,' Clive said.

Chapter 75

Zoe sat beside Clive in the conference room in the New Scotland Yard office opposite Bhatt and Lance.

The damp patches on her clothes had dried, but had left thin, dark, jagged rings at the edge of their existence. Clive had stopped steaming, and his suit had a brittle, crisp look to it. He emitted an odour that reminded Zoe of a trip to a farm as a kid. They hadn't wanted to break the journey for clean clothes. Too important a case. Too much risk of Lilou trying to escape.

Not that she had tried. She seemed as determined as them to find Serge. She was in an interview room somewhere below them, answering Lance's team's questions.

Bhatt beamed. 'Congratulations you two. Excellent work.'

Lance was frowning and looking into the distance, like he was trying to detach himself from Bhatt's words.

'Clive, taking the hand like that was reckless and stupid,' Bhatt continued. Then with a soft shake of her head, 'And very brave.'

Clive gave a dismissive shrug and his leg started jiggling under the table. Zoe reached over and touched him on the shoulder to comfort him. His hands had shaken most of the journey back to London and he still seemed like he was somewhere else. Thinking about something else. Someone else.

Zoe pulled her hand away, remembering the water that had drenched him and wiped her hand on her trousers. Everything would be straight in the clothes processor when she got home.

'Don't you agree, Lance?' Bhatt said.

Lance shifted in his seat. 'Sure, yeah. Of course. London was the obvious target and I'm glad that I sent these two to Wales. Important to cover all the possibilities on a case like this.'

Zoe couldn't believe Lance's blatant twist on reality, but he was too many ranks above her to challenge him. Clive didn't even seem to notice.

As Bhatt looked at Lance, Zoe thought there was a cold, assessing glare in Bhatt's eyes, like her bullshit detector had flashed red.

Zoe allowed herself a small smile. *Bhatt has the measure of Lance.*

'Clive,' Bhatt said softly, but he didn't respond so Zoe risked another gentle touch on his shoulder.

'Boss.'

Clive seemed to become aware of the room and his eyes focused on Zoe, then Bhatt.

'Clive, Zoe told me that you blame yourself for Ava, but you mustn't. She was unbelievably brave and saved lives. It was her decision. We'll all miss her, but it wasn't your fault.'

Clive dropped his head but said nothing.

When he looked up again, he said, 'We need to find the bastards behind the attack. They need to pay for what they did to Ava.'

'I agree,' Bhatt said. 'Give me ideas.'

'It's a state-sponsored terror attack from a foreign power trying to destabilise the country. We've had lots of groups claiming responsibility,' Lance said.

'Any look like they actually did it?' Bhatt asked.

'Nothing yet, ma'am.'

Zoe noticed Clive's leg was jiggling again, and the shake was back in his hands. He slid his hands under the desk. Must be delayed shock, Zoe thought.

'Ma'am?' Zoe said, hesitant to venture too much unsolicited.

'What is it?'

'Um,' Zoe said. 'Clive and I were watching the news streams in the car on the way back to London.'

'And.'

'Obviously lots of people were talking about the explosions. They might have more local motives for the attacks.'

'Really?' Lance said with a dismissive sneer. 'You need serious clout to put this attack together.'

'Sure,' Clive said with a crack in his voice. 'But you need something to gain from it. Otherwise, it's pointless.'

'Terror attacks are,' Lance said, keeping the sneer in his voice strong. 'They want to prove they have the capability to hit hard at the centre of us. Try and scare us.'

'Clive and I discussed some other possibilities,' Zoe offered.

Lance let out a half-laugh, but Bhatt said, 'Go on.'

'The Church of the New Modelists have seen a surge of new members since the attacks started. Lots of people are deserting the traditional faiths because they feel that they're not relevant to modern life.'

'That's a cult not a church,' Lance said.

'That's more reason it could be them. Their Ultras have a hard edge to them,' Clive said.

'And Issac Townsend was talking about a new political arm on the news today,' Zoe added.

'Not very likely,' Lance said. 'Load of nutcases. Anyway, the Model doesn't like risks and they live by the Model.'

'The Model controls their risks. Not foreigners. So, they could have used foreigners to do their dirty work,' Clive said.

But Lance was shaking his head. 'You got anything better than that?'

'Climate catastrophe protesters,' Zoe said. 'They're everywhere at the moment.'

'But they're all liberal do-gooders,' Lance said.

'And all the protests have been very peaceful,' Bhatt added.

'There were lots of interviews with protesters fed up with the empty promises of a government claiming to focus on climate change and then doing nothing.'

'Don't think so,' Lance said.

'You don't think that a few protesters might consider that eleven lives lost now is a fair price to save the planet?' Zoe said. 'Your generation has done nothing but damage the planet. You've done nothing to save my generation's future.' She ended with emphasis, worrying she had gone too far. But it was true.

Lots of talk and promises, but no change. It might already be too late to save the planet. What about any children Zoe might have? *What sort of world would they live in? If any?*

Bhatt and Lance looked at Zoe.

'I don't like your tone, Zoe,' Bhatt said. 'But I hear your point.'

Lance scoffed next to her.

'Then there's iMe,' Clive said.

'Oh, here we go.' Lance laughed. 'Enter the inevitable government conspiracy theory – from the anti-iMe detective.'

Clive shrugged. 'Doesn't stop it being a possibility. The Ministry of Well-being and Health are already calling for more powers to counter the threat and add new functions to the iTourist. They're asking for more iMe controls as well. It wouldn't be the first time that a government department was behind domestic violence and used the public's fear to increase their own budget and power.'

'Look, Lussac,' Lance said. 'I deal with cyber attacks from foreign governments every day. They're always probing and looking for weakness. That's where we need to focus.'

'You got any evidence?' Clive asked, but Lance flicked a dismissive hand in Clive's direction.

'Run along home and change out of that stinky suit and leave the thinking to the grown-ups. You too, Jordan.'

Chapter 76

Lance had given Zoe a disinterested 'whatever' when she asked if it was OK to work from the PCU office today. 'The real terrorists are abroad, not in Slough,' he had added.

Bhatt was more supportive and had messaged: 'I need to show my support for Lance in his Cyber Terrorism work, but I've been thinking about your suggestions. They have merit. Carry on digging.'

Now, Clive and Zoe were perched on the edges of the corral of desks in the PCU office.

'You're still a scruffy mess, Boss,' Zoe sighed.

Clive had stuffed his suit in the clothes processor when he got home but forgotten to take it out when the buzzer sounded. It should have been nice and clean, and crisp, but instead his suit wore stubborn creases that had refused to fall out with wearing.

Clive shrugged. 'I'm an old dog and that clothes processor is definitely a new trick.' He looked at the display wall in the PCU office, which was connected to Zoe's HUD and had one word on it: *Serge*.

Clive could still feel Ava's presence in the room, a sweet, little voice saying, *Find them, Clive*. The voice changed and became hard and demanding. *Don't let my death be in vain*.

He owed it to Ava. He couldn't fail, whatever Lance bloody Grannum said.

'So, while the *grown-ups* think about foreign governments and diplomacy,' Clive started and pushed his hands into his pockets. 'We need to find out about Serge.'

'Sounds good, Boss.' Zoe put a little smiling emphasis on 'Boss'. Clive half-smiled back. It was good to work with her again in the PCU offices, but Ava's absence drained the room.

'Ideas?'

'What PCU always do. Trace iMe signals.'

Clive frowned. 'Serge won't have a signal.'

Zoe lifted her eyebrows. 'Obviously.'

She selected a contact on her HUD and pressed her jaw to make a call.

'Tech Support, this is Rob,' the voice said over the display wall speaker.

'Hi, Rob, been a while. This is Zoe.'

'Zoe, how's tricks?' He seemed pleased to hear from her. They had spoken a lot on the last case.

'You know the four iTourist disconnects? I need the details of anyone who searched for them before they disconnected.'

'OK. Wait.' Clive could hear sighing and clicks as Rob ran a search. After a few seconds, he said, 'You're in luck, Zoe. Multiple searches, but all from the same account: Chile Gaming Services, Inc.'

'OK. Any other details?'

'The account was set up a month ago. It only ran searches for those four and is now closed. I'll send you the details.'

'Thanks, Rob,' Zoe said and dropped the call.

'Chile is a long way from Rouen, but it must be Serge if he's the one controlling the game,' Clive said.

'Agreed.'

The message from Rob arrived on Zoe's HUD as he promised. Zoe took the details and opened windows and ran searches. The results all told the same story. Chile Gaming Services, Inc was a shell company set-up for the game. It was open for only a few months, but the bank account had been very active.

The accounts showed a lot of money coming into the account from all over the world. Millions of Pan-European dollars. The only outgoing payments were the ones to pay for the iMe searches and a single payment to a Cayman Islands bank that emptied the account.

'We need to tell iMe to be more thorough on their account set up process,' Clive said. 'Otherwise, it's a dead end.'

'Maybe not,' Zoe said. 'Cyber might be able to trace the location of the computer that set up the account and ran the searches.'

'Oh, they can do that?'

'Maybe, depends on how clever Serge is.'

'Send them a request for a search,' Clive said, but Zoe shook her head.

'It's better to send them one request with everything. And I think there's more we need to ask them.'

'OK,' Clive conceded. Zoe knew better than him how Cyber worked. 'Let's look at the account Lilou gave us on the gamers' forum.'

Zoe had started the login process before Clive had finished talking. She entered Lilou's username and password and pressed 'Login'.

The screen opened onto an 'AR Gamerplay Elite' window.

Lilou had hundreds of unread messages, which all seemed to be about the 'Forbidden Island' or other gamers' support for her.

Zoe scrolled down. And down. She found the message Lilou had described with her joining instructions for the selection process. Her meeting point inside Rouen Cathedral.

It didn't tell them anything that she hadn't already said, except Lilou couldn't remember the exact name of the account that the message had come from. She'd only remembered CGS even though she had played a lot of their games. Now they knew the full name: 'CGS Game Master'.

'CGS has got to be Chile Gaming Services,' Zoe said as she took copies of the message and the details of the account. She added them to a draft message she was composing for Cyber.

Clive didn't respond. He was scratching his ear like a dog chasing a flea. Finally, he cornered an idea he was hunting down.

'Femi was the only one of The Four who got to their target. His controller could have recognised that he was at the finish, but Tatsuko was clearly trying to get somewhere else when her's...' He gulped. 'When... you know. Lilou's finish wasn't the water and Sully's wasn't at that military base.'

'So?'

'So, those game controllers definitely had GPS tracking to tell the players where they were and how far they had left. I don't think they blew up on their own. Serge was watching their progress. Like he did when they still wore the iTourist. Lilou's controller started counting down after the car started moving faster than a person walking. I think that Serge sent a message to the controller to get it to blow up.'

'Plausible,' Zoe said.

'Can you ask if Cyber can trace those messages as well?'

'I can.'

Zoe went silent as she spent a few minutes on the message to Cyber with their three requests for more information. Their three chances.

Finally, Zoe pressed *'Send'.*

And they waited. Hoping for some good news.

Clive touched his shoulder where he imagined Ava waited for him to avenge her.

Give me something to work with, he thought.

Chapter 77

Several hours later, there was still no information from Cyber.

The display wall showed one of the news channels. They had nothing new to report and had reverted to their usual speculation and scare mongering, dressed as fact. The experts on terror, religion, politics and the impact on the economy all had a lot to say. Nearly all of it started, 'It might mean...' or 'It could mean...' There was speculation on when and where the next attacks would be. Speculation about Russia, China and Pan-Europe. All opinion dressed as news.

As the hours passed, the news channels seemed to be in a loop. The same faces: the Prime Minister's statement from the morning, the Home Secretary, experts, Issac Townsend, the eco-catastrophe protests, Miles Raven, the shots of the impromptu tributes and flowers at the broken steps of Stormont and the scorched grass of Parliament Square. Even candles by the water in Cardiff.

They repeated. Different experts saying the same thing. The only thing that changed was the growing size of the shrines at the bomb sites.

It was like the whole country was holding its breath, waiting. Praying.

The PCU *'Requiring Action'* queue stayed thankfully empty. No more missing tourists.

'We're all so used to a crime-less existence, that the fear from these attacks is magnified tenfold,' Clive said.

'I know. We need to find who's responsible,' Zoe agreed, not taking her eyes from her messages.

'Anything?' Clive asked for the hundredth time.

'No,' Zoe said, with the forced patience of a parent answering the 'are we there yet' question from the back seat of a car.

'Have you seen this?' Clive asked and threw an image at the PCU office display wall.

The wall showed an image of Rouen Cathedral. Built all those centuries ago, before power tools and cranes. The spectacular Flamboyant Gothic architecture with its pinnacles, gables and statues must have taken years. *No one has the time, money or skills to build something like that now,* Clive thought.

The cathedral's two towers framed each edge of the image, with three arched doors and intricate stone carvings joining the towers. From the angle of the image, only the top of the huge central spire was visible.

'Yep,' Zoe said. 'So what?'

'That tower on the right, the yellower one. You know it's called the Butter Tower?'

'Yes, because of the colour.'

Clive shook his head. 'That's one story, but I prefer the story about the citizens of Rouen missing their local butter so much during Lent, that they bribed the church to let them carry on eating it. Catholics call it Indulgencies. Eat what you like and then pay away your sins. Look at the size of the tower. That's a lot of butter eaten to build something that big.'

'So?' Zoe shrugged and carried on looking at her message queue.

'Zoe, come on,' Clive nagged. 'It's like now. The Model Citizen and Freedom Units are like Lent all year round, telling you what you can and can't eat. We should have Indulgences built into the iMe. I'd pay for chocolate.'

Zoe rolled her eyes. 'Mum told me about your diabetes. How can you still think about food and breaking out of the Model, when it's keeping control of your diabetes? You could die.'

Clive looked down at his feet and swung his leg back and forward under him. He was so much older than Zoe, but he had a very clear vision of his mum telling him off in the kitchen with half-melted chocolate around his mouth.

'I like it,' was all he said.

I need it, was what he was thinking. What else have I got?

***

Four o'clock in the afternoon and Clive and Zoe were still waiting. He could feel his guilt of Ava's death pressing down on his shoulders.

'They'll be snowed under with requests,' Zoe said in answer to Clive's latest request about a response from Cyber.

Clive went back to looking at the display wall and his throat closed and caught in a half-cough. The cameras were at the site of Ava's death. A large crowd had gathered. Lots of eco-protesters, plus some others waiting for the promised attendance of the Prime Minister to lay some flowers as a tribute, but she was already late. The debate in the Commons had gone on longer than expected and the news channel's presenter was struggling to fill the time. She had tried a few people waiting on the edge of the grass, but only got some bland 'super sad' or terrified 'what's the government doing' style responses.

She looked around, desperate for someone to talk to when there were shouts and complaints to her left. The camera tracked to the noise and showed a group of about ten figures in half-green, half-black robes forcing a path through to the front of the crowd. Issac Townsend walked serenely in the middle of the group holding a large floral arrangement that spelt the word Ava.

The presenter started her own pushing and shoving trying to get to Issac. 'Sorry, excuse me. Sorry,' she kept repeating as the camera followed her.

Issac stepped onto the grass and approached the black section of grass already covered in flowers. 'Ava's Shrine' the press were calling it now. Issac stood for a few seconds before he laid his flowers and returned to his Ultras.

Don't want flowers, Clive thought he heard Ava say. *I want justice.*

The news channel's presenter got to the edge of the Ultras and was blocked by a large man.

'Let her through,' Issac said, and the Ultra stepped to one side.

'Issac,' the presenter said, pointing at a cluster of Control Rebellion placards. 'Are your members simply brainwashed slaves to the Model?'

Issac pushed his palms together, fingers together and pointing away from his body, in the New Modelists' horizontal sign of prayer. 'The church brings contentment and peace to its faithful. Control Rebellion are nothing but hedonistic anarchists looking for chaos and gluttony.'

A couple of Ultras took a step towards the presenter.

'Er... OK, so what do you make of the government's response to the attacks?'

'Have they made a response?' he said, smiling at the camera. His eyes glittered with malice. 'I think all Parliament does is generate hot air. It's a major contributor to climate warming.'

He waved into the distance at the eco-catastrophe protesters who flanked one side of Parliament Square with their *'Action Now'* placards.

'Ask them how much action the government has taken. We all grow impatient. Perhaps these attacks might be a catalyst for change.'

'Amen,' the Ultras said.

Now Issac looked straight into the camera. His eyes held Clive, there was something persuasive in them.

'We need changes to the Model to limit consumption. We need to address the unending population boom–'

The display wall changed to show Zoe's HUD and Issac was cut off mid-flow.

Zoe had opened a long message from Cyber, but in a font too small for Clive to read easily.

'Tell me what it says, Zoe.'

'There's a lot of detail of different routers and dead ends, but basically, Serge was very careful and very clever. He hid his tracks well, but he isn't as clever as Cyber. They can't get an exact location, but all three leads can be traced back to the Rouen area. It looks like Rouen is a permanent base rather than a temporary place selected only for the game.'

'Oh, that's all? No physical address?'

'No.'

'Doesn't really get us anywhere does it?'

'Well, it says that Rouen is at the centre of this,' Zoe said.

'We knew that,' Clive said and stopped. He had seen that look in Zoe's eyes before. She was holding something back, edging him down a dark alley, before leading him to sunshine. 'What, Zoe? Tell me.'

Zoe didn't say anything. Instead, she threw an advert for a lecture tour titled Climate Change: A Catastrophe of Population.

Issac Townsend's smiling face beamed back at them from the advert.

'Look at the second date down.'

Clive did. Four months ago, stop two on the tour was in Rouen. The eleventh date was today. In London. *Can't be a coincidence*, Clive thought.

He beamed. 'Zoe, you're a superstar.'

'Yeah, I know.'

Chapter 78

'Waste of time,' Lance had said, when Zoe told him their news, but Bhatt's message said, 'Go.'

The lecture was a sell out for weeks before the attacks, but the fear had caused a renewed push for more tickets. The Church had moved the venue to a much bigger hall. It had sold out in a flash and there was still a huge waiting list.

As Clive approached the entry to the hall, he put his left hand on the barrier. Instead of opening, it flashed 'No valid ticket found' on a small screen, and he heard a harsh little buzz of denial. With his left hand still touching the barrier, he used his right hand to select the 'Menu' in the top left of his HUD, selected 'PCU', then 'Overrides' and then 'Locks'.

The barrier flashed 'PCU' and opened. To his right, Zoe was completing the same process at her barrier.

They both stepped through and headed to the main lecture hall doors. The hall was packed, and they were hit by a wall of warm air. Everyone was staring at the floodlit stage and Issac. Not a spare seat anywhere, so they stood at the back and leant against the wall.

A young man in a bow tie that seemed to be the uniform of the lecture hall staff approached them in a fast walk.

'You can't stand there. It's a fire risk. This is an emergency evacuation route.'

'We won't still be standing here if there's a fire,' Clive said.

'You still can't stand–' he started, but Zoe must have thrown her Cyber-Terror Police ID at him and he shot off like a mouse seeing a cat.

Clive had misused his police powers and checked on Sophia. She was here somewhere. He scanned the seats, taking in the silence of the audience's rapt attention, but couldn't see her. He focused on the stage. Issac was in full flow.

Zoe was reading something on her HUD. 'He's been going a while, but there's an interval halfway through,' she said. 'Maybe ten minutes more.'

Clive nodded.

Issac moved to the centre of the stage. The massive display wall behind him changed to show what looked like blue discs and jagged, purple balls. The caption read 'What is cancer?'. Clive guessed that the blue discs were meant to represent normal cells and the purple balls must be cancer cells. He frowned, not sure what cancer had to do with religion or climate or even population.

Issac spoke. Clear and compelling.

'A cancer is an uncontrolled multiplication of cells. The world's population has exploded: 1bn in 1800, 1.6bn in 1900, 2.5bn in 1950 to 10bn now. It's an uncontrolled multiplication of people. When we behave like this, humankind is a cancer on our planet.'

A line-graph of the world population over time overlaid the image of the coloured discs. The scale made the line seem almost vertical.

'All of the world leaders' efforts are focused on the treatment of the symptoms. It hasn't worked. The disease of humankind is so far advanced that only radical surgery will give the planet a chance of survival. We need to cut out our cancer. The operation will demand the strength to make difficult decisions. The pain may be intense.'

He paused and the image on the display wall changed to a graveyard.

'Before modern medicine, death eliminated people almost as quickly as birth produced them. The population rose very slowly, then rich countries developed modern medicine – "instant death control". Death rates plunged. They wiped out major diseases. Now science threatens to wipe us out.'

Issac pushed his hands together into his usual horizontal prayer. 'Why have people insisted on breeding way past the point of no return? The birth rate is driven by the ceaseless biological urge to dominate through numbers, with no thought of the burden it places on the planet.'

The screen changed again. Half of it showed a field of lush corn, the other showed a post-apocalypse field scorched of vegetation.

Issac opened his arms wide to suggest a question.

'The root of the environmental catastrophe is clear to see. It's "Too Many". Too many factories, too many flights, too many pesticides, too many carbon pollutants. But these are effects. The *cause* is too many people. We need a conscious regulation of both consumption *and* human numbers. We need to bring the world population under control, by reducing the growth rate to zero or making it go negative. We need to do it now.'

There was a swell of agreement from the crowd.

Issac gave a small bow. 'After the break, I will outline the optimum population-environment goals for the world.'

***

Clive and Zoe walked along the corridor that ran behind the lecture theatre's stage. There were lots of doors, but it was obvious that Issac must be behind the one the two Ultras were guarding.

The Ultras both took a half-pace towards the centre of the door as Clive approached, completely blocking the door.

'Move,' he said, but they looked past him like he wasn't there.

'Issac Townsend,' Clive shouted. 'Police. We sent you a message. We need to talk to you. Now.'

Nothing happened, and then the door opened. Issac smiled out at them. 'Citizens, please allow them to pass,' he said, and the Ultras parted and allowed Clive and Zoe into the room.

It was a simple dressing room with a plain table and chair. The table had a jug of water on it.

'Drink?' Issac asked, but both Clive and Zoe shook their heads.

'All that rhetoric about population control, is that Church policy now?' Clive asked.

'It always has been. We've always been against consumption and excess. Excess includes people and their constant need for instant gratification. How can we save the planet when people want to click a button and have the product delivered? Do they think of the cost? The carbon production of the factory in China, the aeroplane flying it here. The car delivering the package may be electric, but so much electricity is still produced by burning carbon fuels. It's all part of the human disease.'

He likes the sound of his own voice, Clive thought.

'And you planned the recent terror attacks to promote your population control agenda,' Clive said.

Issac seemed puzzled. 'How am I implicated? You have proof?' he asked.

'All of the activity and planning for the attacks came from Rouen. You were there recently.'

Now Issac laughed.

'And the hundred thousand or so people who live there. Are you going to arrest them all?'

'You can't be serious about population control,' Zoe said.

'No, Ms Jordan? What's your solution to the climate disaster?'

'You could manufacture things locally and avoid the air freight.'

Issac looked pityingly at Zoe. 'Then you have hundreds of people all doing the same thing. Wasting scarce resources on inefficient duplication. You'll make it worse.'

Issac leant forward, and beckoned Clive and Zoe closer like fellow conspirators.

'I doubt you'll stay for the second half of the lecture, but the solution is clear. Let the purity of a life conforming to the

Model bless each of you, for iMe can control consumption.' He lowered his voice.

'And with upgrades, it can provide the population control we need. We can turn the unworthy off.'

Chapter 79

The morning brought a cloudy but bright day. The clouds seemed to have somewhere else they wanted to be, as they scuttled past, pushed along by a strong breeze.

At least the health and safety clowns hadn't stooped to naming a breeze as a health hazard, Clive thought, but how soon would it be before the rustling of the leaves and swaying twigs were a 'falling from height' risk? Or the seeds picked up and carried on the wind a 'risk to eye and lung health'?

Clive pushed through the PCU office door.

Zoe was already there, fingers waving as she used her HUD, but she looked tired. 'Morning, Boss. Can't get that Issac out of my head. He wants to turn people off. Kept me up all night.'

'Me too. I'd be on his unworthy list for sure.'

'It's not all about you, Boss,' Zoe scolded.

One of the window seals in the PCU office must have failed as the wind was whistling inside the office. It made the wind sound much stronger than it was, and made the office sound like they were trapped in a remote cabin, surrounded by something sinister. Something scary.

The problem was that if Issac got his way, the something scary was already embedded in their necks. Would it be like the game controllers? A ten second countdown to death? No time to say goodbye to those you loved.

They had no evidence on Issac other than a trip to Rouen. With no iMe in France there was no way of tracking where he went and who he met. No way to find a secret meeting with Serge.

'You manage to find any other links to Rouen, Zoe?'

Zoe pursed her lips and dropped her eyes. 'Nothing. I scanned the last year. Loads of events, loads of travel, but nothing that looks like a lead.'

Maybe Lance was right. The whole 'game' had been well organised, but did a foreign government really have all the local agents needed to transport the game controllers, find the butchers shops, and the drop off points?

The wind sounded stronger, adding to Clive's sense of isolation.

Ava waited on Clive's shoulder. Her tone was more demanding. *Try harder.*

***

The wind noise in the office had dropped during the late morning. The lack of progress was compounded by Clive's research on terrorist conviction rates and made his mood darker.

The common theme seemed to be that the actual terrorist committing the offence might get convicted if they didn't blow themselves up or get shot by the police, but the power behind the attacks – the planners, financiers, and ultimate leaders blended into the background. They hid behind cells where members knew as little as possible and couldn't give any real evidence that hurt their leaders. They got away. They planned their next attack.

The Terror department were busy chasing the people who had claimed responsibility, but when Clive checked their progress on his HUD, there was nothing concrete.

They were all chasing smoke.

Clive decided to follow a trail of research that centred on Issac. The Church of the New Modelists seemed to have some conflicting gender identity arguments. Their website touched on 'binary-gender church membership' to 'engender a strong and worthy citizenship', but Issac had written papers arguing that outside of the church's members, an individual's choice to live outside traditional gender roles was acceptable. Desirable even, as a proliferation of same sex partnerships was likely to lower birth rates compared to heterosexual partnerships.

Clive followed the references in one of Issac's papers to an old paper written by the Vatican called *Male and Female He Created Them*. Clive didn't read all thirty odd pages, but it seemed to be advocating the same binary gender definitions and countering the scientific view that gender was a spectrum. The paper pitted the church against science, and Clive ran that as a new search.

It produced over a million results. He tried a different search: *'Church versus science, gender, Rouen'* and pressed *'Send'*.

Two hundred thousand results. He added *'Issac Townsend'* to the search string.

A much smaller set of results and on page four, mixed in with all the papers he had found earlier was the gold.

'Zoe,' he said, the excitement bursting out of him. 'Look.'

Zoe's head snapped up, but the display wall still showed the scrolling *'Safety First and Safety Last'* briefings from the government's latest initiative. 'What?'

'Wait. Got overexcited and forgot to throw my HUD.' Clive flicked his wrist and the display wall redrew to show a large group of people, bunched together, all trying to seem the most important and the most involved. They were standing under a long, covered walkway, with steps and market stalls behind them.

'Look at the hairstyles. That's a long time ago,' Zoe said. 'What's so exciting?'

'Pre-iMe,' Clive agreed. 'Look at the faces, age them a bit.' Clive moved the mouse over a young woman in a grey power-dressing suit with big shoulders.

'That's the Prime Minister.'

'Yep, she was a junior minister then. See who's two rows behind her?'

'Karli Neilson, she worked for the Gender Equality Commission back then.' Zoe's eyes were darting over the faces, trying to see who else was there. 'Issac,' she shouted, matching the excitement of Clive's earlier outburst.

'Yes, and look on the far right of the picture. It would have been his far left so he could have stood there on purpose.'

Zoe scanned the edge of the image, yelped, and ran to the screen. Her finger touched on a face, partly hidden by the person in front of them. 'Miles Raven.'

'Bingo. They're all there.'

'What's the picture from?'

'A conference against gender intolerance, but best of all... It's in Rouen. It's the Church of St Joan of Arc in the Place du Vieux-Marche. Apparently, it's on the site where Joan of Arc was burned for heresy and cross-dressing in 1431. The conference used her positive image as a brave woman who had to dress as a man as a symbol of hope about the changing times. Probably, also a dig at the Catholic Church.'

'All these people have a link to Rouen.' Zoe turned to look at Clive, her eyebrows narrowing. 'Strange Issac didn't mention it yesterday.'

Chapter 80

'Before we take this to Bhatt and Lance. I've got something for you, Boss,' Zoe said.

'What?'

'You remember both Lilou and Sully said the selection process went from ten to seven to five to four? Well I've had lots of searches running over the last thirty-six hours. Looking for that pattern.'

'And?'

Zoe pinched her finger and threw her HUD. 'One finally came back with something useful. What do you think about this?'

The display wall redrew to show the tweets of a film blogger called FilmOPhil.

'The account belongs to someone called Phillipe Blanc. It's been open for years and he has thousands of followers, but Phillipe died six months ago. Not surprisingly, there are no posts for a while and then recently they started again. But the style of the entries is different.'

'OK... like someone bought his account?'

'Exactly, there are still a lot of tweets, but these are the ones the search found.' Zoe's fingers moved upwards, and the display wall scrolled up and showed four tweets:

> 'Hi to all you film fans, horrible day outside so I'm going to settle down and watch "10 Items or Less". Should be exciting.'

> 'Hi to all you film fans, quick poll. Which film do you prefer "Se7en" or "The Magnificent Seven"? Both classics – you decide.'

> 'Hi to all you film fans, enjoying a sci-fi classic today. "The Fifth Element".'

> 'Hi, film fans. Going old-school and watching "The Fantastic Four" tonight.'

'The dates of the tweets match the dates of the selection process,' Zoe said as Clive nodded, a smile growing on his face.

'That's brilliant, Zoe.'

'That's not all. When I looked in detail at all the tweets sent since Phillipe's death, I found more.' Zoe moved her fingers up again and the display wall obeyed. It showed another tweet.

'To all you Reece Witherspoon fans, just finished watching "Overnight Delivery".'

'The date of that tweet matches the delivery that Jay said he picked up. Then there's these.' More finger movement and two tweets scrolled into view.

'Hi to all you film fans, I'm watching "The Departed" and enjoying every minute.'

'Hi to all you film fans, a sports comedy theme today. I was tempted by "Run Fat Boy Run", but I settled on "Ready to Rumble".'

'They match the dates when Lilou said they travelled and then when the game started.'

Clive started clapping, his smile so big that it almost stretched to his ears. 'Zoe, you're brilliant. These tweets must be progress reports to someone who can't risk receiving a real message. Someone whose messages are saved by iMe.'

Zoe nodded. 'Someone here in the UK. Not a foreign government.'

***

Clive's knee jiggled under the table of the New Scotland Yard conference table again.

Zoe settled in the chair next to him and pushed her elbow into Clive's arm. He looked at her, surprised, but when he saw Zoe's sharp nod down, he got the message and told his leg to stop.

While they waited, Zoe threw her HUD at the conference room's wall and prepared a set of stacked windows, with the tweets and photos of the conference in Rouen.

The door opened and Lance's hand appeared. He must have ushered Bhatt through ahead of him as she appeared before Lance.

'Creep,' muttered Clive.

Zoe jabbed him in the arm again. 'Senior officer first,' Zoe hissed.

'So why did you come in here before me?' Clive said, but Zoe was already standing up.

'Show us what you've got,' Bhatt said, as always cutting out all option for small talk.

Zoe talked and swiped and scrolled her way through the tweets and the photo of the conference.

'All you've got is some people at an ancient conference that hundreds attended, and some tweets from a dead man's account,' Lance said.

'No,' Clive said, his voice cracking as he tried not to swear at Lance. 'We have a link between Rouen and the Prime Minister, Karli Neilson, Miles Raven and Issac Townsend. Those cryptic messages mean that the person behind this is in the UK and not a foreign government.'

Lance shook his head. 'When you're wrong, you're wrong. I've just come from a briefing with the PM and there's growing concern that the French link means the attack is from Pan-Europe. Certainly not the PM herself.'

'She and Karli stand to gain more power. They're using this to squash any pretence at privacy and upgrade iMe,' Clive said, trying not to think about the upgrade that Issac wanted.

'There's more,' Zoe said. 'Miles Raven is a subscriber to those tweets and Cyber have confirmed that the recent post came from a place called Poses. It's only twenty-one miles from Rouen.'

'Did Miles Raven start following the film blogger recently?' Bhatt asked.

'Uh… No, ma'am.' Zoe stumbled over her words.

'When?'

'A year ago, ma'am.'

'Look I know it seems a long time ago, but they must have been planning this for a long time. Those controllers needed building, the network of people…' Clive faltered, he didn't have anything conclusive, but there was definitely something there.

Lance snorted. 'He likes films – lock him up. Sorry, ma'am, this is a waste of time.'

Bhatt raised her hand to think.

'I think that the leads have some merit.' She looked at Lance. 'Can you still spare these officers?'

'They've no value to me.'

Bhatt looked at Clive and Zoe. 'Spend some more time digging, but we would have to be very certain of our facts before acting.'

'But ma'am–' Lance started, but Bhatt's raised hand stopped his complaint in its tracks.

Chapter 81

Clive and Zoe got back to the PCU office in time for their shift to end. Clive trudged home and was officially off duty, but Ava's presence kept him working.

Clive's shoulders ached from the time on his HUD and he stopped and rolled his shoulder. His right shoulder gave the usual clunk-clunk crunch on each revolution, but it didn't ease the stiffness.

After all his research he knew a lot more about the Prime Minister, Karli, Miles and Issac. It didn't help him. No leads. Nothing concrete. Dead end after dead end.

Clive's Buddy scampered across the bottom of his HUD dragging a *'New Message'* banner.

Clive clicked on the message icon and watched it morph into the message header. It was a reply from Inspector Bisset, in the French police.

Probably a brush off, Clive thought. He scrolled down to the body of the letter and almost fell off his chair.

> *'FAO Inspector Lussac,*
>
> > *Re: Terror bombings in UK*
> > *Suspect Request "Serge"*
> > *Location: Rouen and surrounding area*
> > *ID: FaceFit profile*
>
> > *Following your request to locate suspect "Serge", in connection with the recent terrorist bombings in UK, I forwarded your request to the local Rouen police. As expected, they have acted with typical efficiency and have detained M. Serge Wischard.*
>
> > *He is being held in Rouen Police Station awaiting questioning. As we can only hold the suspect for twenty-four hours without formal arrest, and allowing for the journey time for UK officers to attend in person, I respectfully offer the capability of a remote interview. English speaking officers from the Rouen police will be present to aid in translation.*
>
> > *Cordially,*
> > *Inspector Bisset'*

Clive grabbed the message and clicked *'Forward To'*. He selected DCS Bhatt and Zoe and paused. With slow reluctance, he added Lance and pressed *'Send'*.

He clicked on DCS Bhatt's name and touched his jaw to make a call.

'Bhatt.' The tone was curt but not unduly upset. Clive sighed with relief; she was probably still at work.

'Sorry to disturb you, ma'am, but I've just forwarded you a message from the French police. They've detained Serge.'

'Wait,' Bhatt said.

Clive waited, listening to silence at the other end.

'Good work, Clive,' Bhatt said eventually. 'I'll liaise with Lance.'

'I'd like to be involved in the interview, ma'am. And Zoe. After all it was us who found him.'

'Not happening, Clive. This is a Terror case. Lance will handle it.'

'But–'

'No buts, Clive.'

The line went silent again and Clive crossed his fingers. Maybe she was reconsidering. Maybe he would be at the front of the interview.

'Best I can do is send you a link to the interview stream. You can watch and listen, but absolutely no questions from you.'

'Thank you, ma'am,' Clive said.

It was better than being out in the cold.

***

Clive sat on his sofa, staring at the display wall. His HUD screen was split in two. On one side, he had the link for the interview open. He was online early and all he could see was an empty room. Uniform dull grey walls, a table and four chairs. On the other side of his HUD, he had a one-to-one TrueMe chat window open with Zoe.

Clive saw the door to the French interview room open and a uniformed officer entered the room leading two men. The first was a perfect match to the FaceFit that Lilou had provided of Serge. The second man was younger, fitter and carried a briefcase.

The message half of Clive's screen blinked and the words *'Serge – great match. And solicitor'* flashed up from Zoe.

He typed a quick *'Yep'* reply, and was in time to see two women arrive in the room and sit opposite Serge and his solicitor. The camera angle was behind the women's backs so Clive couldn't see their faces, but he had a clear front-on view of Serge.

From the movement of her head, it looked like the female police officer on the right spoke. There seemed to be a lot of discussions in French which Clive guessed was the formal procedural beginning of the interview. It ended with Serge giving a shrug and blowing a short breath out of the side of his mouth.

Then the police officer spoke in English.

'Monsieur Wischard has confirmed that he is happy to conduct the interview in English. Chief Inspector Grannum, are you ready?'

'Yes.'

Clive grimaced as Lance's voice came through the speakers. Lance had done nothing to find Serge, but here he was running the show. 'May I call you Serge?' Lance asked.

'OK,' Serge said.

'Serge, can you confirm that you organised and ran a game called Forbidden Island?'

Serge ducked his head to listen to some whispered words from his solicitor.

'I sent some emails. I collected ten people and I ran some exercises. That's it,' he said and emphasised the end with a quick upturning of his hands.

'Did your selection process result in four contestants for the game?'

'Oui.'

'Did you send four people to the UK, provide them with game controllers and then cause the game controllers to explode?'

Serge's solicitor muttered something, and Serge said, 'No. I gave them tickets. No more.'

'How do you explain the explosions?'

'I saw in the news, they have an electronic hand and it exploded. Maybe it was broken. A fault.'

Clive slouched back into his sofa. The interview wasn't going well. Lance's questions seemed messy and unstructured, but he had no way to intervene. Clive watched the interview go from bad to worse, before Serge's solicitor spoke in rapid French to the two officers in the room.

The officer on the left nodded. Serge sat back in his chair and placed his hands casually in his lap.

His solicitor cleared his throat and said, 'My client has given all of the information that he can. He admits that he ran a selection exercise from his executive training facility at the request of a company in Chile. This is my client's legitimate business. This is the full extent of my client's involvement. He has no knowledge of any game controllers or explosions. Unless the English chief inspector can provide any evidence other than the bogus claims of two terrorists, then I demand you release my client.'

The room was silent. The female officer said, 'Chief Inspector, do you have the evidence?'

Clive jumped to his feet. 'Come on, Lance, do something.'

Lance said, 'No concrete evidence at this time.'

Serge smiled at his solicitor, and they rose to leave.

'Shit,' shouted Clive, and collapsed back onto the sofa.

Chapter 82

A bad night's sleep worsened Clive's mood. He banged around in the kitchen, each cabinet door closed unnecessarily hard, cutlery thrown in drawers, plates moved with no care.

It didn't help and all he had to show for it was a small chip on a plate. He dabbed his index finger on the end of his tongue and touched the now homeless little piece of blue ceramic, using the moisture on his finger to pick it up. He flicked it onto the floor in front of the sleeping cleaning robot. Harry woke with a whir of fans and rotating brushes and rushed out to see what had arrived on the floor like a dog hoping for a carelessly discarded scrap of food. He tracked back and forth over the ceramic and headed back to his charging point to rest.

If only this case was so easy to clean up, Clive thought, examining his over-long fingernails and reminding himself to trim them.

Had Lance been deliberately useless in the interview of Serge? The questions had been clumsy and disjointed. True there wasn't a lot of evidence, but he could have tried to trick and trap Serge.

The case went around and around in Clive's head during the journey to the PCU office, like a wheel of fortune, except that it didn't stop. Instead, it clicked past labels for Terror, Miles, Issac, Government, iMe, Karli, PM, Lance, Ava. Back to Terror. Round and around.

As the car arrived at PCU and the door opened, Clive added another segment to the wheel. Money.

***

Clive and Zoe perched on their habitual desks and looked at the PCU office display wall.

A glass of water balanced on the edge of Clive's desk. He wanted coffee. Strong, black and full of caffeine. The office vending machine had other ideas.

Some recent incentive had changed the coffee suppliers and the organic, eco-friendly coffee tasted like soggy cardboard.

According to his FU allowance page on his HUD, even the caffeinated version was so low in caffeine that it wasn't worth suffering the flavour.

The display wall was showing Miles Raven's bank statements. They were trawling through looking for payments to Serge, or someone else who might have funded the game, just as they had already done with Issac, Karli and the PM.

'For a socialist, there are a lot of credits in his accounts,' Clive said. 'Salary, speaking engagements, endorsements.'

'How is that relevant?' Zoe asked with a frown.

'Just saying.'

'We need to focus on what leads us to Serge, Boss.'

'Sure.' Clive flicked his eyes to the debit column as Zoe paged down.

Miles' personal account showed nothing incriminating.

Zoe closed down the accounts and changed the search to the bank statements of Miles' Eco-Socialist Democracy party.

There were pages and pages of results.

'Can you filter out the donations to start with?' Clive asked.

Zoe clicked a menu and the number of pages halved and she started paging down through salary payments, office rent, advertising and a thousand other expenses.

Three years into the accounts Zoe said, 'There.' She moved the mouse over a payment to 'ReGrow SARL.'

'What is it?'

'Some sort of eco-farming project. Its name came up on some other searches.'

'Not unreasonable for an eco-socialist party to fund eco-projects, Zoe.' Then Clive noticed her smile.

'What?'

'It's based at the same address as ExecUGrow SARL.'

Clive frowned in confusion. 'They're growing what?'

'Executives. It's Serge's executive training company.'

***

Clive stared out of the car window replaying Lance's words: *Lussac, the payment doesn't prove anything. Leave it to me.*

But Miles had been in Rouen, saw the film tweets and made the payments. Clive had been forced to leave the interview with Serge to Lance, and that was a disaster. This, he would do himself.

He'd left Zoe at PCU, tricked by a small lie. Of course she didn't want to come with him to his latest hospital appointment. If she bothered to track his signal it would be too late. She'd see him go past the hospital and then head towards Hammersmith.

She'd see him arrive at Miles Raven's meeting for his constituents where they could air their worries and grievances.

Clive wasn't a constituent, but he had a big grievance. Ava's was bigger.

**

The meeting was in the old Hammersmith library. Miles' party had 'recycled' it into their main offices when it had shut down, and all the books had been removed and sent to be recycled themselves. No one cut down trees to make paper for books anymore. Not when the HUD provided a nice, clean, zero-carbon footprint version.

Clive waited with his back to a wall that might once have held shelving but now was bland and empty. He watched Miles Raven talking to an old couple in the centre of the room. Not much privacy for their concerns about their safety and what their neighbours were up to.

Clive had been given the number fifty-seven when he arrived, and he waited. The couple had got up and shuffled over to talk to Miles when the display wall flashed the number fifty-six.

Finally, the couple shook hands with Miles, and they shuffled off.

The number on the display wall clicked up one and Clive walked over.

'Mr Lussac,' Miles said, still standing from saying goodbye to the couple. 'I can see from your registration that you're not a constituent, but I'm happy to talk to everyone. We're all trapped in the government's eco-catastrophe.' He waved at a chair. 'Please.'

Clive sat. The plastic of the old chair had retained the heat from the old man's visit.

'How can I help you?'

'I want to know your thoughts about the bombings.'

'Terrible. Terrible business, but if they can be a catalyst for change then the deaths of the innocents might save many more lives.'

'Easy to use empty words when it's not your friend blown up.'

Miles sat back in his chair and gave Clive a hard, flat look, like he was re-evaluating the conversation.

'Who did you know?' he asked.

Clive could see a calculation running in Miles' eyes – only bombers, scientists or police had died. Miles' fingers moved like he was trying to use his HUD without being too obvious.

'Ava. She was brave and good and sacrificed herself to save lives,' Clive said.

'Ah, I see. *Inspector* Lussac.'

'Why did you do it?' Clive asked. It was a clumsy attempt to trick Miles into admitting his involvement, but Clive's brain was jumbled with memories of Ava and his own failure to win her justice.

Miles looked shocked. 'Do what?'

'Run the game with Serge. Kill people. Kill Ava.' Clive's voice was almost a shout and the meeting room fell silent as the waiting people turned to stare.

'I don't know what you're talking about,' Miles said, but Clive could see him calculating again. 'You're mad. I had nothing to do with that game.' The volume of Miles' voice was directing the words to the room and not only Clive. 'You've no proof.'

Clive's frustration flipped into a broiling sea of anger. 'You. Killed. Ava,' he said, each word punctuated with a hard, sharp prod of his finger into Miles' chest.

'Security!' Miles called. 'Get this mad man away from me.'

Two large figures in black stirred and moved towards Clive, but he jumped up said, 'OK, I'll go. But if I find proof, I'll break through anything to get to you.'

Clive stormed to the doorway, face red and hands shaking, feeling that he had done well to keep some tiny amount of control and not smash a fist into Miles' face.

He turned and glanced back.

Miles was staring at him, calculations running in his eyes.

Chapter 83

'What were you thinking, Lussac?' Lance screamed.

Clive deliberately looked at Bhatt, and not at Lance or Cathie from Employee Wellness. The pastel tones and soft sofas of the Employee Wellness 'Meeting Haven' weren't soothing him. Clive's fists were clenched tight at his sides, and he rocked forward onto his toes.

Lance saw the motion and swayed backwards.

'This is meant to be a safe, caring space,' Cathie said. Her words were soothing and conflicted with how fiercely her hair had been dragged back into a ponytail and the severity of the cut of the dark jacket she wore. 'We're here to acknowledge Clive's feelings as well as explore his actions.'

Clive bit down hard on his lip. It wouldn't help if he shouted at Cathie, but what a load of bollocks. He'd spent his whole life avoiding the F word, and now he was meant to 'Acknowledge his *feelings*'.

'With respect, *sir*,' Clive said, making sure that Lance was clear that no respect was present. 'You're ignoring evidence, you mishandled the interview with Serge, and Miles Raven is walking free while Ava... Ava is in a coffin.' Clive looked at Cathie. 'So, I'm *feeling* fucking angry.'

'How dare you,' shouted Lance. 'You're the one acting unprofessionally, Defective Inspector.'

Cathie crossed her arms and gave Clive a look as cold as a mid-winter blizzard. 'I have noted your abusive language.'

Cathie and Bhatt seemed not to have noticed Lance's use of defective instead of detective. Lance sneered. Not a slip of the tongue.

'Let's all calm down,' Bhatt said. 'Miles Raven has made a formal complaint against you for harassment and violent assault.'

'Violent assault?' Clive snorted. 'I prodded his chest.'

'The complaint is for violent assault that led to extensive bruising and temporary loss of use of his left arm.'

Clive shook his head, wishing that he could jump into a parallel universe where everyone wasn't wounded and offended by everything. Maybe he needed a time machine instead to jump back in time.

'Oh dear. How sad,' Clive said and added the 'never mind' in his head.

'Empathising with a victim is a wonderful step on the road to healing,' Cathie said.

Clive pinched his lips together. He had caught a look in Bhatt's eye. She had been around the block enough times with real crooks as well. Bhatt looked away, a glitter of amusement in her eye, and Clive pushed his lips harder together to suppress the giggle.

'This is no laughing matter, Lussac,' Lance snapped.

'Indeed,' said Bhatt, back in control. 'Inspector Lussac, you are transferred back to PCU from your assignment with Terror, pending a formal investigation into your conduct and the complaint brought against you by Miles Raven.'

***

Clive looked at the empty *'Requiring Action'* message queue and then around the PCU office.

Zoe had been recalled to Cyber Crime, and Clive had the empty tables and chairs for company.

And Ava.

'It's Miles. He's the only one with the links to Serge. I just can't prove it,' Clive told her, but the only response was Ava's disappointed silence.

He had failed Ava again. Sighing, he checked the time. He had an hour until the car was due to take him back to New Scotland Yard for his disciplinary hearing.

Was this the end of his career? Not that this was much of a job anymore. It wasn't like in the old days, but there was no point thinking about it. There was no going back. Life expectancy was over ninety-five now, so he had forty more working years. But doing what?

He wasn't sure he would make it with Ava watching him.

Clive trolled around online, scouring websites for possible leads, but there was nothing. No definitive proof against Miles. Or Issac. Or anyone. Only a gut feeling.

He sighed and read the broadcast banner that his Buddy dragged out: *'Statement from the Prime Minister starting in one minute'*.

Clive turned the display wall on to show the iconic black doorway of 10 Downing Street. A glass lectern stood waiting for the PM, not that she would put paper on it, but it provided a place for the microphones and sponsorship messages of the big corporates.

The black door opened, and the Prime Minister came out. She gave a small wave and a tight smile and crossed to the lectern.

She paused and ignored some shouted questions before looking into the cameras.

'We live in times of great challenges not only for the people of the United Kingdom, but the world. The global fight against pollution and climate change continues despite the recent terror attacks. I want to assure the public that there is no evidence that the eco-protesters on our streets are behind the attacks.'

She paused once more and Clive admired her delivery skill, if not her misdirection. She said the words 'no evidence' softly, so that most people would focus on the 'eco-protesters on our streets are behind the attacks' and not the 'no evidence' part.

'Our focus has to be on real environmental change, but we cannot sacrifice the economy in doing so. There are too many jobs at stake. We cannot allow eco-socialism to decimate our industries and food production and plunge us back into a medieval lifestyle where each day is spent in a survivalist's search for food.'

Clive stopped listening. He was staring at the lectern and the stylised NM logo that he hadn't noticed before.

'...so, to that end,' the Prime Minister said, 'I am announcing a number of new initiatives. This first is an enlarging of the Ministry of Well-being and Health. Karli will oversee the strengthening of iMe controls to prevent the atrocity of the recent bombings happening again. The second is to welcome new experts to our Environmental Policy Group, and I am pleased to announce that Issac Townsend, head of the Church of the New Modelists will be one of those. He and his growing members fully embrace the Model Citizen that is central to government policy and—'

Clive hit the display wall's off switch.

He'd had enough politics. Enough of them twisting Ava's death to suit their own agenda.

Issac Townsend advising on environmental policy. Issac, the advocate of population control.

He shuddered and touched the back of his neck. He could feel the small bump and scar where his iMe lived.

Maybe Clive didn't have to worry about surviving forty more years.

Chapter 84

Clive paced backwards and forwards outside the Employee Wellness meeting haven. The jury was out, well, not a jury, but the three people on the disciplinary committee.

He had been entitled to a serving officer to act as his witness, and Zoe had been happy to help. Now she sat on her hands, rocking back and forth on her chair.

'You're making me nervous, Boss. Can't you sit down.'

'*You're* nervous?' Clive laughed. 'You heard how it went. I might have been alright if the so-called *assault* was only on a civilian. Not an MP.'

Zoe shrugged and Clive resumed his pacing.

After what felt like another lifetime had passed, the door to the meeting haven opened and Cathie's face appeared.

Her usual hard, expressionless face gave nothing away. *She must be brilliant at poker*, Clive thought.

He pushed the thought aside and followed her into the room. Zoe brought up the rear.

The other members of the committee were already waiting and for a moment the only noise was of fabric rustling as they sat on the sofa.

The world seemed to stop for Clive. The silent room was like the calm before the storm.

Cathie gave a small cough to mark the resumption of business. 'Clive, as you have admitted to assaulting Miles Raven, we have no option but to uphold his complaint.'

The other members nodded. Cathie looked straight at Clive. Nothing moved on her face. No 'tells', no hint.

'The recommended tariff for this complaint is a double red notice – immediate removal from office, loss of salary and pension.'

Clive's head dropped to his chin. Shit.

His brain clung on to the word 'recommended'.

'The hurdle that this committee has to clear in determining the tariff is whether you are "fit for purpose".'

Doesn't that phrase relate to machines, not people? Clive thought.

'Here the committee was split.'

Clive looked up at the older committee member, he had seemed to be on Clive's side during the hearing.

Cathie continued, 'I argued that you were, and the other committee members argued that you were not.'

Clive spun his head to Cathie, possibly his unlikely saviour. Still no visible emotion.

'The police force has a duty of care to its officers, and as you were sent to Cardiff before Ava's tragic death, you slipped through our list of Victims of Grief. You should have been offered mandatory grief counselling, but were not. That was a failing of Employee Wellness and I believe it left you with a chink in your emotional armour which your anger escaped through.'

Clive blinked. Had he heard an actual apology from Employee Wellness? Not quite, but close.

'This is a strong mitigation factor in the tariff calculation, and it is the decision of the committee to drop it to a double yellow notice. You will remain employed by the police force, but will undertake restricted duties until you have successfully completed three months without any other issues. Do you understand?'

Clive gave her a tight smile and nodded. It was much better than he had expected, or dared hope.

'And you will undertake an extensive course of grief counselling and our new initiative of Feeling Re-centring. This is a month-long, off-site, immersive programme that will bring your feelings' centre of gravity back into spiritual balance.'

Fuck, sounds like torture, thought Clive.

He was sure he heard Zoe suppress a laugh.

**

Clive followed Zoe along the corridor of New Scotland Yard and back to her desk in Lance's section.

She had all her things in a cardboard box ready to be moved back to Cyber.

'Sorry I screwed your job here,' Clive said.

Zoe touched him gently on the arm. 'Not your fault. I made all my own decisions.'

The other officers in the room started to huddle around the display wall.

'What's happening?' Zoe asked one of them.

'It's a day for press conferences. This one's Miles Raven.'

Clive and Zoe rushed towards the display wall and peered around heads and shoulders to see the screen. Lance sat at the front, elbows on knees and head in his palms.

Miles stood in front of a lectern in the old library that was bare of any corporate sponsors' logos.

'After the Prime Minister's statement and other recent events, I felt it was imperative to set the record straight, before the capitalist spin distorts the truth and, once again, we ignore the environmental catastrophe that is engulfing us,' he said.

Something in his tone made the terror officers hang on his words. No one spoke. They hardly dared breathe.

'Capitalism is happy to enlist the environmental movement for convenience and to deflect our calls for action, but we still have meat and dairy production fuelling global warming. We're locked into "within-system" approaches. But these approaches, like carbon offsets, are simply a capitalist game that turns pollution into a new source of profit.'

Miles paused, allowing his point to sink in.

'A martyr is somebody who suffers persecution and death for refusing to renounce a belief. The capitalists refuse to renounce profit and will make martyrs of us all. Capitalist barbarism now guarantees eco-catastrophe.'

Clive could hear shouted agreement from inside the library.

'The environmentalists have paraphrased the great Rosa Luxemburg's socialism or barbarism into *eco*-socialism or barbarism, but this is weak and full of appeasement of the capitalists. The truth is that it is eco-socialism or *extinction*. There is no third way.'

Miles took a sip of water and now Clive could hear cheering from inside the library.

'iMe has led to great socialist reforms. The tyranny of possession is broken. The rich can't parade their wealth and status in environmentally barbarous cars. We finally have equality in consumption between rich and poor, but our democratic processes have failed us. The Prime Minister will drive us to extinction in the name of growth. We must recognise the truth – that the struggle for an ecologically rational world must include a struggle for the state.'

Miles waited for more cheering from the people in the library to subside.

'The term "terrorist" is often used as a political label. Nelson Mandela was labelled a terrorist for being right and challenging the South African government. Eco-protesters are not terrorists, they are freedom fighters. They are the saviours of our planet – the saviours of our children's future. A government that's killing its people and the planet has no legitimate moral grounds to govern. Some may claim that violence is the rupturing of our ecosystems, and that terrorism is absolutely wrong, but we face a supreme emergency. There is an imminent threat of extermination, yet nothing stops the capitalists. We can't wait any longer. We need to act now. The only way to change is to shock the system into change.'

Miles took another sip and stared into the camera.

'It is time to uncuff ourselves from the yoke of capitalism. I sent four glorious eco-warriors to the symbols of power to relight the fire of our democracy. If the government labels my actions as terrorism, then so be it. Let history judge me, but the path of eco-socialism is the only way to prevent global extinction. People of the United Kingdom, people of the world, rise, rise and seize control. Seize the future. Give us a future, give us–'

The display from the library snapped off and was replaced by a *'Technical Fault'* message.

Clive forced his way through the stunned silence that followed and stood in front of Lance. 'Told you,' he said.

Clive raised his hand, finger extended to jab some sense into Lance. Lance smiled and leaned towards it, trying to initiate contact, but Clive heard Cathie's 'without other issues' warning and dropped his hand. 'This is my arrest.'

'No way. This is *my* case,' Lance said and turned from Clive. 'Arrest team. On me. Let's go.'

The room seemed to empty in a second and left Clive and Zoe standing alone. The arrest and all the action was happening around them. They were like two static rocks in a turbulent river.

They had been right.

They were discarded.

Chapter 85

Clive and Zoe stared at the New Scotland Yard display wall. The *'Technical Fault'* message cleared and showed a flustered presenter. 'We seem to have lost the coverage from Miles Raven,' he said. 'But we can cut to our cameras at Ava's Shrine.'

The display wall changed to show an image panning along the crowd. A small group of Control Rebellion hoodies jumped and cheered, but most were eco-protesters. From their angry shouts and urgent discussions, they must have all seen Miles' call to arms.

They faced a wall of Uniforms.

'Shit,' Clive said, 'if Miles' revolution is going to kick off, then now is the time.'

The banks of protesters rippled backwards and forwards but didn't surge forward. It was like the starter of a race had said 'go' but no one moved.

'Look at the demographic of the protesters,' Clive said. 'It's hard to fight the police when your young kids are standing next to you holding a "Give us a future" banner. They'd get trampled.'

'I guess,' said Zoe. 'Maybe Miles' supporters agree with his view of capitalism and the environment, but don't support violence.'

Zoe turned to look at Clive. She rolled her eyes at something she saw in his face. 'Let me guess, in the old days...'

'Sorry, Zoe,' Clive said with a smile. 'In the old days, people might have rioted. It's one thing to chuck a petrol bomb at the police when you're anonymous in a crowd wearing a mask, but you can't hide like that now. We know who you are. You'd go straight to jail... Not that you can get petrol anyway.'

The seconds ticked away. A lone child's voice started singing 'Save the World' and the tension seemed to drain out of the protesters. They joined in the singing.

The video snapped away from the protesters to show the inside of Miles' library headquarters.

Miles was surrounded by supporters and TV crews; he clearly had no intention of running. He was talking to journalists, probably giving them access to him during the run-up to the trial that would be watched by the world.

If it got that far. There was no proof other than his 'confession'. He was a politician. He could probably twist his way out of it and reframe the argument to be about the environment. Clive could imagine Miles already rehearsing his speeches. He would get a massive media platform to continue his calls for change.

Clive saw blue lights strobing into the library and Lance's team arrived.

He watched the shambles of the arrest.

'Lance even cocked up Miles' arrest,' Clive said. 'And that was the easy bit.'

Zoe seemed lost in silent thought.

'What?' Clive asked.

'Miles was completely wrong to use bombs… and kill.' She paused, seeming reluctant to say it. 'But that doesn't mean we don't need to change. We do need a future.'

'Of course we do,' Clive said, but he had no belief that politicians would even try to deliver it.

***

Part of Clive's Employee Wellness recuperation and grief counselling plan involved him 'avoiding the inherent stress of the work environment'. In reality, it meant him staying at home and watching a lot of old films. And a lot of news.

One of his favourites was Miles' arrest. Not only for Ava.

Lance's team's arrival was captured by the news crews in all its glorious detail.

Clive had saved it so that he could play it again and again.

Miles was in the centre of the library, surrounded by a crush of his supporters. Maybe fifteen deep and encircling him. When Lance and his team arrived, Miles' supporters linked arms and refused to move. They were a moat around the castle, there to block an invasion and protect their king.

Lance and his team tried pushing and shoving, cajoling and threatening.

Lance's face was vivid red by the time he got to Miles.

'Here are the fascist puppets of our criminal government,' Miles shouted.

The supporters jeered and pushed back, sending Lance stumbling to the floor.

That brought a loud cheer from the supporters and a laugh from Miles. 'The puppet fell over.'

The supporters launched into a repeating chant: 'He fell over. He fell over.'

Lance recovered his balance. His anger blazed from him and he launched a swinging punch into Miles' face.

Clive pressed pause as Lance's fist landed. 'Double red notice, Lance.'

***

A few weeks later, Clive's duties involved sitting in a car on a round trip to Birmingham.

Lilou was due for deportation to the place of her entry into the UK. She was headed for a state funded flight back to Berlin and then was on her own.

The courts had said she had no case to answer, that she was a victim of Miles' deception. A victim of self-harm. The prosecution had also tried for a conviction for damaging the property of the UK Border forces, but her defence lawyers had been sent a recommissioning and recalibration report of her iTourist. It had come off her severed hand with no issues and the report confirmed that it worked perfectly. Some tourist was probably walking around the UK with it on their arm now.

When they arrived at the airport and the UK Border Security officers took Lilou away, the door of the car closed, and Clive burst into tears.

All he could think of was Ava, and the time they dropped dozy Brett at Gatwick's East terminal after he overstayed his time limit.

Chapter 86

Clive was lounging on his sofa, looking at his display wall watching Julia Roberts kicking ass in *Erin Brockovich*. He'd seen it so many times that he knew the story by heart. He pressed pause.

All he could think about was chocolate. Again.

Winter was still threatening him, and his restricted duties gave him too much spare time. Being at home didn't help. There was no legitimate chocolate in the fridge, but the contraband chocolate was still hidden in the cupboard. He was within Model, but he held himself back. He was trying to be a better Clive.

But why bother? On one side, the government and Issac were clamping down more and how soon would it be before they turned people off? On the other, the calls for a ban on meat and dairy production to ease global warming were deafening. That meant no steak, but worse no milk. No milk meant no real chocolate.

Mmmm, chocolate, he thought.

A bing broke his daydream and Clive groaned as he looked at the message his Buddy rolled out: *'Your next self-healing course is available to view'*.

He knew that as he was technically at work, he had ten minutes' grace in starting the course. Six more of these videos and he would be back at PCU. Then he could sit around and do nothing in the PCU office rather than at home.

Clive clicked on the message and his display wall redrew to show a face. The man was bald, but with a huge beard. It made his head look like it was on upside down.

'Please pay attention,' the man said. 'This self-healing course uses proximity scanning and eye direction monitoring from your HUD camera to ensure that you are fully engaged with the learning programme. Please blink twice to confirm your acceptance.'

Clive blinked twice and the screen changed to a picture of bars and bars of chocolate.

'Welcome to *Food Searches Us Out*,' the man's voice said. 'In the old days, humans spent the majority of their time searching for and preparing food. Now modern life has plentiful food and iMe's learning software adjusts your diet to keep you in optimal health. This benefit requires little effort on your part. It's all done automatically. It frees our time, but that can present different challenges in the form of cravings. When we crave food, it is usually due to our emotional state, rather than actual hunger. Think back to your own cravings. Do they appear when you are bored, anxious, or depressed? Your cravings are nothing more than your brain trying to self-medicate...'

Clive sat through the rest of his self-healing course. It all made sense, but...

He stifled a yawn. He shouldn't be tired at eleven o'clock in the morning, so he headed down the hall to the bathroom. He ducked down to the sink and splashed water on his face.

Better, he thought and reached for the towel.

He rubbed his face dry and looked hard in the mirror. His skin was red from the towel and he thought he saw Ava staring at him. His eyes dropped to his body and his favourite 'Spirit of a Honey Badger' T-shirt.

Was he really a honey badger anymore? Was he ferocious? Fearless?

No. He was choosing to eat salad and avoiding chocolate unless he cowered behind a bracelet. Watching bloody self-help videos.

Worse. He was seeing the validity of the arguments in the self-help crap.

He was whipped. Broken. No fighting spirit left. He was a puppy rolling on its back and begging for a tummy rub.

He needed a Spirit of a Gerbil T-shirt.

Clive's face reddened more, and he curled his hands into fists.

Bang. Bang. Bang. He rained punches on his head.

'What the fuck have you become?' he screamed.

Clive ran through his bedroom, along the corridor and into the kitchen. He yanked open a cupboard door and pulled down a Health Bank bracelet. He sneered at it and tossed it into the sink.

No more hiding.

He reached to the back of the cupboard, fingers darting around to find it.

There.

His hand touched thin packaging, he could feel ridges and indentations.

He pulled the bar of chocolate out and stared at its perfection.

Clive's long thumbnail sliced a cut through the packaging three rows of blocks back. Six cubes of heaven.

After some frantic tearing the cubes were naked. Two went into his mouth.

'Arghh...' Clive said, and his knees almost gave way as his taste buds exploded.

Clive's Buddy ran out, waving his finger at him in rebuke, and unfurled another banner: *'Freedom Unit violation reported to the Ministry of Well-being and Health'*.

He ignored it, and pushed the four remaining cubes of chocolate into his mouth, savouring every delicious morsel.

***

Clive licked the last of the chocolate from his fingers. He felt warm and snug, comforted by its creamy perfection. Momentarily at peace.

Until his Buddy jogged onto his HUD, trailing an *'Urgent New Message'* banner. Clive clicked on the banner and his Buddy threw the message text onto the HUD.

'Sender: Special Investigator Winter, Freedom Unit Enforcement, Ministry of Well-being and Health.'

'Subject: Health Reorientation Camp joining instructions.'

'Message: A car will pick you up at 05:30 tomorrow and take you to the Dartmoor Health Reorientation Camp…'

Clive's legs collapsed under him, and he dropped his head. He let out a long, 'Nooooo.'

The high from the chocolate had evaporated, nothing more than a transient sugar-rush. The self-help beardie had been right, his act of defiance was a simple act of self-medication. It didn't solve anything.

He looked around his kitchen. He was alone. No Ava, no Sophia and worse, the continual presence of his nemesis, the Model Citizen.

He was controlled.

Energy surged through Clive, 'But no more,' he screamed.

He jumped up and ran to the nearest drawer. He yanked it open and grabbed a large knife.

'Shit, more health and safety bollocks,' he said. Every knife he had was blunt. The baby training knives his parents used at mealtimes were sharper. He tried anyway, testing the edge of the blade across his wrist. It left a thin white line that faded as the blood returned.

Even when trying to end it all, he was controlled.

He pushed his right thumb into his mouth, and nibbled at his nail. Shaping it into a crude, but sharp point.

Issac's words replayed in his head – *We can turn the unworthy off.*

Clive grabbed the back of his neck with his left hand, feeling for the bump where the iMe was. He didn't care if it killed him, it was coming out.

He brought his right thumb up and jabbed the point of his nail into the soft flesh. He pushed and hacked and broke the skin.

Blood oozed down his neck.

He worked his thumb deeper, then pulled it out. Now that knife should be of some use. He grabbed it and pushed the blunt corner into the opening his nail had made. He used it as a lever, tearing the skin, forcing the blade in.

Bile started to rise in Clive's mouth, and despite shivering, sweat appeared on his brow. He had to stop and wait for a wave of dizziness to pass.

Clenching his jaw tight, he pushed the blade again, working it back and forth. The skin deformed as the knife made progress, outlining the shape of the blade.

It reached the centre of his neck.

The angle of Clive's wrist changed, and he started pushing the blade down, battling the pain and waves of nausea.

He gagged. Then again and a mouthful of vomit escaped his mouth and splattered onto the floor.

The knife was just above the iMe, he was sure. He paused, scanning the room, but saw nothing to change his mind, and pushed harder down.

The blade touched something metal. He thought he heard a tiny 'fut' of an electrical short-circuit, and Clive's HUD flashed a blinding white. Pain exploded in his neck and spread like surging, breaking waves. It enveloped him before he collapsed.

***

Clive unpeeled his right eye. His whole body hurt, every nerve ending was in rebellion, firing pulses that swamped his brain.

He tried to lift his hand, but couldn't.

'Don't,' a gentle voice said. 'Try and stay still.'

His eye rose, millimetre by agonising millimetre. 'What… Where?'

It was all he could manage.

'You're in… hospital. You nearly died, but Harry saved you. He came out to clean up your vomit and his sensors picked up blood. He messaged for help.'

Good old Harry. His only friend.

But maybe, not. 'That you, Zoe?' he croaked.

'Of course. You're such an idiot.'

He listened for another person, a hint of their breathing. He sniffed, willing for a trace of a familiar perfume in the air. 'Is Sophia here?'

'Sorry. No.'

Clive didn't have any time to think about what her absence really meant before he heard a door crash open and a voice he couldn't help recognise – Special Investigator Winter, full of righteous anger. 'Inspector, you missed another appointment, but getting locked up in a psychiatric hospital doesn't get you off the hook.'

Clive glanced at his right hand and saw that he was strapped to the bed. Winter crowded in over him and laughed.

Clive curled up his middle finger and jabbed it up as much as the straps allowed.

'Winter, I see you got my application to join Control Rebellion.'

With thanks…

To Rax, James, Georgie and my family and friends for all their support.

To Oonagh for the dreams about pirates.

To Amanda, my editor at Let's Get Booked.

To Abbie at Abbie Editorial.

To the *TrashFiction* crew for all the support and jokes.

Dear Reader,

Thank you for reading *No Signal*. I hope you found its blend of thriller and near future both plausible and thought-provoking. Real life provides so much inspiration for fiction and I would love to hear your views.

If you enjoyed the story, I'd be extremely grateful if you would write a review. Getting feedback from readers is extremely rewarding and also helps persuade others to pick up one of my books for the first time.

For news about the next in the series, please visit me at my website – www.jemtugwell.com or join me on Twitter @JemTugwell and Facebook @JemTugwellAuthor.

All the best,

Jem

Read **PROXIMITY**, the first book in the iMe series.

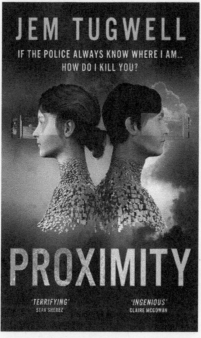

Leading the trend in speculative crime thrillers, Jem Tugwell's thrilling and thought-provoking debut sits alongside *Black Mirror* and *The City and the City* in an unsettling exploration of our near future.

DI Clive Lussac has forgotten how to do his job. Ten years of embedded technology – 'iMe' – has led to complete control and the eradication of crime.

Then the impossible happens. A body is found, and the killer is untraceable.

With new partner Zoe Jordan, Clive must re-sharpen his detective skills and find the killer without technology, before time runs out for the next victim…